Felix Mendelssohn Bartholdy

Letters from Italy and Switzerland

Felix Mendelssohn Bartholdy

Letters from Italy and Switzerland

ISBN/EAN: 9783743374102

Hergestellt in Europa, USA, Kanada, Australien, Japan

Cover: Foto ©Andreas Hilbeck / pixelio.de

Manufactured and distributed by brebook publishing software (www.brebook.com)

Felix Mendelssohn Bartholdy

Letters from Italy and Switzerland

LETTERS

FROM

ITALY AND SWITZERLAND

BY

FELIX MENDELSSOHN BARTHOLDY.

Translated from the German

BY

LADY WALLACE.

WITH A BIOGRAPHICAL NOTICE

BY

JULIE DE MARGUERITTES.

THIRD EDITION.

PHILADELPHIA:
FREDERICK LEYPOLDT.
NEW YORK: F. W. CHRISTERN.

1865.

FELIX MENDELSSOHN BARTHOLDY.

Felix Mendelssohn Bartholdy was born at Hamburg, on the third of February, 1809. The name to which he was destined to add such lustre, was already high in the annals of fame. Moses Mendelssohn, his grandfather, a great Jewish philosopher, one of the most remarkable men of his time, was the author of profound Metaphysical works, written both in German and Hebrew. To this great power of intellect, Moses Mendelssohn added a purity and dignity of character worthy of the old stoics. The epigraph on the bust of this ancestor of the composer, shows the esteem in which he was held by his contemporaries:

"Faithful to the religion of his fathers, as wise as Socrates, like Socrates teaching the immortality of the soul, and like Socrates leaving a name that is immortal."

One of Moses Mendelssohn's daughters married Frederick Schlegel, and swerving from the religion in which both had been brought up, both became Roman Catholics.

Joseph Mendelssohn, the eldest son of this great old man, was also distinguished for his literary taste, and has left two excellent works of very different characters, one on Dante, the other on the system of a paper currency.

In conjunction with his brother, Abraham, he founded the banking-house of Mendelssohn & Company at Berlin, still flourishing under the management of the sons of the original founders, the brothers and cousins of Felix, the subject of this memoir.

George Mendelssohn the son of Joseph, was also a distinguished political writer and Professor in the University at Bonn.

With such an array of intellectual ancestry, the Mendelssohn of our day came into the world at Hamburg, on the third of February, 1809. He was named Felix, and a more appropriate name could not have been found for him, for in character, circumstance and endowment, he was supremely happy. Goethe, speaking of him, said "the boy was born on a lucky day." His first piece of good fortune, was in having not only an excellent virtuous woman for his mother, but a woman who, besides these qualities, possessed extraordinary intellect and had received an education that fitted her to be the mother of children endowed as hers were. She professed the Lutheran creed, in which her children were brought up. Being of a distinguished commercial family and an heiress, her husband added her name of Bartholdy to his own. Mme. Mendelssohn Bartholdy's other children were, Fanny her first-born, whose life is entirely interwoven with that of her brother Felix, and Paul and Rebecca, born some years later.

When yet a boy, Felix removed with his parents to Berlin, probably at the time of the formation of the banking house. The Prussian capital has often claimed the honor of being his birthplace, but that distinction really belongs to Hamburg.

His extraordinary musical talent was not long in developing itself. His sister Fanny, his "soul's friend" and constant companion, almost as richly endowed as himself, aroused his emulation, and they studied music together first as an art, and then as a science, to be the foundation of future works of inspiration and genius.

Zelter, severe and classic, profoundly scientific, inexorable for all that was not true science, became the teacher of these two gifted children in composition and in counterpoint. For piano-forte playing, Berger was the professor, though some years later Moscheles added the benefit of his counsels, and Felix was fond of calling himself the pupil of Moscheles, with whom in after life he contracted a close friendship. Zelter was exceedingly proud of his pupil, soon discovering that instead of an industrious and intelligent child, one of the greatest musical geniuses ever known was dawning on the world. When he was but fifteen, Zelter took the young musician to Weimar, and secured for him the acquaintance and good will of Goethe, which as long as Goethe lived, seemed to be the necessary consecration of all talent in Germany. By this time not only was he an admirable performer on the piano, possessed of a talent for improvisation and a memory so wonderful, that not only could he play almost all Bach, Händel, Haydn, Mozart and Beethoven by heart, but he could also without hesitation accompany a whole opera from memory, provided he had but seen the score once. The overture to Midsummer Night's Dream, so popular now in every country, was composed before he was seventeen, and was played for the first time as a duet on the piano by his sister Fanny and himself on the 19th November, 1826. This is indeed the inspiration of youth with its brilliancy, its buoyancy, its triumphant joy, full of the poetry of a young heart, full of the imagination of a mind untainted by the world. It was not till some years after, that Mendelssohn completed the music to Shakspeare's great play. In 1827, Felix left the University of Berlin with great honors. He was a profound classical scholar, and has left as a specimen of his knowledge, a correct, graceful and elegant translation of Terence's comedy of Andria, a work greatly approved of by Goethe. He excelled in gymnastics, was an elegant rider, and like Lord Byron, a bold and accomplished swimmer. The year he left the University, he went to England, where Henrietta Sonntag was in the height of her fame. He played in several concerts where she sang, as well as with Moscheles, his old friend and teacher, now established in London.

On his return to Germany in 1830, he visited Goethe at Weimar, and there planned his journey to Italy, a country which all men of genius yearn after, as the promised land of inspiration. When in Rome, Felix Mendelssohn began the grand Cantata of the Walpurgis Night, to Goethe's words, at which he worked for some years. On his return from his travels, Mendelssohn, who had now all the assurance and self-possession of an artist, was appointed chapel-master at Düsseldorf, a position which gave him the direction of the grand musical festivals held at that time in this city and in Aix-la-Chapelle. It was during his residence in Düsseldorf, that he composed his oratorio of St. Paul, and also, the first set of his "Songs without Words" for the piano, where the music, by its varied expression and its intensity, alone told the story of the poet. These compositions were a novelty for piano-forte players, and inaugurated a new style, full of interest, gradually setting aside the variations and sonatas which had become so meaningless and tedious. The oratorio of St. Paul was not given until 1836, when it was produced at Düsseldorf, under his own special superintendence. Mendelssohn composed very rapidly, but he was cautious in giving his works to the public, until they thoroughly satisfied his judgment, the most critical to which they could be submitted.

In the latter part of 1836, having gone to Frankfort, to direct a concert of the Ceciliaverein, he became acquainted with Cecilia Jeanrenaud, a beautiful and accomplished girl, the second daughter of a clergyman of the Reformed Church, and in the spring of 1837 she became his wife. The marriage had been delayed some months by Mendelssohn's ill health; he had begun to feel the first symptoms of the nervous disease, affecting the brain, from which he was destined henceforth to suffer, and of which, finally, he was fated to die.

After his marriage he undertook the direction of the Leipzig Concerts. All over Germany, Mendelssohn was in requisition; his immense genius as a composer, his great skill as a conductor, his gentle, fascinating manners, gave him extraordinary popularity. It was England, however, after all, who appreciated him most. Sacred music seems to appeal especially to the English taste. Haydn, Händel, Beethoven have all found more patronage and appreciation in England than in their own country. So it was with Mendelssohn; the greatest musical triumph ever achieved, was the performance of the oratorio of Elijah, given at Birmingham, the work on which Mendelssohn's fame will rest. He was nine years in composing this oratorio; and notwithstanding the most flattering ovation, Mendelssohn's serene temperament was not moved to vanity or conceit. In the very moment of his success, he sat down modestly to correct many things that had not satisfied him. The trio for three female voices (without accompaniment) one of the most beautiful pieces in the oratorio, was added by the composer after the public had declared itself satisfied with the work as it originally stood. Elijah was produced in 1847, but Mendelssohn had been several times to England before this, playing at the ancient and Philharmonic concerts; at that time, the resort of the élite in London.

It was during one of these visits in 1842, that Prince Albert, who as a German and a musician, had sought his acquaintance, introduced him to Queen Victoria. The visit was entirely devoid of formality, for without any previous announcement, the Prince conducted Mendelssohn from his private apartments, to the Queen's study, where they found her surrounded by papers, and just terminating her morning's work. The Queen receiving him most graciously, apologized to the composer for the untidiness of the room, beginning herself to put it in order and laughingly accepting his assistance. After some agreeable conversation Mendelssohn sat down to the piano and played whatever the Queen asked of him. When at length he rose, Prince Albert asked the Queen to sing, and gracefully choosing one of Mendelssohn's own compositions, she complied with the request. Mendelssohn of course applauded, but the Queen laughingly told him, that she had been too frightened to sing well. "Ask Lablache," (Lablache was her singing master) added the Queen, "he will tell you that I can sing better than I have done to-day." Prince Albert and the Queen were ever warm patrons and friends of Mendelssohn.

During all this time so brilliantly filled up, Mendelssohn's health was continually and gradually declining. His nervous susceptibility was such that he was often obliged to abstain from playing for weeks together, his gentle and affectionate wife watching him and keeping him as much as possible from composition. This was a very difficult task, for Mendelssohn was a great worker. Even when travelling, he would take out pen and ink from his pocket and compose at one corner of the table, whilst the dinner was getting ready.

Little was Mendelssohn prepared, either mentally or physically at this time, to bear the one great sorrow that overwhelmed this happy life, on which the sun of prosperity had ever shone. His sister Fanny, to whom many of his letters were written, and who had been the companion of his studies, possessing the same tastes and a great deal of the same genius; his sister Fanny, who was the nearest and dearest affection of his life, was suddenly taken from him. She had married and was living in Frankfort, where she was the ornament of society, in this enlightened and art-loving city, when in the midst of a rehearsal of Faust, a symphony of her own composition, she was struck with apoplexy and fell back dead in her chair. There is no doubt that this shock considerably increased the disease from which Mendelssohn was suffering, and though he used to rally and even appear resigned, this sorrow, until the day of his death, lay heavy at his heart. Again he tried to find health and peace in travel; he went to Switzerland with his wife, who strove to keep him from all occupation and labor, but he would gently urge her to let him work. " The time is not far off, when I shall rest ; I must make the most of the time given me." "I know not how short a time it may be," would he say to her. On his return from Switzerland and Baden-Baden, he went to Berlin; and once more all that remained of this tenderly attached family, were united for a short time. At length he returned to his home in Leipzig, serene as ever, but worn to a shadow by the acute and continued pains in the head for which he could obtain no relief. On the 9th of October, he went to the house of a friend, one of the artists of the Leipzig concerts, and entreated her to sing for him a song he had that night composed. By a strange coincidence, this song began with these words, "Vanished has the light of day." It was Mendelssohn's last composition, the last music he heard on earth, for whilst the lady was singing it, he was seized with vertigo and was carried insensible back to his house. He recovered, however, comparatively from this attack, but a second stroke of apoplexy placed his life in extreme peril, and a third, on the 3rd of November, made him utterly unconscious. Towards nine o'clock on the evening of the 4th, (1847,) he breathed his last, going to his everlasting rest as easily and as calmly as a tired child sinks to sleep. He was in the thirty-ninth year of his age.

Mendelssohn's death was looked upon, throughout Germany, as a public calamity. The funeral ceremonies at Leipzig were of a most imposing character, and all the way from Leipzig to Berlin, where the corpse was taken, to be buried in the family vault, the most touching honors greeted it. Nearly all the crowned heads of Europe wrote letters of condolence to his widow.

Mendelssohn as a musician is profoundly original. In his oratorios "Paul" and "Elijah" he has swerved from the conventional religious style; eschewing all fugues, his oratorios are full of power, and contain great dramatic effects—at once grand and solemn. His other music is remarkable for the sweetness of its melodies—its earnest simplicity. His instrumentality is scientific without being pedantic or heavy, and utterly devoid of antiquated formalism; though pathetic often, there is always a vigor and life in all his inspirations; the low mournful wail that runs through all Chopin's works, arising from a morbid condition of health and heart, is never felt in Mendelssohn. There is none of the bitterness, the long suffering that artists' lives entail and that artists infuse into their works, for Mendelssohn was a happy man from first to last.

Mendelssohn the happy, "the boy born on a lucky day," has left a life-record that amid the gloomy heart-rending and often degrading histories of artists, shines with a chaste and holy life. Nature, the world and circumstance had done every thing for him. To the great and all-sufficient gift of his musical genius he added many others,—he had the eye of a painter, the heart of a poet, his intellect was of the highest order; he was tall, handsome, graceful, his social position one of the finest in Berlin, rich, and surrounded by the tenderest family affections. With all these advantages, with all the success that attended him, with all the flattery lavished on him, Mendelssohn was never vain or proud, and throughout his life was utterly free from envy. His fine, fearless, childlike spirit, led him through the world, unconscious of evil, undaunted by it. With all the temptations that must have assailed the young, handsome, rich man, there is not one moment of his life over which his friends would wish to draw a veil. On such a life as that of Felix Mendelssohn, it is good for every one to look, for once, genius is not set forth as a dazzling screen to hide and to excuse disorder and crime, but genius, that one great gift from heaven, was employed as heaven would have directed it, each action, each succeeding year of his life, bringing forth in various but harmonious ways, that extraordinary moral and intellectual worth, that rare beauty of character that endeared him to all who knew him, ensured him the unvarying love of kindred and friends, and the admiration of the whole world.

PREFACE.

Last year a paragraph was inserted in the newspapers, requesting any one who possessed letters from Felix Mendelssohn Bartholdy to send them to Professor Droysen, or to myself, with the view of completing a selection from his correspondence which we contemplated publishing. Our design in this was twofold.

In the first place, we wished to offer to the public in Mendelssohn's own words, which always so truly and faithfully mirrored his thoughts, the most genuine impression of his character; and secondly, we thought that the biographical elements contained in such a correspondence, might be of infinite use in the compilation of a memoir—which we reserve for a future day—and serve as its precursor and basis.

There are difficulties, however, opposed to the immediate fulfilment of our original purpose to its full extent; and at present it is impossible to decide when these can be removed.

I have, therefore, formed the resolution to carry out my plan in the meantime within more circumscribed limits, but which leaves me unfettered.

On Mendelssohn's return from his first visit to England, in the year 1829, he came to Berlin for a short time to attend a family festivity, and thence in 1830 proceeded to Italy, returning through Switzerland to France, and in the beginning of 1832 visiting England for the second time.

This period, which to a certain degree forms a separate section of his life, and which, through the vivid impressions it made, assuredly exercised an important influence on Mendelssohn's development (we may mention that he was only one-and-twenty at the commencement of his journey), supplies us with a number of letters addressed to his parents, and to his sisters, Fanny and Rebecca, as well as to myself. I have also added some communications of the same date, to various friends, partly entire and partly in extracts, and now present them to the public in their original integrity.

Those who were personally acquainted with Mendelssohn, and who wish once more to realize him as he was when in life,—and those also who would be glad to acquire a more definite idea of his individuality than can be found in the general inferences deduced from his musical creations,—will not lay down these letters dissatisfied. Along with this particular source of interest they offer a more universal one, as they prove how admirably Mendelssohn's superior nature, and perceptions of Art, mutually pervaded and regulated each other.

With this view, it appeared to me a duty to give to the public these letters, stored up in the peaceful home for which they were originally destined and exclusively intended, and thus to make them accessible to a more extended circle. They begin by a visit to Goethe. May his words then accompany these Letters, as an appropriate convoy :—

> " Be sure the works of mighty men,
> The good, the faithful, the sublime,
> Stored in the gallery of Time,
> Repose awhile—to wake again."*

PAUL MENDELSSOHN BARTHOLDY.

BERLIN, *March*, 1861.

a " Was in der Zeiten Bildersaal
Jemals ist trefflich gewesen,
Das wird immer einer einmal
Wieder auffrischen und lesen."

LETTERS.

Weimar, May 21st, 1830.

Never, in the whole course of my travels, do I remember a more glorious and inspiriting day for a journey than yesterday. At an early hour in the morning the sky was grey and cloudy, but the sun presently burst forth; the air was cool and fresh, and being Ascension Sunday the people were all dressed in their best. In one village I saw them crowding into church as I passed, in another coming away from divine service, and, last of all, playing at bowls. The gardens were bright with tulips, and I drove quickly past, eagerly looking at everything. At Weissenfels they gave me a little basket carriage, and at Naumburg an open droschky. My effects, including my hat and cloak, were piled upon it behind. I bought a few bunches of lilies-of-the-valley, and thus I travelled on through the country, as if on a pleasure excursion.

Some collegians came up to me beyond Naumburg, and envied me. We then drove past President G——, seated in a small carriage, which

(1

evidently had some difficulty in containing him, and his daughters or *wives;* in short, the two ladies with him, who appeared equally envious of my position. We actually *trotted* up the Kösen Hill, for the horses scarcely drew bridle, and overtook several heavily-laden carriages, the drivers of which no doubt also envied me, for I was really to be envied. The scenery had a charming air of spring— so cheerful and gay, and blooming. The sun sank solemnly behind the hills, and presently we came up with the Russian minister and his suite, in two heavy carriages, each with four horses, in true ponderous official array; and my light droschky darted past him like a hare.

In the evening I got a pair of restive horses, so that I had my little annoyance also, (according to my theory, enhancing pleasure,) and not a single bar did I compose all day, but enjoyed complete idleness. It was a delicious day, and one I shall not soon forget. I close this description with the remark, that the children in Eckartsberge dance merry rounds hand-in-hand, just as ours do at home, and that the appearance of a stranger did not in the least disturb them, in spite of his distinguished air; I should have liked to join in their game.

May 24th.

I wrote this before going to see Goethe, early in the forenoon, after a walk in the park; but I could not find a moment to finish my letter till now. I shall probably remain here for a couple of days, which is no sacrifice, for I never saw the old gentleman so cheerful and amiable as on this occasion, or so talkative and communicative. My especial reason however for staying two days longer, is a very agreeable one, and makes me almost vain, or I ought rather to say proud, and I do not intend to keep it secret from you,—Goethe, you must know, sent me a letter yesterday addressed to an artist here, a painter, which I am to deliver myself; and Ottilie confided to me that it contains a commission to take my portrait, as Goethe wishes to place it in a collection of likenesses he has recently commenced of his friends. This circumstance gratified me exceedingly; as however I have not yet seen the complaisant artist who is to accomplish this, nor has he seen me, it is probable that I shall have to remain here until the day after to-morrow. I don't in the least regret this, for, as I have told you, I live a most agreeable life here, and thoroughly enjoy the society of the old poet. I have dined with him every day, and am invited again to-day. This evening there is to be a party at his house, where I am to play. It is quite delightful to hear him conversing on every subject, and seeking information on all points.

I must however tell you everything regularly and in order, so that you may know each separate detail.

Early in the day I went to see Ottilie, who, though still delicate, and often complaining. I thought more cheerful than formerly, and quite as kind and amiable as ever towards myself. We have been constantly together since then, and it has been a source of much pleasure to me to know her more intimately. Ulrike is more agreeable and charming than formerly; a certain earnestness pervades her whole nature, and she has now a degree of repose, and a depth of feeling, that render her one of the most attractive creatures I have ever met. The two boys, Walter and Wolf, are lively, studious, cordial lads, and to hear them talking about "Grandpapa's Faust," is most pleasant.

But to return to my narrative. I sent Zelter's letter at once to Goethe, who immediately invited me to dinner. I thought him very little changed in appearance, but at first rather silent and apathetic; I think he wished to see how I demeaned myself. I was vexed, and thought that possibly he was always now in this mood. Happily the conversation turned on the *Frauen-Vereine* in Weimar, and on the 'Chaos,' a humorous paper circulated among themselves by the ladies here, I having soared so high as to be a contributor to this undertaking. All at once the old man became quite gay, laughing at the two ladies about their charities and intellectualism, and their subscriptions and hospital work, which he seems cordially to detest. He called on me to aid him in his onslaught, and as I did not require to be asked twice, he speedily became just what he used to be, and at last more kind and confidential than I had ever seen him. The assault soon became general. The 'Robber Bride' of Ries, he said contained all that an artist in these days required to live happily,—a robber and a bride; then he attacked the young people of the present day for their universal tendency to languor and melancholy, and related the story of a young lady to whom he had once paid court, and who also felt some interest in him; a discussion on the exhibitions followed, and a fancy bazaar for the poor, where the ladies of Weimar were the shopwomen, and where he declared it was impossible to purchase anything because the young people made a private agreement among themselves, and hid the different articles till the proper purchasers appeared.

After dinner he all at once began—"Gute Kinder—hübsche Kinder—muss immer lustig sein—tolles Volk," etc., his eyes looking like those of a drowsy old lion. Then he begged me to play to him, and said it seemed strange that he had heard no music for so long; that he supposed we had made great progress, but he knew nothing of it. He wished me to tell him a great deal on the subject, saying "Do let us have a little rational conversation together;" and turning to Ottilie, he said, "No doubt you have already made your own wise arrangements, but they must yield to my express orders, which are, that you must make tea here this evening, that we may be all together again." When in return she asked him if it would not make him too late, as Riemer was coming to work with him, he replied, "As you gave your children a holiday from their Latin to-day, that they might hear Felix play, I think you might also give me one day of relaxation from *my* work." He invited me to return to dinner, and I played a great deal to him in the evening.

My three Welsh pieces, dedicated to three English sisters, have great success here;* and I am trying to rub up my English. As I had begged Goethe to address me as *thou*, he desired Ottilie to say to me on the following day, in that case I must remain longer than the two days I had fixed, otherwise he could not regain the more familiar habit I wished. He repeated this to me himself, saying that he did not think I should lose much by staying a little longer, and invited me always to dine with him when I had no other engagement. I have consequently been with him every day, and yesterday I told him a great deal about Scotland, and Hengstenberg, and Spontini, and Hegel's 'Æsthetics.'† He sent me to Tiefurth with the ladies, but prohibited my driving to Berka, because a very pretty girl lived there, and he did not wish to plunge me into misery.

I thought to myself, this was indeed the Goethe of whom people will one day say, that he was not one single individual, but consisted of several little *Goethiden.* I am to play over to him to-day various pieces of Bach, Haydn, and Mozart, and thus lead him on, as he said, to the present day.

---

* Three pieces for the piano, composed in 1829 for the album of three young English ladies; subsequently published as Opus 16.

† Felix Mendelssohn attended the Berlin University as a matriculated student for more than a year; a vast number of sheets written by him at this period, during the lectures, are still extant.

I should indeed have been very foolish to have regretted my delay; besides, I am a conscientious traveller, and have seen the Library, and 'Iphigenia in Aulis.' Hummel has struck out all the octaves, etc.

FELIX.

Weimar, May 25th, 1830.

I have just received your welcome letter, written on Ascension Day. I cannot help myself, but must still write to you from this place. I will soon send you, dear Fanny, a copy of my symphony; I am having it written out here, and mean to forward it to Leipzig (where perhaps it will be performed), with strict orders to deliver it into your own hands, as soon as possible. Try to collect opinions as to the title I ought to select; Reformation Symphony, Confession Symphony, Symphony for a Church Festival, Juvenile Symphony, or whatever you like. Write to me on this subject, and instead of a number of stupid suggestions, send me one clever one; still, I should rather like to hear some of the nonsensical ones sure to be devised on the occasion.

Yesterday evening I was at a party at Goethe's, and played alone the whole evening—the Concert-Stück, the Invitation à la Valse, and Weber's Polonaise in C, my three Welsh pieces, and my Scotch Sonata. It was over by ten o'clock, but I of course stayed till twelve o'clock, when we had all sorts of fun, dancing and singing; so you see I lead a most jovial life here. The old gentleman goes to his room regularly at nine o'clock, and as soon as he is gone, we begin our frolics, and never separate before midnight.

To-morrow my portrait is to be finished; a large black-crayon sketch, and very like; but I look rather sulky. Goethe is so friendly and kind to me, that I don't know how to thank him sufficiently, or what to do to deserve it. In the forenoon he likes me to play to him the compositions of the various great masters, in chronological order, for an hour, and also tell him the progress they have made, while he sits in a dark corner, like a *Jupiter tonans*, his old eyes flashing on me. He did not wish to hear anything of Beethoven's, but I told him that I could not let him off, and played the first part of the Symphony in C minor. It seemed to have a singular effect on him; at first he said, "This causes no emotion, nothing but astonishment; it is *grandios*." He continued grumbling in this way, and after a long pause he began again,—"It is very grand, very wild; it makes one fear that the house is about to fall down; and what must it be when played by a number of men together!" During dinner, in the midst of another subject, he alluded to it again. You know that I dine with him every day, when he questions me very minutely, and is always so gay and communicative after dinner, that we generally remain together alone for an hour, while he speaks on uninterruptedly.

I have no greater pleasure than when he brings out engravings, and explains them to me, or gives his opinion of Ernani, or Lamartine's Elegies, or the theatre, or pretty girls. He has several times lately invited people, which he rarely does now, so that most of the guests had not seen him for a long time. I then play a great deal, and he compliments me before all these people, and "*ganz stupend*" is his favourite expression. To-day he has invited a number of Weimar beauties on my account, because he thinks that I ought to enjoy the society of young people. If I go up to him on such occasions, he says, "My young friend, you must join the ladies, and make yourself agreeable to them." I am not however devoid of tact, so I contrived to have him asked yesterday whether I did not come too often; but he growled out to Ottilie, who put the question to him, that "he must now begin to speak to me in good earnest, for I had such clear ideas, that he hoped to *learn much from me*." I became twice as tall in my own estimation, when Ottilie repeated this to me. He said so to me himself yesterday; and when he declared that there were many subjects he had at heart that I must explain to him, I *said*, "Oh, certainly!" but I *thought*, "This is an honour I can never forget,"— often it is the very reverse.

FELIX.

Munich, June 6th, 1830.

It is a long time since I have written to you, and
I fear you may have been anxious on my account.
You must not be angry with me, for it was really
no fault of mine, and I have been not a little annoyed about it. I expedited my journey as well as
I could, inquiring everywhere about diligences, and
invariably receiving false information. I travelled
through one night on purpose to enable me to
write to you by this day's post, of which I was told
at Nürnberg; and when at last I arrive, I find that
no post leaves here to-day: it is enough to drive
one wild, and I feel out of all patience with Germany and her petty Principalities, her different
kinds of money, her diligences, which require an
hour and a quarter for a German mile, and her
Thuringian forests, where there is incessant rain
and wind,—nay, even with her 'Fidelio' this very
evening, for, though dead beat, I must do my duty
by going to see it, when I would far rather go to bed.
Pray do not be angry with me, or scold me for my
delay in writing; I do assure you that this very
night while I was travelling, I thought I saw peeping through the clouds the shadow of your threat-
ning finger; but I shall now proceed to explain
why I could not write sooner.

Some days after my last letter from Weimar, I
wished, as I told you, to set off for this place, and
said so during dinner to Goethe, who made no
reply. After dinner however he withdrew with
Ottilie into the recess of a window, and said, "You

must persuade him to remain." She endeavoured to prevail on me to do so, and walked up and down in the garden with me. I wished however to show 'hat I was a man of determination, so I remained teady to my resolve. Then came the old gentle-man himself, and said he saw no use in my being in such a hurry; that he had still a great deal to tell one, and I had still a great deal to play to him ; and what I had told him as to the object of my journey, was really all nonsense,—Weimar was my present object,—and he could not see that I was likely to find in *tables-d'hôte* elsewhere, what I could not obtain here : I would see plenty of hotels in my travels. 'Ie talked on in this style, which touched my heart, especially as Ottilie and Ulrike added their persua-sions, assuring me that the old gentleman much more often insisted on people going away, than on their remaining; and as no one can be so sure of enjoying a number of happy days, that he can afford to throw away those that cannot fail to be pleasant, and as they promised to go with me to Jena, I resolved *not* to be a man of determination, and agreed to stay.

Seldom in the course of my life have I so little regretted any resolution as on this occasion, for the following day was by far the most delightful that I ever passed in Goethe's house. After an early drive, I found old Goethe very cheerful ; he began to converse on various subjects, passing from the 'Muette de l'ortici' to Walter Scott, and thence to the beauties in Weimar ; to the 'Students,' and the

'Robbers,' and so on to Schiller; then he spoke on uninterruptedly for more than an hour, with the utmost animation, about Schiller's life and writings, and his position in Weimar. He proceeded to speak of the late Grand-Duke, and of the year 1775, which he designated as the intellectual spring of Germany, declaring that no man living could describe it so well as he could; indeed, it had been his intention to have devoted the second volume of his life to this subject; but what with botany, and meteorology, and other stuff of the same kind, for which no one cared a straw, he had not yet been able to fulfil his purpose. He proceeded to relate various anecdotes of the time when he was director of the theatre, and when I wished to thank him, he said, "It is mere chance, it all comes to light incidentally,—called forth by your welcome presence." These words sounded marvellously pleasant to me; in short, it was one of those conversations that a man can never forget so long as he lives. Next day he made me a present of a sheet of the manuscript of 'Faust,' and at the bottom of the page he wrote, "To my dear young friend F. M. B., mighty, yet delicate master of the piano—a friendly souvenir of happy May days in 1830. J. W. von Goethe." He also gave me three letters of introduction to take with me.

If that relentless 'Fidelio' did not begin at so early an hour, I could tell you much more, but as it is, I have only time to detail my farewell interview with the old gentleman. At the very beginning of my visit to Weimar, I spoke of a print taken from Adrian von Ostade, of a peasant family praying, which nine years ago made a deep impression on me. When I went at an early hour to take leave of Goethe, I found him seated beside a large portfolio, and he said, "So you are actually going away? I must try to keep all right till you return; but at all events we won't part now without some pious feelings, so let us once more look at the praying family together." He told me that I must sometimes write to him—(courage! courage! I mean to do so from this very place), and then he embraced me, and we drove off to Jena, where the Frommans received me with much kindness, and where the same evening I took leave of Ottilie and Ulrike, and came on here.

Nine o'clock.—'Fidelio' is over; and while waiting for supper I add a few words.

Schechner is very much gone off; the quality of her voice has become husky; she repeatedly sang flat, yet there were moments when her expression was so touching, that I wept in my own fashion; all the others were bad, and there was also much to censure in the performance. Still, there is great talent in the orchestra, and the style in which they played the overture was very good. Certainly our Germany is a strange land; producing great people, but not appreciating them; possessing many fine singers and intellectual artists, but none sufficiently modest and subordinate to render their parts faithfully, and without false pretension. Marzeline intro-

duces all sorts of flourishes into her part; Jaquino
is a blockhead; the minister a simpleton: and when a
German like Beethoven writes an opera, then comes
a German like Stuntz or Poissl (or whoever it may
have been) and strikes out the ritournelle, and
similar unnecessary passages; another German adds
a trombone part to his symphonies; a third declares
that Beethoven is overloaded: and thus is a great
man sacrificed.

Farewell! be happy and merry; and may all my
heartfelt wishes for you be fulfilled.   FELIX.

To Fanny Hensel.

Munich, June 14th, 1830.

My dearest Sister,

I received your letter of the 5th this morning; I
see from it that you are not yet quite well. I wish
I were with you, and could see you, and talk to
you; but this is impossible, so I have written a
song for you expressive of my wishes and thoughts.
You were in my mind when I composed it, and
I was in a tender mood. There is indeed nothing
very new in it. You know me well, and what I am;
in no respect am I changed, so you may smile at
this and rejoice. I could say and wish many other
things for you, but none better; and this letter too
shall contain nothing else. You know that I am
always your own; and may it please God to bestow
on you all that I hope and pray.

Andante.
mf

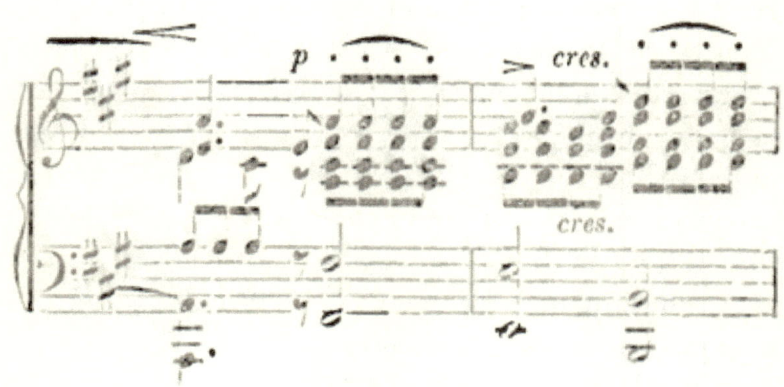
p
cres.
cres.

sf
f   p
dolce.

f   espress.

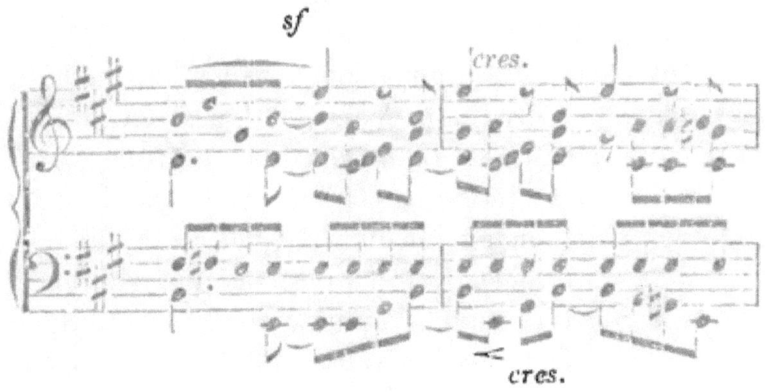
sf
cres.
cres.

Linz, August 11th, 1830.

Dearest Mother,

"How a travelling musician bore his bad luck in Salzburg." A fragment from the unwritten journal of Count F. M. B. (continuation.) After I had finished my last letter to you, a regular day of misfortunes commenced for me. I took up my pencil, and so entirely destroyed two of my pet sketches, taken in the Bavarian mountains, that I was obliged to tear them from my book, and to throw them out

2*

of the window. This provoked me exceedingly; so
to divert my mind, I went to the Capuchin Hill: of
course I contrived to lose my way, and at the very
moment, when I at last found myself on the summit,
it began to rain so furiously that I was forced to
run down again with all speed under the shelter of
an umbrella. Well! I resolved at all events to
have a look at the monastery at the foot of the
hill, so I rang the bell, when I suddenly recollected
that I had not sufficient money to give the monk
who was to show the building, and as this is a kind
of thing that they take highly amiss, I hurried away
without waiting till the porter appeared.

I then closed my packet of letters for Leipzig,
and took it myself to the post, but there I was told,
that it must first be examined at the Custom-house;
so thither I went. They kept me waiting a whole
hour, till they composed a certificate of three lines,
and behaved so saucily that I was forced to quarrel
with them. Hang Salzburg! thought I; so I
ordered horses for Ischl, where I hoped to escape
from all my bad luck. No horses were to be had
without a permission from the police. I went to
the police office. "No permission can be granted
till you bring your passport." Why pursue the
subject? After innumerable delays, and running
about hither and thither, the wished-for post-car-
riage arrived. My dinner was over, my luggage
ready, and I thought that at last all was in good
train: my bill and the servants fees were paid.

Just as I reached the door, I saw two handsome

open carriages approaching at a foot's pace, and the people of the inn hurrying to receive the travellers, who were following on foot. I however paid no attention to the new arrivals, but jumped into my carriage. I observed, that at the same moment, one of the travelling carriages drew up close to mine, and that a lady was seated in it,—but what a lady! That you may not instantly jump to the conclusion that I had suddenly fallen in love, which would have been the crowning point of my unlucky day, I must tell you that she was an elderly lady; but she looked very amiable and benevolent; she wore a black dress, and a massive gold chain, and smiled good-humouredly when she paid the postilion his fare. Heaven knows why I continued to arrange my luggage instead of driving off. I did look across continually at the other carriage, and though the lady was an entire stranger to me I felt a strong inclination to address her. It might be mere imagination on my part, but I do think that she too looked at the dusty traveller in his student's cap. At length she got out of the carriage, and stood close to the door of my vehicle, leaning her hand on it, and I required all my knowledge of the common proprieties of travelling, not to get out myself and say to her, "Dear lady, what may your name be?" Routine however conquered, and I called out with an air of dignity, "Postilion! go on!" on which the lady quickly withdrew her hand, and we set off. I felt in no very pleasant humour, and while thinking over the events of the day, I fell asleep.

A carriage with two gentlemen passing us, woke me up, and the following dialogue ensued between the postilion and myself. *I.* These gentlemen are coming from Ischl, so I shall probably find no horses there. *He.* Oh! the two carriages that stopped at the Inn were also from Ischl; still there is no doubt you will get horses. *I.* Are you sure they came from Ischl? *He.* Quite sure: they go there every year, and were here last summer also; I drove them. It is a baroness from Vienna, (Heavens! thought I,) and she is dreadfully rich, and has such handsome daughters. When they went to Berchtesgaden to visit the mines, I drove them, and very nice they looked in their miner's dresses: they have a grand estate, and yet they speak to us quite familiarly. Halt! cried I; what name?—Don't know.—Pereira?*—Not sure.—Drive back,—said I in a resolute tone.—If I do, we shall not reach Ischl to-night, and we have got over the worst hill; you can learn the name at the next stage.—I hesitated, and we drove on. They did not know the name at the next stage, nor at the following one either. At length, at the end of seven long wearisome hours, we arrived, and before I left the carriage, I said, who were the party who drove to Salzburg this morning in two carriages? and received the quiet reply,—Baroness Pereira; she proceeds to Gastein early to-morrow morning, but returns four or five days hence. Now I had arrived at a certainty, and I

---

* A relation of the family.

also spoke to her driver, who said that none of the
family were here. The two gentlemen I met in a carriage on the road, were sons of the Baroness (the
very two I had never seen). In addition to all this, I
remembered a wretched portrait that I had once
got a glimpse of at our aunt H——'s, and the lady
in the black dress was Baroness Pereira! Heaven
knows when I may have another opportunity of
seeing her! I do not think that she ever could
have made a more pleasing impression on me, and
I shall not assuredly soon forget her attractive
appearance, and her kind expression of counte-
nance.

Nothing is more unsatisfactory than a presentiment; we all experience them, but we never
discover till too late, that they really were presen-
timents. I would have returned then and there,
and travelled through the night, but I reflected that
I should only overtake her at the very moment of
her departure, or that possibly she might have left
Salzburg before my arrival, and that I should thus
frustrate all the plan of my journey to Vienna. At
one moment I thought of going to Gastein, but I
could not help feeling that Salzburg had treated
me very badly, so I once more said adieu, and went
to bed very crest-fallen. Next morning I desired
that her empty house should be pointed out to me,
and made a sketch of it for you, dear mother. My
bad luck, however, was still growling in the distance, for I could find no favourable spot to take
my sketch from. Besides, they charged me more

than a ducat at the inn for one night's entertainment, etc., etc. I gave utterance to various anathemas, both in English and German, and drove away, laying aside among the things of the past, Ischl, Salzburg, Baroness Pereira, and the Traunsee; and so I came on here, where I have taken a day's rest.

To-morrow I intend to pursue my journey, and (D. V.) to sleep in Vienna the day after. I will write to you further from thence. Thus ended my day of misfortunes; "truth, and *no* poetry," not even the leaning the hand against the door of my carriage is invention; all is a portrait taken from life. The most incomprehensible thing is that I should have totally overlooked Flora, who it seems was also there, for the old lady in a tartan cloak, who went into the inn, was Frau von W——, and the old gentleman with green spectacles who followed her, could not well have been Flora? In short, when things once take a wrong turn, they will have their course. I can write no more to-day, for my disappointment is still too recent; in my next letter I will describe the Salzkammergut, and all the beauties of my journey yesterday.' How right Devrient was to advise me to take this route! The Traunstein also, and the Traun Falls, are wonderfully fine; and after all, the world is a very pleasant world, and it is fortunate for me that you are in it, and that I shall find letters from you the day after to-morrow, and possibly much that is agreeable besides. Dear Fanny, I mean now to

compose my *Non nobis,* and the symphony in A
minor. Dear Rebecca, if you could hear me singing
" Im warmen Thal " in a spasmodic fashion, you
would think it rather deplorable; you could sing it
better. Oh, Paul! can you declare that you understand the Schein Gulden, W. W. Gulden, heavy
Gulden, light Gulden, Conventions Gulden, and the
devil and his grandmother's Gulden? I don't, one
bit. I wish therefore that you were with me, but
for many reasons besides this one. Farewell!

Presburg, September 27th, 1830.

Dear Brother,

Peals of bells, drums and music, carriages on carriages, people hurrying in all directions, everywhere
gay crowds, such is the general aspect around me,
for to-morrow is to be the coronation of the King,
which the whole city has been expecting since
yesterday, and are now imploring that the sky may
clear up, and wake bright and cheerful, for the
grand ceremony which ought to have taken place
yesterday was obliged to be deferred on account of
the torrents of rain. This afternoon the sky is blue
and beautiful, and the moon is now shining down
tranquilly on the tumult of the city. To-morrow at
a very early hour the Crown Prince is to take his
oaths (as King of Hungary) in the large Market-
place; he is then to go to church in grand proces

sion, attended by a whole array of bishops and nobles of the realm, and afterwards rides up the Königsberg, which lies opposite my windows, in order to wave his sword towards the banks of the Danube and the four quarters of the globe, in token that he takes possession of his new realm.

This excursion has made me acquainted with a new country; for Hungary with her magnates, her high dignitaries, her Oriental luxury, and also her barbarism, is to be seen here, and the streets offer a spectacle which is to me both novel and striking. We really seem here to approach closer to the East; the miserably obtuse peasants or serfs; the troops of gipsies; the equipages and retainers of the nobles overloaded with gold and gems, (for the grandees themselves are only visible through the closed windows of their carriages); then the singularly bold national physiognomy, the yellow hue, the long moustaches, the soft foreign idiom—all this makes the most motley impression in the world.

Early yesterday I went alone through the streets. First came a long array of jovial officers, on spirited little horses; behind them a crew of gipsies, making music; succeeded by Vienna fashionables, with eyeglasses and kid gloves, conversing with a Capuchin monk; then a couple of uncivilized peasants in long white coats, their hats pressed down on their foreheads, and their straight black hair cut even all round, (they have reddish-brown complexions, a languid gait, and an indescribable expression of savage stupidity and indifference); then came a couple of sharp, acute-looking students of theology. in their long blue coats, walking arm-in-arm; Hungarian proprietors in their dark blue national costume; court servants; and numbers of carriages every moment arriving, covered with mud. I followed the crowd as they slowly moved on up the hill, and so at last I arrived at the dilapidated castle, which commands an extensive view of the whole city and the Danube. People were looking down on all sides from the ancient white walls, and from the towers and balconies; in every corner boys were scribbling their names on the walls for the benefit of posterity; in a small chamber (perhaps once on a time a chapel, or a sleeping-apartment) an ox was in the act of being roasted whole, and as it turned on the spit, the people shouted with delight; a succession of cannons bristled before the castle, destined to bellow forth their appropriate thunders at the coronation.

Below, on the Danube, which runs very rapidly here, darting with the speed of an arrow through the pontoon bridge, lay a new steamer, that had just arrived, laden with strangers; then the extensive view of the flat but wooded country, and meadows overflowed by the Danube; of the embankments and streets swarming with human beings, and mountains clothed with Hungarian vines—all this was not a little strange and foreign. Then the pleasant contrast of living in the same house with the best and most friendly people in the world, and finding novelty doubly interesting in their society.

These were really among the happy days, dear brother, that a kind Providence so often and so richly bestows on me.

September 28th, one o'clock.

The King is crowned—the ceremony was wonderfully fine. How can I even try to describe it to you? An hour hence we will all drive back to Vienna, and thence I pursue my journey. There is a tremendous uproar under my windows, and the Burgher-guards are flocking together, but only for the purpose of shouting "*Vivat!*" I pushed my way through the crowd, while our ladies saw everything from the windows, and never can I forget the effect of all this brilliant and almost fabulous magnificence.

In the great square of the Hospitallers the people were closely packed together, for there the oaths were to be taken on a platform hung with cloth; and afterwards the people were to be allowed the privilege of tearing down the cloth for their own use; close by was a fountain spouting red and white Hungarian wine. The grenadiers could not keep back the people; one unlucky hackney coach that stopped for a moment was instantly covered with men, who clambered on the spokes of the wheels, and on the roof, and on the box, swarming on it like ants, so that the coachman, unable to drive on, without becoming a murderer, was forced to wait quietly where he was. When the procession arrived, which was received bare-headed, I had the utmost difficulty in taking off my hat, and holding it above my head; an old Hungarian, however, behind me, whose view it intercepted, quickly devised a remedy, for without ceremony he made a snatch at my unlucky hat, and in an instant flattened it to the size of a cap; then they yelled as if they had all been spitted, and fought for the cloth; in short they were a mob; but my Magyars! the fellows look as if they were born noblemen, and privileged to live at ease, looking very melancholy, but riding like the devil.

When the procession descended the hill, first came the court servants, covered with embroidery, the trumpeters and kettle drums, the heralds and all that class, and then suddenly galloped along the street a mad Count, *en pleine carrière*, his horse plunging and capering, and the caparisons edged with gold; the Count himself a mass of diamonds, rare herons' plumes, and velvet embroidery (though he had not yet assumed his state uniform, being bound to ride so madly—Count Sandor is the name of this furious cavalier.) He had an ivory sceptre in his hand with which he urged on his horse, causing it each time to rear, and to make a tremendous bound forward.

When his wild career was over, a procession of about sixty more magnates arrived, all in the same fantastic splendour, with handsome coloured turbans, twisted moustaches, and dark eyes. One rode a white horse covered with a gold net; another a dark grey, the bridle and housings studded with

diamonds ; then came a black charger with purple
cloth caparisons. One magnate was attired from
head to foot in sky blue, thickly embroidered with
gold, a white turban, and a long white dolman ;
another in cloth of gold, with a purple dolman;
each one more rich and gaudy than the other, and
all riding so boldly and fearlessly, and with such
defiant gallantry, that it was quite a pleasure to
look at them. At length came the Hungarian
Guards, with Esterhazy at their head, dazzling in
gems and pearl embroidery. How can I describe
the scene ? You ought to have seen the procession
deploy and halt in the spacious square, and all the
jewels and bright colours, and the lofty golden
mitres of the bishops, and the crucifixes glittering
in the brilliant sunshine like a thousand stars !

Well, to-morrow, God willing, I proceed on my
journey. Now, dear brother, you have a letter, so
pray write soon, and let me hear how you are getting on. So you have had an *émeute* in Berlin ?
and that, too, an *émeute* of tailors' apprentices ?
What did it all mean ? Once more I send you my
farewell from Germany, my dear parents, and
brother and sisters. I am leaving Hungary for
Italy, and thence I hope to write to you more frequently and more at leisure. Be of good cheer,
dear Paul, and go forwards in a confident spirit ;
rejoice with those that rejoice, and do not forget
the brother who is wandering about the world.

Yours,   FELIX.

Venice, October 10th, 1830.

Italy at last ! and what I have all my life considered as the greatest possible felicity, is now begun, and I am basking in it. The day has been so fruitful in enjoyment, that I must, now that it is evening, endeavour to collect my thoughts a little to write to you, my dear parents, and to thank you for having bestowed such happiness on me. You also, my dear brother and sisters, are often in my thoughts. How much I wish for you, Paul, to be with me here, once more to enjoy your delight in our rapid travels by sea and by land; and I should like to prove to you, Hensel, that the "Assumption of the Blessed Virgin" is the most divine work ever produced by the hands of man. You are not here, however, so I am obliged to give vent to my enthusiasm in bad Italian to the *laquais de place*, who stands still and listens.

I shall however become quite confused, if things are to go on as they have done on this first day, when every hour brought with it so much never to be forgotten, that I do not know where to find sufficient grasp of intellect to comprehend it all properly. I saw the "Assumption," then a whole gallery of paintings in the Manfrini Palace; then a church festival in the church where hangs Titian's St. Peter; afterwards St. Mark's, and in the afternoon I had a row on the Adriatic, and visited the public gardens, where the people lie on the grass and eat. I then returned to the Piazza of St. Mark, where in the twilight there is always an im

mense crowd and crush of people; and all this I
was obliged to see to-day, because there is so much
that is novel and interesting to be seen to-morrow.

But I must now relate methodically how I came
hither by water, (for, as Telemachus says, to do so
by land would be no easy matter,) and so I begin
my history at Gratz, which is certainly the most
tiresome hole in the world, and where you yawn all
day; and why should I have stayed a single day
longer, on account of a (he) relation ? How can a
traveller with any experience possibly accept of a
brother, who is also an ensign, in the place of a
charming mother and sister ? In short, the man did
not know what to do with me, for which I forgive
him freely, and shall not defame him to his mother,
when I perform my promise and write to her; but
he took me to the theatre to see the " Rehbock,"
the most wretched, silly, objectionable piece that
the late Kotzebue ever wrote; and moreover he
declared it to be very good and very amusing, and
this is not to be forgiven, for this *Rehbock* has such
a *haut goût* or *fumet*, that it could not even please
a cat : but at all events I have left Gratz, for here
I am in Venice.

My old vetturino woke me up at four o'clock in
the dark, and the horse crawled off with us both.
I thought of you, dear father, at least a hundred
times during our journey of two days. You would
certainly have gone wild with impatience, and possibly assaulted the coachman also, for at every
little declivity, he got slowly off the box, deliber-

ately put on the drag, and crept up the smallest hill at a snail's pace; then he thought fit to walk beside his horses for a time, to stretch his legs: every possible conveyance passed us on the road, even when drawn by dogs or donkeys, and when at last, at a steep hill, the fellow put on two oxen as leaders, whose pace exactly corresponded with that of his horse, I had the greatest difficulty in not belabouring him, indeed I did so more than once; but he then gravely assured me that we were going at a capital pace, and I had no means of proving the contrary. Moreover he always passed the night in the most detestable pot-houses, starting again at four o'clock in the morning, so on arriving at Klagenfurt I was fairly worn out; but when in answer to my question as to the time the Venetian diligence set out, I received the answer,—in an hour hence,—I seemed to revive. I was promised a place, and I also got a good supper. The diligence, indeed, did not arrive for two hours after its time, having been detained by deep snow on the Sömmering, but still it came at last. Three Italians were inside, and chattered so that I could scarcely get to sleep, but my snoring fairly silenced them after a time.

At last morning broke, and as we drove into Resciutta, the driver said, that on the other side of the bridge there, no one understood a word of German. I therefore took leave of my mother tongue for a long time to come, and we drove over the bridge. The style of the houses immediately beyond was entirely different. The flat roofs with their convex tiles, the deep windows, the high white walls, and lofty square towers, all betokened another land. The pale olive faces of the men, the innumerable beggars who besieged the carriage, the various small chapels, brightly and carefully painted on every side with flowers, the nuns, monks, and so forth, were all symptomatic of Italy. The monotonous character of the whole scenery however, and of the road we were travelling, passing through bare white rocks, along the banks of a river with a rough rocky bed, in summer creeping along in the form of a tiny brook, certainly does not seem characteristic of Italy. "I purposely made this passage rather meagre, in order that the *subject* might be more distinctly heard," says Abt Vogler; and I almost think that Providence has done pretty much the same here, for when we had passed Ospedaletto the *subject* did come out well, and a fine sight it was. I had imagined that the first impression of Italy would be like that of a sudden explosion, violent and startling; I have not hitherto found this to be the case. The effect produced on me has been rather that of a genial warmth, mildness and cheerfulness, and an indescribable sensation of pervading content and satisfaction.

After passing Ospedaletto we entered a plain, leaving the blue mountains behind us; the sun shone bright and warm through the foliage of the vines; the road winding through orchards, in which the trees were connected by trailing boughs. I felt as

if I were at home again, and knew every object, and
was once more about to take possession of it all.
The carriage too seemed to *fly* over the smooth
road, and towards evening we arrived at Udine,
where we passed the night, when for the first time
I ordered my supper in Italian, my tongue skating
as if on slippery ice, first gliding into English, and
then stumbling afresh. Moreover next morning I
was famously cheated, but I did not in the least
care, and on we went. It happened to be Sunday,
and on every side people were coming along, in
bright southern costumes, and flowers; the women
with roses in their hair. Light single-horse carriages drove past, and men were riding to church
on donkeys; at the inns, groups of idlers were to
be seen in the most picturesque, indolent attitudes:
among others, one man placed his arm quietly
round his wife's waist, and swung round with her
and then they went on their way; this sounds trivial
enough, and yet it had a pretty effect. Venetian
villas now were occasionally visible from the road,
and by degrees became more frequent, till at length
our way led past houses, trees, and gardens like a
park. The whole country had a gay festive air,
as if a Prince were expected to make his grand
entry, and the vine-branches with their rich purple
grapes hanging in festoons from the trees, made
the most lovely of all festive wreaths. The inhabitants were all gaily dressed and adorned, and a few
scattered cypresses only enhanced the general
effect.

In Treviso there was an illumination, paper lanterns suspended in every part of the great square, and a large gaudy transparency in the centre. Some most lovely girls were walking about, in their long white veils and scarlet petticoats. It was quite dark when we arrived at Mestre last night, when we got into a boat, and in a dead calm, gently rowed across to Venice. On our passage thither, where nothing but water is to be seen, and distant lights, we saw a small rock which stands in the midst of the sea; on this a lamp was burning; all the sailors took off their hats as we passed, and one of them said, this was the "Madonna of Tempests," which are often most dangerous and violent here. We then glided quietly into the great city, under innumerable bridges, without sound of post-horns, or rattling of wheels, or toll-keepers; the passage now became more thronged, and numbers of ships were lying near; past the theatre, where gondolas in long rows lie waiting for their masters, just as our own carriages do at home, then into the great canal, past the church of St. Mark, the Lions, the palace of the Doges, and the Bridge of Sighs. The obscurity of night only enhanced my delight on hearing the familiar names, and seeing the dark outlines.

And so I am actually in Venice! Well, to-day I have seen the finest pictures in the world, and have at last personally made the acquaintance of a very admirable man, whom hitherto I only knew by name —I allude to a certain Signor Giorgione, an inimi-

table artist—and also to Pordenone, who paints the
most noble portraits, both of himself and many of
his simple scholars, in such a devout, faithful, and
pious spirit, that you seem to converse with him,
and to feel an affection for him. Who would not
have been confused by all this? But if I am to
speak of Titian, I must do so in a more reverent
mood. Till now, I never knew that he was the feli-
citous artist I have this day seen him to be. That
he thoroughly enjoyed life, in all its beauty and ful-
ness, the picture in Paris proves; but he has fathomed
the depths of human sorrow, as well as the joys of
Heaven. His glorious "Entombment," and also
the "Assumption," fully evince this. How Mary
floats on the cloud, while a waving movement seems
to pervade the whole picture; how you see at a
glance her very breathing, her awe, and piety, and
in short a thousand feelings,—all words seem poor
and commonplace in comparison! The three angels
too, on the right of the picture, are of the highest
order of beauty,—pure, serene loveliness, so unconscious, so bright and so seraphic. But no more of
this! or I must perforce become poetical, or indeed
am so already, and this does not at all suit me; but
I shall certainly see it every day.

I must however say a few words about the " Entombment," as you have the engraving. Look at it,
and think of me. This picture represents the conclusion of a great tragedy: so still, so grand, and
so acutely painful. Magdalene is supporting Mary,
fearing that she will die of anguish; she endeavours

to lead her away, but looks round herself once more, evidently wishing to imprint this spectacle indelibly on her heart, thinking that it is for the last time; it surpasses everything; and then the sorrowing John, who sympathizes and suffers with Mary; and Joseph, who absorbed in his piety, and occupied with the tomb, directs and conducts the whole; and Christ himself, lying there so tranquil, having endured to the end: then the blaze of brilliant colour, and the gloomy mottled sky! It is a composition that speaks to my heart and fills me with enthusiasm, and will never leave my memory.

I believe few things I have yet to see in Italy will affect me so deeply; but you know that I am devoid of all prejudices, and I give you a fresh proof of this by telling you that the "Martyrdom of St. Peter," from which I expected the most, pleased me the least of the three; it did not strike me as being a complete whole; the landscape, which is very fine, seemed to me to predominate too much. Then I was dissatisfied with the disposition in the picture of *two* victims and only *one* murderer; (for the small figure in the distant background does not remedy this). I could not bring myself to consider it a martyrdom. But probably I am in error, and I intend to study it more carefully to-morrow; my contemplation of it, besides, was disturbed by some one strumming most sacrilegiously on the organ, and these sacred forms were forced to listen to such miserable opera *finales!* But this matters not; where such pictures are, I require no organist. I play the organ in my thoughts

for myself, and feel as little irritated by such trash,
as I should be by an ignorant rabble. Titian, however, was a man well adapted to improve others; so
I shall try to profit by him, and to rejoice that I am
in Italy. At this moment the gondoliers are shouting to each other, and the lights are reflected in the
depths of the waters; one is playing a guitar, and
singing to it. It is a charming night. Farewell!
and think of me in every happy hour as I do of you.

FELIX.

To PROFESSOR ZELTER.*

Venice, October 16th, 1830.

Dear Professor,

I have entered Italy at last, and I intend this
letter to be the commencement of a regular series
of reports, which I purpose transmitting to you, of
all that appears to me particularly worthy of notice.
Though I only now for the first time write to you, I
must beg you to impute the blame to the state of
constant excitement in which I lived, both in Munich
and in Vienna. It was needless for me to describe to
you the parties in Munich, which I attended every
evening, and where I played the piano more unremittingly than I ever did in my life before; one *soirée*
succeeding another so closely, that I really had

---

* Mendelssohn's instructor in the theory of music.

4

not a moment to collect my thoughts. Moreover, it would not have particularly interested you, for after all, "good society which does not offer materials for the smallest epigram," is equally vapid in a letter. I hope that you have not taken amiss my long silence, and that I may expect a few lines from you, even if they contain nothing save that you are well and cheerful.

The aspect of the world at this moment is very bleak and stormy, and much that was once thought durable and unchangeable, has been swept away in the course of a couple of days. It is then doubly welcome to hear well-known voices, to convince us that there are certain things which cannot be annihilated or demolished, but remain firm and steadfast. You must know that I am at this moment very uneasy at not having received any news from home for some weeks past. I found no letters from my family, either at Trieste or here, so a few lines from you, written in your old fashion, would both cheer and gratify me, especially as it would prove that you think of me with the same kindness that you have always done from my childhood to the present time.

My family have no doubt told you of the exhilarating impression made on me by the first sight of the plains of Italy. I hurry from one enjoyment to another hour by hour, and constantly see something novel and fresh; but immediately on my arrival I discovered some masterpieces of art, which I study with deep attention, and contemplate daily for a couple of hours at least. These are three pictures by Titian. The "Presentation of Mary as a Child in the Temple;" the "Assumption of the Virgin;" and the "Entombment of Christ." There is also a portrait by Giorgione, representing a girl with a cithern in her hand, plunged in thought, and looking forth from the picture in serious meditation (she is apparently about to begin a song, and you feel as if you must do the same): besides many others.

To see these alone would be worth a journey to Venice; for the fruitfulness, genius, and devotion of the great men who painted these pictures, seem to emanate from them afresh as often as you gaze at their works, and I do not much regret that I have scarcely heard any music here; for I suppose I must not venture to include the music of the angels, in the "Assumption," encircling Mary with joyous shouts of welcome; one gaily beating the tambourine, a couple of others blowing away on strange crooked flutes, while another charming group are singing—or the music floating in the thoughts of the cithern player. I have only once heard anything on the organ, and miserable it was. I was gazing at Titian's "Martyrdom of St. Peter" in the Franciscan Church. Divine service was going on, and nothing inspires me with more solemn awe than when on the very spot for which they were originally created and painted, those ancient pictures in all their grandeur, gradually steal forth out of the darkness in which the long lapse of time has veiled them.

As I was earnestly contemplating the enchanting
evening landscape with its trees, and angels among
the boughs, the organ commenced. The first sound
was quite in harmony with my feelings; but the
second, third, and in fact all the rest, quickly roused
me from my reveries, and sent me straight home,
for the man was playing in church and during
divine service, and in the presence of respectable
people, thus:

with the "Martyrdom of St. Peter" actually close
beside him! I was therefore in no great hurry to
make the acquaintance of the organist. There is
no regular Opera here at this moment, and the gondoliers no longer sing Tasso's stanzas; moreover,

what I have hitherto seen of modern Venetian art,
consists of poems framed and glazed on the subject of Titian's pictures, or Rinaldo and Armida,
by a new Venetian painter, or a St. Cecilia by a
ditto, besides various specimens of architecture in
no style at all; as all these are totally insignificant,
I cling to the ancient masters, and study how they
worked. Often, after doing so, I feel a musical inspiration, and since I came here I have been busily
engaged in composition.

Before I left Vienna, a friend of mine made me a
present of Luther's Hymns, and on reading them
over I was again so much struck by their power, that
I intend to compose music for several next winter.
I have nearly completed here the choral " Aus tiefer
Noth," for four voices *a capella;* and the Christmas
hymn, " Vom Himmel hoch," is already in my head.
I wish also to set the following hymns to music:
"Ach Gott, vom Himmel sieh darein," " Wir glauben
all' an einen Gott," " Verleih uns Frieden," " Mitten wir im Leben sind," and finally " Ein' feste
Burg." The latter, however, it is my intention to
compose for a choir and orchestra. Pray write to
me about this project of mine, and say whether you
approve of my retaining the ancient melodies in
them all, but not adhering to them too strictly:
for instance, if I were to take the first verse of
" Vom Himmel hoch " as a separate grand chorus.
Besides this, I am hard at work at an orchestral
overture, and if an opportunity for an opera offered
it would be most welcome.

I finished two pieces of sacred music in Vienna —a choral in three movements for chorus and orchestra ("O! Haupt voll Blut und Wunden") and an Ave Maria for a choir of eight voices, *a capella*. The people I associated with there were so dissipated and frivolous, that I became quite spiritually-minded, and conducted myself like a divine among them. Moreover, not one of the best pianoforte players there, male or female, ever played a note of Beethoven, and when I hinted that he and Mozart were not to be despised, they said, "So you are an admirer of classical music?"—"Yes," said I.

To-morrow I intend to go to Bologna to have a glance at the St. Cecilia, and then proceed by Florence to Rome, where I hope (D. V.) to arrive eight or ten days hence I will then write to you more satisfactorily. I only wished to make a beginning to day, and to beg you not to forget me, and kindly to accept my heartfelt wishes for your health and happiness.   Your faithful

FELIX.

Florence, October 23rd, 1830.

Here am I in Florence, the air warm and the sky bright; everything is beautiful and glorious, " wo blieb die Erde," as Goethe says. I have now received your letter of the 3rd, by which I see that you are all well, that my anxiety was needless, that you are all going on as usual, and thinking of me;

so I feel happy again, and can now see everything, and enjoy everything, and am able to write to you; in short, my mind is at rest on the main point. I made my journey here amid a thousand doubts and fears, quite uncertain whether to go direct to Rome, because I did not expect any letters at Florence. Fortunately, however, I decided on coming here, and now it is of no consequence how the misunderstanding arose, that caused me to wait for letters in Venice, while you had written to Florence; all I can promise is to endeavour in future to be less over-anxious. My driver pointed out a spot between the hills, on which lay a blue mist, and said "*Ecco Firenze!*" I eagerly looked towards the place, and saw the round dome looming out of the mist before me, and the spacious wide valley in which the city is situated. My love of travel revived when at last Florence appeared. I looked at some willow-trees (as I thought) beside the road, when the driver said, "Buon olio," and then I saw that they were hanging full of olives.

My driver, as a genus, is undoubtedly a most villanous knave, thief, and impostor; he has cheated me and half-starved me, and yet I think him almost amiable from his enthusiastic animal nature. About an hour before we arrived in Florence he said that the beautiful scenery was now about to commence; and true it is that the fair land of Italy does first begin then. There are villas on every height, and decorated old walls, with sloping terraces of roses and aloes, flowers and grapes and olive leaves, the sharp points of cypresses, and the flat tops of pines, all sharply defined against the sky; then handsome square faces, busy life on the roads on every side, and at a distance in the valley, the blue city.

So I drove confidently into Florence in my little open carriage, and though I looked shabby and dusty, like one coming from the Apennines, I cared little for that. I passed recklessly through all the smart equipages from which the most refined English ladies looked at me; while I thought it may one day actually come to pass that you who are now looking down on the *roturier*, may shake hands with him, the only difference being a little clean linen and so forth. By the time that we came to the *battisterio*, I no longer felt diffident, but gave orders to drive to the Post, and then I was really happy, for I received three letters,—yours of the 22nd and the 3rd, and my father's also. I was now quite delighted, and as we drove along beside the Arno, to Schneider's celebrated hotel, the world seemed once more a very pleasant world.

October 24th.

The Apennines are really not so beautiful as I had imagined; for the name always suggested to me richly wooded, picturesque hills, covered with vegetation, whereas they are merely a long chain of melancholy bleak hills; and the little verdure there is, not gratifying to the eye. There are no dwellings to be seen, no merry brooks or rills; only an occasional stream, its broad bed dried up, or a little

water-channel. Add to this the shameful roguery
of the inhabitants: really, at last, I became quite
confused and perplexed, by their incessant cheating,
and could scarcely discover for what object they
were lying. I therefore, once for all, invariably
protested against every demand they made, and
declared that I would not pay at all if they asked
more than I chose to give; so in this way I managed
very tolerably.

Last night I was again in grand quarters: I had
made an agreement with the vetturino for board
and lodging, and all I required. The natural consequence was, that the fellow took me to the most
detestable little inns, and actually starved me. So
late yesterday we arrived at a solitary pothouse,
the filth of which no pen can describe. The stair
was strewed with heaps of dead leaves and firewood;
moreover the cold was intense, and they invited me
to warm myself in the kitchen, which I agreed to
do. A bench was placed for me beside the fire; a
whole troop of peasants were standing about, also
warming themselves. I looked quite regal from my
bench on the hearth among this rough set of fellows,
who, in their broad-leaved hats, lit up by the fire, and
babbling in their incomprehensible dialect, looked
vastly suspicious characters. I made them prepare
my soup under my own eyes, giving moreover good
advice on the subject; but, after all, it was not
eatable.

I entered into conversation with my subjects
from my throne on the hearth, and they pointed out

to me a little hill in the distance incessantly vomiting forth flames, which had a singular effect in the dark ("Raticosa" is the name of the hill), and then I was conducted to my bed-room. The landlord took hold of the sackcloth sheets, and said, " Very fine linen !" but I slept as sound as a bear, and before falling asleep I said to myself, Now you are in the Apennines : and next morning, after getting no breakfast, my vetturino civilly asked me how I liked my night's entertainment. The fellow talked a great deal of nonsense about politics, and the present state of France, abused his horse in German for being born in Switzerland, and spoke French to the beggars who swarmed round the cabriolet, while I corrected many a fault in his pronunciation.

October 25th.

I now intend to go once more to the Tribune, to be inspired with feelings of reverence. There is a particular place where I like to sit, as the little Venus de' Medici is directly opposite, and above, that of Titian, and by turning rather to the left, I have a view of the Madonna del Cardello, a favourite picture of mine, and which invariably reminds me of *la belle Jardinière*, and seems to me a kindred creation; and also the Fornarina, which made no great impression on me from the first, for I know the engraving, which is very faithful, and the face has, I think, a most disagreeable and even ordinary expression. In gazing thus, however, at the two Venuses, their loveliness inspires a feeling of piety;

it is as if the two spirits who could produce such creations, were flying through the hall and grasping you as they passed.

Titian must have been a marvellous man, and enjoyed his life in his works; still the fair Medici is not to be slighted, and then the divine Niobe with all her children : while we gaze at her, we can find no words. I have not yet been to the Pitti Palace, which possesses the Saint Ezekiel, and the Madonna della Sedia, of Raphael. I saw the gardens of the palace yesterday in sunshine; they are superb, and the thick solid stems of the myrtles and laurels, and the innumerable cypresses, made a strange exotic impression on me; but when I declare that I consider beeches, limes, oaks, and firs, ten times more beautiful and picturesque, I think I hear Hensel exclaim, "Oh, the northern bear!"

October 30th.

After the soft rain of yesterday, the air is so mild and genial, that I am at this moment seated at the open window writing to you; and indeed it is pleasant enough to see the people going about the streets, offering the prettiest baskets of flowers, fresh violets, roses, and pinks. Two days ago, being satiated with all pictures, statues, vases, and museums, I resolved to take a long walk till sunset; so after buying a bunch of narcissuses and heliotropes, I went up the hill through the vineyards. It was one of the most delightful walks I ever remember;

every one must feel revived and refreshed at the
sight of nature in such a garb as this, and a thous-
and happy thoughts passed through my mind.

First of all, I went to a villa called Bello
Sguardo, whence the whole of Florence and its spacious valley are to be seen, and I thoroughly enjoyed
the view of the superb city and its massive towers
and palaces. But most of all I admired the count-
less villas, covering every hill and every acclivity
as far as the eye can reach, as if the city extended
beyond the mountains into the far distance. And
when I took up a telescope and looked down on the
valley through the blue mists, every portion of it
seemed thickly dotted with bright objects and white
villas, while such a large circle of dwellings inspired
me with a feeling of home and comfort.

I proceeded far over the hills to the highest point
I could see, on which stood an ancient tower, and
when I reached it I found all the people throughout
the building busily engaged in making wine, drying
grapes, and repairing casks. It proved to be
Galileo's tower, from which he used to make his
discoveries and observations; from here also there
was a very extensive view, and the girl who took
me to the roof of the tower related a number of
stories in her peculiar dialect, which I scarcely
understood at all; but she afterwards presented me
with some of her sweet dried grapes, which I ate
with great gusto. And so I went on to another
tower I saw at a distance, but could not manage to
find my way; and examining my map as I went

along, I stumbled on a traveller busily searching his map also; the only difference between us being, that he was an old Frenchman with green spectacles, who addressed me thus, "È questo S. Miniato al Monte, Signor?" With admirable decision I replied, "Si, Signor;" and it turned out that I was right. A. F—— immediately recurred to my memory, as she had advised me to see this monastery, which is indeed wonderfully fine.

When I tell you I went from there to the Boboli Gardens, where I saw the sun set, and at night enjoyed the brightest moonlight, you may imagine how much I was invigorated by my ramble. I will write to you about the pictures here some other time, for to-day it is too late, as I have still to take leave of the Pitti Palace and the great Gallery, and to gaze once more at my Venus, who is not indeed mentioned before ladies, but whose beauty is truly divine. The courier goes at five o'clock, and God willing, I shall be in Rome the day after to-morrow. From thence you shall hear again.

FELIX.

————————————

Rome, November 2nd, 1830.

.. I refrain from writing longer in this melancholy strain; for just as your letter, after a lapse of fourteen days, has saddened me, my answer will have the same effect on you fourteen days hence.

5

You would write to me in the same style, and so it might go on for ever. As four weeks must pass before I can receive any answer, I feel that I ought to restrict myself to relating events past and present, and not dwell much on the particular frame of my mind at the moment, which is indeed usually sufficiently manifest in the narrative given, and the various occurrences described.

I have scarcely yet arrived at the conviction that I am now actually in Rome; and when yesterday, just as day was breaking, I drove across a bridge with statues, under a deep blue sky, and in dazzling white moonlight, and the courier said, "Ponte Molle," it all seemed to me like a dream, and at the same moment I saw before me my sick-bed in London a year ago, and my rough Scotch journey, and Munich, and Vienna, and the pines on these hills. The journey from Florence to Rome has very few attractions. Siena, which is, I understand, worth seeing, we passed through during the night. It was unpleasant to see a regular Government courier compelled to take a military escort, which was doubled at night; still it must be absolutely necessary, as he is obliged to pay for it. In these days this ought not to be the case. In the meantime everything progresses, and there are moments when the bound forwards is actually visible.

I was still in Florence, waiting for the departure of the post, reading a French newspaper, when at the very moment the bell sounded, I read among the advertisements, "Vie de Siebenkäs, par Jean

Paul." Many reflections occurred to me as to so many men of renown gradually vanishing from our sight, and our great geniuses having such homage paid to them after their death, and yet during their *life*, Lafontaine's novels and French vaudevilles alone make any impression on their fellow-countrymen; while *we* only strive to appreciate the very refuse of the French, and neglect Beaumarchais and Rousseau. However, it matters little after all.

The first thing connected with music that I met with here, was the "Tod Jesu," by Graun, which an Abbate here, Fortunato Santini, has translated faithfully and admirably into Italian. It appears that the music of this heretic has been sent along with the translation to Naples, where it is to be produced this winter at a great festival, and I hear that the musical world there are quite enchanted with it, and are studying the work with infinite love and enthusiasm. I understand that the Abbate has been long impatiently expecting me, because he hopes to obtain considerable information from me about German music, and thinks I may also have the score of Bach's " Passion." Thus music progresses onwards, as sure to pierce through as the sun ; if mists still prevail, it is merely a sign that the spring-time has not yet come, but come again it must and will ! Farewell ! and from my heart I say,—May a merciful Providence preserve you all in health and happiness !

Felix.

Rome, November 8th, 1830.

I must now write to you of my first week in Rome; how I have arranged my time, how I look forward to the winter, and what impression the glorious objects by which I am surrounded have made on me; but this is no easy task. I feel as if I were entirely changed since I came here. Formerly when I wished to check my haste and impatience to press forward, and to continue my journey more rapidly, I attributed this eagerness merely to the force of habit, but I am now fully persuaded that it arose entirely from my anxiety to reach this goal. Now that I have at last attained it, my mood is so tranquil and joyous, and yet so earnest, that I shall not attempt to describe it to you. What it is that thus works on me I cannot exactly define; for the awe-inspiring Coliseum, and the brilliant Vatican, and the genial air of spring, all contribute to make me feel thus, and so do the kindly people, my comfortable apartments, and everything else. At all events I am different from what I was. I am better in health and happier than I have been for a long time, and take delight in my work, and feel such an inclination for it, that I expect to accomplish much more than I anticipated; indeed, I have already done a good deal. If it pleases Providence to grant me a continuation of this happy mood, I look forward to the most delightful and productive winter.

Picture to yourself a small house, with two windows in front, in the Piazza di Spagna, No. 5 which

all day long enjoys the warm sun, and an apartment
on the first floor, where there is a good Viennese
grand piano: on the table are some portraits of
Palestrina, Allegri, etc., along with the scores of
their works, and a Latin psalm-book, from which I
am to compose the *Non Nobis;*—such is my present
abode. The Capitol was too far away, besides I
had a great dread of the cold air, which here I have
no cause to guard against; for when I look out of
my window in the morning across the square, I see
every object sharply defined in the sunshine against
the blue sky. My landlord was formerly a captain
in the French army, and his daughter has the most
splendid contralto voice I ever heard. Above me
lives a Prussian captain, with whom I talk politics,
—in short, the situation is excellent.

When I come into the room early in the morning,
and see the sun shining so brightly on the breakfast-
table (you see I am marred as a poet), I feel so
cheerful and comfortable, for it is now far on in the
autumn, and who in our country at this season looks
for warmth, or a bright sky, or grapes and flowers?
After breakfast I begin my work, and play, and
sing, and compose till near noon. Then Rome in
all her vast dimensions lies before me like an interesting problem to enjoy; but I go deliberately to
work. daily selecting some different object apper-
taining to history. One day I visit the ruins of the
ancient city; another I go to the Borghese gallery,
or to the Capitol, or St. Peter's, or the Vatican.
Each day is thus made memorable, and as I take

my time, each object becomes firmly and indelibly impressed on me. When I am occupied in the forenoon I am willing to leave off, and should like to continue my writing, but I say to myself that I must see the Vatican, and when I am actually there, I equally dislike leaving it; thus each of my occupations causes me the most genuine pleasure, and one enjoyment follows another.

Just as Venice, with her past, reminded me of a vast monument: her crumbling modern palaces, and the perpetual remembrance of former splendour, causing sad and discordant sensations; so does the past of Rome suggest the impersonation of history; her monuments elevate the soul, inspiring solemn yet serene feelings, and it is a thought fraught with exultation that man is capable of producing creations, which, after the lapse of a thousand years, still renovate and animate others. When I have fairly imprinted an object like this on my mind, and each day a fresh one, twilight has usually arrived and the day is over.

I then visit my friends and acquaintances, when we mutually communicate what each has done, which means *enjoyed* here, and are reciprocally pleased. I have been most evenings at Bendemann's and Hübner's, where German artists usually assemble, and I sometimes go to Schadow's. The Abbate Santini is a valuable acquaintance for me, as he has a very complete library of ancient Italian music, and he kindly gives or lends me anything I like, for no one can be more obliging. At night he

makes either Ahlborn or me accompany him home,
as an Abbate being seen alone at night in the
streets would bring him into evil repute. That
such youngsters as Ahlborn and I should act as
duennas to a priest of sixty is diverting enough.

The Duchess of —— gave me a list of old music
which she was anxious to procure copies of if possible. Santini's collection contains all this, and I am
much obliged to him for having furnished me with
copies, for I am now looking through them all, and
becoming acquainted with them. I beg you will
send me for him, as a token of my gratitude, the six
cantatas of Sebastian Bach, published by Marx at
Simrock's, or some of his pieces for the organ. I
should however prefer the cantatas: he already has
the "Magnificat" and the Motets, and others. He
has translated the "Singet dem Herrn ein neues
Lied," and intends it to be executed at Naples, for
which he deserves a reward. I am writing to Zelter
all particulars about the Papal singers, whom I
have heard three times,—in the Quirinal, in the
Monte Cavallo, and once in San Carlo.

I look forward with delight to seeing Bunsen;
we shall have much to discuss together, and I have
likewise an idea that he has got some work for me;
if I can conscientiously undertake it, I will do so
gladly, and render it all the justice in my power.
Among my home pleasures I include that of reading
for the first time Goethe's Journey to Italy; and I
must avow that it is a source of great satisfaction
to me to find that he arrived in Rome the very

same day that I did; that he also went first to the Quirinal, and heard a Requiem there; that he was seized with the same fit of impatience in Florence and Bologna; and felt the same tranquil, or as he calls it, solid spirit here: indeed, everything that he describes, I exactly experience myself, so I am pleased.

He speaks in detail of a large picture of Titian's in the Vatican, and declares that its meaning is not to be devised; only a number of figures standing beautifully grouped together. I fancy, however, that I have discovered a very deep sense in it, and I believe that whoever finds the most beauties in Titian, is sure to be most in the right, for he was a glorious man. Though he has not had the opportunity of displaying and diffusing his genius here, as Raphael has done in the Vatican, still I can never forget his three pictures in Venice, and to these I may add the one in the Vatican, which I saw for the first time this morning. If any one could come into the world with full consciousness, every object around would smile on him with the same vivid life and animation, that these pictures do on us. "The School of Athens," and the "Disputa." and the "Peter," stand before us precisely as they were created; and then the entrance through splendid open arches, whence you can see the Piazza of St. Peter's, and Rome, and the blue Alban hills; and above our heads figures from the Old Testament, and a thousand bright little angels, and arabesques of fruit, and garlands of flowers; and then on to the gallery!

You may well be proud, dear Hensel, for your copy of the "Transfiguration" is superb! The pleasing emotion which seizes me, when I see for the first time some immortal work, and the pervading idea and chief impression it inspires, I did not experience on this occasion from the original, but from *your* copy. The first effect of this picture to-day, was precisely the same that yours had previously made on me; and it was not till after considerable research and contemplation that I succeeded in finding out anything new to me. On the other hand, the Madonna di Foligno dawned on me in the whole splendour of her loveliness. I have passed a happy morning in the midst of all these glorious works; as yet I have not visited the statues, but have reserved my first impression of them for another day.

November 9th, morning.

Thus every morning brings me fresh anticipations, and every day fulfils them. The sun is again shining on my breakfast-table and I am now going to my daily work. I will send you, dear Fanny, by the first opportunity, what I composed in Vienna, and anything else that may be finished, and my sketch-book to Rebecca; but I am far from being pleased with it this time, so I intend to study attentively the sketches of the landscape painters here, in order to acquire if possible a new manner. I tried to produce one of my own, but it would not do!

To-day I am going to the Lateran, and the ruins of ancient Rome; and in the evening to a kind English family, whose acquaintance I made here. Pray send me a good many letters of introduction. I am exceedingly anxious to know numbers of people, especially Italians. So I live on happily, and think of you in every pleasant moment. May you also be happy, and rejoice with me at the prospect which lies before me here!

FELIX M. B.

Rome, November 16th, 1830.

Dear Fanny,

No post left this the day before yesterday, and I could not talk to you, so when I remembered that my letter must necessarily remain two days before it left Rome, I felt it impossible to write; but I thought of you times without number, and wished you every happiness, and congratulated myself that you were born a certain number of years ago. It is, indeed, cheering to think what charming, rational beings, are to be found in the world; and you are certainly one of these. Continue cheerful, bright, and well, and make no great change in yourself. I don't think you require to be much better; may good fortune ever abide with you!

And now I think these are all my birthday good wishes; for really it is not fair to expect that a man of my *calibre* should wish you also a fresh stock of musical ideas; besides you are very unreasonable in complaining of any deficiency in that respect. *Per Bacco!* if you had the inclination, you certainly have sufficient genius to compose, and if you have no desire to do so, why grumble so much? If I had a baby to nurse, I certainly should not write any scores, and as I have to compose *Non Nobis*, I cannot unluckily carry my nephew about in my arms. But to speak seriously, your child is scarcely six months old yet, and you can think of anything but Sebastian?* (not Bach!) Be thankful that you have him. Music only retreats when there is no longer a place for her, and I am not surprised that you are not an unnatural mother. However, you have my best wishes on your birthday, for all that your heart desires; so I may as well wish you half-a-dozen melodies into the bargain; not that this will be of much use.

In Rome here, we celebrated the 14th of November by the sky shining, in blue and festive array, and breathing on us warm genial air. So I went on pleasantly towards the Capitol and into church, where I heard a miserable sermon from ——, who is no doubt a very good man, but to my mind has a most morose style of preaching; and any one who could irritate me on *such* a day, in the Capitol, and in church, must have an especial talent for so doing. I afterwards went to call on Bunsen, who had just arrived. He and his wife received me

---

* The name of the child.

most kindly, and we conversed on much that was interesting, including politics and regrets for your absence. *Apropos*, my favourite work that I am now studying is Goethe's 'Lili's Park,' especially three portions: "Kehr' ich mich um, und brumm:" then, "Eh la menotte;" and best of all, "Die ganze Luft ist warm, ist blüthevoll," where decidedly clarionets must be introduced. I mean to make it the subject of a scherzo for a symphony.

Yesterday, at dinner at Bunsen's, we had among others a German musician. Oh, heavens! I wish I were a Frenchman! The man said to me, "Music must be *handled* every day." "Why?" replied I, which rather embarrassed him. He also spoke of earnest purpose; and said that Spohr had no earnest purpose, but that he had distinctly discerned gleams of an earnest purpose in my *Tu es Petrus*. The fellow, however, has a small property at Frascati, and is about to *lay down* the profession of music. We have not got so far as that yet!

After dinner came Catel, Eggers, Senf, Wolf, then a painter, and then two more, and others. I played the piano, and they asked for pieces by Sebastian Bach, so I played numbers of his compositions, which were much admired. I also explained clearly to them the mode in which the "Passion" is executed; for they seemed scarcely to believe it. Bunsen possesses it, arranged for the piano; he showed it to the Papal singers, and they said before witnesses, that such music could not possibly be executed by human voices. I think the contrary.

It seems, however, that Trautwein is about to publish the score of the Passion of St. John. I suppose I must order a set of studs for Paris, *à la Bach*.

To-day Bunsen is to take me to Baini's, whom he has not seen for a year, as he never goes out except to hear confessions. I am glad to know him, and shall endeavour to improve my intimacy with him, for he can solve many an enigma for me. Old Santini continues as kind as ever. When we are together in society, if I praise any particular piece or am not acquainted with it, next morning he is sure to knock gently at my door, and to bring me the piece in question carefully wrapped up in a blue pocket-handkerchief; I, in return, accompany him home every evening; and we have a great regard for each other. He also brought me his *Te Deum*, written in eight parts, requesting me to correct some of the modulations, as G major predominates too much; so I mean to try if I cannot introduce some A minor or E minor.

I am now very anxious to become acquainted with a good many Italians. I visit at the house of a certain Maestro di San Giovanni Laterano, whose daughters are musical, but not pretty, so this does not count for much. If therefore you can send me letters, pray do so. I work in the morning; at noon I see and admire, and thus the day glides away till sunset; but I should like in the evening to associate with the Roman world. My kind English friends have arrived from Venice; Lord Harrowby and his family are to pass the winter here.

Schadow, Bendeman, Bunsen, Tippelskirch, all receive every evening; in short I have no lack of
acquaintances, but I should like to know some
Italians also.

The present, dear Fanny, that I have prepared
for your birthday, is a psalm, for chorus and orchestra, *Non nobis, Domine.* You know the melody well; there is an air in it which has a good
ending, and the last chorus will I hope please you.
I hear that next week I shall have an opportunity
of sending it to you, along with a quantity of new
music. I intend now to finish my overture, and
then (D.V.) to proceed with my symphony. A
pianoforte concerto, too, that I wish to write for
Paris, begins to float in my head. If Providence
kindly bestows on me success and bright days, I
hope we shall enjoy them together. Farewell!
May you be happy!

FELIX.

⎯⎯⎯⎯⎯⎯

Rome, November 22nd, 1830.

My dear Brother and Sisters,

You know how much I dislike, at a distance of
two hundred miles, and fourteen days' journey from
you, to offer good advice. I mean to do so, however, for once. Let me tell you therefore of a
mistake in your conduct, and in truth the same that
I once made myself. I do assure you that never in
my life have I known my father write in so irritable

a strain as since I came to Rome, and so I wish to ask you if you cannot devise some domestic recipe to cheer him a little? I mean by forbearance and yielding to his wishes, and in this manner, by allowing my father's view of any subject to predominate over your own; then, not to speak at all on topics that irritate him; and instead of saying shameful, say unpleasant; or instead of superb, very fair. This method has often a wonderfully good effect; and I put it, with all submission to yourselves, whether it might not be equally successful in this case? For, with the exception of the great events of the world, ill-humour often seems to me to proceed from the same cause that my father's did when I chose to pursue my own path in my musical studies. He was then in a constant state of irritation, incessantly abusing Beethoven and all visionaries; and this often vexed me very much, and made me sometimes very unamiable. At that very time something new came out, which put my father out of sorts, and made him I believe not a little uneasy. So long therefore as I persisted in extolling and exalting my Beethoven, the evil became daily worse; and one day, if I remember rightly, I was even sent out of the room. At last, however, it occurred to me that I might speak a great deal of truth, and yet avoid the particular truth obnoxious to my father; so the aspect of affairs speedily began to improve, and soon all went well.

Perhaps you may have in some degree forgotten that you ought now and then to be forbearing, and

not aggressive. My father considers himself both
much older and more irritable than, thank God, he
really is; but it is our duty always to submit our
opinion to his, even if the truth be as much on our
side, as it often is on his, when opposed to us.
Strive, then, to praise what he likes, and do not
attack what is implanted in his heart, more especially ancient established ideas. Do not commend
what is new till it has made some progress in the
world, and acquired a name, for till then it is a
mere matter of taste. Try to draw my father into
your circle, and be playful and kind to him. In
short, try to smooth and to equalize things; and remember that I, who am now an experienced man of
the world, never yet knew any family, taking into
due consideration all defects and failings, who have
hitherto lived so happily together as ours.

Do not send me any answer to this, for you will
not receive it for a month, and by that time no
doubt some fresh topic will have arisen; besides, if
I have spoken nonsense, I do not wish to be scolded
by you; and if I have spoken properly, I hope you
will follow my good advice.

November 23rd.

Just as I was going to set to work at the " Hebrides," arrived Herr B——, a musical professor from
Magdeburg. He played me over a whole book of
songs, and an Ave Maria, and begged to have the
benefit of my opinion. I seemed in the position of
a juvenile Nestor, and made him some insipid

speeches, but this caused me the loss of a morning in Rome, which is a pity. The Choral, "Mitten wir im Leben sind," is finished, and is certainly one of the best sacred pieces that I have yet composed. After I have completed the Hebrides, I think of arranging Händel's Solomon for future performance, with proper curtailments, etc. I then purpose writing the Christmas music of "Vom Himmel hoch," and the symphony in A minor; perhaps also some pieces for the piano, and a concerto, etc., just as they come into my head.

I own I do sadly miss some friend to whom I could communicate my new works, and who could examine the score along with me, and play a bass or a flute; whereas now when a piece is finished I must lay it aside in my desk without its giving pleasure to any one. London spoiled me in this respect. I can never again expect to meet all together such friends as I had there. Here I can only say the half of what I think, and leave the best half unspoken; whereas there it was not necessary to say more than the half, because the other half was a mere matter of course, and already understood. Still, this is a most delightful place.

We young people went lately to Albano, and set off in the most lovely weather. The road to Frascati passed under the great aqueduct, its dark brown outlines standing out sharply defined against the clear blue sky; thence we proceeded to the monastery at Grotta Ferrata, where there are some beautiful frescoes by Domenichino; then to Marino, very picturesquely situated on a hill, and proceeding along the margin of the lake we reached Castel Gandolfo. The scenery, like my first impression of Italy, is by no means so striking or so wonderfully beautiful as is generally supposed, but most pleasing and gratifying to the eye, and the outlines undulating and picturesque, forming a perfect whole, with its *entourage* and distribution of light.

Here I must deliver a eulogy on monks; they finish a picture at once, giving it tone and colour, with their wide loose gowns, their pious meditative gait, and their dark aspect. A beautiful shady avenue of evergreen oaks runs along the lake from Castel Gandolfo to Albano, where monks of every order are swarming, animating the scenery and yet marking its solitude. Near the city a couple of begging monks were walking together; further on, a whole troop of young Jesuits; then we saw an elegant young priest in a thicket reading; beyond this two more were standing in the wood with their guns, watching for birds. Then we came to a monastery, encircled by a number of small chapels. At last all was solitude; but at that moment appeared a dirty, stupid-looking Capuchin, laden with huge nosegays, which he placed before the various shrines, kneeling down in front of them before proceeding to decorate them.

As we passed on, we met two old prelates engaged in eager conversation. The bell for vespers was ringing in the monastery of Albano, and even on the summit of the highest hill stands a Passionist convent, where they are only permitted to speak for a single hour daily, and occupy themselves solely in reading the history of the passion of Christ. In Albano, among girls with pitchers on their heads, vendors of flowers and vegetables, and all the crowd and tumult, we saw a coal-black dumb monk, returning to Monte Cavo, who formed a singular contrast to the rest of the scene. They seem to have taken entire possession of all this splendid country, and form a strange melancholy ground-tone for all that is lively, gay, and free, and the ever-living cheerfulness bestowed by nature. It is as if men, on that very account, required a counterpoise. This is not however my case, and I need no contrast to enable me to enjoy what I see.

I am often with Bunsen, and as he likes to turn the conversation on the subject of his Liturgy and its musical portions, which I consider very deficient, I am perfectly plain-spoken, and give him a straightforward opinion; and I believe this is the only way to establish a mutual understanding. We have had several long, serious discussions, and I hope we shall eventually know each other better. Yesterday Palestrina's music was performed at Bunsen's house (as on every Monday), and then for the first time I played before the Roman musicians *in corpore*. I am quite aware of the necessity in every foreign city of playing so as to make myself understood by the audience. This makes me usually feel rather embarrassed, and such was the case with me yesterday. After the Papal singers finished Palestrina's music,

it was my turn to play something. A brilliant piece
would have been unsuitable, and there had been
more than enough of serious music; I therefore
begged Astolfi, the Director, to give me a theme, so
he lightly touched the notes with one finger thus :—

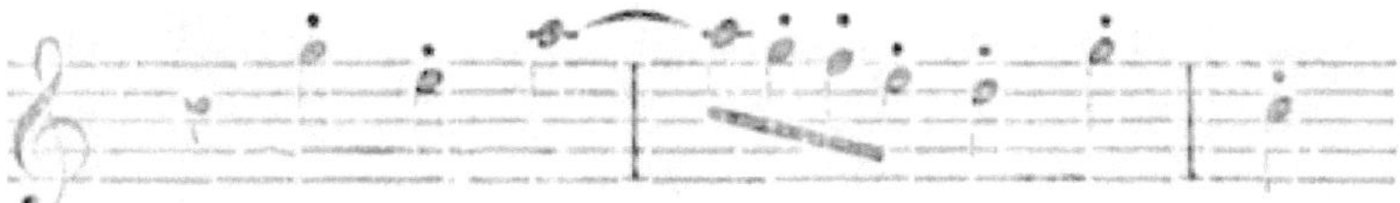

smiling as he did so. The black-frocked Abbati
pressed round me and seemed highly delighted. I
observed this, and it inspirited me so much that
towards the end I succeeded famously; they clapped
their hands like mad, and Bunsen declared that I
had astounded the clergy; in short, the affair went
off well. There is no encouraging prospect of any
public performance here, so society is the only resource, which is fishing in troubled waters.

Yours,   FELIX.

Rome, November 30th, 1830.

To come home from Bunsen's by moonlight, with
your letter in my pocket, and then to read it through
leisurely at night,—this is a degree of pleasure I
wish many may enjoy. In all probability I shall stay
here the whole winter, and not go to Naples till
April. It is so delightful to look round on every
side, and to appreciate it all properly. There is

much that must be thought over, in order to receive a due impression from it. I have also within myself so much work requiring both quiet and industry, that I feel anything like haste would be utter destruction; and though I adhere faithfully to my system, to receive each day only one fresh image into my mind, still I am sometimes compelled even then to give myself a day of rest, that I may not become confused. I write you a short letter to-day, because I must for the present adhere to my work; and yet I cannot refrain from culling all the beauty that lies at my feet. The weather, too, is *brutto* and cold, so that I am not in a very communicative mood. The Pope is dying, or possibly dead by this time. "We shall soon get a new one," say the Italians, coolly. His death will not affect the Carnival, nor the church festivals, with their pomps and processions, and fine music; and as there will be in addition to these, solemn requiems, and the lying-in-state at St. Peter's, they care little about it, provided it does not occur in February.

I am delighted to hear that Mantius sings my songs, and likes them. Give him my kind regards, and ask him why he does not perform his promise, and write to me. I have written to him repeatedly in the shape of music. In the "Ave Maria," and in the choral "Aus tiefer Noth," some passages are composed expressly for him, and he will sing them charmingly. In the "Ave," which is a salutation, a tenor solo takes the lead of the choir (I thought of a disciple all the time). As the piece is in A major, and goes rather high at the words *Benedicta tu*, he must prepare his high A; it will vibrate well. Ask him to sing you a song I sent to Devrient from Venice, "Von schlechtem Lebenswandel." It is expressive of mingled joy and despair; no doubt he will sing it well. Show it to no one, but confine it solely to forty eyes. Ritz* too never writes, and yet I am constantly longing for his violin and his depth of feeling when he plays, which all recurs to my mind when I see his welcome writing. I am now working daily at the "Hebrides," and will send it to Ritz as soon as it is finished. It is quite a piece to suit him—so very singular.

Next time I write I will tell you more of myself. I work hard, and lead a pleasant, happy life; my mirror is stuck full of Italian, German, and English visiting-cards, and I spend every evening with one of my acquaintances. There is a truly Babylonian confusion of tongues in my head, for English, Italian, German and French are all mixed up together in it. Two days ago I again extemporized before the Papal singers. The fellows had contrived to get hold of the most strange, quaint theme for me, wishing to put my powers to the test. They call me, however, *l'insuperabile professorone*, and are particularly kind and friendly. I much wished to have described to you the Sunday music in the Sistina, a *soirée* at Torlonia's, the Vatican, St.

---

* The violin player, Edward Ritz, an intimate friend of Mendelssohn's.

Onofrio, Guido's Aurora, and other small matters, but I reserve them for my next letter. The post is about to set off, and this letter with it. My good wishes are always with you, to-day and ever.

Yours,

FELIX.

Rome, December 7th, 1830.

I cannot even to-day manage to write to you as fully as I wish. Heaven knows how time flies here! I was introduced this week to several agreeable English families, and so I have the prospect of many pleasant evenings this winter. I am much with Bunsen. I intend also to cultivate Baini. I think he conceives me to be only a *brutissimo Tedesco*, so that I have a famous opportunity of becoming well acquainted with him. His compositions are certainly of no great value, and the same may be said of the whole music here. The wish is not wanting, but the means do not exist. The orchestra is below contempt. Mdlle. Carl,* (who is engaged as *prima donna assoluta* for the season, at both the principal theatres here,) is now arrived, and begins to make *la pluie et le beau temps.* The Papal singers even are becoming old; they are almost all unmusical, and do not execute even the most established pieces in tune. The whole choir consists of thirty-two

---

* Formerly a singer in the Royal Theatre at Berlin.

singers, but that number are rarely together. Concerts are given by the so-called Philharmonic Society, but only with the piano. There is no orchestra, and when recently they wished to perform Haydn's "Creation," the instrumentalists declared it was impossible to play it. The sounds they bring out of their wind instruments, are such as in Germany we have no conception of.

The Pope is dead, and the Conclave assembles on the 14th. A great part of the winter will be occupied with the ceremonies of his funeral, and the enthronement of the new Pope. All music therefore and large parties must be at an end, so I very much doubt whether I shall be able to undertake any public performance during my stay here; but I do not regret this, for there are so many varied objects to enjoy inwardly, that my dwelling on these and meditating on them is no disadvantage. The performance of Graun's "Passion" in Naples, and more especially the translation of Sebastian Bach's, prove that the good cause is sure eventually to make its way, though it will neither kindle enthusiasm, nor will it be appreciated. It is no worse however with regard to music—in fact, rather better—than with their estimate of every other branch of the fine arts; for when some of Raphael's Loggie are with inconceivable recklessness and disgraceful barbarism actually defaced, to give place to inscriptions in pencil; when the lower parts of the arabesques are totally destroyed, because Italians with knives, and Heaven knows what else besides, inscribe their insignificant

names there; when one person painted in large
letters under the Apollo Belvedere, 'Christ;' when
an altar has been erected in front of Michael Angelo's "Last Judgment," so large that it hides the
centre of the picture, thus destroying the whole
effect; when cattle are driven through the splendid
saloons of the Villa Madama, the walls of which are
painted by Giulio Romano, and fodder is stored in
them. simply from indifference towards the beautiful,
—all this is certainly much worse than a bad orchestra, and painters must be even more distressed
by such things than I am by their miserable music.

The fact is, that the people are mentally ener-
vated and apathetic. They have a religion, but
they do not believe in it; they have a Pope and a
Government, but they turn them into ridicule; they
can recall a brilliant and heroic past, but they do
not value it. It is thus no marvel that they do not
delight in Art, for they are indifferent to all that is
earnest. It is really quite revolting to see their
unconcern about the death of the Pope, and their
unseemly merriment during the ceremonies. I myself saw the corpse lying in state, and the priests
standing round incessantly whispering and laughing; and at this moment, when masses are being
said for his soul, they are in the very same church
hammering away at the scaffolding of the catafalque.
so that the strokes of the hammers and the noise of
the workpeople entirely prevent any one hearing
the religious services. As soon as the Cardinals
assemble in conclave, satires appear against them,

where, for instance, they parody the Litanies, and instead of praying to be delivered from each particular sin, they name the bad qualities of each well-known cardinal; or, again, they perform an entire opera, where all the characters are Cardinals, one being the *primo amoroso*, another the *tiranno assoluto*, a third, stage candle-snuffer, etc. This could not be the case where the people took any pleasure in Art. Formerly it was no better, but they had faith then; and it is this which makes the difference. Nature, however, and the genial December atmosphere, and the outlines of the Alban hills, stretching as far as the sea, all remain unchanged. There they can scribble no names, or compose no inscriptions. These every one can still individually enjoy in all their freshness, and to these I cling. I feel much the want of a *friend* here, to whom I could freely unbosom myself; who could read my music as I write it, thus making it doubly precious in my eyes; in whose society I could feel an interest, and enjoy repose; and honestly learn from him, (it would not require a very wise man for this purpose.) But just as trees are not ordained to grow up into the sky, so probably such a man is not likely to be found here; and the good fortune I have hitherto so richly enjoyed elsewhere, is not to fall to my share at present; so I must hum over my melodies to myself, and I dare say I shall do well enough.

FELIX.

Rome, December 10th, 1830.

Dear Father,

It is a year this very day since we kept your birthday at Hensel's, and now let me give you some account of Rome, as I did at that time of London. I intend to finish my Overture to the "Einsame Insel"* as a present to you, and if I write under it the 11th December, when I take up the sheets I shall feel as if I were about to place them in your hands. You would probably say that you could not read them, but still I should have offered you the best it was in my power to give; and though I desire to do this every day, still there is a peculiar feeling connected with a birthday. Would I were with you! I need not offer you my good wishes, for you know them all already, and the deep interest I, and all of us, take in your happiness and welfare, and that we cannot wish any good for you, that is not reflected doubly on ourselves. To-day is a holiday. I rejoice in thinking how cheerful you are at home; and when I repeat to you how happily I live here, I feel as if this were also a felicitation. A period like this, when serious thought and enjoyment are combined, is indeed most cheering and invigorating. Every time I enter my room I rejoice that I am not obliged to pursue my journey on the following day, and that I may quietly postpone many things till the morrow—that I am in Rome!

---

* Afterwards published under the name of "Overture to the Hebrides."

Hitherto much that passed through my brain was swept away by fresh ideas, each new impression chasing away the previous one, while here, on the contrary, they are all in turn properly developed. I never remember having worked with so much zeal, and if I am to complete all that I have projected, I must be very industrious during the winter. I am indeed deprived of the great delight of showing my finished compositions to one who could take pleasure in them, and enter into them along with me; but this impels me to return to my labours, which please me most when I am fairly in the midst of them. And now this must be combined with the various solemnities, and festivals of every kind, which are to supplant my work for a few days; and as I have resolved to see and to enjoy all I possibly can, I do not allow my occupation to prevent this, and shall then return with fresh zeal to my composition.

This is indeed a delightful existence! My health is as good as possible, though the hot wind, called here the *sirocco*, rather attacks my nerves, and I find I must beware of playing the piano much, or at night; besides it is easy for me to refrain from doing so for a few days, as for some weeks past I have been playing almost every evening. Bunsen, who often warns me against playing if I find it prejudicial, gave a large party yesterday, where nevertheless I was obliged to play; but it was a pleasure to me, for I had the opportunity of making so many agreeable acquaintances. Thorwaldsen, in particu-

lar, expressed himself in so gratifying a manner
with regard to me, that I felt quite proud, for I
honor him as one of the greatest of men, and
always have revered him. He looks like a lion,
and the very sight of his face is invigorating. You
feel at once that he must be a noble artist; his
eyes look so clear, as if with him every object must
assume a definite form and image. Moreover he is
very gentle, and kind, and mild, because his nature
is so superior; and yet he seems to be able to enjoy
every trifle. It is a real source of pleasure to see
a great man, and to know that the creator of works
that will endure for ever stands before you in person; a living being with all his attributes, and
individuality, and genius, and yet a man like others.

December 11th, morning.

Now your actual birthday is arrived! A few
lines of music suggested themselves to me on the
occasion, and though they may not be worth much,
the congratulations I have been in the habit of offering, were of quite as little value. Fanny may add
the second part. I have only written what occurred
to my mind as I entered the room, the sun shining,
on your birthday :—

7*

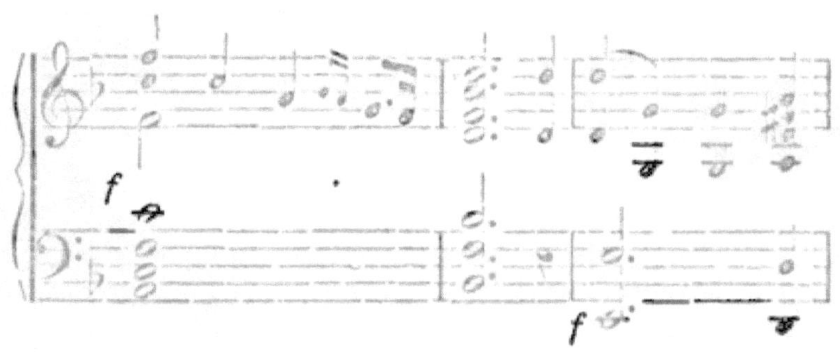
f
f

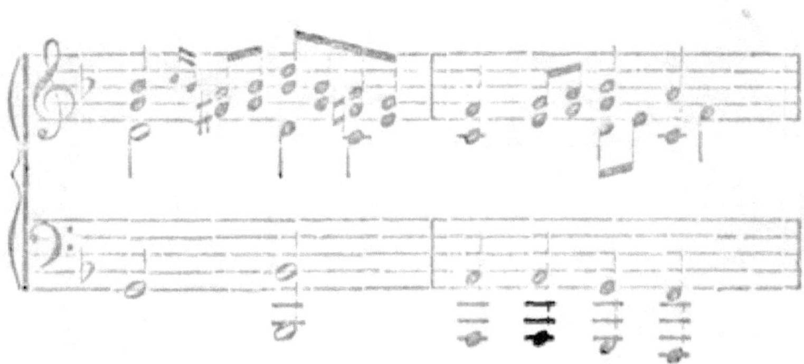

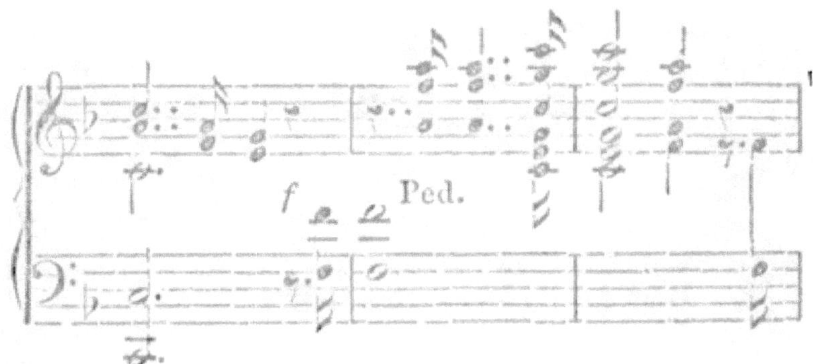
f
Ped.

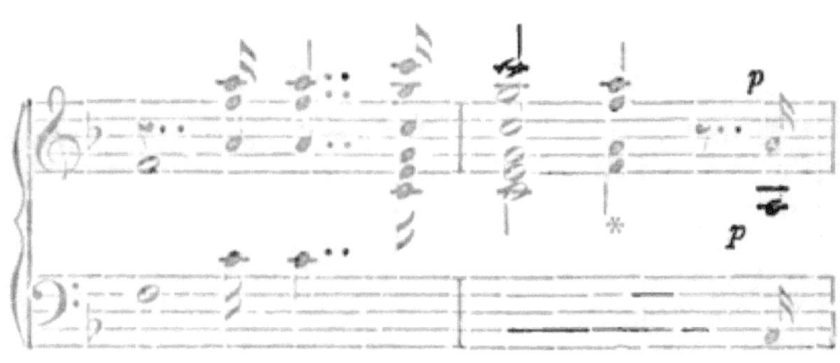
p
p

f
ETC.

Bunsen has just been here, and begs me to send you his best regards and congratulations. He is all kindness and courtesy towards me, and as you wish to know, I think I may say that we suit each other remarkably well. The few words you wrote about P—— recalled him to my memory in all his offensiveness. The Abbate Santini ought to be an obscure man compared with him, for he never attempts to magnify his own importance by impertinence or self-sufficiency. P—— is one of those collectors who make learning and libraries distasteful to others by their narrow-mindedness, whereas Santini is a genuine collector, in the best sense of the word, caring little whether his collection be of much value in a pecuniary point of view. He therefore gives everything away indiscriminately, and is only anxious to procure something new, for his chief object is the diffusion and universal knowledge of ancient music. I have not seen him lately, as every morning now he figures, *ex officio*, in his violet gown at St. Peter's; but if he has made use of some ancient text, he will say so without scruple, as he has no wish to be thought the first discoverer. He is, in fact, a man of limited capacity; and this I consider great praise in a certain sense, for though he is neither a musical nor any other luminary, and even bears some resemblance to Lessing's inquisitive friar, still he knows how to confine himself within his own sphere. Music itself does not interest him much, if he can only have it on his shelves; and he is, and esteems himself to be, simply a quiet, zealous collector. I must admit that he is fatiguing, and not altogether free from irritability; still I love any one who adopts and perseveres in some particular pursuit, prosecuting it to the best of his ability. and endeavouring to perfect it for the benefit of mankind, and I think every one ought to esteem him just the same, whether he chance to be tiresome or agreeable.

I wish you would read this aloud to P——. It always makes me furious when men who have no pursuit, presume to criticize those who wish to effect something, even on a small scale; so on this very account I took the liberty of rebuking lately a certain musician in society here. He began to speak of Mozart, and as Bunsen and his sister love Palestrina, he tried to flatter their tastes by asking me, for instance, what I thought of the worthy Mozart, and all his sins. I however replied, that so far as I was concerned, I should feel only too happy to renounce all *my* virtues in exchange for Mozart's sins: but that of course I could not venture to pronounce on the extent of *his* virtues. The people all laughed, and were highly amused. How strange it is that such persons should feel no awe of so great a name!

It is some consolation, however, that it is the same in every sphere of art, as the painters here are quite as bad. They are most formidable to look at, sitting in their *Café Greco.* I scarcely ever go there, for I dislike both them and their favourite places of resort. It is a small dark room, about eight feet square, where on one side you may smoke, but not on the other; so they sit round on benches, with their broad-leaved hats on their heads, and their huge mastiffs beside them; their cheeks and throats, and the whole of their faces covered with hair, puffing forth clouds of smoke (only on one side of the room), and saying rude things to each other, while the mastiffs swarm with vermin. A neckcloth or a coat would be quite innovations. Any portion of the face visible through the beard, is hid by spectacles; so they drink coffee, and speak of Titian and Pordenone, just as if they were sitting beside them, and also wore beards and wide-awakes! Moreover, they paint such sickly Madonnas and feeble saints, and such milk-sop heroes, that I feel the strongest inclination to knock them down. These infernal critics do not even shrink from discussing Titian's picture in the Vatican, about which you asked me; they say that it has neither subject nor meaning; yet it never seems to occur to them, that a master who had so long studied a picture with due love and reverence, must have had quite as deep an insight into the subject as they are likely to have, even with their coloured spectacles. And if in the course of my life I accomplish nothing but this, I am at all events determined to say the most harsh and cutting things to those who show no reverence towards their masters, and then I shall at least have performed one good work. But there they stand, and see all the splendour of those creations, so far transcending their own conceptions, and yet dare to criticize them.

In this picture there are three stages, or whatever

they are called, the same as in the " Transfiguration."
Below, saints and martyrs are represented in suffering and abasement; on every face is depicted sadness, nay almost impatience; one figure in rich
episcopal robes looks upwards, with the most eager
and agonized longing, as if weeping, but he cannot
see all that is floating above his head, but which *we*
see, standing in front of the picture. Above, Mary
and her Child are in a cloud, radiant with joy, and
surrounded by angels, who have woven many garlands; the Holy Child holds one of these, and seems
as if about to crown the saints beneath, but his
Mother withholds his hand for the moment. The
contrast between the pain and suffering below,
whence St. Sebastian looks forth out of the picture
with such gloom and almost apathy, and the lofty
unalloyed exultation in the clouds above, where
crowns and palms are already awaiting him, is truly
admirable. High above the group of Mary, hovers
the Holy Spirit, from whom emanates a bright
streaming light, thus forming the apex of the whole
composition. I have just remembered that Goethe,
at the beginning of his first visit to Rome, describes
and admires this picture; but I no longer have the
book to enable me to read it over, and to compare
my description with his. He speaks of it in considerable detail. It was at that time in the Quirinal,
and subsequently transferred to the Vatican;
whether it was painted on a given subject, as some
allege, or not, is of no moment. Titian has imbued
it with his genius and his poetical feeling, and has

thus made it his own. I like Schadow much, and am often with him; on every occasion, and especially in his own department, he is mild and clear-judging, doing justice with due modesty to all that is truly great; he recently said that Titian had never painted an indifferent or an uninteresting picture, and I believe he is right; for life and enthusiasm and the soundest vigour are displayed in all his productions, and where these are, it is good to be also. There is one singular and fortunate peculiarity here: though all the objects have been, a thousand times over, described, discussed, copied, and criticized, in praise or blame, by the greatest masters, and the most insignificant scholars, cleverly or stupidly, still they never fail to make a fresh and sublime impression on all, affecting each person according to his own individuality. Here we can take refuge from man in all that surrounds us; in Berlin it is often exactly the reverse.

I have this moment received your letter of the 27th, and am pleased to find that I have already answered many of the questions it contains. There is no hurry about the letters I asked for, as I have now made almost more acquaintances than I wish; besides, late hours, and playing so much, do not suit me in Rome, so I can await the arrival of these letters very patiently: it was not so at the time I urged you to send them. I cannot however understand what you mean by your allusion to *coteries* which I ought to have outgrown, for I know that I, and all of us, invariably dreaded and detested what is usually so called,—that is, a frivolous, exclusive circle of society, clinging to empty outward forms. Among persons, however, who daily meet, while their mutual objects of interest remain the same, who have no sympathy with public life (and this is certainly the case in Berlin, with the exception of the theatre), it is not unnatural that they should form for themselves a gay, cheerful, and original mode of treating passing events, and that this should give rise to a peculiar, and perhaps monotonous style of conversation; but this by no means constitutes a *coterie*. I feel convinced that I shall never belong to one, whether I am in Rome or Wittenberg. I am glad that the last words I was writing when your letter arrived, chanced to be that in Berlin you must take refuge in society from all that surrounds you; thus proving that I had no spirit of *coterie*, which invariably estranges men from each other. I should deeply regret your observing anything of the kind in me or in any of us, except indeed for the moment. Forgive me, my dear father, for defending myself so warmly, but this word is most repugnant to my feelings, and you say in your letters that I am always to speak out what I think in a straightforward manner, so pray do not take this amiss.

I was in St. Peter's to-day, where the grand solemnities called the absolutions have begun for the Pope, and which last till Tuesday, when the Cardinals assemble in conclave. The building surpasses all powers of description. It appears to me like some great work of nature, a forest, a mass of rocks, or something similar; for I never can realize the idea that it is the work of man. You strive to distinguish the ceiling as little as the canopy of heaven. You lose your way in St. Peter's, you take a walk in it, and ramble till you are quite tired; when divine service is performed and chanted there, you are not aware of it till you come quite close. The angels in the Baptistery are monstrous giants; the doves, colossal birds of prey; you lose all idea of measurement with the eye, or proportion; and yet who does not feel his heart expand, when standing under the dome, and gazing up at it? At present a monstrous catafalque has been erected in the nave in this shape.* The coffin is placed in the centre under the pillars; the thing is totally devoid of taste, and yet it has a wondrous effect. The upper circle is thickly studded with lights, so are all the ornaments; the lower circle is lighted in the same way, and over the coffin hangs a burning lamp, and innumerable lights are blazing under the statues. The whole structure is more than a hundred feet high, and stands exactly opposite the entrance. The guards of honour, and the Swiss, march about in the quadrangle; in every corner sits a Cardinal in deep mourning, attended by his servants, who hold large burning torches, and then the singing commences with responses, in the simple and monotonous tone you no doubt remember. It is the only occasion when there is any

---

* A little sketch of the catafalque was enclosed in the letter.

singing in the middle of the church, and the effect is wonderful. Those who place themselves among the singers (as I do) and watch them, are forcibly impressed by the scene: for they all stand round a colossal book from which they sing, and this book is in turn lit up by a colossal torch that burns before it; while the choir are eagerly pressing forward in their vestments, in order to see and to sing properly: and Baini with his monk's face, marking time with his hand, and occasionally joining in the chant with a stentorian voice. To watch all these different Italian faces, was most interesting; one enjoyment quickly succeeds another here, and it is the same in their churches, especially in St. Peter's, where by moving a few steps the whole scene is changed. I went to the very furthest end, whence there was indeed a wonderful *coup d'œil*. Through the spiral columns of the high altar, which is confessedly as high as the palace in Berlin, far beyond the space of the cupola, the whole mass of the catafalque was seen in diminished perspective, with its rows of lights, and numbers of small human beings crowding round it. When the music commences, the sounds do not reach the other end for a long time, but echo and float in the vast space, so that the most singular and vague harmonies are borne towards you. If you change your position, and place yourself right in front of the catafalque, beyond the blaze of light and the brilliant pageantry, you have the dusky cupola replete with blue vapour; all this is quite indescribable. Such is Rome!

This has become a long letter, so I must conclude; it will reach you on Christmas-day. May you all enjoy it happily! I send each of you presents, which are to be dispatched two days hence, and will arrive in time for the anniversary of your silver wedding-day. Many glad festivals are thus crowded together, and I scarcely know whether to imagine myself with you to-day, and to wish you, dear father, all possible happiness, or to arrive with my letter at Christmas, and not to be allowed by my mother to pass through the room with the Christmas-tree. I am afraid I must be contented with thinking of you.—Farewell all! May you be happy!

FELIX.

I have just received your letter, which brings me the intelligence of Goethe's illness. What I personally feel at this news I cannot express. This whole evening his words, "I must try to keep all right till your return," have sounded continually in my ears, to the exclusion of every other thought: when he is gone, Germany will assume a very different aspect for artists. I have never thought of Germany without feeling heartfelt joy and pride that Goethe lived there; and the rising generation seem for the most part so weakly and feeble, that it makes my heart sink within me. He is the last; and with him closes a happy prosperous period for us! This year ends in solemn sadness.

Rome, December 20th, 1830.

In my former letter I told you of the more serious aspect of Roman life; but as I wish to describe to you how I live, I must now tell you of the gayeties that have prevailed during this week.

To-day we have the most genial sunshine, a blue sky, and a transparent atmosphere, and on such days I have my own mode of passing my time. I work hard till eleven o'clock, and from that hour till dark, I do nothing but breathe the air. For the first time, for some days past, we yesterday had fine weather. After therefore working for a time in the morning at "Solomon," I went to the Monte Pincio, where I rambled about the whole day. The effect of this exhilarating air is quite magical; and when I arose to-day, and again saw bright sunshine, I exulted in the thoughts of the entire idleness I was again about to indulge in. The whole world is on foot, revelling in a December spring. Every moment you meet some acquaintance, with whom you lounge about for a time, then leave him, and once more enjoy your solitary revery. There are swarms of handsome faces to be seen. As the sun declines, the appearance of the whole landscape, and every hue, undergo a change. When the Ave Maria sounds, it is time to go to the church of Trinità de' Monti, where French nuns sing; and it is charming to hear them. I declare to heaven that I am become quite tolerant, and listen to bad music with edification; but what can I do? the composition is positively ridiculous; the organ playing even

8*

more absurd. But it is twilight, and the whole of the small bright church is filled with persons kneeling, lit up by the sinking sun each time that the door is opened; both the singing nuns have the sweetest voices in the world, quite tender and touching, more especially when one of them sings the responses in her melodious voice, which we are accustomed to hear chanted by priests in a loud, harsh, monotonous tone. The impression is very singular; moreover, it is well known that no one is permitted to see the fair singers,—so this caused me to form a strange resolution. I have composed something to suit their voices, which I observed very minutely, and I mean to send it to them,— there are several modes to which I can have recourse to accomplish this. That they will sing it, I feel quite assured; and it will be pleasant for me to hear my chant performed by persons whom I never saw, especially as they must in turn sing it to the *barbaro Tedesco*, whom they also never beheld. I am charmed with this idea. The text is in Latin, —a Prayer to Mary. Does not this notion please you ?*

After church I walk again on the hill until it is quite dark, when Madame Vernet and her daughter, and pretty Madame V—— (for whose acquaintance I have to thank Roesel), are much admired by us Germans, and we form groups round them, or follow, or walk beside them. The background is

---

* This piece appeared afterwards as Opus 39.

formed by haggard painters with terrific beards; they smoke tobacco on the Monte Pincio, whistle to their huge dogs, and enjoy the sunset in their own way.

As I am in a frivolous mood to-day, I must relate to you, dear sisters, every particular of a ball I lately attended, and where I danced with a degree of zeal I never did before. I had spoken a few fair words to the *maître de danse* (who stands in the middle here, and regulates everything), consequently he allowed the galop to continue for more than half an hour, so I was in my element, and pleasantly conscious that I was dancing in the Palazzo Albani, in Rome, and also with the prettiest girl in it, according to the verdict of the competent judges (Thorwaldsen, Vernet, etc.) The way in which I became acquainted with her is also an anecdote of Rome. I was at Torlonia's first ball, though not dancing, as I knew none of the ladies present, but merely looking at the people. Suddenly some one tapped me on the shoulder, saying, "So you also are admiring the English beauty; I am quite dazzled." It was Thorwaldsen himself standing at the door, lost in admiration; scarcely had he said this, when we heard a torrent of words behind us,—"Mais où est-elle donc, cette petite Anglaise? Ma femme m'a envoyé pour la regarder. Per Bacco!" It was quite clear that this little thin Frenchman, with stiff, grey hair, and the ribbon of the Legion of Honour, must be Horace Vernet. He now discussed the youthful beauty with Thorwaldsen, in the

most earnest and scientific manner; and it was
quite a pleasure to me to see these two old masters
admiring the young girl together, while she was
dancing away, quite unconcerned. They were then
presented to her parents, but I felt very insignificant, as I could not join in the conversation. A
few days afterwards, however, I was with some
acquaintances whom I knew through the Attwoods,
at Venice, they having invited me for the purpose
of presenting me to some of their friends; and
these friends turned out to be the very persons I
have been speaking of; so your son and brother was
highly delighted.

My pianoforte playing is a source of great gratification to me here. You know how Thorwaldsen
loves music, and I sometimes play to him in the
morning while he is at work. He has an excellent
instrument in his studio, and when I look at the
old gentleman and see him kneading his brown
clay, and delicately fining off an arm, or a fold of
drapery,—in short, when he is creating what we must
all admire when completed, as an enduring work,
—then I do indeed rejoice that I have the means of
bestowing any enjoyment on him. Nevertheless, I
have not fallen into arrear with my own tasks.
The " Hebrides " is completed at last, and a strange
production it is. The chant for the nuns is in my
head; and I think of composing Luther's choral
for Christmas, but on this occasion I must do so
quite alone; and it will be a more serious affair this
time, and so will the anniversary of your silver

wedding-day, when I intend to have a great many lights, and to sing my "Liederspiel," and to have a peep at my English *bâton*. After the new year, I intend to resume instrumental music, and to write several things for the piano, and probably a symphony of some kind, for two have been haunting my brain.

I have lately frequented a most delightful spot,—the tomb of Cecilia Metella. The Sabine hills had a sprinkling of snow, but it was glorious sunshine; the Alban hills were like a dream or a vision. There is no such thing as distance in Italy, for all the houses on the hills can be counted, with their roofs and windows. I have thus inhaled this air to satiety; and to-morrow in all probability, more serious occupations will be resumed, for the sky is cloudy, and it is raining hard, but what a spring this will be !

December 21st.

This is the shortest day, and very gloomy, as might have been anticipated; so to-day nothing can be thought of but fugues, chorals, balls, etc. But I must say a few words about Guido's "Aurora," which I often visit; it is a picture the very type of haste and impetus; for surely no man ever imagined such hurry and tumult, such sounding and clashing. Painters maintain that it is lighted from two sides,—they have my full permission to light *theirs* from three if it will improve them,—but the difference lies elsewhere.

I really cannot compose a tolerable song here, for who is there to sing it to me? But I am writing a grand fugue, "Wir glauben all," and sing it to myself in such a fashion that my friend the Captain rushes downstairs in alarm, puts in his head, and asks what I want. I answer—a counter theme. But how much I do really want; and yet how much I have got! Thus life passes onwards.

FELIX.

Rome, December 28th, 1830.

Rome in wet weather is the most odious, uncomfortable place imaginable. For some days past we have had incessant storms and cold, and streams of water from the sky; and I can scarcely comprehend how, only one week ago, I could write you a letter full of rambles and orange-trees and all that is beautiful: in such weather as this everything becomes ugly. Still, I must write to you about it, otherwise my previous letter would not have the advantage of contrast, and of that there is no lack. If in Germany we can form no conception of the bright winter days here, quite as little can we realize a really wet winter day in Rome; everything is arranged for fine weather, so the bad is borne like a public calamity, and in the hope of better times. There is no shelter anywhere; in my room, which is usually so comfortable, the water pours in through the windows, which will not shut fast; the wind whistles through the doors, which will not close; the stone floor chills you in spite of double mattings, and the smoke from the chimney is driven into the room, because the fire will not burn; foreigners shiver and freeze here like tailors.

All this is, however, actual luxury when compared with the streets; and when I am obliged to go out, I consider it a positive misfortune. Rome, as every one knows. is built on seven large hills; but there are a number of smaller ones besides, and all the streets are sloping, so the water pours down them, and rushes towards you; nowhere is there a raised footpath, or a *trottoir;* at the stair of the Piazza di Spagna, there is a flood like the great water-works in Wilhelms-Höhe; the Tiber has overflowed its banks, and inundated the adjacent streets: this, then, is the water from below. From above come violent showers of rain, but that is the least part. The houses have no water-spouts, and the long roofs slant precipitously, but, being of different lengths, this causes an incessant violent inundation on both sides of the street, so that go where you will, close to the houses, or in the middle of the streets, beside a barber's shop or a palace, you are sure to be deluged, and, quite unawares, you find yourself standing under a tremendous shower-bath, the water pelting on your umbrella, while a stream is running before you that you cannot jump over, so you are obliged to return the way you came: this is the water overhead. Then the carriages drive as rapidly as possible, and close to the houses, so that you must retreat into the doorways till they are past; they not only splash men and houses, but each other, so that when two meet, one must drive into the gutter, which, being a rapid current, the consequences are lamentable. Lately I saw an Abbate hurrying along, whose umbrella chancing to knock off the broad-brimmed hat of a peasant, it fell with the crown exposed to one of these deluges, and when the man went to pick it up, it was quite filled with water. "Scusi," said the Abbate. "Padrone," replied the peasant. The hackney coaches moreover only ply till five o'clock, so if you go to a party at night, it costs you a scudo. *Fiat justitia et pereat mundus*—Rome in rainy weather is vastly disagreeable.

I see by a letter of Devrient's, that one I wrote to him from Venice, and which I took to the post myself on the 17th of October, had not reached him on the 19th of November. It would appear also, that another which I sent the same day to Munich had not arrived; both these letters contained music, and this accounts for the loss. At that very time in Venice they carried off all my manuscripts to the Custom-house, after visiting my effects at night, shortly before the departure of the post, and I only received them again here, after much worry and writing backwards and forwards. Every one assured me that the cause of this was a secret correspondence being suspected in cipher in the manuscript music. I could scarcely credit such intolerable stupidity; but as my two letters from

Venice containing music have not arrived, and these only, the thing is clear enough. I intend to complain of this to the Austrian ambassador here, but it will do no good, and the letters are lost, which I much regret. Farewell!

FELIX.

————•————

Rome, January 17th, 1831.

For a week past we have had the most lovely spring weather. Young girls are carrying about nosegays of violets and anemones, which they gather early in the morning at the Villa Pamfili. The streets and squares swarm with gaily attired pedestrians; the Ave Maria has already been advanced twenty minutes, but what is become of the winter? Some little time ago it indeed reminded me of my work, to which I now mean to apply steadily, for I own that during the gay social life of the previous weeks, I had rather neglected it. I have nearly completed the arrangement of " Solomon," and also my Christmas anthem, which consists of five numbers; the two symphonies also begin to assume a more definite form, and I particularly wish to finish them here. Probably I shall be able to accomplish this during Lent, when parties cease (especially balls) and spring begins, and then I shall have both time and inclination to compose, in which case I hope to have a good store of new works. Any performance of them here is quite out of the question. The orchestras are worse than any one could believe ; both musicians, and a right feeling for music, are wanting. The two or three violin performers play just as they choose, and join in when they please ; the wind instruments are tuned either too high or too low ; and they execute flourishes like those we are accustomed to hear in farm-yards, but hardly so good ; in short the whole forms a Dutch concert, and this applies even to compositions with which they are familiar.

The question is, whether all this could be radically reformed by introducing other people into the orchestra, by teaching the musicians time, and by instructing them in first principles. I think in that case the people would no doubt take pleasure in it ; so long, however, as this is not done, no improvement can be hoped for, and every one seems so indifferent on the subject, that there is not the slightest prospect of such a thing. I heard a solo on the flute, where the flute was more than a quarter of a tone too high ; it set my teeth on edge, but no one remarked it, and when at the end a shake came, they applauded mechanically. If it were even a shade better with regard to singing ! The great singers have left the country. Lablache, David, Lalande, Pisaroni, etc., sing in Paris, and the minor ones who remain, copy their inspired moments, which they caricature in the most insupportable manner.

We in Germany may perhaps wish to accomplish

something false or impossible, but it is, and always will be, quite *dissimilar;* and just as a *cicisbeo* will for ever be odious and repulsive to my feelings, so is it also with Italian music. I may be too obtuse to comprehend either; but I shall never feel otherwise; and recently, at the Philharmonic, after the music of Pacini and Bellini, when the Cavaliere Ricci begged me to accompany him in "Non più andrai," the very first notes were so utterly different and so infinitely remote from all the previous music, that the matter was clear to me then, and never will it be equalized, so long as there is such a blue sky, and such a charming winter as the present. In the same way the Swiss can paint no beautiful scenery, precisely because they have it the whole day before their eyes. "Les Allemands traitent la musique comme une affaire d'état," says Spontini, and I accept the axiom. I lately heard some musicians here talking of their composers, and I listened in silence. One quoted ——, but the others interrupted him, saying he could not be considered an Italian, for the German school still clung to him, and he had never been able to get rid of it; consequently he had never been at home in Italy: we Germans say precisely the reverse of him, and it must be not a little trying to find yourself so *entre deux,* and without any fatherland. So far as I am concerned I stick to my own colours, which are quite honourable enough for me.

Last night a theatre that Torlonia has undertaken and organized, was opened with a new opera of Pacini's. The crowd was great, and every box filled with handsome, well-dressed people ; young Torlonia appeared in a stage-box with his mother, the old Duchess, and they were immensely applauded. The audience called out *Bravo, Torlonia, grazie, grazie !* Opposite to him was Jerome, with his suite, and covered with orders : in the next box Countess Samoilow, etc. Over the orchestra is a picture of Time pointing to the dial of the clock, which revolves slowly, and is enough to make any one melancholy. Pacini then appeared at the piano, and was kindly welcomed. He had prepared no overture, so the opera began with a chorus, accompanied by strokes on an anvil tuned in the proper key. The Corsair came forward, sang his *aria*, and was applauded, on which the Corsair above, and the Maestro below, bowed (this pirate is a contralto, and sung by Mademoiselle Mariani); a variety of airs followed, and the piece became very tiresome. This seemed to be also the opinion of the public, for when Pacini's grand *finale* began, the whole pit stood up, talking to each other as loud as they could, laughing and turning their backs on the stage. Madame Samoilow fainted in her box, and was carried out. Pacini glided away from the piano, and at the end of the act, the curtain fell in the midst of a great tumult. Then came the grand ballet of *Barbe Bleue,* followed by the last act of the opera. As the audience were now in a mood for it, they hissed the whole ballet from the very beginning, and accompanied the second act also with hooting and laughter. At the close Torlonia was called for, but he would not appear.

This is the matter-of-fact narrative of a first performance at the opening of a theatre in Rome. I had anticipated much amusement, so I came away considerably out of humour; still, if the music had made *furore*, I should have been very indignant, for it is so wretched that it really is beneath all criticism. But that they should turn their backs on their favourite Pacini, whom they wished to crown in the Capitol, parody his melodies, and sing them in a ludicrous style, this does, I confess, provoke me not a little, and is likewise a proof of how low such a musician stands in the public opinion. Another time they will carry him home on their shoulders; but this is no compensation. They would not act thus in France with regard to Boieldieu; independent of all love of art, a sense of propriety would prevent their doing so: but enough of this subject, for it is too vexatious.

Why should Italy still insist on being the land of Art, while it is in reality the Land of Nature, thus delighting every heart! I have already described to you my walks to the Monte Pincio. I continue them daily. I went lately with the Vollards to Ponte Nomentano, a solitary dilapidated bridge in the spacious green Campagna. Many ruins from the days of ancient Rome, and many watch-towers from the Middle Ages, are scattered over this long succession of meadows; chains of hills rise towards the horizon, now partially covered with snow, and fantastically varied in form and colour by the shadows of the clouds. And there is also the enchanting, vapoury vision of the Alban hills, which change their hues like a chameleon, as you gaze at them,—where you can see for miles little white chapels glittering on the dark ground of the hills, as far as the Passionist Convent on the summit, and whence you can trace the road winding through thickets, and the hills sloping downwards to the Lake of Albano, while a hermitage peeps through the trees. The distance is equal to that from Berlin to Potsdam, say I as a good Berliner; but that it is a lovely vision, I say in earnest. No lack of music *there;* it echoes and vibrates *there* on every side; not in the vapid, tasteless theatres. So we rambled about, chasing each other in the Campagna, and jumping over the fences, and when the sun went down we drove home, feeling so weary, and yet so self-satisfied and pleased, as if we had done great things; and so we have, if we *rightly appreciated* it all.

I have now applied myself again to drawing, and have latterly put in some tints, as I should be glad to be able to recall some of these bright hues, and practice quickens the perceptions. I must now tell you, dear mother, of a great, very great pleasure I recently enjoyed, because you will rejoice with me. Two days ago I was for the first time in a small circle with Horace Vernet, and played there. He had previously told me that his most favourite and esteemed music was "Don Juan," especially the Duet and the Commendatore at the end; and as

I highly approved of such sentiments on his part, the result was, that while playing a prelude to Weber's *Concert-Stück*, I imperceptibly glided further into extemporizing—thought I would please him by taking these themes, and so I worked them up fancifully for some time. This caused him a degree of delight far beyond what I ever knew my music produce in any one, and we became at once more intimate. Afterwards he suddenly came up to me, and whispered that we must make an exchange, for that he also was an improvisatore; and when I was naturally curious to know what he meant, he said it was his secret. He is however like a little child, and could not conceal it for more than a quarter of an hour, when he came in again, and taking me into the next room, he asked me if I had any time to spare, as he had stretched and prepared a canvas, and proposed painting my portrait on it, which I was to keep in memory of this day, or roll it up and send it to you, or take it with me, just as I chose. He said he should have no easy task with his improvisation, but at all events he would attempt it. I was only too glad to give my consent, and cannot tell you how much I was enchanted with the delight and enthusiasm he evidently felt in my playing.

It was in every respect a happy evening; as I ascended the hill with him. all was so still and peaceful, and only one window lit up in the large dark villa.* Fragments of music floated on the

---

* Vernet lived in the Villa Medici.

air, and its echoes in the dark night, mingled with
the murmuring of fountains, were sweeter than I can
describe. Two young students were drilling in the
anteroom, while the third acted the part of lieutenant, and commanded in good form. In another
room my friend Montfort, who gained the prize for
music in the Conservatorium, was seated at a piano,
and others were standing round, singing a chorus;
but it went very badly. They urged another young
man to join them, and when he said that he did not
know how to sing, his friend rejoined, "Qù'est-ce
que ça fait? c'est toujours une voix de plus!" I
helped them as I best could, and we were well
amused. Afterwards we danced, and I wish you
could have seen Louisa Vernet dancing the Salta-
rella with her father. When at length she was
forced to stop for a few moments, and snatched up
a tambourine, playing with the utmost spirit,
and relieving us, who could really scarcely any
longer move our hands, I wished I had been a
painter, for what a superb picture she would have
made! Her mother is the kindest creature in the
world, and the grandfather, Charles Vernet (who
paints such splendid horses), danced a quadrille the
same evening with so much ease, making so many
entrechats, and varying his steps so gracefully, that
it is a sad pity he should actually be seventy-two
years of age. Every day he rides, and tires out two
horses, paints and draws a little, and spends the
evening in society.

In my next letter I must tell you of my acquaintance with Robert, who has just finished an admirable picture, "The Harvest," and also describe my recent visits with Bunsen to the studios of Cornelius, Koch, Overbeck, etc. My time is fully occupied, for there is plenty to do and to see; unluckily I cannot make time elastic, however much I may strive to extend it. I have as yet said nothing of Raphael's portrait as a child, and Titian's "Nymphs Bathing," who in a piquant enough fashion are designated "Sacred and Profane Love," one being in full gala costume, while the other is devoid of all drapery,* or of my exquisite "Madonna di Foligno," or of Francesco Francia, the most guileless and devout painter in the world; or of poor Guido Reni, whom the bearded painters of the present day treat with such contempt, and yet he painted a certain Aurora, and many other splendid objects besides; but what avails description? It is well for me that I can revel in the sight of them. When we meet, I may perhaps be able to give you a better idea of them.

Your

FELIX.

Rome, February 1st, 1831.

I intended not to write to you till my birthday, but possibly two days hence I may not be in a writing mood, and must drive all fancies away by hard work. It does not seem probable that the Papal mili-

---

* This picture is in the Borghese Gallery.

tary band will surprise me in the morning,* and as I have told all my acquaintances that I was born on the 25th, I think the day will glide quietly by; I prefer this to a trivial half-and-half celebration. I will place your portrait before me in the morning, and feel happy in looking at it and in thinking of you. I shall then play over my military overture, and select my favourite dish for dinner, from the *carte* at the *Lepre*. It is not unprofitable to be obliged to do all this for one's self, both on birth-days and other days. I feel isolated enough, and am rather partial to the other extreme. At night the Torlonias are so obliging as to give a ball to eight hundred persons; on Wednesday, the day before, and on Friday, the day after my birthday, I am invited to the house of some English friends. During the previous week, I have been busily engaged in sight-seeing, and revisited many well-known objects; —thus I was in the Vatican, the Farnesina, Corsini, the Villa Lante, Borghese, etc. Two days ago I saw the frescoes for the first time in Bartholdy's house ;† inasmuch as the English ladies who reside there, and who have transformed the painted saloon into a sleeping apartment, with a four-post bed, would never hitherto permit me to enter it. So this was my first visit to my uncle's house, where at last I saw his pictures, and the view of the city. It was

---

* On the 3rd of February, 1830, the bands of some regiments in Berlin gave Mendelssohn a serenade in honour of his birthday.

† The Prussian Consul-General Bartholdy, who died in Rome, and was an uncle of Felix Mendelssohn's.

a noble, regal idea to have these frescoes; and the execution of such a sublime thought, in spite of every kind of impediment and annoyance, simply in order that the design should be carried out, seems to me very charming.

But to turn to an entirely different subject. In many circles here, it is the fashion to consider piety and dulness synonymous, and yet they are very different; our German clergyman here is not behindhand in this respect. There are men in Rome with an amount of fanaticism credible in the sixteenth century, but quite monstrous in the present day; they all wish to make converts, abusing each other in a Christian manner, and each ridiculing the belief of his neighbour, till it is quite too sad to hear them. As if to have simplicity, and to be simple, were the same thing! Unfortunately I must here retract my favourite axiom, that *goodwill* can effect all things, *ability* must accompany it; but I am soaring too high, and my father will lecture me. I wish this letter were better, but we have snow on the ground; the roofs in the Piazza di Spagna are quite white, and heavy clouds of snow are gathering; nothing can be more odious to us Southerners, and we are freezing. The Monte Pincio is a mass of ice. Your Northern Lights have their revenge on us. Who can write or think with any degree of warmth? I was so pleased at the idea of being a whole winter without snow, but now I must give up that notion. The Italians say that spring breezes will come in a few days; then gay life, and gay letters, will be resumed. Farewell! may you enjoy every good, and think of me.   FELIX.

Rome, February 8th, 1831.

The Pope is elected : the Pope is crowned. He performed mass in St. Peter's on Sunday, and conferred his benediction; in the evening the dome was illuminated, succeeded by the Girandola; the Carnival began on Saturday, and pursues its headlong course in the most motley forms. The city has been illuminated each evening. Last night there was a ball at the French Embassy; to-day the Spanish Ambassador gives a grand entertainment. Next door to me they sell *confetti*, and how they do shout! And now I might as well stop, for why attempt to describe what is, in fact, indescribable? You ought to make Hensel tell you of these splendid *fêtes*, which in pomp, brilliancy, and animation, surpass all the imagination can conceive, for my sober pen is not equal to the task. What a different aspect everything has assumed during the last eight days, for now the mildest and most genial sun is shining, and we remain in the balcony enjoying the air till after sunset. Oh, that I could enclose for you, in this letter, only one quarter of an hour of all this pleasure, or tell you how life actually flies in Rome, every minute bringing its own memorable delights! It is not difficult to give *fêtes* here; if the simple architectural outlines are lighted up, the dome of St. Peter's blazes forth in the dark purple atmosphere, calmly shining. If there are fireworks, they brighten the gloomy solid walls of the Castle of St. Angelo, and fall into the Tiber; when they commence their fantastic *fêtes* in February, the most lustrous sun shines down on them and beautifies them. It is a wondrous land.

But I must not forget to tell you that I spent my birthday very differently from what I expected. I must however be brief, for an hour hence I go to join the Carnival in the Corso. My birthday had three celebrations—the eve, the birthday itself, and the day after. On the 2nd of February, Santini was sitting in my room in the morning, and in answer to my impatient questions about the Conclave, he replied with a diplomatic air, that there was little chance of a Pope being elected before Easter. Herr Brisbane also called, and told me that after leaving Berlin, he had been in Constantinople, and Smyrna, etc., and inquired after all his acquaintances in Berlin, when suddenly the report of a cannon was heard, and then another, and the people rushed across the Piazza di Spagna, shouting with all their might. We three started off, Heaven knows how, and ran breathlessly to the Quirinal, where the man was just retreating, who had shouted through a broken window—"Annuncio vobis gaudium magnum; habemus Papam R. E. dominum Capellari, qui nomen assumsit Gregorius XVI." All the Cardinals now crowded into the balcony, to breathe fresh air, and laughed, and talked together.

It was the first time they had been in the open air for fifty days, and yet they looked so gay, their red caps shining brightly in the sun; the whole Piazza was filled with people, who clambered on the obelisk, and on the horses of Phidias, and the statues projected far above in the air. Carriage after carriage drove up, amid jostling and shouting. Then the new Pope appeared, and before him was borne the golden cross, and he blessed the crowd for the first time, while the people at the same moment prayed, and cried " Hurrah ! " All the bells in Rome were ringing, and there was firing of cannons, and flourishes of trumpets, and military music. This was the *eve* of my birthday.

Next morning I followed the crowd down the long street to the Piazza of St. Peter's, which looked finer than I had ever seen it, lit up brightly by the sun, and swarming with carriages; the Cardinals in their red coaches, driving in state to the sacristy, with servants in embroidered liveries, and people innumerable, of every nation, rank, and condition; and high above them the dome and the church seeming to float in blue vapour, for there was considerable mist in the morning air. And I thought that Capellari would probably appropriate all this to himself when he saw it; but I knew better. It was all to celebrate my birthday; and the election of the Pope, and the homage, a mere spectacle in honour of me; but it was well and naturally performed; and so long as I live, I shall never forget it.

The Church of St. Peter's was crowded to the

door. The Pope was borne in on his throne, and fans of peacocks' feathers carried before him, and then set down on the High Altar, when the Papal singers intoned, " *Tu es sacerdos magnus.*" I only heard two or three chords, but it required no more; the sound was enough. Then one Cardinal succeeded another, kissing the Pope's foot and his hands, when he in turn embraced them. After surveying all this for a time, standing closely pressed by a crowd, and unable to move, to look suddenly aloft to the dome, as far as the lantern, inspires a singular sensation. I was with Diodati, among a throng of Capuchins; these saintly men are far from being devotional on an occasion of this kind, and by no means cleanly. But I must hasten on; the Carnival is beginning, and I must not lose any portion of it.

At night, (in honour of my birthday,) barrels of pitch were burned in all the streets, and the Propaganda illuminated. The people thought this was owing to its being the former residence of the Pope, but *I* knew it was because I lived exactly opposite, and I had only to lean out of my window to enjoy it all. Then came Torlonia's ball, and in every corner were seen glimpses of red caps above, and red stockings below. The following day they worked very hard at scaffoldings, platforms, and stages for the Carnival; edicts were posted up about horse-racing, and specimens of masks were displayed at the windows, and (in celebration of the day following my birthday) the illumination of the dome, and the Gi-

randola were fixed for Sunday. On Saturday all the
world went to the Capitol, to witness the form of the
Jews' supplications to be suffered to remain in the
Sacred City for another year; a request which is
refused at the foot of the hill, but after repeated
entreaties, granted on the summit, and the Ghetto is
assigned to them. It was a tiresome affair; we
waited two hours, and after all, understood the
oration of the Jews as little as the answer of the
Christians. I came down again in very bad humour,
and thought that the Carnival had commenced
rather unpropitiously. So I arrived in the Corso
and was driving along, thinking no evil, when I was
suddenly assailed by a shower of sugar comfits. I
looked up; they had been flung by some young ladies
whom I had seen occasionally at balls, but scarcely
knew, and when in my embarrassment I took off my
hat to bow to them, the pelting began in right earnest.
Their carriage drove on, and in the next was Miss
T——, a delicate young Englishwoman. I tried to
bow to her, but she pelted me too, so I became quite
desperate, and clutching the *confetti*, I flung them
back bravely; there were swarms of my acquaintances, and my blue coat was soon as white as that of
a miller. The B——s were standing on a balcony,
flinging *confetti* like hail at my head; and thus pelting and pelted, amid a thousand jests and jeers, and
the most extravagant masks, the day ended with
races.

The following day there was no carnival, but as a
compensation, the Pope conferred his benediction

from the Loggia, in the Piazza of St. Peter's; he was consecrated as Bishop in the Church, and at night the dome was lighted up. The sudden, nay *instantaneous* change the illumination of the building effects, you must ask Hensel to paint or to describe, whichever he prefers. Nothing can be more startling than the sudden and surprising vision, of so many hundred human beings, previously invisible, now revealed as it were in the air, working and moving about—and the glorious Girandola,—but who can conceive it! Now the gaieties recommence. Farewell! in my next letter I mean to continue my description. Yesterday, at the Carnival, flowers and *bonbons* were indiscriminately thrown, and a mask gave me a bouquet, which I have dried, and mean to bring home for you. All idea of occupation is out of the question at present; I have only composed one little song; but when Lent comes, I intend to be more industrious. Who can at such a moment think either of writing or music? I must go out, so farewell, dear ones. Felix.

———————◆———————

Rome, February 22nd, 1831.

A thousand thanks for your letter of the 8th, which I received yesterday, on my return from Tivoli. I cannot tell you, dear Fanny, how much I am delighted with your plan about the Sunday music. This idea of yours is most brilliant, and I do entreat of you, for Heaven's sake, not to let it die away again; on the contrary, pray give your travelling brother a commission to write something new for you. He will gladly do so, for he is quite charmed with you, and with your project. You must let me know what voices you have, and also take counsel with your subjects as to what they like best (for the people, O Fanny, have rights). I think it would be a good plan to place before them something easy, interesting and pleasing,—for instance, the Litany of Sebastian Bach. But to speak seriously, I recommend the "Shepherd of Israel," or the "Dixit Dominus," of Hændel.

Do you mean to play something during the intervals to these people? I think this would not be unprofitable to either party, for they must have time to take breath, and you must study the piano, and thus it would become a vocal and instrumental concert. I wish so much that I could be one of the audience, and compliment you afterwards. Be discreet and indulgent, and avoid fatiguing either yourself or the voices of your singers. Do not be irritable when things go badly; say very little on the subject to any one. Lastly, above all, endeavour to prevent the choir feeling any tedium, for this is the principal point. One of my pieces certainly owes its birth to this Sunday music. When you wrote to me about it lately, I reflected whether there was anything I could send you, thus reviving an old favourite scheme of mine, which has however now assumed such vast proportions, that I cannot let you have any part of it by E——, but you shall have it at some future time.

Listen and wonder! Since I left Vienna I have partly composed Goethe's first "Walpurgis Night," but have not yet had courage to write it down. The composition has now assumed a form, and become a grand Cantata, with full orchestra, and may turn out well. At the opening there are songs of spring, etc., and plenty of others of the same kind. Afterwards, when the watchmen with their " Gabeln, und Zacken, und Eulen," make a great noise, the fairy frolics begin, and you know that I have a particular foible for them; the sacrificial Druids then appear, with their trombones in C major, when the watchmen come in again in alarm, and here I mean to introduce a light mysterious tripping chorus; and lastly to conclude with a grand sacrificial hymn. Do you not think that this might develop into a new style of Cantata? I have an instrumental introduction, as a matter of course, and the effect of the whole is very spirited. I hope it will soon be finished. I have once more begun to compose with fresh vigour, and the Italian symphony makes rapid progress; it will be the most sportive piece I have yet composed, especially the last movement. I have not yet decided on the *adagio*, and think I shall reserve it for Naples. "Verleih uns Frieden" is completed, and "Wir glauben all" will also be ready in a few days. The Scotch symphony alone is not yet quite to my liking; if any brilliant idea occurs to me, I will seize it at once, quickly write it down, and finish it at last.   Felix.

Rome, March 1st, 1831.

While I write this date, I shrink from the thought of how time flies. Before this month is at an end the Holy Week begins, and when it is over, my stay in Rome will be drawing to a close. I now try to reflect whether I have made the best use of my time, and on every side I perceive a deficiency. If I could only compass one of my two symphonies! I must and will reserve the Italian one till I have seen Naples, which must play a part in it, but the other also seems to elude my grasp; the more I try to seize it, and the nearer the end of this delightful quiet Roman period approaches, the more am I perplexed, and the less do I seem to succeed. I feel as if it will be long indeed before I can write again as freely as here, and so I am eager to finish what I have to do, but I make no progress. The "Walpurgis Night" alone gets on quickly, and I hope it will soon be accomplished. Besides, I cannot resist every day sketching, that I may carry away with me reminiscences of my favourite haunts. There is still much that I wish to see, so I perfectly well know that this month will suddenly come to an end, and much remain undone; and indeed it is quite too beautiful here.

Rome is considerably changed, and neither so gay nor so cheerful as formerly.* Almost all my acquaintances are gone; the promenades and streets

---

* Some disturbances had in the meantime broken out in the Ecclesiastical States, at Bologna.

are deserted, the galleries closed, and it is impossible to gain admittance into them. All news from without almost entirely fails us, (for we saw the details about Bologna first in the 'Allgemeine Zeitung' yesterday;) people seldom or never congregate together; in fact, everything has subsided into entire rest; but then the weather is lovely, and no one can deprive us of this warm, balmy atmosphere. Those who are most to be pitied in the present state of affairs are the Vernet ladies, who are unpleasantly situated here. The hatred of the entire Roman populace is, strangely enough, directed against the French Pensionaries, believing that their influence alone could easily effect a revolution. Threatening anonymous letters have been repeatedly sent to Vernet; indeed he one day found an armed Transteverin stationed in front of the windows of his studio, who however took to flight when Vernet fetched his gun: and as the ladies are now entirely alone, and isolated in the villa, their family are naturally very uneasy. Still all continues quiet and serene within the city, and I am quite convinced it will remain so.

The German painters are really more contemptible than I can tell you. Not only have they cut off their whiskers and moustaches, and their long hair and beards, openly declaring that as soon as all danger is at an end they will let them grow again, but these tall stalwart fellows go home as soon as it is dark, lock themselves in, and discuss their fears together. They call Horace Vernet a braggart, and yet he is very different from these miserable creatures, whose conduct makes me cordially despise them. Latterly I occasionally visited some of the modern studios. Thorwaldsen has just finished a statue in clay of Lord Byron. He is seated amidst ancient ruins, his feet resting on the capital of a column, while he is gazing into the distance, evidently about to write something on the tablets he holds in his hand. He is represented not in Roman costume, but in a simple modern dress, and I think it looks well, and does not destroy the general effect. The statue has the natural air and easy pose so remarkable in all this sculptor's works, and yet the poet looks sufficiently gloomy and elegiac, though not affected. I must some day write you a whole letter about the 'Triumph of Alexander,' for never did any piece of sculpture make such an impression on me; I go there every week, and stand gazing at that alone, and enter Babylon along with the Conqueror. I lately called on A——; he has brought with him some admirable pencil sketches from Naples and Sicily, so I should be glad to take some hints from him, but I fear that he is a considerable exaggerator, and does not sketch faithfully. His landscape of the Colosseum, at H. B., is a beautiful romance; for I cannot say that in the original I ever perceived woods of large cypresses and orange-trees, or fountains or thickets in the centre, extending to the ruins. Moreover, *his* moustaches have also disappeared.

I have something amusing to tell you in conclusion. I wish, O my Fanny, that as a contrast to your Sunday harmony you had heard the music we perpetrated last Sunday evening. We wished to sing the Psalms of Marcello, being Lent, and the best dilettanti consequently assembled. A Papal singer was in the middle, a *maestro* at the piano, and we sang. When a soprano solo came, all the ladies pressed forward, each insisting on singing it, so it was executed as a *tutti*. The tenor by my side never alighted on the right note, and rambled about in the most insecure regions. When I chimed in as second tenor, he dropped into my part, and when I tried to assist him, he seemed to think that was my original part, and kept steadily to his own. The Papal singer at one instant sang in the soprano falsetto, and presently took the first bass; soon after he quaked out the *alt*, and when all that was of no avail, he smiled sorrowfully across at me, and we nodded mysteriously to each other. The *maestro*, in striving to set us all right, repeatedly lost his own place, being a bar behind, or one in advance, and thus we sang with the most complete anarchy, just as we thought fit. Suddenly came a very solemn solo passage for the bass, which *all* attacked valiantly, but at the second bar broke into a chorus of loud laughter, in which we unanimously joined, so the affair ended in high good-humour. The people who had come as audience talked at the pitch of their voices, and then went out and dispersed. Eynard came in and listened to our music for a time, then made a horrid grimace, and was seen no more. Farewell! Health and happiness attend you all!   FELIX.

Rome, March 15th, 1831.

The letters of introduction that R—— sent me, have been of no use to me here. L—— likewise, to whom I was presented by Bunsen, has not taken the smallest notice of me, and tries to look the other way when we meet. I rather suspect the man is an aristocrat. Albani admitted me, so I had the honour of conversing for half an hour with a Cardinal. After reading the introductory letter, he asked me if I was a pensioner of the King of Hanover. "No," said I. He supposed that I must have seen St. Peter's? "Yes," said I. As I knew Meyerbeer, he assured me that he could not endure his music; it was too scientific for him; indeed, everything he wrote was so learned, and so devoid of melody, that you at once saw that he was a German, and the Germans, *mon ami*, have not the most remote conception of what melody is! "No," said I. "In *my* scores," continued he, "all sing; not only the voices sing, but also the first violin sings, and the second violin also, and the oboe sings, and so it goes on, even to the horns, and last of all the double-bass sings too." I was naturally desirous, in all humility, to see some of his music; he was modest, however, and would show me nothing, but he said that wishing to make my stay in Rome a agreeable as possible, he hoped I would pay a visit to his villa, and I might take as many of my friends with me as I chose. It was near such and such a place. I thanked him very much, and subsequently boasted considerably of this gracious permission; but presently discovered that this villa is open to the public, and any one can go there who chooses. Since that time I have heard no more of him, and as this and some other instances have inspired me with respect, mingled with aversion, towards the highest Roman circles, I resolved not to deliver the letter to Gabrielli, and was satisfied by having the whole Bonaparte family pointed out to me on the promenade, where I met them daily.

I think Mizkiewicz very tiresome. He possesses that kind of indifference which bores both himself and others, though the ladies persist in designating it melancholy and lassitude; but this makes it no better in my eyes. If he looks at St. Peter's, he deplores the times of the hierarchy; if the sky is blue and beautiful, he wishes it were dull and gloomy; if it is gloomy, he is freezing; if he sees the Colosseum, he wishes he had lived at that period. I wonder what sort of a figure he would have made in the days of Titus!

You inquire about Horace Vernet, and this is, indeed, a pleasant theme. I believe I may say that I have learned something from him, and every one may do the same. He produces with incredible facility and freshness. When a form meets his eye which touches his feelings, he instantly adopts it, and while others are deliberating whether it can be called beautiful, and praising or censuring, he has long completed his work, entirely deranging our æsthetical standard. Though this facility cannot be acquired, still its principle is admirable, and the serenity which springs from it, and the energy it calls forth in working, nothing else can replace.

Among the alleys of evergreen trees, where at this season of blossoms the fragrance is so charming, in the midst of the shrubberies and gardens of the Villa Medicis, stands a small house, in which as you approach you invariably hear a tumult,—shouting and wrangling, or a piece executed on a trumpet, or the barking of dogs; this is Vernet's *atelier*. The most picturesque disorder everywhere prevails; guns, a hunting-horn, a monkey, palettes, a couple of dead hares or rabbits; the walls covered with pictures, finished and unfinished. "The Investiture of the National Cockade" (an eccentric picture which does not please me), portraits recently begun of Thorwaldsen, Eynard, Latour-Maubourg, some horses, a sketch of Judith, and studies for it; the portrait of the Pope, a couple of Moorish heads, bagpipers, Papal soldiers, my unworthy self, Cain and Abel, and last of all a drawing of the interior of the place itself, all hang up in his studio.

Lately his hands were quite full, owing to the number of portraits bespoken from him; but in the street he saw one of the Campagna peasants, who are armed and mounted by Government, and ride about **Rome.** The singular **costume caught the** artist's eye, and next day he began a picture representing a similar **peasant, sitting on his horse in bad** weather in the Campagna, and seizing **his gun in** order to take aim **at some one** with it; in the **distance are visible a small** troop of soldiers, and the desolate **plain.** The minute **details of the** weapon, **where the** peasant peeps through the soldier's uniform, **the** wretched horse and **its shabby trappings, the dis-**comfort prevalent throughout, **and the Italian** phlegm in the bearded fellow, make **a charming little** picture; and no one **can help envying him, who sees** the real delight with **which his brush traverses the stretched canvas, at one moment putting in a little** rivulet, **and a couple of soldiers, and a button on the saddle; then lining the soldier's great-coat with** green. **Numbers of people come to look on: during** my **first** sitting twenty persons, **at least, arrived one** after the **other. Countess E——— asked him to allow her to be present when he was at work; but when he darted on it as a hungry man does on food, her amazement was great. The whole family are, as I told you, good people, and when** old Charles **talks about his father Joseph, you must feel respect for them, and I maintain that they are noble. Good-bye, for it is late, and I must send my letter to the Post.**

Fanny.

————◆————

Rome, March 29th, 1831.

In the midst of the Holy Week. To-morrow for
the first time I am to hear the Miserere, and while
you last Sunday performed "The Passion," the Cardinals and all the priesthood here received twisted
palms and olive-branches. The Stabat Mater of
Palestrina was sung, and there was a grand procession. My work has got on badly during the last
few days. Spring is in all her bloom; a genial blue
sky without, such as we at most only dream of,
and a journey to Naples in my every thought; so
even a quiet time to write is not to be found. O——,
who is usually a cool fellow, has written me such a
glowing letter from Naples! The most prosaic men
become poetical when they speak of it. The finest
season of the year in Italy, is from the 15th of April
to the 15th of May. Who can wonder that I find it
impossible to return to my misty Scotch mood? I
have therefore laid aside the Scotch symphony for
the present, but hope to write out the " Walpurgis
Night" here. I shall manage to do so if I work hard
to-day and to-morrow, and if we have bad weather,
for really a fine day is too great a temptation. As
soon as an impediment occurs, I hope to find some
resource in the open air, so I go out and think of
anything and everything but my composition, and do
nothing but lounge about, and when the church bells
begin to ring, it is the Ave Maria already. All I
want now is a short overture. If I can accomplish
this, the thing is complete, and I can write it out in a

couple of days. Then I have done with music, and leaving all music-paper here, I shall go off to Naples, where, please God, I mean to do nothing.

Two French friends of mine have tempted me to *flâner* with them a good deal of late. When they are together, it is either a perpetual tragedy, or comedy,—as you will. Y—— distorts everything, without a spark of talent, always groping in the dark, but esteeming himself the creator of a new world; writing moreover the most frightful things, and yet dreaming and thinking of nothing but Beethoven, Schiller, and Goethe; a victim at the same time to the most boundless vanity, and looking down condescendingly on Mozart and Haydn, so that all his enthusiasm seems to me very doubtful. Z—— has been toiling for three months at a little rondo on a Portuguese theme; he arranges neatly and brilliantly, and according to rule, and he now intends to set about composing six waltzes, and is in a state of perfect ecstasy if I will only play him over a number of Vienna waltzes. He has a high esteem for Beethoven, but also for Rossini and for Bellini, and no doubt for Auber,—in short, for everybody. Then my turn comes to be praised, who would be only too glad to murder Y——, till he chances to eulogize Gluck, when I can quite agree with him. I like nevertheless to walk about with these two, for they are the only musicians here, and both very pleasant, amiable persons. All this forms an amusing contrast.

You say, dear mother, that Y—— must have a

fixed aim in his art; but this is far from being my opinion. I believe he wishes to be married, and is in fact worse than the other, because he is by far the most affected of the two. I really cannot stand his obtrusive enthusiasm, and the gloomy despondency he assumes before ladies,—this stereotyped genius in black and white; and if he were not a Frenchman, (and it is always pleasant to associate with them, as they have invariably something interesting to say,) it would be beyond endurance. A week hence, I shall probably write you . my last letter from Rome, and then you shall hear of me from Naples. It is still quite uncertain whether I go to Sicily or not; I almost think not, as in any event I must have recourse to a steamboat, and it is not yet settled that one is to go.

In haste, yours, FELIX.

Rome, April 4th, 1831.

The Holy Week is over, and my passport to Naples prepared. My room begins to look empty, and my winter in Rome is now among my reminiscences of the past. I intend to leave this in a few days, and my next letter (D. V.) shall be from Naples. Interesting and amusing as the winter in Rome has been, it has closed with a truly memorable week; for what I have seen and heard far surpassed my expectations, and being the conclusion, I will endeavour in this, my last letter from

Rome, to give you a full description of it all. People have often both zealously praised and censured the ceremonies of the Holy Week, and have yet omitted, as is often the case, the chief point, namely its perfection as a complete whole. My father may probably remember the description of Mdlle. de R——, who after all only did what most people do, who write or talk about music and art, when in a hoarse and prosaic voice she attempted at dinner to give us some idea of the fine clear Papal choir. Many others have given the mere music, and been dissatisfied, because external adjuncts are required to produce the full effect. Those persons may be in the right; still so long as these indispensable externals are there, and especially in such entire perfection, so long will it impress others; and just as I feel convinced that place, time, order, the vast crowd of human beings awaiting in the most profound silence the moment for the music to begin, contribute largely to the effect, so do I contemn the idea of deliberately separating what ought in fact to be indivisible, and this for the purpose of exhibiting a certain portion, which may thus be depreciated. That man must be despicable indeed, on whom the devotion and reverence of a vast assemblage did not make a corresponding impression of devotion and reverence, even if they were worshipping the Golden Calf; let him alone destroy this, who can replace it by something better.

Whether one person repeats it from another, whether it comes up to its great reputation, or is merely the effect of the imagination, is quite the same thing. It suffices that we have a perfect totality, which has exercised the most powerful influence for centuries past, and still exercises it, and therefore I reverence it, as I do every species of real perfection. I leave it to theologians to pronounce on its religious influence, for the various opinions on that point are of no great value. There is more to be considered than the mere ceremonies: for me it is sufficient, as I already said, that in any sphere the object should be fully carried out, so far as ability will permit, with fidelity and conscientiousness, to call forth my respect and sympathy. Thus you must not expect from me a formal critique on the singing, as to whether they intoned correctly or incorrectly, in tune or out of tune, or whether the compositions are fine. I would rather strive to show you, that as a whole the affair cannot fail to make a solemn impression, and that everything contributes to this result, and as last week I enjoyed music, forms, and ceremonies, without severing them, revelling in the perfect whole, so I do not intend to separate them in this letter. The technical part, to which I naturally paid particular attention, I mean to detail more minutely to Zelter.

The first ceremony was on Palm Sunday, when the concourse of people was so great, that I could not make my way through the crowd to my usual place on what is called the Prelates' Bench, but was forced to remain among the Guard of Honour, where indeed I had a very good view of the solemnities, but could not follow the singing properly, as they pronounced the words very indistinctly, and on that day I had no book. The result was that on this first day, the various antiphons, Gospels, and Psalms, and the mode of chanting, instead of reading, which is employed here in its primitive form, made the most confused and singular impression on me. I had no clear conception what rule they followed with regard to the various cadences. I took considerable pains gradually to discover their method, and succeeded so well, that at the end of the Holy Week I could have sung with them. I thus also escaped the extreme weariness, so universally complained of during the endless Psalms before the Miserere; for I quickly detected any variety in the monotony, and when perfectly assured of any particular cadence, I instantly wrote it down; so I made out by degrees (which indeed I deserved) the melodies of eight Psalms. I also noted down the antiphons, etc., and was thus incessantly occupied and interested.

The first Sunday, however, as I already told you, I could not make it all out satisfactorily: I only knew that the choir sang " Hosanna in excelsis," and intoned various hymns, while twisted palms were offered to the Pope, which he distributed among the Cardinals. These palms are long branches decorated with buttons, crosses, and crowns, all entirely made of dried palm-leaves, which makes them look like gold. The Cardinals, who are seated in the Chapel in the form of a quadrangle, with the abbati at their feet, now advance each in turn to receive their palms, with which they return to their places; then come the bishops, monks, abbati, and all the other orders of the priesthood; the Papal singers, the knights, and others, who receive olive-branches entwined with palm-leaves. This makes a long procession, during which the choir continues to sing unremittingly. The abbati hold the long palms of their cardinals like the lances of sentinels, slanting them on the ground before them, and at this moment there is a brilliancy of colour in the chapel that I never before saw at any ceremony. There were the Cardinals in their gold embroidered robes and red caps, and the violet abbati in front of them, with golden palms in their hands, and further in advance, the gaudy servants of the Pope, the Greek priests, the patriarchs in the most gorgeous attire; the Capuchins with long white beards, and all the other religious Orders; then again the Swiss, in their popinjay uniforms, all carrying green olive-branches, while singing is going on the whole time; though certainly it is scarcely possible to distinguish what is being sung, yet the mere sound is sufficient to delight the ear.

The Pope's throne is then carried in, on which he is elevated in all processions, and where I saw Pius VIII. enthroned on the day of my arrival (*vide* the 'Heliodorus' of Raphael, where he is portrayed). The Cardinals, two and two, with their palms, head the procession, and the folding doors of the chapel being thrown open, it slowly defiles through them. The singing, which has hitherto incessantly prevailed,

like an element, becomes fainter and fainter, for the
singers also walk in the procession, and at length are
only indistinctly heard, the sound dying away in the
distance. Then a choir in the chapel bursts forth
with a query, to which the distant one breathes a
faint response; and so it goes on for a time, till the
procession again draws near, and the choirs reunite.
Let them sing how or what they please, this cannot
fail to produce a fine effect; and though it is quite
true that nothing can be more monotonous, and even
devoid of form, than the hymns *all' unisono*, being
without any proper connection, and sung *fortissimo*
throughout, still I appeal to the impression that as
a *whole* it must make on every one. After the procession returns, the Gospel is chanted in the most
singular tone, and is succeeded by the Mass. I must
not omit here to make mention of my favourite moment; I mean the Credo. The priest takes his place
for the first time in the centre, before the altar, and
after a short pause, intones in his hoarse old voice
the Credo of Sebastian Bach. When he has finished, the priests stand up, the Cardinals leave
their seats, and advance into the middle of the
chapel, where they form a circle, all repeating the
continuation in a loud voice, " Patrem omnipoten-
tem," etc. The choir then chimes in, singing the
same words. When I for the first time heard my
well-known

and all the grave monks round me began to recite in loud and eager tones, I felt quite excited, for this is the moment I still like the best of all. After the ceremony, Santini made me a present of his olive-branch, which I carried in my hand the whole day when I was walking about, for the weather was beautiful. The Stabat Mater which succeeds the Credo, made much less effect; they sang it incorrectly and out of tune, and likewise curtailed it considerably. The 'Sing Akademie' executes it infinitely better. There is nothing on Monday or Tuesday; but on Wednesday, at half-past four, the nocturns begin.

The Psalms are sung in alternate verses by two choirs, though invariably by one class of voices, basses or tenors. For an hour and a half, therefore, nothing but the most monotonous music is heard; the Psalms are only once interrupted by the Lamentations, and this is the first moment when, after a long time, a complete chord is given. This chord is very softly intoned, and the whole piece sung *pianissimo*, while the Psalms are shouted out as much as possible, and always upon one note, and the words uttered with the utmost rapidity, a cadence occurring at the end of each verse, which defines the different characteristics of the various melodies. It is not therefore surprising that the mere soft sound (in G major) of the first Lamentation, should produce so touching an effect. Once more the single tone recommences; a wax light is extinguished at the end of each Psalm, so that in the course of an hour and a half the fifteen lights round the altar are all out; six large-sized candles still burn in the vestibule. The whole strength of the choir, with alti and soprani, etc., intone *fortissimo* and *unisono*, a new melody, the "Canticum Zachariæ," in D minor, singing it slowly and solemnly in the deepening gloom; the last remaining lights are then extinguished. The Pope leaves his throne, and falls on his knees before the altar, while all around do the same, repeating a paternoster *sub silentio;* that is, a pause ensues, during which you know that each Catholic present says the Lord's Prayer, and immediately afterwards the Miserere begins *pianissimo* thus :—

This is to me the most sublime moment of the whole. You can easily picture to yourself what follows, but not this commencement. The continuation, which is the Miserere of Allegri, is a simple sequence of chords, grounded either on tradition, or what appears to me much more probable, merely embellishments, introduced by some clever *maestro* for the fine voices at his disposal, and especially for a very high soprano. These *embellimenti* always recur on the same chords, and as they are cleverly constructed, and beautifully adapted for the voice, it is invariably pleasing to hear them repeated. I could not discover anything unearthly or mysterious in the music; indeed, I am perfectly contented that its beauty should be earthly and comprehensible. I refer you, dearest Fanny, to my letter to Zelter. On the first day they sang Baini's Miserere.

On Thursday, at nine o'clock in the morning, the solemnities recommenced, and lasted till one o'clock. There was High Mass, and afterwards a procession. The Pope conferred his benediction from the Loggia of the Quirinal, and washed the feet of thirteen priests, who are supposed to represent the pilgrims, and were seated in a row, wearing white gowns and white caps, and who afterwards dine. The crowd of English ladies was extraordinary, and the whole affair repugnant to my feelings. The Psalms began again in the afternoon, and lasted on this occasion till half past seven. Some portions of the Miserere were taken from Baini, but the greater part were Allegri's. It was almost dark in the chapel when the Miserere commenced. I clambered up a tall ladder standing there by chance, and so I had the whole chapel crowded with people, and the kneeling Pope and his Cardinals, and the music, beneath me. It had a splendid effect. On Friday forenoon the chapel was stripped of every decoration, and the Pope and Cardinals in mourning. The history of the Passion, according to St. John, the music by Vittoria, was sung; then the Improperia of Palestrina, during which the Pope and all the others, taking off their shoes, advance to the cross and adore it. In the evening Baini's Miserere was given, which they sang infinitely the best.

Early on Saturday, in the baptistery of the Lateran, Heathens, Jews, and Mahomedans were baptized, all represented by a little child, who screeched the whole time, and subsequently some young priests received consecration for the first time. On Sunday the Pope himself performed High Mass in the Quirinal, and subsequently pronounced his benediction on the people, and then all was over. It is now Saturday, the 9th of April, and to-morrow at an early hour I get into a carriage and set off for Naples, where a new style of beauty awaits me. You will perceive by the end of this letter that I write in haste. This is my last day, and a great deal yet to be done. I do not therefore finish my letter to Zelter, but will send it from Naples. I wish my description to be correct, and my approaching journey distracts my attention sadly. Thus I am off to Naples; the weather is clearing up, and the sun shining, which it has not done for some days past. My passport is prepared, the carriage ordered, and I am looking forward to the months of spring. Adieu!   FELIX.

<hr>

Naples, April 13th, 1831.

Dear Rebecca,

This must stand in lieu of a birthday letter : may it wear a holiday aspect for you! It arrives late in

the day, but with equally sincere good wishes. Your
birthday **itself I** passed in a singular but delightful
manner, though I could not write, having neither
pens nor ink ; in fact, I was **in the** very middle of the
Pontine Marshes. May the ensuing year bring you
every happiness, **and may we** meet somewhere ! If
you were thinking of me on that day, our thoughts
must have met either on the Brenner or at Inspruck ;
for I was constantly thinking of you. Even without
looking at the date **of this letter,** you will at once
perceive by its tone that I am in Naples. I have not
yet **been able to** compass one serious quiet reflection.
there is everywhere such jovial life here, inviting you
to do nothing, and to think of nothing, and even the
example of so many thousand people has an irresisti-
ble influence. I do not indeed intend that this **should**
continue, but I see plainly that it must go on for the
first few days. I stand **for hours** on my balcony,
gazing **at** Vesuvius and the Bay.

But I must now endeavour to resume my old descriptive style, or my materials will accumulate so
much that I shall become confused, and I fear you
may not be able to follow me properly. So much
that is novel crowds on me, that a journal would **be**
requisite **to detail to you my life and my state of ex-**
citement. **So I begin by acknowledging that I deeply**
regretted **leaving Rome. My life there was so** quiet,
and yet so full of interest, **having made** many kind
and friendly acquaintances, with **whom** I had become
so domesticated, that the last days of my stay, with
all their discomforts and perpetual running about,

seemed doubly odious. The last evening I went to Vernet's to thank him for my portrait, which is now finished, and to take leave of him. We had some music, talked politics, and played chess, and then I went down the Monte Pincio to my own house, packed up my things, and the next morning drove off with my travelling companions. As I gazed out of the cabriolet at the scenery, I could dream to my heart's desire. When we arrived at our night quarters, we all went out walking. The two days glided past more like a pleasure excursion than a journey.

The road from Rome to Naples is indeed the most luxuriant that I know, and the whole mode of travelling most agreeable. You fly through the plain; for a very slight gratuity the postilions gallop their horses like mad, which is very advisable in the Marshes. If you wish to contemplate the scenery, you have only to abstain from offering any gratuity, and you are soon driven slowly enough. The road from Albano, by Ariccia and Genzano, as far as Velletri, runs between hills, and is shaded by trees of every kind; uphill and downhill, through avenues of elms, past monasteries and shrines. On one side is the Campagna, with its heather, and its bright hues; beyond comes the sea, glittering charmingly in the sunshine, and above, the clearest sky; for since Sunday morning the weather has been glorious.

Well! we drove into Velletri, our night quarters, where a great Church festival was going on. Handsome women with primitive faces were pacing the alleys in groups, and men were standing together wrapped in cloaks, in the street. The church was decorated with garlands of green leaves, and as we drove past it we heard the sounds of a double bass and some violins; fireworks were prepared in the square; the sun went down clear and serene, and the Pontine Marshes, with their thousand colours, and the rocks rearing their heads one by one against the horizon, indicated the course we were to pursue on the following day. After supper I resolved to go out again for a short time, and discovered a kind of illumination; the streets were swarming with people, and when I at last came to the spot where the church stood, I saw, on turning the corner, that the whole street had burning torches on each side, and in the middle the people were walking up and down, crowding together, and pleased to see each other so distinctly at night. I cannot tell you what a pretty sight it was. The concourse was greatest before the church; I pressed forward into it along with the rest. The little building was filled with people kneeling, adoring the Host, which was exposed; no one spoke a word, nor was there any music. This stillness, the lighted church, and the many kneeling women with white handkerchiefs on their heads, and white gowns, had a striking effect. When I left the church a shrewd, handsome Italian boy explained the whole festival, assuring me that it would have been far finer had it not been for the recent disturbances, for they had been the cause of depriving the people of the horse-races, and barrels of pitch, etc., and on this account it was unlucky that the Austrians had not come sooner.

The following morning, at six o'clock, we pursued our way through the Pontine Marshes. It is a species of Bergstrasse. You drive through a straight avenue of trees along a plain. On one side of the avenue is a continued chain of hills, on the other the Marshes. They are, however, covered with innumerable flowers, which smell very sweet; but in the long-run this becomes very stupefying, and I distinctly felt the oppression of the atmosphere, in spite of the fine weather. A canal runs along beside the *chaussée*, constructed by the orders of Pius VI. to form a conduit for the marshes, where we saw a number of buffaloes wallowing, their heads emerging out of the water, and apparently enjoying themselves. The straight, level road has a singular appearance. You see the chain of hills at the end of the avenue when you come to the first station, and again at the second and third, the only difference being that as you advance so many miles nearer, the hills loom gradually larger. Terracina, which is situated exactly at the end of this avenue, is invisible till you come quite close to it. On making a sudden turn to the left, round the corner of a rock, the whole expanse of the sea lies before you. Citron-gardens, and palms, and a variety of plants of Southern growth, clothe the declivity in front of the town; towers appearing above the thickets, and the harbour projecting into the sea.

To me, the finest object in nature is, and always will be, the ocean. I love it almost more than the sky. Nothing in Naples made a more enchanting impression on my mind than the sea, and I always feel happy when I see before me the spacious surface of waters.

The South, properly speaking, begins at Terracina. This is another land, and every plant and every bush reminds you of it. Above all, the two mighty ridges of hills delighted me, between which the road runs; they were totally devoid of bushes or trees, but clothed entirely with masses of golden wall-flowers, so that they had a bright yellow hue, and the fragrance was almost too strong. There is a great want of grass and large trees. The old robbers' nests of Fondi and Itri looked very piratical and gloomy. The houses are built against the walls of the rocks, and there are likewise some large towers of the date of the Middle Ages. Many sentinels and posts were stationed on the tops of the hills; but we made out our journey without any adventure. We remained all night in Mola di Gaeta; there we saw the renowned balcony whence you look over orange and citron groves to the blue sea, with Vesuvius and the islands in the far distance. This was on the 11th of April. As I had been celebrating your birthday all day long in my own thoughts, I could not in the evening resist informing my companions that it was your birthday; so your health was drunk again and again. An old Englishman, who was of the party, wished me a "happy return to my sister." I emptied the glass to your health, and thought of you. Remain unchanged till we meet again.

With such thoughts in my head, I went in the evening to the citron-garden, close to the sea-shore, and listened to the waves rolling in from afar, and breaking on the shore, and sometimes gently rippling and splashing. It was indeed a heavenly night. Among a thousand other thoughts, Grillparzer's poem recurred to my memory, which it is almost impossible to set to music; for which reason, I suppose, Fanny has composed a charming melody on it; but I do not jest when I say that I sang the song over repeatedly to myself, for I was standing on the very spot he describes. The sea had subsided, and was now calm, and at rest; this was the first song. The second followed next day, for the sea was like a meadow or pure ether as you gazed at it, and pretty women nodded their heads, and so did olives and cypresses; but they were all equally brown, so I remained in a poetic mood.

What is it that shines through the leaves, and glitters like gold? Only cartridges and sabres; for the King had been reviewing some troops in Sant' Agata, and soldiers defiled on both sides of the path, who had the more merit in my eyes because they resembled the Prussians, and for a long time past I have seen only Papal soldiers. Some carried dark-lanterns on their muskets, as they had been marching all night. The whole effect was bold and gay. We now came to a short rocky pass, from which you descend into the valley of Campana, the

most enchanting spot I have ever seen; it is like a
boundless garden, covered entirely with plants and
vegetation as far as the eye can reach.   On one side
are the blue outlines of the sea, on the other an
undulating range of hills above which snowy peaks
project; and at a great distance Vesuvius and the
islands, bathed in blue vapours, start up on the level
surface; large avenues of trees intersect the vast
space, and a verdant growth forces its way from
under every stone.   Everywhere you see grotesque
aloes and cactuses, and the fragrance and vegetation are quite unparalleled.

The pleasure we enjoy in England through men,
we here enjoy through nature; and as there is no
corner there, however small, of which some one has
not taken possession in order to cultivate and adorn
it, so here there is no spot which Nature has not
appropriated, bringing forth on it flowers and herbs,
and all that is beautiful.   The Campana valley is
fruitfulness itself.   On the whole of the vast im-
measurable surface bounded in the far distance by
blue hills and a blue sea, nothing but green meets
the eye.   At last you come to Capua.   I cannot
blame Hannibal for remaining too long there.
From Capua to Naples the road runs uninterruptedly
between trees, with hanging vines, till at the end of
the avenue, Vesuvius, and the sea, with Capri, and
a mass of houses, lie before you.   I am living here
in St. Lucia as if in heaven; for in the first place I
see before me Vesuvius, and the hills as far as Cas-
tellamare, and the bay, and in the second place, I

am living up three stories high. Unfortunately that
traitor Vesuvius does not smoke at all, and looks
precisely like any other fine mountain; but at night
the people float in lighted boats on the Bay, to
catch sword-fish. This has a pretty enough effect.
Farewell!   FELIX.

Naples, April 20th, 1831.

We are so accustomed to find that everything
turns out quite differently from what we expected
and calculated, that you will feel no surprise when
instead of a letter like a journal, you receive a very
short one, merely saying that I am quite well, and
little else.

As for the scenery, I cannot describe it, and if
you have no conception of what it really is, after all
that has been said and written on the subject, there
is little chance of my enlightening you; for what
makes it so indescribably beautiful, is precisely that
it is not of a nature to admit of description. Any
other detail I could send you would be about my
life here; but it is so simple, that a very few words
suffice to depict it. I do not wish to make any acquaintances, for I am resolved not to remain here
longer than a few weeks. I intend to make various
excursions to see the country, and all I desire here,
is to become thoroughly intimate with nature: so I
go to bed at nine o'clock, and rise at five, to refresh
myself by gazing from my balcony at Vesuvius, the

sea, and the coast of Sorrento, in the bright morning light. I have also taken very long solitary rambles, discovering beautiful views for myself, and I have infinite satisfaction in finding that what I consider the loveliest spot of all is almost entirely unknown to the Neapolitans. During these excursions I sought out some house on a height, to which I scrambled up; or else merely followed any path I fancied, allowing myself to be surprised by night and moonshine, and making acquaintance with vine-dressers, in order to learn my way back; arriving at last at home about nine o'clock, very tired, through the Villa Reale. The view from this villa, of the sea and the enchanting Capri by moonlight, is truly charming, and so is the almost overpowering fragrance of the acacias in full bloom, and the fruit-trees scattered all over with rose-coloured blossoms, looking like trees with pink foliage,—all this is indeed quite indescribable.

As I live chiefly with and in nature, I can write less than usual; perhaps we may talk it over when we meet, and the sketches in our sitting-room at home will furnish materials and reminiscences for conversation. One thing I must not however omit, dear Fanny, which is, that I quite approve of your taste when I recall what you told me years ago that your favorite spot was the island of Nisida. Perhaps you may have forgotten this, but I have not. It looks as if it were made expressly for pleasure-grounds. On emerging from the thicket of Bagnuolo, Nisida has quite a startling effect, rising out of the sea, so near, so large and so green; while the other islands, Procida, Ischia, and Capri, stand afar off, and indistinct in their blue tints. After the murder of Cæsar, Brutus took refuge in this island, and Cicero visited him there; the sea lay between them then, and the rocks, covered with vegetation, bent over the sea, just as they do now. *These* are the antiquities that interest me, and are infinitely more suggestive than crumbling mason-work. There is a degree of innate superstition and dishonesty among the people here that is totally inconceivable, and this has often even marred my pleasure in nature; for the Swiss, of whom my father complained so much, are positively guileless, primitive beings, compared with the Neapolitans. My landlord invariably gives me too little change for a piastre, and when I tell him of it, he coolly fetches the remainder. The only acquaintances I intend to make here are musical ones, that I may leave nothing incomplete,—for instance Fodor, who does not sing in public, Donizetti, Coccia, etc.

I now conclude by a few words to you, dear Father. You write to me that you disapprove of my going to Sicily; I have consequently given up this plan, though I cannot deny that I do so with great reluctance, for it was really more than a mere *whim* on my part. There is no danger to be apprehended, and, as if on purpose to vex me, a steamer leaves this city on the 4th of May, which is to make the entire tour; and a good many Germans, and probably the minister here, are to take advantage of it.

I should have liked to see a mountain vomiting forth flames, as Vesuvius has been hitherto so unkind as not even to smoke. Your instructions however have till now so entirely coincided with my own inclinations, that I cannot allow the first opportunity I have of showing my obedience to your wishes (even when opposed to my own), to pass without complying with them, so I have effaced Sicily from my travelling route. Perhaps we may meet sooner in consequence of this; and now farewell, for I am going to walk to Capo di Monte.

FELIX.

Naples, April 27th, 1831.

It is now nearly a fortnight since I have heard from you. I do earnestly hope that nothing unpleasant has occurred, and every day I expect the post will bring me tidings of you all. My letters from Naples are of little value, for I am too deeply absorbed here to be able easily to extricate myself, and to write descriptive letters. Besides, when we had bad weather lately, I took advantage of it to resume my labours, and zealously applied myself to my " Walpurgis Night," which daily increases in interest for me, so I employ every spare moment in completing it. I hope to finish it in a few days, and I think it will turn out well. If I continue in my present mood, I shall finish my Italian symphony also in Italy, in which case I shall have a famous store to bring home with me, the fruits of this winter. Moreover every day I have something new to see. I generally make my excursions with the Schadows.

Yesterday we went to Pompeii. It looks as if it had been burnt down, or like a recently deserted city. As both of these always seem to me deeply affecting, the impression made on me was the most melancholy that I have yet experienced in Italy. It is as if the inhabitants had just gone out, and yet almost every object tells of another religion and another life; in short, of seventeen hundred years ago; and the French and English ladies scramble about as gaily as possible, and sketch it all. It is the old tragedy of the Past and the Present, a problem I never can solve. Lively Naples is indeed a pleasant contrast; but it is painful to see the crowd of wretched beggars who waylay you in every street and path, swarming round the carriage the instant it stops. The old white-haired men particularly distress me, and such a mass of misery exceeds all belief. If you are walking on the sea-shore, and gazing at the islands, and then chance to look round at the land, you find yourself the centre of a group of cripples, who make a trade of their infirmities; or you discover (which lately happened to me) that you are surrounded by thirty or forty children, all whining out their favourite phrase, "Muoio di fame," and rattling their jaws to show that they have nothing to eat. All this forms a most repulsive contrast; and yet to me it is still more repugnant that you must entirely renounce the great pleasure of seeing happy faces; for even when you have given the richest gratuities to guards, waiters, or workpeople, in short, to whom you will, the invariable rejoinder is, "Nienti di più?" in which case you may be very sure that you have given too much. If it is the proper sum, they give it back with the greatest apparent indignation, and then return and beg to have it again. These are trifles, certainly, but they show the lamentable condition of the people. I have even gone so far as to feel provoked with the perpetual smiling aspect of nature, when in the most retired spots troops of beggars everywhere assailed me, some even persisting in following me a long way. It is only when I am quietly seated in my own room, gazing down on the Bay, and on Vesuvius, that being totally alone with them I feel really cheerful and happy.

To-day we are to ascend the hill to visit the Camaldoli Monastery, and to-morrow, if the weather permits, we proceed to Procida and Ischia. I go this evening to Madame Fodor's with Donizetti, Benedict, etc. She is very kind and amiable towards me, and her singing has given me great pleasure, for she has wonderful facility, and executes her *fiorituri* with so much taste, that it is easy to see how many things Sonntag acquired from her, especially the *mezza voce*, which Fodor, whose voice is no longer full and fresh, most prudently and judiciously introduces into many passages. As she is not singing at the theatre, I am most fortunate in having made her acquaintance personally. The theatre is now closed for some weeks, because the blood of St. Januarius is shortly to liquefy. What I heard at the opera previously did not repay the trouble of going. The orchestra, like that in Rome, was worse than in any part of Germany, and not even one tolerable female singer. Tamburini alone, with his vigorous bass voice, imparted some life to the whole. Those who wish to hear Italian operas, must now-a-days go to Paris or London. Heaven grant that this may not eventually be the case with German music also!

I must however return to my "Witches," so you must forgive my not writing any more to-day. This whole letter seems to hover in uncertainty, or rather I do so in my "Walpurgis Night," whether I am to introduce the big drum or not. "Zacken, Gabeln, und wilde Klapperstücke," seem to force me to the big drum, but moderation dissuades me. I certainly am the only person who ever composed for the scene on the Brocken without employing a piccolo-flute, but I can't help regretting the big drum, and before I can receive Fanny's advice, the "Walpurgis Night" will be finished and packed up. I shall then set off again on my travels, and Heaven knows what I may have in my head by that time. I feel convinced that Fanny would say *yes;* still, I feel very doubtful; at all events a vast noise is indispensable.

Oh, Rebecca! can you not procure the words of some songs, and send them to me? I feel quite in the humour for them, and you must require something new to sing. If you can furnish me with some pretty verses, old or new, gay or grave, I will compose something in a style to suit your voice. I am at your service for any compact of this kind. Pray do send me wherewithal to work at, during my journey, in the inns. Now, farewell to you all! May you be as happy as I ever wish you to be, and think of me!   FELIX.

Naples, May 17th, 1831.

On Saturday, the 14th of May, at two o'clock, I told my driver to turn the carriage. We were opposite the Temple of Ceres at Pæstum, the most southern point of my journey. The carriage consequently turned towards the north, and from that moment, as I journey onwards, I am every hour drawing nearer to you. It is about a year now since I travelled with my father to Dessau and Leipzig; the time in fact exactly corresponds, for it was about the half-year. I have made good use of the past year. I have acquired considerable experience and many new impressions. Both in Rome and here I have been very busy, but no change has occurred in my outward circumstances; and till the beginning of the new year, in fact so long as I am in Italy, it will probably be the same. This period has not however been less valuable to me than some when outwardly, and in the opinion of others, I have appeared to make greater progress; for there must always be a close connection between the two. If I have gathered experience, it cannot fail to influence me outwardly, and I shall allow no opportunity to escape to show that it has done so. Possibly some such may occur before the end of my journey, so I may for the present continue to enjoy nature, and the blue sky, during the months that still remain for me in Italy, without thinking of anything else; for *there* alone lies true art, now in Italy,—*there* and in her monuments; and there it will ever remain; and there we shall ever find it, for our instruction and delight, so long as Vesuvius stands, and so long as the balmy air, and the sea, and the trees do not pass away.

In spite of all this, I am enough of a musician to own that I do heartily long once more to hear an orchestra or a full chorus where there is at least some sound, for here there is nothing of the sort. This is *our* peculiar province, and to be so long deprived of such an element, leaves a sad void. The orchestra and chorus here are like those in our second-rate provincial towns, only more harsh and incorrect. The first violinist, all through the opera, beats the four quarters of each bar on a tin candlestick, which is often more distinctly heard than the voices (it sounds somewhat like *obbligati* castanets, only louder); and yet in spite of this the voices are never together. Every little instrumental solo is adorned with old-fashioned flourishes, and a bad tone pervades the whole performance, which is

totally devoid of genius, fire, or spirit. The singers
are the worst Italian ones I ever heard anywhere
(except, indeed, in Italy), and those who wish to
have a true idea of Italian singing must go to Paris
or to London. Even the Dresden company, whom I
heard last year in Leipzig, are superior to any here.
This is but natural, for in the boundless misery that
prevails in Naples, where can the bases of a theatre
be found, which of course requires considerable
capital? The days when every Italian was a born
musician, if indeed they ever existed, are long gone
by. They treat music like any other fashionable
article, with total indifference; in fact, they scarcely
pay it the homage of outward respect, so it is not
to be wondered at that every single person of talent
should, as regularly as they appear, transfer themselves to foreign countries, where they are better
appreciated, their position better defined, and where
they find opportunities of hearing and learning
something profitable and inspiriting.

The only really good singer here is Tamburini;
he has, however, long since been heard in Vienna
and Paris, and I believe in London also; so now,
when he begins to discover that his voice is on the
decline, he comes back to Italy. I cannot admit
either that the Italians alone understand the art of
singing; for there is no music, however florid, I
have ever heard executed by Italians, that Sonntag
cannot accomplish, and in even greater perfection.
She certainly, as she acknowledges, learned much
from Fodor; but why should not another German

in turn learn the same from Sonntag? and Malibran
is a Spaniard. Italy can no longer claim the glorious appellation of " the land of music ;" in truth,
she has already lost it, and possibly she may yet do
so even in the opinion of the world, though this
is problematical. I was lately in company with
some professional musicians, who were speaking of
a new opera by a Neapolitan, Coccia; and one of
them asked if it was clever. " Probably it is," said
another, "for Coccia was long in England, where he
studied, and some of his compositions are much
liked there." This struck me as very remarkable, for
in England they would have spoken exactly in the
same way of Italy; but *quo me rapis?* I say
nothing to you, dear sisters, in this letter, but in the
course of a few days I mean to send you a little
pamphlet dedicated to you. Do not be alarmed, it
is not poetry ; the thing is simply entitled "Journal
of an Excursion to the Islands, in May."

Felix.

Naples, May 28th, 1831.

My dear Sisters,

As my journal is become too stupid and uninteresting to send you, I must at least supply you with
an *abrégé* of my history. You must know, then,
that on Friday, the 20th of May, we breakfasted *in
corpore* at Naples, on fruit, etc.; this *in corpore* includes the travelling party to Ischia, consisting of

Ed. Bendemann, T. Hildebrand, Carl Sohn, and Felix Mendelssohn Bartholdy. My knapsack was not very heavy, for it contained scarcely anything but Goethe's poems, and three shirts; so we packed ourselves into a hired carriage, and drove through the grotto of Posilippo to Pozzuoli. The road runs along by the sea, and nothing can be more lovely; so it is all the more painful to witness the horrible collection of cripples, blind men, beggars, and galley slaves, in short, the poor wretches of every description who there await you, amid the holiday aspect of nature.

I seated myself quietly on the mole and sketched, while the others plodded and toiled through the Temple of Serapis, the theatres, the hot springs, and extinct volcanoes, which I had already seen to satiety on three different occasions. Then, like youthful patriarchs or nomads, we collected all our goods and chattels, cloaks, knapsacks, books and portfolios on donkeys, and placing ourselves also on them, we made the tour of the Bay of Baiæ, as far as the Lake of Avernus, where you are obliged to buy fish for dinner; we crossed the hill to Cumæ (*vide* Goethe's 'Wanderer') and descended on Baiæ, where we ate and rested. We then looked at more ruined temples, ancient baths, and other things of the kind, and thus evening had arrived before we crossed the bay.

At half-past nine we arrived at the little town of Ischia, where we found every corner of the only inn fully occupied, so we resolved to go on to Don Tommaso's; a journey of two hours nominally, but which we performed in an hour and a quarter. The evening was deliciously cool, and innumerable glow-worms, who allowed us to catch them, were scattered on the vine-branches, and fig-trees, and shrubs. When we at last arrived, somewhat fatigued, at Don Tommaso's house, about eleven o'clock, we found all the people still up, clean rooms, fresh fruits. and a friendly deacon to wait on us, so we remained comfortably seated opposite a heap of cherries till midnight. The next morning the weather was bad, and the rain incessant, so we could not ascend the Epomeo, and as we seemed little disposed to converse (we did not get on in this respect, Heaven knows why!) the affair would have become rather a bore, if Don Tommaso had not possessed the prettiest poultry-yard and farm in Europe. Right in front of the door stands a large leafy orange-tree covered with ripe fruit, and from under its branches a stair leads to the dwelling. Each of the white stone steps is decorated with a large vase of flowers, these steps leading to a spacious open hall, whence through an archway you look down on the whole farm-yard, with its orange-trees, stairs, thatched roofs, wine casks and pitchers, donkeys and peacocks. That a foreground may not be wanting, an Indian fig-tree stands under the walled arch, so luxuriant that it is fastened to the wall with ropes. The background is formed by vineyards with summer-houses, and the adjacent heights of the Monte Epomeo. Being protected from the rain by the archway, the party seated themselves there under shelter, and

sketched the various objects in the farm the best
way they could, the whole livelong day. I was on
no ceremony, and sketched along with them, and I
think I in some degree profited by so doing. At
night we had a terrific storm, and as I was lying in
bed, I remarked that the thunder growled tremen-
dously on Monte Epomeo, and the echoes continued
to vibrate like those on the Lake of Lucerne, but
even for a greater length of time.

Next morning, Sunday, the weather was again fine.
We went to Foria, and saw the people going to the
cathedral in their holiday costumes. The women
wore their well-known head-dress of folds of white
muslin placed flat on the head; the men were standing in the square before the church, in their bright
red caps, gossiping about politics, and we gradually
wound our way through these festal villages up the
hill. It is a huge rugged volcano, full of fissures,
ravines, cavities, and steep precipices. The cavities
being used for wine cellars, they are filled with large
casks. Every declivity is clothed with vines and
fig-trees, or mulberry-trees. Corn grows on the sides
of the steep rocks, and yields more than one crop
every year. The ravines are covered with ivy, and
innumerable bright-coloured flowers and herbs, and
wherever there is a vacant space, young chestnut-
trees shoot up, furnishing the most delightful shade.
The last village, Fontana, lies in the midst of verdure and vegetation. As we climbed higher, the
sky became overcast and gloomy, and by the time
we reached the most elevated peaks of the rocks, a

thick fog had come on. The vapours flitted about, and although the rugged outlines of the rocks, and the telegraph, and the cross, stood forth strangely in the clouds, still we could not see even the smallest portion of the view. Soon afterwards rain commenced, and as it was impossible to remain, and wait as you do on the Righi, we were obliged to take leave of Epomeo without having made his acquaintance. We ran down in the rain, one rushing after the other, and I do believe that we were scarcely an hour in returning.

Next day we went to Capri. This place has something Eastern in its aspect, with the glowing heat reflected from its rocky white walls, its palm-trees, and the rounded domes of the churches that look like mosques. The sirocco was burning, and rendered me quite unfit to enjoy anything; for really climbing up five hundred and thirty-seven steps to Anacapri in this frightful heat, and then coming down again, is toil only fit for a horse. True, the sea is wondrously lovely, looking down on it from the summit of the bleak rock, and through the singular fissures of the jagged peaks, so strangely formed.

But above all, I must tell you of the blue grotto, for it is not known to every one, as you can only enter it either in very calm weather, or by swimming. The rocks there project precipitously into the sea, and are probably as steep under the water as above it. A huge cavity has been hollowed out by nature, but in such a manner, that round the whole circumference of the grotto, the rocks rest on the sea in all their breadth, or rather are sunk precip.tously into it, and ascend thence to the vault of the cavern. The sea fills the whole space of the grotto, the entrance to which lies under the water, only a very small portion of the opening projecting above the water, and through this narrow space you can only pass in a small boat, in which you must lie flat. When you are once in, the whole extent of the huge cave and its vault is revealed, and you can row about in it with perfect ease, as if under a dome. The light of the sun also pierces through the opening into the grotto underneath the sea, but broken and dimmed by the green sea water, and thence it is that such magical visions arise. The whole of the rocks are sky-blue and green in the twilight, resembling the hue of moonshine, yet every nook, and every depth, is distinctly visible. The water is thoroughly lighted up and brilliantly illuminated by the light of the sun, so that the dark skiff glides over a bright shining surface. The colour is the most dazzling blue I ever saw, without shadow or cloud, like a pane of opal glass; and as the sun shines down, you can plainly discern all that is going on under the water, while the whole depths of the sea with its living creatures are disclosed. You can see the coral insects and polypuses clinging to the rocks, and far below, fishes of different species meeting and swimming past each other. The rocks become deeper in colour as they go lower into the water, and are quite black at the end of the grotto, where they are closely crowded together, and still further under them, you can see crabs, fishes, and reptiles in the clear waters. Every stroke too of the oars echoes strangely under the vault, and as you row round the wall, new objects come to light. I do wish you could see it, for the effect is singularly magical. On turning towards the opening by which you entered, the daylight seen through it seems bright orange, and by moving even a few paces you are entirely isolated under the rock in the sea, with its own peculiar sunlight: it is as if you were actually living under the water for a time.

We then proceeded to Procida, where the women adopt the Greek dress, but do not look at all prettier from doing so. Curious faces were peeping from every window. A couple of Jesuits, in black gowns and with gloomy countenances, were seated in a gay arbour of vines, evidently enjoying themselves, and made a good picture. Then we crossed the sea to Pozzuoli, and through the grotto of Posilippo again home.

I cannot write to Paul about his change of residence, and his entrance into the great, wide world of London, because he mentions casually, that he will probably leave for London in the course of three weeks, so my letter could not possibly reach him in Berlin; a week hence I shall take my chance, and address to my brother in London. That smoky place is fated to be now and ever my favourite residence; my heart glows when I even think of it, and I paint to myself my return there, passing through Paris, and finding Paul independent, alone, and another man, in the dear old haunts; when he will present me **to his new friends,** and I will present him **to my old ones, and we** shall live and dwell together: so even **at this** moment I am all impatience soon to go there. **I see** by some newspapers my **friends have sent me, that my name is not for-**gotten, and so I **hope when I return to London, to** be able to work **steadily, which I** was previously unable to do, being forced to **go to Italy.** If they make any difficulty in Munich **about my opera,** or if I cannot get a *libretto* that **I** like, I intend **in** that case to compose an opera for London. I know that I could receive a commission **to do so, as** soon as **I chose.** I am also bringing **some new pieces with me for the** Philharmonic, **and so I shall have made good use of** my time.

As my evenings here are at **my own disposal, I read a little French and English.** The "Barricades" and **"Les États de Blois" particularly interest me,** as while **I read them** I realize with horror a period which we have often heard extolled as a vigorous epoch. too soon passed away. Though these books seem to me to **have** many faults, yet the delineation of the two opposite leaders is but too correct ; both were weak, irresolute, miserable hypocrites, and I **thank** God that the so highly-prized middle ages are gone never to return. Say **nothing** of this to any disciple of Hegel's, but it **is so** nevertheless ; and the more I read and think on the subject, the more I feel this to be true. Sterne has become a great favourite of mine. I remembered that Goethe once spoke to me of the 'Sentimental Journey,' and said that it was impossible for any one better to paint what a froward and perverse thing is the human heart. I chanced to meet with the book, and thought I should like to read it. It pleases me very much. I think it very subtle, and beautifully conceived and expressed.

There are very few German books to be had here. I am therefore restricted to Goethe's Poems, and assuredly these are suggestive enough, and always new. I feel especial interest in those poems which he evidently composed in or near Naples, such as Alexis and Dora; for I daily see from my window how this wonderful work was created. Indeed, which is often the case with master-pieces, I often suddenly and involuntarily think, that the very same ideas might have occurred to myself on a similar occasion, and as if Goethe had only by some chance been the first to express them.

With regard to the poem, "Gott segne dich, junge Frau," I maintain that I have discovered its locality and dined with the woman herself; but of course she is now grown old, and the boy she was then nursing is become a stalwart vine-dresser. Her house lies between Pozzuoli and Baiæ, "eines Tempels Trümmern," and is fully three miles from Cumæ. You may imagine therefore with what new light and truth these poems dawn on me, and the different feeling with which I now regard and study them. I say nothing of Mignon's song at present, but it is

14*

singular that Goethe and Thorwaldsen are still living, that Beethoven only died a few years ago, and yet H—— declares that German art is as dead as a rat. *Quod non.* So much the worse for him if he really feels thus; but when I reflect for a time on his conclusions, they appear to me very shallow. *Apropos,* Schadow, who returns to Düsseldorf in the course of a few days, has promised to extract, if possible, some new songs for me from Immermann, which rejoices me much. That man is a true poet, which is proved by his letters, and everything that he has written. Count Platen is a little, shrivelled, wheezing old man, with gold spectacles, yet not more than five-and-thirty! He quite startled me. The Greeks look very different! He abuses the Germans terribly, forgetting however that he does so in German. But farewell for to-day.

FELIX.

◆

Rome, June 6th, 1831.

My dear Parents,

It is indeed high time that I should write to you a rational, methodical letter, for I fear that none of those from Naples were worth much. It really seemed as if the atmosphere there deterred every one from serious reflection, at least I very seldom succeeded in collecting my thoughts or ideas; and now I have been scarcely more than a few hours here, when I once more resume that Roman tranquillity, and grave serenity, which I alluded to in my former letters from this place. I cannot express how infinitely better I love Rome than Naples. People allege that Rome is monotonous, of one uniform hue, melancholy, and solitary. It is certainly true that Naples is more like a great European city, more lively and varied, and more cosmopolitan; but I may say to you confidentially, that I begin gradually to feel the most decided hatred of all that is cosmopolitan;—I dislike it, just as I dislike *many-sidedness*, which, moreover, I rather think I do not much believe in. Anything that aspires to be distinguished, or beautiful, or really great, must be *one-sided;* but then this *one side* must be brought to a state of the most consummate perfection, and no man can deny that such is the case at Rome.

Naples seems to me too small to be called properly a great city; all the life and bustle are confined to two large thoroughfares—the Toledo, and the coast from the harbour to the Chiaja. Naples does not realize to my mind the idea of a centre for a great nation, which London offers in such perfection; chiefly indeed because it is deficient in a people: for the fishermen and lazzaroni I cannot designate as a people, they are more like savages, and their centre is not Naples, but the sea. The middle classes, by which I mean those who pursue various trades, and the working citizens who form the basis of other great towns, are quite subordinate; indeed, I may almost say that such a class is not to be found there. It was this that often made me feel out of humour during my stay in Naples, much as I loved and enjoyed the scenery; but as a dissatisfied feeling constantly recurred, I think I at last discovered the cause to lie within myself. I cannot say that I was precisely unwell during the incessant sirocco, but it was more disagreeable than an indisposition which passes away in a few days. I felt languid, disinclined for all that was serious,—in fact, lazy. I lounged about the streets all day with a morose face, and would have preferred lying on the ground, without the trouble of thinking, or wishing, or doing anything; then it suddenly occurred to me, that the principal classes in Naples live in reality precisely in the same manner; that consequently the source of my depression did not spring from myself, as I had feared, but from the whole combination of air, climate, etc. The atmosphere is suitable for grandees who rise late, never require to go out on foot, never think (for this is heating), sleep away a couple of hours on a sofa in the afternoon, then eat ice, and drive to the theatre at night, where again they do not find anything to think about, but simply make and receive visits. On the other hand, the climate is equally suitable for a fellow in a shirt, with naked legs and arms, who also has no occasion to move about—begging for a few *grani* when he has literally nothing left to live on—taking his afternoon's siesta stretched on the ground, or on the quay, or on the stone pavement (the pedestrians step over him, or shove him aside if he lies right in the middle). He fetches his *frutti di mare* himself out of the sea, sleeps wherever he may chance to find himself at night; in short, he employs every moment in doing exactly what he likes best, just as an animal does.

These are the two principal classes of Naples. By far the largest portion of the population of the Toledo there, consists of gaily dressed ladies and gentlemen, or husbands and wives driving together in handsome equipages, or of those olive *sans-culottes* who sometimes carry about fish for sale, brawling in the most stentorian way, or bearing burdens when they have no longer any money left. I believe there are few indeed who have any settled occupation, or follow up any pursuit with zeal and perseverance, or who like work for the sake of working. Goethe says that the misfortune of the North is, that people there always wish to be doing something, and striving after some end; and he goes on to say, that an Italian was right, who advised him not to think so much, for it would only give him a headache. I suspect however that he was merely jesting; at all events, he did not act in this manner himself, but, on the contrary, like a genuine Northman. If however he means that the difference of character is produced by nature, and subservient to her influence, then there is no doubt that he is quite in the right. I can perfectly conceive that it must be so, and why wolves howl; still it is not necessary to howl along with them. The proverb should be exactly reversed. Those who, owing to their position, are obliged to work, and must consequently both think and bestir themselves, treat the matter as a necessary evil, which brings them in money, and when they actually have it, they too live like the great, or the naked, gentlemen. Thus there is no shop where you are not cheated. Natives of Naples, who have been customers for many years, are obliged to bargain, and to be as much on their guard as foreigners ; and one of my acquaintances, who had dealt at the same shop for fifteen years, told me that during the whole of that period there had been invariably the same battle about a few scudi, and that nothing could prevent it.

Thence it is that there is so little industry or competition, and that Donizetti finishes an opera in ten days; to be sure, it is sometimes hissed, but that does not matter, for it is paid for all the same, and he can then go about amusing himself. If at last however his reputation becomes endangered, he will in that case be forced really to work, which he would find by no means agreeable. This is why he sometimes writes an opera in three weeks, bestowing considerable pains on a couple of airs in it, so that they may please the public, and then he can afford once more to divert himself, and once more to write trash. Their painters, in the same way, paint the most incredibly bad pictures, far inferior even to their music. Their architects also erect buildings in the worst taste ; among others, an imitation, on a small scale, of St. Peter's, in the Chinese style. But what does it matter ? the pictures are bright in colour, the music makes plenty of noise, the build-

ings give plenty of shade, and the Neapolitan grandees ask no more.

My physical mood was similar to theirs, everything inspiring me with a wish to be idle, and to
lounge about, and sleep; yet I was constantly saying to myself that this was wrong; and striving to
occupy myself, and to work, which I could not
accomplish. Hence arose the querulous tone of
some of the letters I wrote to you, and I could only
escape from such a mood by rambling over the hills,
where nature is so divine, making every man feel
grateful and cheerful. I did not neglect the musicians, and we had a great deal of music, but I cared
little in reality for their flattering encomiums.
Fodor is hitherto the only genuine artist, male or
female, that I have seen in Italy; elsewhere I should
probably have found a great many faults with her
singing, but I overlooked them all, because when
she sings it is real music, and after such a long pri-
vation, that was most acceptable.

Now however I am once more in old Rome, where
life is very different. There are processions daily, for
last week was the Corpus Domini; and just as I left
the city during the celebration of the week following the Holy Week, I now return after the Corpus
Christi to find them engaged in the same way. It
made a singular impression on me to see that the
streets had in the interim assumed such an aspect
of summer; on all sides booths with lemons and
iced water, the people in light dresses, the windows
open, and the *jalousies* closed. You sit at the

doors of coffee-houses, and eat *gelato* in quantities; the Corso swarms with equipages, for people no longer walk much, and though in reality I miss no dear friends or relatives, yet I felt quite moved when I once more saw the Piazza di Spagna, and the familiar names written up on the corners of the streets. I shall stay here for about a week, and then proceed northwards.

The Infiorata is on Thursday, but it is not yet quite certain that it will take place, because they have some apprehensions of a revolution; but I hope I shall witness this ceremony. I mean to take advantage of this opportunity to see the hills once more, and then to set off for the north. Wish me a good journey, for I am on the eve of departure. It is a year this very day since I arrived in Munich, heard 'Fidelio,' and wrote to you. We have not met since then; but, please God, we shall see each other again before another year.

FELIX.

Rome, June 16, 1831.

Dear Professor,

It was my intention some time ago to have written you a description of the music during the Holy Week, but my journey to Naples intervened, and during my stay there, I was so constantly occupied in wandering among the mountains, and in gazing at the sea, that I had not a moment's leisure to write; hence arose the delay for which I now beg to apologize. Since then I have not heard a single note worth remembering; in Naples the music is most inferior. During the last two months, therefore, I have no musical reminiscences to send you, save those of the Holy Week, which however made so indelible an impression on my mind, that they will be always fresh in my memory. I already described to my parents the effect of the whole ceremonies, and they probably sent you the letter.

It was fortunate that I resolved to listen to the various Offices with earnest and close attention, and still more so, that from the very first moment I felt sensations of reverence and piety. I consider such a mood indispensable for the reception of new ideas, and no portion of the general effect escaped me, although I took care to watch each separate detail.

The ceremonies commenced on Wednesday, at half past four o'clock, with the antiphon "Zelus domus tuæ." A little book containing the Offices for the Holy Week explains the sense of the various solemnities. "Each Nocturn contains three Psalms, " signifying that Christ died for all, and also sym- " bolical of the three laws, the natural, the written, " and the evangelical. The ' Domine labia mea' and " the ' Deus in adjutorium' were not sung on this " occasion, when the death of our Saviour and Mas- " ter is deplored, as slain by the hands of wicked " godless men. The fifteen lights represent the " twelve apostles and the three Marys." (In this manner the book contains much curious information on this subject, so I mean to bring it with me for you.)

15

The Psalms are chanted *fortissimo* by all the male voices of two choirs. Each verse is divided into two parts, like a question and answer, or rather, classified into A and B; the first chorus sings A, and the second replies with B. All the words, with the exception of the last, are sung with extreme rapidity on one note, but on the last they make a short "melisma," which is different in the first and second verse. The whole Psalm, with all its verses, is sung on this melody, or *tono* as they call it, and I wrote down seven of these *toni*, which were employed during the three days. You cannot conceive how tiresome and monotonous the effect is, and how harshly and mechanically they chant through the Psalms. The first *tonus* which they sang was—

Thus the whole forty-two verses of the Psalm are sung in precisely the same manner; one half of the verse ending in G, A, G, the other in G, E, G. They sing with the accent of a number of men quarrelling violently, and it sounds as if they were shouting out furiously one against another. The closing words of each Psalm are chanted more

slowly and impressively, a long " triad " being sub-
stituted for the "melisma," sung *piano*. For instance, this is the first :—

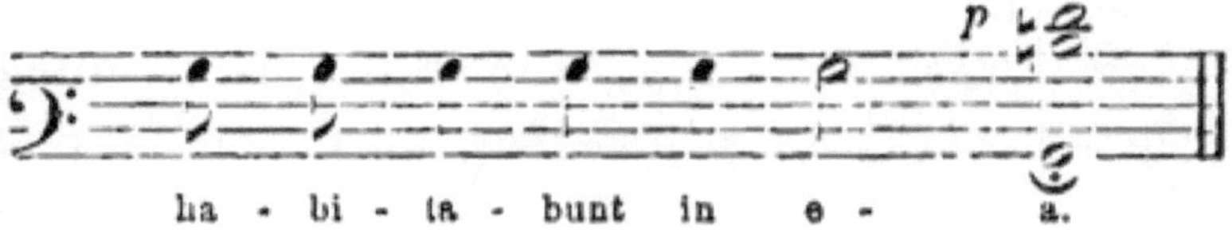

An antiphon, and sometimes more than one,
serves as an introduction to each Psalm. These
are generally sung by two counter-tenor voices, in
canto fermo, in harsh, hard tones; the first half of
each verse in the same style, and the second respon-
ded to by the chorus of male voices that I already
described. I have kept the several antiphons that
I wrote down, that you may compare them with the
book. On the afternoon of Wednesday, the 68th,
69th, and 70th Psalms were sung. (By the bye,
this division of the verses of the Psalms sung in
turns by each chorus, is one of the innovations that
Bunsen has introduced into the Evangelical Church
here; he also ushers in each choral by an antiphon,
composed by Georg, a musician who resides here,
in the style of *canti fermi*, first sung by a few
voices, succeeded by a choral, such as " Ein' feste
Burg ist unser Gott.") After the 70th Psalm
comes a paternoster *sub silentio*—that is, all present

stand up, and a short silent inward prayer ensues, and a pause.

Then commences the first Lamentation of Jeremiah, sung in a low subdued tone, in the key of G major, a solemn and fine composition of Palestrina's. The solos are chanted entirely by high tenor voices, swelling and subsiding alternately, in the most delicate gradations, sometimes floating almost inaudibly, and gently blending the various harmonics; being sung without any bass voices, and immediately succeeding the previous harsh intonation of the Psalms, the effect is truly heavenly. It is rather unfortunate however that those very parts which ought to be sung with the deepest emotion and reverence, being evidently those composed with peculiar fervour, should chance to be merely the titles of the chapter or verse, *aleph*, *beth*, *gimel*, etc., and that the beautiful commencement, which sounds as if it came direct from Heaven, should be precisely on these words, "Incipit Lamentatio Jeremiæ Prophetæ Lectio I." This must be not a little repulsive to every Protestant heart, and if there be any design to introduce a similar mode of chanting into our churches, it appears to me that this will always be a stumbling-block; for any one who sings "chapter first" cannot possibly feel any pious emotions, however beautiful the music may be, let him strive as he will.

My little book indeed says, " Vedendo profetizzato il crocifiggimento con gran pietà, si cantano eziandio molto lamentevolmente *aleph*, e le altre simili parole, che sono le lettere dell' alfabeto Ebreo, perchè erano in costume di porsi in ogni canzone in luogo di lamento, come è questa. Ciascuna lettera ha in se, tutto il sentimento di quel versetto che la segue, ed è come un argomento di esso ; " but this explanation is not worth much. After this the 71st, 72nd, and 73rd Psalms are sung in the same manner, with their antiphons. These are apportioned to the various voices. The soprano begins, " In monte Oliveti," on which the bass voices chime in *forte*, " Oravit ad Patrem : Pater," etc. Then follow the lessons, from the treatise of Saint Augustine on the Psalms. The strange mode in which these are chanted appeared to me very extraordinary when I heard them for the first time on Palm Sunday, without knowing what it meant. A solitary voice is heard reciting on one note, not as in the Psalms, but very slowly and impressively, making the tone ring out clearly.

There are different cadences employed for the different punctuation of the words, to represent a comma, interrogation, and full stop. Perhaps you are already acquainted with these : to me they were a novelty, and appeared very singular. The first, for example, was chanted by a powerful bass voice in G. If a comma occurs, he sings so, on the last word :—

an interrogation thus :—

a full stop :—

For example :—

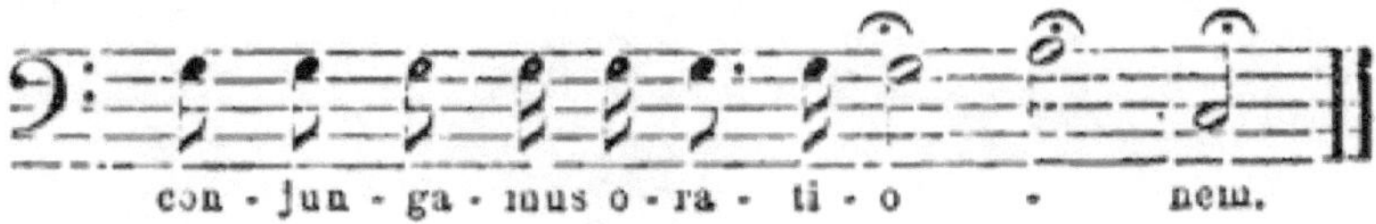

I cannot describe to you how strange the falling
cadence from A to C sounds; especially when the
bass is followed by a soprano, who begins on D, and
makes the same falling cadence from E to G; then
an alto does the same in his key; for they sang
three different lessons alternately with the *canto
fermo.* I send you a specimen of the mode in which
they render the *canto fermo,* regardless both of the
words and the sense. The phrase "better he had
never been born" was thus sung :—

quite *fortissimo* and monotonously. Then came the Psalms 74, 75, and 76, followed by three lessons, succeeded by the Miserere, sung in the same style as the preceding Psalms, in the following *tonus*:—

It will be long before you can improve on this. Then followed Psalms 8, 62, and 66; "Canticum Moysi" in its own tone. Psalms 148, 149, and 150 came next, and then antiphons. During this time the lights on the altar are all extinguished, save one which is placed behind the altar. Six wax candles still continue to burn high above the entrance, the rest of the space is already dim, and now the whole chorus *unisono* intone with the full strength of their voices the "Canticum Zachariæ," during which the last remaining lights are extinguished. The mighty swelling chorus in the gloom, and the solemn vibration of so many voices, have a wonderfully fine effect.

The melody (in **D** minor) is also very beautiful. At the close all is profound darkness. An antiphon begins on the sentence, "Now **he that** betrayed him **gave** them a **sign," and** continues to **the** words "that same is he, hold him fast." Then all present fall on their knees, and one solitary voice softly sings, "Christus factus est pro nobis obediens usque ad mortem;" on the second day is added, "mortem autem crucis;" and on Good Friday, "propter quod et Deus exaltavit illum, et dedit illi Nomen, quod est super omne nomen." A pause ensues, during which each person repeats the Paternoster to himself. During this silent prayer, a death-like silence prevails in the whole church; presently the **Miserere commences, with a chord** softly breathed **by the** voices, **and gradually branching off into two choirs. This beginning, and** its **first harmonious** vibration, certainly made the deepest impression on **me. For an hour and a** half previously, one voice **alone had been heard chanting** almost without any variety; after the pause came an admirably con- structed **chord, which** has the finest possible effect, causing every **one** to feel in their hearts the power **of music; it is** this indeed that is so striking. The **best voices are** reserved for the Miserere, which is sung with the greatest variety **of effect, the** voices swelling and dying away, from **the softest** *piano* to the full strength of the **choir.** No wonder that it should **excite** deep emotion in **every** heart. More- over they **do not** neglect the **power of** contrast; verse after **verse** being **chanted by all** the male voices in unison, *forte*, and harshly. At the beginning of the subsequent verses, the lovely, rich, soft sounds of voices steal on the ear, lasting only for a short space, and succeeded by a chorus of male voices. During the verses sung in monotone, every one knows how beautifully the softer choir are about to uplift their voices; soon they are again heard, again to die away too quickly, and before the thoughts can be collected, the service is over.

On the first day, when the Miserere of Baini was given in the key of B minor, they sang thus:—"Miserere mei Deus" to "misericordiam tuam" from the music, with solo voices, two choirs using the whole strength of voices at their command; then all the bass singers commenced *tutti forte* by F sharp, chanting on that note "et secundum multitudinem" to "iniquitatem meam," which is immediately succeeded by a soft chord in B minor, and so on, to the last verse of all, which they sing with their entire strength; a second short silent prayer ensues, when all the Cardinals scrape their feet noisily on the pavement, which betokens the close of the ceremony. My little book says, "This noise is symbolical of the tumult made by the Hebrews in seizing Christ." It may be so, but it sounded exactly like the commotion in the pit of a theatre, when the beginning of a play is delayed, or when it is finally condemned. The single taper still burning, is then brought from behind the altar, and all silently disperse by its solitary light.

On leaving the chapel, I must not omit to mention the striking effect of the blazing chandelier lighting up the great vestibule, when the Cardinals and their attendant priests traverse the illuminated Quirinal through ranks of Swiss Guards. The Miserere sung on the first day was Baini's, a composition entirely devoid of life or power, like all his works; still it had chords and music, and so it made a certain impression.

On the second day they gave some pieces by Allegri and Bai. On Good Friday all the music was Bai's. As Allegri composed only one verse, on which the rest are chanted, I heard the three compositions which they gave on that day. It is however quite immaterial which they sing, for the *embellimenti* are pretty much the same in all three. Each chord has its *embellimento*, thus very little of the original composition is to be discovered. How these *embellimenti* have crept in they will not say. It is maintained that they are traditional; but this I entirely disbelieve. In the first place no musical tradition is to be relied on; besides, how is it possible to carry down a five-part movement to the present time, from mere hearsay? It does not sound like it. It is evident that they have been more recently added; and it appears to me that the director, having had good high voices at his command, and wishing to employ them during the Holy Week, wrote down for their use ornamental phrases, founded on the simple unadorned chords, to enable them to give full scope and effect to their voices. They certainly are not of ancient date, but are composed with infinite talent and taste, and their effect is admirable; one in particular is often repeated, and makes so deep an impression, that when it begins, an evident excitement pervades all present ; indeed, in any discussion as to the mode of executing this music, and when people say that the voices do not seem like the voices of men, but those of angels from on high, and that these sounds can never be heard elsewhere, it is this particular *embellimento* to which they invariably allude. For example, in the Miserere, whether that of Bai or Allegri (for they have recourse to the same *embellimenti* in both) these are the consecutive chords :—

Instead of this, they sing it so :—

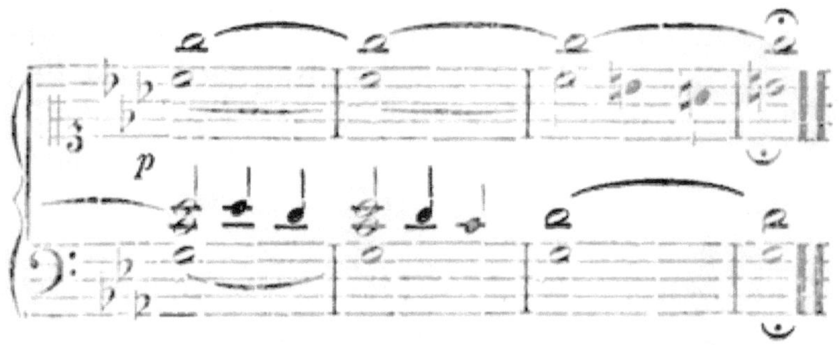

The soprano intones the high C in a pure soft
voice, allowing it to vibrate for a time, and slowly
gliding down, while the alto holds the C steadily, so
that at first I was under the delusion that the high
C was still held by the soprano; the skill, too, with
which the harmony is gradually developed, is truly
admirable. The other *embellimenti* are adapted in
the same way to the consecutive chords; but the
first one is by far the most beautiful. I can give no
opinion as to the particular mode of executing the
music; but what I once read, that some particular
acoustic contrivance caused the continued vibration
of the sounds, is an entire fable, quite as much so as
the assertion that they sing from tradition, and without any fixed time, one voice simply following the
other; for I saw plainly enough the shadow of Baini's
long arm moving up and down; indeed, he sometimes
struck his music-desk quite audibly. There is no
lack of mystery too, on the part of the singers and
others; for example, they never say beforehand
what particular Miserere they intend to sing, but
that it will be decided at the moment, etc., etc.
The key in which they sing, depends on the purity

of the voices. The first day it was in B minor, the second and third in E minor, but each time they finished almost in B flat minor.

The chief soprano, Mariano, came from the mountains to Rome expressly to sing on this occasion, and it is to him I owe hearing the *embellimenti* with their highest notes. However careful and attentive the singers may be, still the negligence and bad habits of the whole previous year have their revenge, consequently the most fearful dissonance sometimes occurs.

I must not forget to tell you that on the Thursday, when the Miserere was about to begin, I clambered up a ladder leaning against the wall, and was thus placed close to the roof of the chapel, so that I had the music, the priests, and the people far beneath me in gloom and shadow. Seated thus alone without the vicinity of any obtrusive stranger, the impression made on me was very profound. But to proceed: you must have had more than enough of Misereres in these pages, and I intend to bring you more particular details, both verbal and written.

On Thursday, at half-past ten o'clock, High Mass was celebrated. They sang an eight-part composition of Fazzini's, in no way remarkable. I reserve for you some *canti fermi* and antiphons, which I wrote down at the time, and my little book describes the order of the various services and the meaning of the different ceremonies. At the " Gloria in Excelsis" all the bells in Rome peal forth, and are not rung again till after Good Friday. The hours are marked in the churches by wooden clappers. The words of the "Gloria," the signal for all the strange tumult of bells, were chanted from the altar by old Cardinal Pacca, in a feeble trembling voice; this being succeeded by the choirs and all the bells, had a striking effect. After the "Credo" they sang the "Fratres ego enim" of Palestrina, but in the most unfinished and careless manner. The washing of the pilgrims' feet followed, and a procession in which all the singers join; Baini beating time from a large book carried before him, making signs first to one, and then to another, while the singers pressed forward to look at the music, counting the time as they walked, and then chiming in,—the Pope being borne aloft in his state chair. All this I have already described to my parents.

In the evening there were Psalms, Lamentations, Lessons, and the Miserere again, scarcely differing from those of the previous day. One lesson was chanted by a soprano solo on a peculiar melody, that I mean to bring home with me. It is an adagio, in long-drawn notes, and lasts a quarter of an hour at least. There is no pause in the music, and the melody lies very high, and yet it was executed with the most pure, clear, and even intonation. The singer did not drop his tone so much as a single comma, the very last notes swelling and dying away as even and full as at the beginning; it was, indeed, a masterly performance. I was struck with the meaning they attach to the word *appoggiatura*. If the melody goes from C to D, or from C to E, they sing thus:—

and this they call an *appoggiatura*. Whatever they may choose to designate it, the effect is most dis-agreeable, and it must require long habit not to be discomposed by this strange practice, which reminds me very much of our old women at home in church; moreover the effect is the same. I saw in my book that the "Tenebræ" was to be sung, and thinking that it would interest you to know how it is given in the Papal chapel, I was on the watch with a sharp-pointed pencil when it commenced, and send you herewith the principal parts. It was sung very quick, and *forte* throughout, without exception. The beginning was:—

Then

I cannot help it, but I own it does irritate me to
hear such holy and touching words sung to such
dull, drawling music. They say it is *canto fermo*,

Gregorian, etc.; no matter. If at that period there was neither the feeling nor the capability to write in a different style, at all events we have now the power to do so, and certainly this mechanical monotony is not to be found in the scriptural words; they are all truth and freshness, and moreover expressed in the most simple and natural manner. Why then make them sound like a mere formula? and, in truth, such singing as this is nothing more! The word "Pater" with a little flourish, the "meum" with a little shake, the "ut quid me"—can this be called sacred music? There is certainly no false expression in it, because there is *none* of any kind; but does not this very fact prove the desecration of the words? A hundred times during the ceremony I was driven wild by such things as these; and then came people in a state of ecstasy, saying how splendid it had all been. This sounded to me like a bad joke, and yet they were quite in earnest!

At Mass early on Friday morning, the chapel is stripped of all its decorations, the altar uncovered, and the Pope and Cardinals in mourning. The "Passion," from St. John, was sung, composed by Vittoria, but the words of the people in the chorus alone are his, the rest are chanted according to an established formula: but more of this hereafter. The whole appeared to me too trivial and monotonous. I was quite out of humour, and, in fact, dissatisfied with the affair altogether. One of the two following modes ought to be adopted. The "Passion" ought either to be recited quietly by the priest, as St.

John relates it, in which case there is no occasion for the chorus to sing "Crucifige eum," nor for the alto to represent Pilate—or else the scene should be so thoroughly realized, that it ought to make me feel as if I were actually present, and saw it all myself. In that event, Pilate ought to sing just as he would have spoken, the chorus shout out "Crucifige" in a tone anything but sacred; and then, through the impress of entire truth, and the dignity of the object represented, the singing would become sacred church music.

I require no under-current of thought when I hear music, which is not to me "a mere medium to elevate the mind to piety," as they say here, but a distinct language speaking plainly to me; for though the sense is *expressed* by the words, it is equally contained in the music. This is the case with the "Passion" of Sebastian Bach; but as they sing it here, it is very imperfect, being neither a simple narrative, nor yet a grand solemn dramatic truth. The chorus sings "Barabbam" to the same sacred chords as "et in terra pax." Pilate speaks exactly in the same manner as the Evangelist. The voice that represents our blessed Saviour commences always *piano*, in order to have one definite distinction, but when the chorus breaks loose, shouting out their sacred chords, it seems entirely devoid of meaning. Pray forgive these strictures. I now proceed to simple narration again. The Evangelist is a tenor, and the mode of chanting, the same as that of the Lessons, with a peculiar falling cadence

at the comma, interrogation, and full stop. The
Evangelist intones on D, and sings thus at a full
stop :—

at a comma :—

and at the conclusion, when another personage
enters, so :—

Christ is represented by a bass, and commences
always thus :—

I could not catch the formula, though I noted down
several parts, which I can show you when I return :
among others, the words spoken on the Cross. All
the other personages,—Pilate, Peter, the Maid, and
the High Priest,—are altos, and sing this melody
only :—

The chorus sings the words of the people from
their places above, while everything else is sung
from the altar. I must really mark down here as a
curiosity the "Crucifige," just as I noted it at the
time :—

The "Barabbam" too is most singular;—very
tame Jews indeed! But my letter is already too
long, so I shall discuss the subject no further.
Prayers are then offered up for all nations and insti-
tutions, each separately designated. When the
prayer for the Jews is uttered, no one kneels, as
they do at all the others, nor is Amen said. They
pray *pro perfidis Judæis,* and the author of my
book discovers an explanation of this also. Then
follows the Adoration of the Cross ; a small crucifix

is placed in the centre of the chapel, and all approach barefooted (without shoes), fall down before it and kiss it; during this time the "Improperia" are sung. I have only once heard this composition, but it seems to me to be one of Palestrina's finest works, and they sing it with remarkable enthusiasm. There is surprising delicacy and harmony in its execution by the choir; they are careful to place every passage in its proper light, and to render it sufficiently prominent without making it too conspicuous—one chord blending softly with the other. Moreover, the ceremony is very solemn and dignified, and the most profound silence reigns in the chapel.

They sing the oft-recurring Greek "Holy" in the most admirable manner, each time with the same smoothness and expression. You will be not a little surprised, however, when you see it written down, for they sing as follows :—

Such passages as that at the commencement, where all the voices sing the very same embellishment, repeatedly occur, and the ear becomes accustomed to them. The effect of the whole is undoubtedly superb. I only wish you could hear the tenors in the first chorus, and the mode in which they take the high A on the word "Theos;" the note is so long-drawn and ringing, though softly breathed, that it sounds most touching. This is repeated again and again till all in the chapel have performed the Adoration of the Cross; but as on this occasion the crowd was not very great, I unluckily had not the opportunity of hearing it as often as I could have wished.

I quite understand why the "Improperias" produced the strongest effect on Goethe, for they are nearly the most faultless of all, as both music and ceremonies, and everything connected with them, are in the most entire harmony. A procession follows to fetch the Host, which had been exposed and adored on the previous evening in another chapel of the Quirinal, lighted up by many hundred wax-lights. The morning service closed at half-past one with a hymn in *canto fermo*. At half-past three in the afternoon the first nocturn began, with the Psalms, Lessons, etc. I corrected what I had written down, heard the Miserere of Baini, and about seven o'clock followed the Cardinals home through the illuminated vestibule—so all was now seen, and all was now over.

I was anxious, dear Professor, to describe the Holy Week to you minutely, as they were memorable days to me, every hour bringing with it something interesting and long anticipated. I also particularly rejoiced in feeling that, in spite of the excitement and the numerous discussions in praise or blame, the solemnities made as vivid an impression on me, as if I had been quite free from all previous prejudice or prepossession. I thus saw the truth confirmed, that perfection, even in a sphere the most foreign to us, leaves its own stamp on the mind. May you read this long letter with even half the pleasure I feel in recalling the period of the Holy Week at Rome.

Yours faithfully,
FELIX MENDELSSOHN BARTHOLDY.

Florence, June 25th, 1831.

Dear Sisters,

On such a day as this my paternal home and those I love are much in my thoughts; my feelings on this point are rather singular. If I feel at any time unwell, or fatigued, or out of humour, I have no particular longing for my own home or for my family; but when brighter days ensue, when every hour makes an indelible impression, and every moment brings with it glad and pleasant sensations, then I ardently wish that I were with you, or you with me; and no minute passes without my thinking of one or other of you, to whom I have something particular to say.

I have to-day passed the whole forenoon, from ten till three, in the gallery; it was glorious! Besides all the beautiful work I saw, from which so much fresh benefit is always to be derived, I wandered about among the pictures, feeling so much sympathy, and such kindly emotions in gazing at them. I now first thoroughly realized the great charm of a large collection of the highest works of art. You pass from one to the other, sitting and dreaming for an hour before some picture, and then on to the next.

Yesterday was a holiday here, so to-day the Palazzo degli Uffizi was crowded with people who had come into the city to see the races, and to visit the far-famed gallery; chiefly peasants, male and female, in their country costumes. All the apartments were thrown open, and as I was about to contemplate them for the last time, I contrived to slip quietly through the crowd, and to remain quite solitary, for I knew that I had not one acquaintance among them.

The busts of the various princes who founded and enriched this collection, are placed near the entrance, at the top of the staircase. I suppose I must have been peculiarly susceptible to-day, for the faces of the Medici interested me exceedingly; they looked so noble and refined, so proud and so dignified. I stood looking at them for a long time, and imprinted on my memory those countenances of world-wide renown.

I then went to the Tribune. This room is so delightfully small you can traverse it in fifteen paces, and yet it contains a world of art. I again sought out my favourite armchair, which stands under the statue of the "Slave Whetting his Knife" (*L'Arrotino*), and taking possession of it, I enjoyed myself for a couple of hours; for here, at one glance, I had the "Madonna del Cardellino,""Pope Julius II.," a female portrait by Raphael, and above it a lovely Holy Family, by Perugino; and so close to me that I could have touched the statue with my hand, the Venus de' Medici; beyond, that of Titian; on the other side, the "Apollino" and the "Wrestlers" (*Lottatori*); in front of the Raphael, the merry Greek Dancing Faun, who seems to feel an uncouth delight in discordant music, for the fellow has just struck two cymbals together, and is listening to the sound, while treading with his foot on a kind of

Pan's pipes, as an accompaniment : what a clown he is! The space between is occupied by other pictures of Raphael's, a portrait by Titian, a Domenichino, etc., and all these within the circumference of a small semicircle, no larger than one of your own rooms. This is a spot where a man feels his own insignificance, and may well learn to be humble.

I occasionally walked through the other rooms, where a large picture by Leonardo da Vinci, only commenced and sketched in, with all its wild dashes and strokes, is very suggestive. I was especially struck with the genius of the monk Fra Bartolommeo, who must have been a man of the most devout, tender, and earnest spirit. There is a small picture of his here, which I discovered for myself. It is about the size of this sheet of paper, in two divisions, and represents the " Adoration" and the " Presentation in the Temple." The figures are about two-thirds of a finger-length in size, but finished in the most exquisite and consummate manner, with the most brilliant colouring, the brightest decorations, and in the most genial sunshine. You can see in the picture itself, that the pious *maestro* has taken delight in painting it, and in finishing the most minute details; probably with the view of giving it away, to gratify some friend. We feel as if the painter belonged to it, and still ought to be sitting before his work, or had only this moment left it. I felt the same with regard to many pictures to-day, especially that of the " Madonna del Cardellino," which Raphael painted as a wedding-gift, and a surprise for his friend. I could not help meditating on all these great men, so long passed away from earth, though their whole inner soul is still displayed in such lustre to us, and to all the world.

While reflecting on these things, I came by chance into the room containing the portraits of great painters. I formerly merely regarded them in the light of valuable curiosities, for there are more than three hundred portraits, chiefly painted by the masters themselves, so that you see at the same moment the man and his work; but to-day a fresh idea dawned on me with regard to them,—that each painter resembles his own productions, and that each while painting his own likeness, has been careful to represent himself just as he really was. In this way you become personally acquainted with all these great men, and thus a new light is shed on many things. I will discuss this point more minutely with you when we meet; but I must not omit to say, that the portrait of Raphael is almost the most touching likeness I have yet seen of him. In the centre of a large rich screen, entirely covered with portraits, hangs a small solitary picture, without any particular designation, but the eye is instantly arrested by it; this is Raphael—youthful, very pale and delicate, and with such onward aspirations, such longing and wistfulness in the mouth and eyes, that it is as if you could see into his very soul. That he cannot succeed in expressing all that he sees and feels, and is thus impelled to go forward, and that he must die an early death,—all this is

written on his mournful, suffering, yet fervid coun-
tenance, and when looking at his dark eyes, which
glance at you out of the very depths of his soul,
and at the pained and contracted mouth, you cannot
resist a feeling of awe.

How I wish you could see the portrait that hangs
above it; that of Michael Angelo, an ugly, muscular,
savage, rugged fellow, in all the vigour of life, looking gruff and morose; and on the other side a wise,
grave man, with the aspect of a lion, Leonardo da
Vinci; but you cannot see this portrait, and I will
not describe it in writing, but tell you of it when we
meet. Believe me, however, it is truly glorious.
Then I passed on to the Niobe, which of all statues
makes the greatest impression on me; and back
again to my painters, and to the Tribune, and
through the Corridors, where the Roman Emperors,
with their dignified yet knavish physiognomies,
stare you in the face; and last of all I took a final
leave of the Medici family.

It was indeed a morning never to be forgotten.

June 26th.

Do not suppose however that I mean to assert
that all days are spent thus. You must battle your
way through the present living mob, before you can
arrive at the nobility, long since dead, and those
who have not a strong arm are sure to come badly
off in the conflict. Such a journey as mine from
Rome to Perugia, and on here, is no joke. Jean
Paul says that the presence of a person who openly

hates you is most painful and oppressive. Such a being is the Roman *vetturino:* he grants you no sleep ; exposes you to hunger and thirst; at night, when he is bound to provide you with your *pranzo,* he contrives that you shall not arrive till midnight, when every one is of course asleep, and you are only too thankful to get a bed. In the morning he sets off before four o'clock, and rests his horses at noon for five hours, but invariably in some solitary little wayside inn, where nothing is to be had. Each day he makes out about six German miles, and drives *piano,* while the sun burns *fortissimo.*

I was very badly off owing to all this, for my fellow-travellers were far from being congenial; three Jesuits inside, and in the cabriolet, where I particularly desired to sit, a most disagreeable Venetian lady. If I wished to escape from her, I was obliged to go inside, and listen to the praises of Charles X., and to hear that Ariosto ought to have been burnt as a corrupt writer, subversive of all morality. It was still worse outside, and we never seemed to get on. The first day, after a journey of four hours, the axletree broke, and we were obliged to remain for nine hours in the same house in the Campagna where we chanced to be, and at last to stay all night. If there was a church on the road that we had an opportunity of visiting, the most beautiful and devotional creations of Perugino, or Giotto, or Cimabue, enchanted our eyes; and so we passed from irritation to delight, and then to irritation again. This was a wretched state to be in. 1

17*

was not in the least amused by it all; and if Nature had not bestowed on us bright moonshine at the Lake of Thrasymene, and if the scenery had not been so wonderfully fine, and if in every town we had not seen a superb church, and if we had not passed through a large city each day as we journeyed on, and if—but you see I am not easily satisfied.

The route however was beautiful, and I must now describe my arrival in Florence, which also includes my whole Italian life of the previous days. At Incisa, half a day's journey from Florence, my *vetturino* became so intolerable from his insolence and abuse, that I found it necessary to take out my luggage, and to tell him to drive to the devil,—which he accordingly did, rather against his will.

It was Midsummer's day, and a celebrated fête was to take place in Florence the same evening, which I would on no account whatever have missed. This is just the kind of thing that the Italians take advantage of, so the landlady at Incisa offered me a carriage at four times the proper fare. When I refused to take it, she said I might try to procure another; and so I accordingly did, but found that no carriages for hire were to be had, only post-horses. I went to the Post, and was there told, to my disgust, that they were at my landlady's, and that she had wished to make me pay an exorbitant price for them. I went back and demanded horses. She said, if I did not choose to pay what she asked, I should have none. I desired to see the regulations, which they are all obliged to have. She said there was no occasion to show them, and turned her back on me. The use of physical strength, which plays a great part here, was resorted to by me on this occasion, for I seized her and pushed her back into a room (for we were standing in the passage) and then hurried down the street to the Podestà. It turned out however that there was no such person in the town, but that he lived four miles off. The affair became every instant more disagreeable, the crowd of boys at my heels increasing at every step. Fortunately a decent-looking man came up, to whom the mob seemed to show some respect; so I accosted him, and explained all that had occurred. He sympathized with me, and took me to a vine-dresser's who had a little carriage for hire.

The whole crowd now congregated before his door, many pressing forward into the house after me, and shouting that I was mad; but the carriage drove up, and I threw a few scudi to an old beggar, on which they all called out that I was a *bravo Signore*, and wished me *buon viaggio*. The moderate price the man demanded more fully showed me the abominable overcharge of the landlady. The carriage was easy, and the horses went on at a good pace, and so we travelled across the hills to Florence. In the course of half an hour we overtook my lazy vetturino. I put up my umbrella to defend me from the sun, and I scarcely ever travelled so pleasantly and so comfortably as during those few hours, having left all annoyances behind me, and before me the prospect of the beautiful fête.

Very soon the Duomo, and the hundreds of villas scattered through the valleys, were visible. Once more we passed by decorated terraces, and the tops of trees seen over them; the Arno valley looking lovelier than ever. And so I arrived here in good spirits and dined; and even while doing so I heard a tumult, and looking out of the window I saw crowds, both young and old, all hurrying in their holiday costumes across the bridges.

I followed them to the Corso, and then to the races; afterwards to the illuminated Pergola, and last of all to a masked ball in the Goldoni Theatre. At one o'clock in the morning I went towards home, thinking that the whole affair was over; but the Arno was still covered with gondolas, illuminated by coloured lamps, and crossing each other in every direction. Under the bridge a large ship was pass ing, hung with green lanterns: the water shone brightly as it rippled along, while a still brighter moon looked down on the whole scene. I recalled to myself the various occurrences of the day, and the thoughts that had chased each other through my mind, and resolved to write them all to you. It is in fact a reminiscence for myself, for it may not be so suggestive to you, but it will one day be of ser- vice to me, enabling me to recall various scenes connected with fair Italy.

Extract from a Letter to Frau von Pereira, in Vienna.

Genoa, July, 1831.

At first I resolved not to answer your letter until I had fulfilled your injunctions, and composed "Napoleon's Midnight Review;" and now I have to ask your forgiveness for not having done so, but there is a peculiarity in this matter. I take music in a very serious light, and I consider it quite inadmissible to compose anything that I do not thoroughly feel. It is just as if I were to utter a falsehood; for notes have as distinct a meaning as words, perhaps even a more definite sense. Now it appears to me almost impossible to compose for a descriptive poem. The mass of compositions of this nature do not militate against this opinion, but rather prove its truth; for I am not acquainted with one single work of the kind that has been successful. You are placed between a dramatic conception or a mere narrative; the one, in the "Erl König," causes the willows to rustle, the child to shriek, and the horse to gallop. The other imagines a ballad singer, calmly narrating the horrible tale, as you would a ghost story, and this is the most accurate view of the two; Reichardt almost invariably adopted this reading, but it does not suit me; the music stands in my way. I feel in a far more spectral spirit when I read such a poem quietly to myself, and imagine the rest, than when it is depicted, or related to me.

It does not answer to look on "Napoleon's Midnight Review" as a narrative, inasmuch as no particular person speaks, and the poem is not written in the style of a ballad. It seems to me more like a clever conception than a poem; it strikes me that the poet himself placed no great faith in his misty forms.

I could indeed have composed music for it in the same descriptive style, as Neukomm and Fischhof, in Vienna. I might have introduced a very novel rolling of drums in the bass, and blasts of trumpets in the treble, and have brought in all sorts of hobgoblins. But I love my serious elements of sound too well to do anything of the sort; for this kind of thing always appears to me a joke; somewhat like the paintings in juvenile spelling-books, where the roofs are coloured bright red, to make the children aware they are intended for roofs; and I should have been most reluctant to write out and send you anything incomplete, or that did not entirely please myself, because I always wish you to have the best I can accomplish.

FELIX.

Milan, July 14th, 1831.

This letter will probably be the last (D.V.) that I shall write to you from an Italian city; I may possibly send you another from the Borromean Islands, which I intend to visit in a few days, but do not rely on this.

My week here has been one of the most agreeable and amusing that I have passed in Italy; and how this could be the case in Milan, hitherto utterly unknown to me, I shall now proceed to relate. In the first place, I immediately secured a small piano, and attacked with *rabbia* that endless "Walpurgis Night," to finish the thing at last; and to-morrow morning it will be completed, except the overture; for as yet I have not quite made up my mind whether it shall be a grand symphony, or a short introduction breathing of spring. I should like to take the opinion of some adept on this point. I must say the conclusion has turned out better than I myself expected. The hobgoblins and the bearded Druid, with the trombones sounding behind him, diverted me immensely, and so I passed two forenoons very happily.

'Tasso' also contributed to my pleasure, which I have now for the first time been able to read with facility; it is a splendid poem. I was glad to be already well acquainted with Goethe's 'Tasso;' being constantly reminded of it by the principal passages of the Italian poet, whose verse, like that of Goethe, is so dreamy, harmonious, and tender, its sweet melody delighting the ear. Your favourite passage, dear father, "Era la notte allor," struck me as very beautiful, but the stanzas that I admire most, are those descriptive of Clorinda's death; they are so wonderfully imaginative, and fine. The close however does not quite please me. Tancred's 'Lamentations' are, I think, more charmingly composed than true to nature; they contain too many clever ideas and antitheses; and even the words of the hermit, which soothe him, sound more like a censure on the hermit himself. I should infallibly have killed him on the spot, if he had talked to me in such a strain.

Recently I was reading the episode of ' Armida ' in a carriage, surrounded by a company of Italian actors, who were incessantly singing Rossini's "Ma trema, trema," when suddenly there recurred to my thoughts Gluck's "Vous m'allez quitter," and Rinaldo's falling asleep, and the voyage in the air— and I felt in a most melting mood. This is genuine music; thus have men felt, and thus have men spoken, and such strains can never die. I do cordially hate the present licentious style. Do not take it amiss; your motto is, Without hatred, no love,— and I did feel so moved when I thought of Gluck, and his grand embodiments.

Every evening I was in society, owing to a mad prank, which however proved very successful. I think I have invented this kind of eccentric proceeding, and may take out a patent for it, as I have already made my most agreeable acquaintances *ex abrupto*, without letters or introductions of any kind.

I asked by chance on my arrival at Milan the name of the Commandant, and the *laquais de place* named General Ertmann. I instantly thought of Beethoven's Sonata in A major, and its dedication; and as I had heard all that was good of Madame

Ertmann, from those who knew her; that she was so kind, and had bestowed such loving care on Beethoven, and played herself so beautifully, I, next morning, at a suitable hour for a visit, put on a black coat, desired that the Government-house should be pointed out to me, and occupied myself on the way thither by composing some pretty speeches for the General's lady, and went on boldly.

I cannot however deny that I felt rather dismayed when I was told that the General lived in the first story, facing the street; and when I was fairly in the splendid vaulted hall, I was seized with a sudden panic, and would fain have turned back: but I could not help thinking that it was vastly provincial on my part to take fright at a vaulted hall, so I went straight up to a group of soldiers standing near, and asked an old man in a short nankeen jacket, if General Ertmann lived there, intending then to send in my name to the lady. Unluckily the man replied, " I am General Ertmann: what is your pleasure?" This was unpleasant, as I was forced to have recourse to the speech I had prepared. The General, however, did not seem particularly edified by my statement, and wished to know whom he had the honour of addressing. This also was far from agreeable, but fortunately he was acquainted with my name, and became very polite: his wife, he said, was not at home, but I should find her at two o'clock, or any hour after that which might suit me.

I was glad that all had gone off so well, and in

the meantime went to the Brera, where I passed the time in studying the 'Sposalizio' of Raphael, and at two o'clock I presented myself to Freifrau Dorothea von Ertmann. She received me with much courtesy, and was most obliging, playing me Beethoven's Sonata in C sharp minor, and the one in D minor. The old General, who now appeared in his handsome grey uniform, covered with orders, was quite enchanted, and had tears of delight in his eyes, because it was so long since he had heard his wife play; he said there was not a person in Milan who cared to hear what I had heard. She mentioned the trio in B major, but said she could not remember it. I played it, and sang the other parts: this enchanted the old couple, and so their acquaintance was soon made.

Since then their kindness to me is so great that it quite overwhelms me. The old General shows me all the remarkable objects in Milan; in the afternoon his lady takes me in her carriage to drive on the Corso, and at night we have music till one o'clock in the morning. Yesterday at an early hour they drove with me in the environs; at noon I dined with them, and in the evening there was a party. They are the most agreeable and cultivated couple you can imagine, and both as much in love with each other as if they were a newly wedded pair,—and yet they have been married for four-and-thirty years. Yesterday he spoke of his profession, of military life, of personal courage, and similar subjects, with a degree of lucidity, and liberality of feeling, that

I scarcely ever met with, except in my father. The General has been now an officer for six-and-forty years, and you should really see him galloping beside his wife's carriage in the park,—the old gentleman looking so dignified and animated !

She plays Beethoven's works admirably, though it is so long since she studied them ; she sometimes rather exaggerates the expression, dwelling too long on one passage, and then hurrying the next ; but there are many parts that she plays splendidly, and I think I have learned something from her. When sometimes she can bring no more tone out of the instrument, and begins to sing in a voice that emanates from the very depths of her soul, she reminds me of you, dear Fanny, though you are infinitely her superior. When I was approaching the end of the adagio in the B major trio, she exclaimed, "The amount of expression here is beyond any one's playing ; " and it is quite true of this passage.

The following day, when I went there again to play her the symphony in C minor, she insisted on my taking off my coat, as the day was so hot. In the intervals of our music she related the most interesting anecdotes of Beethoven, and that when she was playing to him in the evening he not unfrequently used the snuffers as a tooth-pick ! She told me that when she lost her last child, Beethoven at first shrank from coming to her house ; but at length he invited her to visit him, and when she arrived, she found him seated at the piano, and simply saying, "Let us speak to each other by music," he

played on for more than an hour, and, as she expressed it, "he said much to me, and at last gave
me consolation." In short I am now in the most
genial mood, and quite at my ease, having no
occasion to resort to any disguise, or to be silent,
for we understand each other admirably on all
points. She played the Kreutzer Sonata yesterday
with violin accompaniment, and when the violin-
player (an Austrian cavalry officer) made a long
flourish, *à la* Paganini, at the beginning of the
adagio, the old General made such a desperate
grimace, that I nearly fell off my chair from
laughing.

I called on Teschner, as you, dear mother, desired
me to do so ; such a musician however is as depress-
ing as a thick fog. Madame Ertmann has more
soul in her little finger than that fellow has in his
whole body, with his formidable moustaches, behind
which he seems to lie in ambush. There is no
public music in Milan; they still speak with enthusiasm of last winter, when Pasta and Rubini sang
here, but say that they were miserably supported,
and the orchestra and choruses bad. I however
heard Pasta six years ago in Paris, and I can do the
same every year, with the addition of a good orchestra and a good chorus, and many other advantages;
so it is evident that if I wish to hear Italian music,
I must go to Paris or to England. The Germans
however take it amiss when you say this, and persist
par force in singing, playing, and acquiring new
ideas here, declaring this is the land of inspiration ;

while I maintain that inspiration is peculiar to no country, but floats about in the air.

Two days ago I was in the morning theatre here, and was well amused. There you can see more of the life of the people than in any other part of Italy. It is a large theatre with boxes, the pit filled with wooden benches, on which you can find places if you come early; the stage is like every other stage, but there is no roof either over the pit or boxes, so that the bright sun shines into the theatre and into the eyes of the actors. Moreover, the piece they gave was in the Milanese dialect. You feel as if you were secretly watching all these complicated and diverting situations, and might take part in them if necessary, and thus the most familiar comic dilemmas become novel and interesting; and the public seem to feel the most lively interest in them. And now, good night. I wished to talk to you a little before going to bed, and so it has become a letter.

FELIX.

———————

EXTRACTS FROM TWO LETTERS TO EDWARD DEVRIENT.

Milan, July 15th, 1831.

You reproach me with being two-and-twenty without having yet acquired fame. To this I can only reply, had it been the will of Providence that I should be renowned at the age of two-and-twenty, I no doubt should have been so. I cannot help it, for

18*

I no more write to gain a name, than to obtain a
Kapellmeister's place. It would be a good thing if
I could secure both. But so long as I do not
actually starve, so long is it my duty to write only
as I feel, and according to what is in my heart, and
to leave the results to *Him* who disposes of other
and greater matters. Every day, however, I am
more sincerely anxious to write exactly as I feel,
and to have even less regard than ever to external
views; and when I have composed a piece just as it
sprang from my heart, then I have done my duty
towards it; and whether it brings hereafter fame,
honour, decorations, or snuff-boxes, etc., is a matter
of indifference to me. If you mean, however, that I
have neglected, or delayed perfecting myself, or my
compositions, then I beg you will distinctly and
clearly say in what respect and wherein I have done
so. This would be indeed a serious reproach.

You wish me to write operas, and think I am
unwise not to have done so long ago. I answer,
place a right libretto in my hand, and in two months
the work shall be completed, for every day I feel
more eager to write an opera. I think that it may
become something fresh and spirited, if I begin it
now; but I have got no words yet, and I assuredly
never will write music for any poetry that does not
inspire me with enthusiasm. If you know a man
capable of writing the libretto of an opera, for
Heaven's sake tell me his name, that is all I want.
But till I have the words, you would not wish me to
be idle—even if it were possible for me to be so?

I have recently written a good deal of sacred music; that is quite as much a necessity to me, as the impulse that often induces people to study some particular book, the Bible, or others, as the only reading they care for at the time. If it bears any resemblance to Sebastian Bach, it is again no fault of mine, for I wrote it just according to the mood I was in; and if the words inspired me with a mood akin to that of old Bach, I shall value it all the more, for I am sure you do not think that I would merely copy his form, without the substance; if it were so, I should feel such disgust and such a void, that I could never again finish a composition. Since then I have written a grand piece of music which will probably impress the public at large—the first "Walpurgis Night" of Goethe. I began it simply because it pleased me, and inspired me with fervour, and never thought that it was to be performed; but now that it lies finished before me, I see that it is quite suitable for a great *Concertstück*, and you must sing the Bearded Pagan Priest at my first subscription concert in Berlin. I wrote it expressly to suit your voice; and as I have hitherto found that the pieces I have composed with least reference to the public are precisely those which gave them the greatest satisfaction, so no doubt it will be on this occasion also. I only mention this to prove to you that I do not neglect *the practical*. To be sure this is invariably an after-thought, for who the deuce could write music, the most unpractical thing in the world—the very reason why I love it so dearly—and yet think all the time of the practical! It is just as if a lover were to bring a declaration of love to his mistress in rhyme and verse, and recite it to her.

I am now going to Munich, where they have offered me an opera, to see if I can find a man there who is a poet, for I will only have a man who has a certain portion of fire and genius. I do not expect a giant, and if I fail in meeting with a poet there, I shall probably make Immermann's acquaintance for this express purpose, and if he is not the man either, I shall try for him in London. I always fancy that the right man has not yet appeared; but what can I do to find him out? He certainly does not live in the Reichmann Hotel, nor next door; so where does he live? Pray write to me on this subject; although I firmly believe that a kind Providence, who sends us all things in due time when we stand in need of them, will supply this also if necessary; still we must do our duty, and look round us—and I do wish the libretto were found.

In the meantime I write as good music as I can, and hope to make progress, and we already agreed, when discussing this affair in my room, that, as I said before, I am not responsible for the rest. But enough now of this dry tone. I really have become once more almost morose and impatient, and yet I had so firmly resolved never again to be so!

Lucerne, August 27th, 1831.

I quite feel that any opera I were to write now, would not be nearly so good as any second one I might compose afterwards; and that I must first enter on the new path I propose to myself, and pursue it for some little time, in order to discover whither it will lead, and how far it will go, whereas in instrumental music I already begin to know exactly what I really intend. Having worked so much in this sphere, I feel much more clear and tranquil with regard to it,—in short, it urges me onwards. Besides, I have been made very humble lately, by a chance occurrence that still dwells on my mind.

In the valley of Engelberg I found Schiller's 'Wilhelm Tell," and on reading it over again, I was anew enchanted and fascinated by such a glorious work of art, and by all the passion, fire, and fervour it displays. An expression of Goethe's suddenly recurred to my mind. In the course of a long conversation about Schiller, he said that Schiller had been able to *supply* two great tragedies every year, besides other poems. This business-like term *supply*, struck me as the more remarkable on reading this fresh, vigorous work; and such energy seemed to me so wonderfully grand, that I felt as if in the course of my life I had never yet produced anything of importance; all my works seem so isolated. I feel as if I too must one day *supply* something. Pray do not think this presumptuous; but rather believe that I only say so because I know what *ought* to be, and what *is not*. Where I am to find the opportunity, or even a glimpse of one, is hitherto to me quite a mystery. If however it be my mission, I firmly believe that the opportunity will be granted, and if I do not profit by it another will; but in that case I cannot divine why I feel such an impulse to press onwards. If you could succeed in not thinking about singers, decorations, and situations, but feel solely absorbed in representing men, nature, and life, I am convinced that you would yourself write the best libretto of any one living; for a person who is so familiar with the stage as you are, could not possibly write anything undramatic, and I really do not know what you could wish to change in your poetry. If there be an innate feeling for nature and melody, the verses cannot fail to be musical, even though they sound rather lame in the libretto; but so far as I am concerned, you may write prose if you like, I will compose music for it. But when one form is to be moulded into another, when the verses are to be made musically, but not *felt* musically, when fine words are to replace outwardly what is utterly deficient in fine feeling inwardly—there you are right—this is a dilemma from which no man can extricate himself; for as surely as pure metre, happy thoughts, and classical language do not suffice to make a good poem, unless a certain flash of poetical inspiration pervades the whole, so an opera can only become thoroughly musical, and accordingly thoroughly dramatic, by a vivid feeling of life in all the characters.

There is a passage on this subject in Beau-marchais, who is censured because he makes his personages utter too few fine thoughts, and has put too few poetical phrases into their mouths. He answers, that this is not his fault. He must confess that during the whole time he was writing the piece, he was engaged in the most lively conversation with his *dramatis personœ :* that while seated at his writing table he was exclaming, " Figaro, prends garde, le Comte sait tout!—Ah ! Comtesse, quelle imprudence !—vite, sauve-toi, petit page :" and then he wrote down their answers, whatever they chanced to be,—nothing more. This strikes me as being both true and charming.

The sketch of the opera introducing an Italian Carnival, and the close in Switzerland, I already knew, but was not aware that it was **yours.** Be so good however as to describe Switzerland with great vigour, and immense spirit. **If you** are to depict an effeminate Switzerland, with *jodeln* and languishing, **such** as I saw here in the theatre last night in the 'Swiss Family,' **when** the very mountains and Alpine horns became sentimental, I shall lose all **patience, and criticize you** severely in Spener's paper. I beg you will make it full of **animation, and write** to me again on the **subject.**

Isola Bella, July 24th, 1831.

You no doubt imagine that **you** inhale **the fra-**grance of orange-flowers, see blue sky, and a bright

sun, and a clear lake, when you merely read the
date of this letter. Not at all! The weather is
atrocious, rain pouring down, and claps of thunder
heard at intervals;—the hills look frightfully bleak,
as if the world were enshrouded in clouds; the lake
is grey, and the sky sombre. I can smell no orange-
flowers, and this island might quite as appropriately
be called "Isola Brutta!" and this has gone on for
three days! My unfortunate cloak! I am confessedly the "spirit of negation" (I refer to my
mother), and as it is at present the fashion with
every one not to consider the Borromean Islands
"by any means so beautiful," and somewhat formal;
and as the weather seems resolved to disgust me
with this spot,—from a spirit of opposition I maintain that it is perfectly lovely. The approach to
these islands, where you see crowded together green
terraces with quaint statues, and many old-fashioned
decorations, along with verdant foliage, and every
species of southern vegetation, has a peculiar charm
for me, and yet something affecting and solemn too.
For what I last year saw in all the luxuriance and
exuberance of wild nature, and to which my eye had
become so accustomed, I find now cultivated by art,
and about to pass away from me for ever. There
are citron-hedges and orange-bushes; and sharp-
pointed aloes shoot up from the walls—it is just as
if, at the end of a piece, the beginning were to be
repeated; and this, as you know, I particularly like.

In the steamboat was the first peasant girl I have
seen here in Swiss costume; the people speak a bad

half-French Italian. This is my last letter from Italy, but believe me the Italian lakes are not the least interesting objects in this country; *anzi,*—I never saw any more beautiful. People tried to persuade me that the gigantic forms of the Swiss Alps that have haunted me from my childhood* had been exaggerated by my imagination, and that after all a snowy mountain was not in reality so grand as I thought. I almost dreaded being undeceived, but at first sight of the foreground of the Alps from the Lake of Como, veiled in clouds, with here and there a surface of bright snow, sharp black points rearing their heads, and sinking precipitously into the lake, the hills first scattered over with trees and villages, and covered with moss, and then bleak and desolate, and on every side deep ravines filled with snow,—I felt just as I formerly did, and saw that I had exaggerated nothing.

In the Alps all is more free, more sharply defined; more uncivilized, if you will: yet I always feel there both healthier and happier. I have just returned from the gardens of the Palace, which I visited in the midst of the rain. I wished to imitate Albano,† and sent for a barber to open a vein: he however misunderstood my purpose, and shaved me instead, —a very pardonable mistake. Gondolas are landing on every part of the island, for to-day is the fête following the great festival of yesterday, in honour of which the P. P. Borromeo sent for singers and

---

* The whole family had been in Switzerland in the year 1821.
† In the 'Titan' of Jean Paul.

19

musicians from Milan, to sing and play to the islanders. The gardener asked me if I knew what a wind instrument was. I said with a clear conscience that I did; and he replied that I ought to try to imagine the effect of thirty such instruments, and violins and basses, all played at once; but indeed I could not possibly imagine it, for it must be heard to be believed. The sounds (continued he) seemed to come from Heaven, and all this was produced by *philharmony*. What he meant by this term I know not; but the music had evidently made more impression on him, than the best orchestra often does on musical connoisseurs. At this moment some one has just begun to play the organ in the church for Divine service, in the following strain :—

Full organ in the bass, Bourdon 16, and reed stops, have a very fine effect. The fellow has come all the way from Milan, too, expressly to make this disturbance in the church. I must go there for a little, so farewell for a few moments. I intend to remain here for the night, instead of crossing the lake again, for I am so much pleased with this little island. I certainly cannot say that I have slept soundly for the last two nights ; one night owing to the innumerable claps of thunder, the next owing to the innumerable fleas ; and, in all probability, I have to-night the prospect of both combined. But as the following morning I shall be speaking French, and have left Italy, and crossed the Simplon, I mean to ramble about all this day and to-morrow in true Italian fashion.

I must now relate to you historically how I happened to come here. At the very last moment of my stay in Milan, the Ertmanns came to my room to bid me farewell, and we took leave of each other more cordially than I have done of any one for many a long day. I promised to send you many kind wishes from them, though they are unacquainted with you, and I also agreed to write to them occasionally. Another valued acquaintance I made there, is Herr Mozart, who holds an office in Milan ; but he is a musician, heart and soul. He is said to bear the strongest resemblance to his father, especially in disposition ; for the very same phrases that affect the feelings in his father's letters, from their candour and simplicity, constantly recur in the conversation of the son, whom no one can fail to love from the moment he is known. For instance, I consider it a very charming trait in him, that he is as jealous of the fame and name of his father, as if he were an incipient young musician ; and one evening, at the Ertmanns', when a great many of Beethoven's works had been played, the Baroness asked me in a whisper to play something of Mozart's, otherwise his son would be quite mortified ; so when I played the overture to "Don Juan," he began to thaw, and begged me to play also the overture to the "Flauto Magico" of his "*Vatter*," and seemed to feel truly filial delight in hearing it : it is impossible not to like him.

He gave me letters to some friends near the Lake of Como, which procured me for once a glimpse of Italian provincial life, and I amused myself famously there for a few days with the Doctor, the Apothecary, the Judge, and other people of the locality. There were very lively discussions on the subject of Sand, and many expressed great admiration of him ; this appeared strange to me, as the occurrence is of such distant date that no one any longer argues on the subject. They also spoke of Shakspeare's plays, which are now being translated into Italian. The Doctor said that the tragedies were good, but that there were some plays about witches that were too stupid and childish ; one, in particular, "Il Sonno d' una Notte di Mezza State." In it the stale device occurred of a piece being rehearsed in the play, and it was full of anachronisms and childish ideas ;

on which they all chimed in that it was very silly, and advised me not to read it.* I remained meekly silent, and attempted no defence! I bathed frequently in the Lake, and sketched, and yesterday rowed on the Lake of Lugano, which frowned sternly on us with its cascades and dark canopy of clouds; then across the hills to Luvino, and to-day I came here by steam.

Evening.—I have this moment returned from the Isola Madre, and most splendid it is; spacious, and full of terraces, citron-hedges, and evergreen shrubs. The weather has at last become less inclement; thus the large white house on the island, with its ruins and terraces, looked very pretty. It is indeed a unique land, and I only wish I could bring with me to Berlin a portion of the same balmy air that I inhaled when in the boat to-day. You have nothing like it, and I would rather you enjoyed it, than all the people who imbibe it here. A fiercely moustachioed German was with me in the boat, who examined all the beautiful scenery as if he were about to purchase it and thought it too dear. Presently I heard a trait quite in the style of Jean Paul. When we were walking on the island, surrounded by verdure, an Italian, who was of the party, observed that this was a spot well adapted for lovers to ramble in, and to enjoy the charms of nature. " Ah! yes!" said I, in a languishing tone. " It was on

---

* The overture to the "Midsummer Night's Dream" was composed by Mendelssohn as early as the year 1826.

this account," continued he, " that I separated from my wife ten years ago; I established her at Venice in a small tobacconist's shop, and now I live as I please. You must one day do the same."

The old boatman told us that he had rowed General Bonaparte on this lake, and related various anecdotes of him and Murat. He said Murat was a most extraordinary man; all the time that he was rowing him on the lake, he never ceased singing to himself for a single moment, and once when setting off on a journey he gave him his spirit-flask, and said he would buy another for himself in Milan. I cannot tell why these little traits, especially the singing, seemed to realize the man in my mind more than many a book of history.

The " Walpurgis Nacht " is finished and revised, and the overture will soon be equally far advanced. The only person who has heard it as yet, is Mozart, and he was so delighted with it that the well-known composition caused me fresh pleasure; he insisted on my publishing it immediately. Pray forgive this letter, written in true student phraseology. You no doubt perceive from its style that I have not worn a neckcloth for a week past; but I wished you to know how gay and happy I have been during the days spent among the mountains, and with what pleasure I look forward to those that yet await me.

Yours,   FELIX.

A l'Union-prieuré de Chamounix, end of July, 1831.

My dear Parents,

I cannot refrain from writing to you from time to time, to thank you for my wondrously beautiful journey; and if I ever did so before, I must do so again now, for more delightful days than those on my journey hither, and during my stay here, I never experienced. Fortunately you already know this valley, so there is no occasion for me to describe it to you; indeed, how could I possibly have done so? But this I may say, that nowhere has nature in all her glory met my eyes in such brightness as here, both when I saw it with you for the first time and now; and as every one who sees it, ought to thank God for having given him faculties to comprehend, and to appreciate such grandeur, so I must also thank you for having supplied me with the means of enjoying such a pleasure.

I had been told that I exaggerated the forms of the mountains in my imagination; but yesterday, at the hour of sunset, I was pacing up and down in front of the house, and each time that I turned my back on the mountains, I endeavoured vividly to represent to myself these gigantic masses, and each time when I again faced them, they far exceeded my previous conceptions. Like the morning that we drove away from this when the sun was rising* (no doubt you remember it) the hills have been clear and lovely ever since I arrived. The snow pure, and sharply defined, and apparently near in the dark

---

* In the year 1821.

blue atmosphere; the glaciers thundering unremittingly, as the ice is melting: when clouds gather, they lie lightly on the base of the mountains, the summits of which stand forth clear above. Would that we could see them together! I have passed this whole day here quietly, and entirely alone. I wished to sketch the outlines of the mountains, so I went out and found an admirable point of view, but when I opened my book, the paper seemed so very small that I hesitated about attempting it. I have indeed succeeded in giving the outlines what is called *correctly*,—but every stroke looks so formal, when compared with the grace and freedom which everywhere here pervade nature. And then the splendour of colour! In short, this is the most brilliant point of my travels; and the whole of my excursion on foot, so solitary, independent, and enjoyable, is something new to me, and a hitherto unknown pleasure.

I must however **relate how I** came here, otherwise my letter at last will contain **nothing** but exclamations. As I previously wrote to you, I had the most odious weather **on the** Lago Maggiore, and the Islands. It continued so incessantly stormy, cold, and wet, that the same evening I took my place in the diligence in rather a sulky humour, and we drove **on** towards the Simplon. Scarcely had we been **journeying for** half an hour, when the moon came **out, the clouds** dispersed, and **next morning** the weather was most bright and **beautiful. I felt** almost ashamed **of this** undeserved **good fortune, and** I

could now thoroughly enjoy the glorious scenery;
the road winding first through high green valleys,
then through rocky ravines and meadows, and at
last past glaciers and snowy mountains. I had with
me a little French book on the subject of the Simplon road, which both pleased and affected me; for
the subject was Napoleon's correspondence with the
Directoire about the projected work, and the first
report of the General who crossed the mountain.
With what spirit and vigour these letters are
written! and yet a little swagger too, but with such
a glow of enthusiasm that it quite touched me, as I
was driven along this capital level road by an
Austrian postilion. I compared the fire and poetry
displayed in every description contained in these
letters (I mean those of the subaltern General) with
the eloquence of the present day, which leaves you
so terribly cold and is so odiously prosaic in all its
philanthropic views, and so lame—where there is
plenty of *fanfaronnade*, but no genuine youth—and
I could not but feel that a great epoch has passed
away for ever. I was unable to divest myself of the
idea that Napoleon never saw this work—one of his
favourite conceptions—for he never crossed the
Simplon when the road was finished, and was thus
deprived of this great gratification. High up, in
the Simplon village, all is bleak, and I actually
shivered from cold for the first time during the last
year and a half. A neat civil Frenchwoman keeps
the inn on the summit, and it would not be easy to
describe the sensation of satisfaction caused by its

thrifty cleanliness, which is nowhere to be found in Italy.

We then descended into the Valais, as far as Brieg, where I stayed all night, overjoyed to find myself once more among honest, natural people, who could speak German, and who plundered me into the bargain in the most infamous manner. The following day I drove through the Valais—an enchanting journey: the road all along, like those you have seen in Switzerland, ran between two lofty ranges of mountains, their snowy peaks starting up at intervals, and through avenues of green, leafy walnut-trees, standing in front of pretty brown houses,—below, the wild grey Rhone,—past Lenk, and every quarter of an hour a village with a little church. From Martigny I travelled for the first time in my life literally on foot, and as I found the guides too dear I went on quite alone, and started with my cloak and knapsack on my shoulders. About a couple of hours later I met a stout peasant lad, who became my guide, and also carried my knapsack; and so we went on past Forclas to Trient, a little dairy village, where I breakfasted on milk and honey, and thence to the Col de Balme.

The whole valley of Chamouni, and Mont Blanc, with all its precipitous glaciers, lay before me bathed in sunshine. A party of gentlemen and ladies (one of the latter very pretty and young) came from the opposite side on mules, with a number of guides; scarcely had we all assembled under one roof, when subtle vapours began to rise, shrouding first the

mountain and then the valley, and at last thickly
covering every object, so that soon nothing was to
be seen. The ladies were afraid of going out into
the fog. just as if they were not already in the midst
of it ; at last they set off, and from the window I
watched the singular spectacle of the caravan
leaving the house, all laughing, and talking loudly
in French and English and *patois*. The voices
presently became indistinct ; then the figures likewise ; and last of all I saw the pretty girl in her wide
Scotch cloak ; then only glimpses of grey shadows
at intervals, and they all disappeared. A few minutes later I ran down the opposite side of the mountain with my guide ; we soon emerged once more into
sunshine, and entered the green valley of Chamouni
with its glaciers ; and at length arrived here at the
Union. I have just returned from a ramble to
Montanvert, the Mer de Glace, and to the source of
the Arveiron. You know this splendid scenery, and
so you will forgive me, if, instead of going to Geneva
to-morrow, I first make the tour of Mont Blanc, that
I may become acquainted with this personage from
the southern side also, which is I hear the most
striking. Farewell, dear parents ! May we have a
happy meeting !—Yours, FELIX.

Charney, August 6th, 1831.
My dear Sisters,
You have. I know, read Ritter's " Afrika" from
beginning to en 1, but still I do not think you know

where Charney is situated, so fetch out Keller's old travelling map, that you may be able to accompany me on my wanderings. Trace with your finger a line from Vevay to Clarens, and thence to the Dent de Jaman; this line represents a footpath; and where your finger has been my legs also went this morning —for it is now only half-past seven, and I am still fasting. I mean to breakfast here, and am writing to you in a neat wooden room, waiting till the milk is made warm for me; without, I have a view of the bright blue lake; and so I now begin my journal, and mean to continue it as I best can during my pedestrian tour.

After breakfast.—Heavens! here is a pretty business. My landlady has just told me with a long face, that there is not a creature in the village to show me the way across the Dent, or to carry my knapsack, except a young girl; the men being all at work. I usually set off every morning very early and quite alone, with my bundle on my shoulders, because I find the guides from the inns both too expensive and too tiresome; a couple of hours later I hire the first honest-looking lad I see, and so I travel famously on foot. I need not say how enchanting the lake and the road hither were; you must recall for yourself all the beauties you once enjoyed there. The footpath is in continued shade, under walnut-trees and up hill.—past villas and castles,—along the lake which glitters through the foliage; villages everywhere, and brooks and streams rushing along from every nook, in every village;

then the neat tidy houses,—it is all quite too charming, and you feel so fresh and so free. Here comes the girl with her steeple hat. I can tell you she is vastly pretty into the bargain, and her name is Pauline; she has just packed my things into her wicker basket. Adieu!

Evening, Château d'Oex, candle-light.

I have had the most delightful journey. What would I not give to procure you such a day! But then you must first become two youths and be able to climb actively, and drink milk when the opportunity offered, and treat with contempt the intense heat, the many rocks in the way, the innumerable holes in the path, and the still larger holes in your boots, and I fear you are rather too dainty for this; but it was most lovely! I shall never forget my journey with Pauline; she is one of the nicest girls I ever met, so pretty and healthy-looking, and naturally intelligent; she told me anecdotes about her village, and I in return told her about Italy; but I know who was the most amused.

The previous Sunday, all the young people of *distinction* in her village had gone to a place far across the mountain, to dance there in the afternoon. They set off shortly after midnight, arrived while it was still dark, lighted a large fire and made coffee. Towards morning the men had running and wrestling matches before the ladies, (we passed a broken hedge testifying to the truth of this;) then they danced, and were at home again by Sunday evening, and early on

Monday morning they all resumed their labours in the vineyards. By Heavens, I felt a strong inclination to become a Vaudois peasant, while I was listening to Pauline, when from above she pointed out to me the villages where they dance when the cherries are ripe, and others where they dance when the cows go to pasture in the meadows and give milk. To-morrow they are to dance in St. Gingolph ; they row across the lake, and any one who can play, takes his instrument with him ; but Pauline is not to be of the party, because her mother will not allow it, from dread of the wide lake, and many other girls also do not go for the same reason, as they all cling together.

She then asked my leave to say good-day to a cousin of hers, and ran down to a neat cottage in the meadow ; soon the two girls came out together and sat on a bench and chattered ; on the Col de Jaman above, I saw her relations busily mowing, and herding the cows.

What cries and shouts ensued ! Then those above began to *jodel,* on which they all laughed. I did not understand one syllable of their *patois,* except the beginning, which was, Adieu Pierrot ! All these sounds were taken up by a merry mad echo, that shouted and laughed and *jodelled* too. Towards noon we arrived at Allière. When I had rested for a time, I once more shouldered my knapsack, for a fat old man provoked me by offering to carry it for me ; then Pauline and I shook hands, and we took leave of each other. I descended into the meadows, and if you do not care about Pauline, or if I have bored you with her, it is not my fault, but that of the mode in which I have described her; nothing could be more pleasant in reality, and so was my further journey. I came to a cherry-orchard, where the people were gathering the fruit, so I lay down on the grass and ate cherries for a time along with them. I took my mid-day rest at Latine, in a clean wooden house. The carpenter who built it gave me his company to some roast lamb, and pointed out to me with pride every table, and press, and chair.

At length I arrived here, at night, through dazzling green meadows, interspersed with houses, surrounded by fir-trees and rivulets: the church here stands on a velvet green eminence; more houses in the distance, and still further away, huts and rocks; and in a ravine, patches of snow still lying on the plain. It is one of those idyllic spots such as we have seen together in Wattwyl, but the village smaller and the mountains more green and lofty. I must conclude however to-day by a high eulogy on the Canton de Vaud. Of all the countries I know this is the most beautiful, and it is the spot where I should most like to live when I become really old. The people are so contented, and look so well, and the country also. Coming from Italy it is quite touching to see the honesty that still exists in the world,—happy faces, a total absence of beggars, or saucy officials: in short, there is the most complete contrast between the two nations. I thank God for having created so much that is beautiful; and may it be His gracious will to permit us all, whether in Berlin, England, or in the Château d'Oex, to enjoy a happy evening and a tranquil night!

Boltigen, August 7th, evening.

The lightning and thunder are terrific outside, and torrents of rain besides; in the mountains you first learn respect for weather. I have not gone further, for it would have been such a pity to traverse the lovely Simmen valley under an umbrella. It was grey morning, but delightfully cool for walking in the forenoon. The valley at Saanen, and the whole road, is incredibly fresh and gay. I am never weary of looking at the verdure. I do believe that if during a long life I were always gazing at undu. lating verdant meadows, dotted over with reddish-brown houses, I should always experience the same pleasure in looking at them. The road winds the whole way through meadows of this kind, and past running streams.

At noon I dined at Zweisimmen, in one of those enormous Bernese houses, where everything glitters with neatness and cleanliness, and where even the smallest detail is carefully attended to. I there dispatched my knapsack by the diligence to Interlaken, and am now about to walk as a regular pedestrian through the country; a shirt in my pocket, a brush and comb, and my sketch-book, this is all I require; but I am very tired. May the weather be fine to-morrow!

Wimmis, the 8th.

A pretty affair! the weather is three times as bad as ever. I must give up my plan of going to Interlaken to-day, as there is no possibility of getting on. For the last few hours the water has been pouring straight down, as if the clouds above had been fairly squeezed out; the roads are as soft as feather-beds; only occasional shreds of the mountains are to be seen, and even these but rarely. I almost thought sometimes that I was in the Margravate of Brandenburg, and the Simmen valley looked perfectly flat. I was obliged to button my waistcoat tight over my sketch-book, for very soon my umbrella was of no use whatever, and so I arrived here to dinner about one o'clock. I had my breakfast in the following place. [*Vide* page 234.]

Weissenburg, August 8th.

I sketched this on the spot with a pen, so do not laugh at the bold stream. I passed the night very uncomfortably at Boltigen. There was no room in the inn, owing to a fair, so I was obliged to lodge in an adjacent house, where there were swarms of vermin quite as bad as in Italy, a creaking house clock, striking hoarsely every hour, and a baby that screeched the whole night. I really could not help for a time noticing the child's cries, for it screamed in every possible key, expressive of every possible emotion; first angry, then furious, then whining, and when it could screech no longer, it grunted in a deep bass. Let no one tell me that we must wish to return to the days of our childhood, because chil-

20*

dren are so happy. I am convinced that such a little mortal as this, flies into a rage just as we do, and has also his sleepless nights, and his passions, and so forth.

This philosophical view occurred to me this morning, while I was sketching Weissenburg, and so I wished to communicate it to you on the spot; but I

took up the 'Constitutionnel,' in which I read that
Casimir Périer wishes to resign, and many other
things that furnish matter for reflection; among
others a most remarkable article on the cholera,
which I should like to transcribe, for it is so extraordinary. The existence of this disease is totally
and absolutely denied; only one person had it in
Dantzic,—a Jew,—and he got well. Then followed
a number of "Hegelisms" in French, and the election of the deputies—oh world!—As soon as I had
finished reading the paper, I was obliged to set off
again in the rain through the meadows. No such
enchanting country as this is to be seen, even in a
dream; in the worst weather, the little churches, and
the numerous houses, and shrubs, and rills are still
truly lovely. The verdure to-day was quite in its
element. Dinner has been long over, and it is still
pouring. I intend to go no further than Spiez this
evening. I regret much that I can neither see this
place, which seems beautifully situated, nor Spiez,
which I know from Rösel's sketches. This is, in
fact, the climax of the whole Simmen valley, and
thence the old song says :—

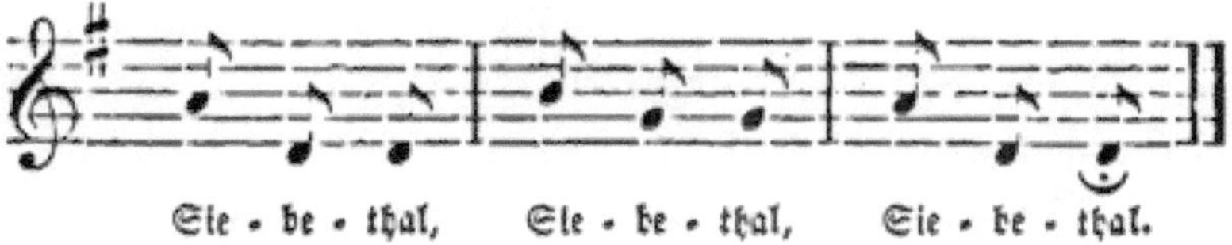

I sang this the whole day while walking along.
The Siebethal, however, showed no gratitude for the
compliment, and the rain continued unremittingly.

Wyler, evening.

They could not take me in at Spiez, for there is
no inn there where you can lodge, so I was obliged
to return here. I very much admired the situation
of Spiez; it is built on a rock, which projects into
the lake, with numbers of turrets, and gables, and
peaks. There I saw a manor-house, with an oran-
gery; a sulky-looking nobleman with two sporting
dogs at his heels; a little church, and terraces with
bright flowers. It was all very lovely. To-morrow
I shall see it from the other side, if the weather permits. To-day it has rained for three hours consecu-
tively, and I was well soaked on the way here. The
mountain streams are superb in such weather, for
they leap and rage furiously. I crossed one of these
demons, the Kander, which seemed to have taken
leave of its senses, leaping and blustering, and
foaming; the water looked quite brown, and scattered its yellow spray in all directions. A black
peak of the mountains was here and there visible
through the rain-laden clouds, which hung deeper
into the valley than I ever before saw them. Yet
the day was most enjoyable.

Wyler, the 9th, morning.

To-day the weather is worse than ever. It has rained the whole night through, and this morning too it is pouring. I have however intimated that I shall not set out in such weather, and if it continues I shall write to you again to-night from Wyler. In the meantime I have an opportunity of making acquaintance with my Swiss host. They are very primitive. I could not get on my shoes, because they had shrunk, owing to the rain. The landlady asked if I wished to have a shoe-horn; and as I said I did, she brought me a tablespoon; but it answered the purpose. And moreover they are eager politicians. Over my bed hangs a horrible distorted face, under which is written, "Brinz Baniadofsgi." If he had not a kind of Polish costume, it would be difficult to discover whether it is intended for a man or a woman, for neither the portrait itself nor the inscription throw much light on the subject.

Evening, at Untersee.

All jesting is turned into sad earnest, which in these days may easily be the case. The storm has raged furiously, and caused great damage and devastation; the people here say that they remember no more violent storm and rain for many years; and the hurricane rushes on with such incredible rapidity. This morning early the weather was merely wet and disagreeable, and yet this afternoon all the bridges are swept away, and every passage blocked up for the moment. There has been a landslip at the Lake of Brienz, and everything is in an uproar.

I have just heard here that war has been proclaimed in Europe; so the world certainly bears a wild, bleak aspect at this time, and I ought to feel thankful, that at all events for the present I have a warm room here, and a comfortable roof over my head. The rain ceased for a time early this morning, and I thought that the clouds were fairly exhausted; so I left Wyler, but soon found that the roads were sadly cut up; but worse was to come; the rain began again gently, but came down so violently about nine o'clock, and in such sudden squalls, that it was evident something strange was brewing. I crept into a half built hut, where a great mass of fodder was lying, and nestled comfortably among the fragrant hay. A soldier of the Canton, who was on his way to Thun, also crept in from the other side, and in the course of an hour, as the weather did not improve, we went on our different paths.

I was obliged to take shelter again under a roof at Leisengen, and waited there a long time; but as my luggage was at Interlaken, a distance of only two hours from thence, I thought that I would set the weather at defiance; so about one o'clock I set out for Interlaken. There was literally nothing to be seen but the grey surface of the lake,—no mountains, and seldom even the outlines of the opposite shore. The little springs,which as you may remember often run along by the footpaths, had swollen into streams, through which I was obliged to wade; and where the road was hilly, the waters accumulated in the hollows and formed a pool, so I was forced to jump over dripping hedges, into marshy meadows; the small blocks of wood—by means of which brooks are crossed here—lay deep under the water; at one moment I found myself between two of these brooks, which had run into each other, and for a considerable time I was obliged to walk against the current, above my ankles in water. All the streams are black, or chocolate-brown, looking like earth flowing along. Torrents poured down from above; the wind shook down the water from the dripping walnut-trees; the waterfalls which tumble into the lake thundered frightfully from both shores. You could trace the course of the brown muddy streaks, rushing along through the pure waters of the lake, which, in the midst of all this uproar, remained perfectly tranquil, its surface scarcely ruffled, quietly receiving all the blustering streams that poured into its bosom.

A man now came up, who had taken off his shoes and stockings, and turned up his trowsers. This made me feel rather nervous. Presently I met two women, who said that I could not go through the village, for all the bridges were gone. I asked how far it was to Interlaken. "A good hour," they said. I could not make up my mind to turn back, so I went on towards the village, where the people shouted to me from the windows, that I could come no further, because the waters were rushing down so impetuously from the mountains; and certainly there was a fine commotion in the middle of the village. The muddy stream had swept everything along with it, eddying round the houses, and running along the meadows and footpaths, and finally thundering down into the lake. Luckily there was a little boat there, in which I was ferried across to Neuhaus, though this expedition in an open boat, in torrents of rain, was far from pleasant. My condition, when I arrived at Neuhaus, was miserable enough; I looked as if I wore long black boots over my light-coloured trowsers, my shoes and stockings quite up to my knees, dark brown; then came the original white, then a soaked blue paletôt; even my sketch-book, that I had buttoned under my waistcoat, was wet through.

I arrived in this plight at Interlaken, where I was very ill received, for the people there either could not or would not find room for me, and so I was forced to return to Untersee, where I am famonsly lodged, and most comfortable. Singularly enough, I had been all along anticipating with such pleasure revisiting the inn at Interlaken, of which I had so many reminiscences, and I drove up in my little Neuhaus carriage to the Nuss-Baum Platz, and saw the well-known glass gallery; the pretty landlady, too, came to the door, but somewhat aged and altered. Neither the dreadful storms, nor the various discomforts I had endured, annoyed me half so much as not being able to remain at Interlaken, consequently for the first time since I left Vevay I was out of humour for half an hour, and obliged to

sing Beethoven's adagio in A flat major, three or
four times over, before I could recover my equanimity.   I learned here, for the first time, the damage
the storm had already done, and may yet do, for the
rain is still incessant.

Half-past Nine o'clock at Night.—The bridge at
Zweilütschenen is carried away; the *vetturini* from
Brienz, and Grindelwald, will not encounter the risk
of driving home, from the fear of some rock falling
on their heads.   The water here has risen to within
a foot and a half of the Aar bridge; the gloom of
the sky I cannot describe.   I mean to wait here patiently; besides, I do not require the aid of localities,
to enable me to summon up my reminiscences.   They
have given me a room where there is a piano; it
indeed bears the date of the year 1794, and somewhat resembles in tone the little old "Silbermann"
in my room at home, so I took a fancy to it at the
very first chord I struck, and it also recalls you to
my mind.   This piano has outlived many things, and
probably never dreamt that I was likely to compose
by its aid, as I was not born till 1809, now fully
two-and-twenty years ago; in the meantime, the
piano, though seven-and-thirty years old, has plenty
of good material in it yet.

I have some new "Lieder" in hand, dear sisters
You have not seen my favourite one in E major
21

"Auf der Reise,"—it is very sentimental. I am now composing one which will not, I fear, be very good; but it will, at all events, please us three, for it is at least well intended. The words are Goethe's, but I don't say what they are; it is very daring in me to compose for this poetry, and the words are by no means suitable for music, but I thought them so divinely beautiful, that I could not resist singing them to myself. Enough for to-day; so good night, dear ones.

August 10th.

The weather this morning is clear and bright, and the storm has passed away; would that all storms ended as quickly, and were as soon allayed! I have passed a glorious day, sketching, composing, and inhaling fresh air. In the afternoon I went on horseback to Interlaken, for no man can go there on foot at this moment. The whole road is flooded, so that even on horseback I got very wet. In this place, too, every street is inundated and impassable. How beautiful Interlaken is! How humble and insignificant we feel when we see how splendid the good Lord has made this world; and nowhere can you see it in greater magnificence than here. I sketched for my father one of the walnut-trees he so much admires, and for the same reason I mean to send him a faithful drawing of one of the Bernese houses. Various parties of ladies and gentlemen, and children, drove past and stared at me; I thought to myself that they were now enjoying the same luxury I formerly did, and would fain have called out to them not to forget this! Towards evening, the snowy mountains were glowing in the clearest outlines and in the loveliest hues.

When I came back, I asked for some music paper, and they referred me to their Pastor, and he to the Forest-ranger, whose daughter gave me two pretty neat sheets. The "Lied" which I alluded to yesterday is now finished; I cannot help after all telling you what it is—but you must not laugh at me—it is actually,—but don't think I am seized with hydrophobia —a sonnet, "Die Liebende schreibt."* I am afraid its merit is not great; I think it was more inwardly felt than outwardly well expressed; still there are some good passages in it, and to-morrow I am going to set to music a little poem of Uhland's; a couple of pieces for the piano are also in progress. I can unfortunately form no judgment of my new compositions; I cannot tell whether they are good or bad; and this arises from the circumstance that all the people to whom I have played anything for the last twelve months, forthwith glibly declared it to be wonderfully beautiful, and that will never do. I really wish that some one would let me have a little rational blame once more, or what would be still more agreeable, a little *rational* praise, and then I should find it less indispensable to act the censor towards myself, and to be so distrustful of my own powers. Nevertheless, I must go on writing in the meantime.

* In the " Liederheft," Opus 15 of his posthumous works.

When I was at the Forest-ranger's, I heard that
the whole country was devastated, and the most sad
intelligence comes from all sides. All the bridges in
the Hasli valley are entirely swept away, and also
many houses and cottages. A man came here to-day
from Lauterbrunnen, and he was up to his shoulders
in water; the high road is ruined, and what sounded
most dismal of all to me, a quantity of furniture and
household things were seen floating down the Kander, coming no one knows whence. Happily the
waters are beginning to subside, but the damage they
have done cannot so easily be repaired. My travelling plans have also been considerably disturbed by
these inundations, for, if there be any risk, I shall
certainly not go into the mountains.

The 11th.

So I now close the first part of my journal, and
send it off to you. To-morrow I shall begin a new
one, for I intend then to go to Lauterbrunnen. The
road is practicable for pedestrians, and not an idea
of any danger; travellers from thence have come
here to-day, but for carriages, the road will not be
passable during the remainder of the year. I purpose, therefore, proceeding across the Lesser Scheideck to Grindelwald, and by the Great Scheideck
to Meiringen; by Furka and Grimsel to Altorf, and
so on to Lucerne; storms, rain, and everything else
permitting,—which means, if God will. This morning early, I was on the Harder, and saw the mountains in the utmost splendour. I never remember
the Jungfrau so clear and so glowing as both yester-

day evening and at early dawn to-day. I rode back
to Interlaken, where I finished my sketch of the
walnut-tree. After that I composed for a time, and
wrote three waltzes for the Forest-ranger's daughter
on the remaining music-paper she had given me,
politely presenting them to her myself. I have just
returned from a watery expedition to an inundated
reading-room, as I wished to see how the Poles are
getting on—unluckily there is no reference to them
in the papers. I must now occupy myself till the
evening in packing, but I am most reluctant to leave
this room, where I am so comfortable, and shall
sadly miss my little piano. I intend to sketch the
view from this window with my pen on the back of
my letter, and also to write out my second " Lied,"
and then Untersee will soon also belong to my
reminiscences. " Ach! wie schnell!" I quote
myself, which is not over-modest, but these lines
recur to me but too often when the days are short-
ening, the leaves of the travelling map turned over,
and first Weimar, then Munich, and lastly Vienna,
are all things of the past year. Well! here you
have my window! [*Vide* page 246.]

An hour later.—My plans are altered, and I stay
here till the day after to-morrow. The people say that
by that time the roads will be considerably better, and
there is plenty here both to see and to sketch. The
Aar has not risen to such a height for seventy years.
To-day people were stationed on the bridge, with
poles and hooks, watching to catch any fragments
of the broken-down bridges. It did look so strange

to see a black object come swimming along in the
distance from the hills, which was at last recognized
to be a piece of balustrade, or a cross-beam, or
something of the sort, when all the people made a
rush at it, and tried to fish it up with their hooks,
and at length succeeded in dragging the monster
out of the water. But enough of water,—that is,
of my journal. It is now evening, and dark. I am
writing by candle-light, and should be so glad if I
could knock at your door, and take my seat beside
you at the round table. It is the old story over
again. Wherever it is bright and cheerful, and I

am well and happy, I most keenly feel your absence, and most long to be with you again. Who knows, however, whether we may not come here together in future years, and then think of this day, as we now do of former ones? But as none can tell whether this may ever come to pass, I shall meditate no longer on the subject, but write out my "Lied," take another peep of the mountains, wish you all happiness and good fortune, and thus close my journal.

Lauterbrunnen, August 13th, 1831.

I have just returned from an expedition on foot to the Schmadri Bach, and the Breithorn. All that you can by possibility conceive as to the grandeur and imposing forms of the mountains here, must fall far short of the reality of nature. That Goethe could write nothing in Switzerland but a few weak poems, and still weaker letters, is to me as incomprehensible as many other things in this world. The road here is again in a lamentable state; where, six days ago, there was the most beautiful highway, there is now only a desolate mass of rocks; numbers of huge blocks lying about, and heaps of rubbish and sand. No trace whatever of human hands to be seen. The waters, indeed, have entirely subsided, but they are still in a troubled state, for from time to time you can hear the stones tossed about, and the waterfalls also in the midst of their white foam, roll down black stones into the valley.

My guide pointed out to me a pretty new house, standing in the midst of a wild turbulent stream;

he said that it belonged to his brother-in-law and formerly stood in a beautiful meadow, which had been very profitable; the man was obliged to leave the house during the night; the meadow has disappeared for ever, and masses of pebbles and stones have usurped its place. "He never was rich, but now he is poor," said he, in concluding his sad story. The strangest thing is, that in the very centre of this frightful devastation,—the Lütschine having overflowed the whole extent of the valley—among the marshy meadows, and masses of rocks, where there is no longer even a trace of a road, stands a *char-à-banc*—and is likely to stand for some time to come. It chanced that the people in it wished to drive through at the very time of the hurricane; then came the inundation, so they were forced to leave the carriage and everything else to fate, thus the *char-à-banc* is still standing waiting there. It was a very frightful sight when we reached the spot, where the whole valley, with its roads and embankments, is a perfect rocky sea; and my guide, who went first, kept whispering to himself, "'sisch furchtbar!" The torrent had carried into the middle of the stream some large trunks of trees, which are standing aloft; for at the same moment some huge fragments of rocks having been flung against them, the bare trees were closely wedged in betwixt them, and they now stand nearly perpendicular in the bed of the river.

I should never come to an end were I to try to tell you all the various forms of havoc which I saw between this place and Untersee. Still the beauty of the valley made a stronger impression on me than I can describe. It is much to be regretted, that when you were in this country, you went no further than Staubbach; for it is from there that the valley of Lauterbrunnen really begins. The Schwarzer Mönch, and all the other snowy mountains in the background, become more mighty and grand, and on every side bright foaming cascades tumble into the valley. You gradually approach the mountains covered with snow, and the glaciers in the background, through pine woods, and oaks, and maple-trees. The moist meadows, too, were covered with a profusion of brilliant flowers—snakewort, the wild scabious, campanulas, and many others. The Lütschine had accumulated masses of stones at the sides, having swept along fragments of rocks, as my guide said, "bigger than a stove," then the carved brown wooden houses, and the hedges; it is all beautiful beyond measure! Unfortunately we could not get to the Schmadri Bach, as bridges, paths, and fords, were all gone; but it was a walk I can never forget.

I also tried to sketch the Mönch; but what can you hope to do with a small pencil? Hegel indeed says, "that every single human thought is more sublime than the whole of Nature;" but in this place I consider that too presumptuous; the axiom sounds indeed very fine, but is a confounded paradox nevertheless. I am quite contented, in the meantime, to adhere to Nature, which is the safest of the two.

You know the situation of the inn here, and if you
cannot recall it, refer to my former Swiss drawing
book, where you will find it sketched, badly enough,
and where I put in a footpath in front, from imagination, which made me laugh heartily to-day, when I
thought of it. I am at this moment looking out of
the same window, and gazing at the dark mountains,
for it is late in the evening, that is, a quarter to
eight o'clock, and I have an idea, which is "more
sublime than the whole of Nature" —I mean to go
to bed; so good night, dear ones.

The 14th, ten o'clock in the forenoon.

From the dairy hut on the Wengern Alp, in
heavenly weather, I send you my greetings.

Grindelwald, evening.

I could not write more to you early this morning ;
I was most reluctant to leave the Jungfrau. What
a day this has been for me ! Ever since we were
here together I have wished to see the Lesser
Scheideck once more. So I woke early to-day, with
some misgivings, for so much might intervene—bad
weather, clouds, rain, fogs—but none of these
occurred. It was a day as if made on purpose for
me to cross the Wengern Alp. The sky was flecked
with white clouds, floating far above the highest
snowy peaks; no mists below on any of the mountains, and all their pinnacles glittering brightly in
the morning air; every undulation, and the face of
every hill, clear and distinct. Why should I even
attempt to portray it ? You have already seen the

Wengern Alp, but at that time we had bad weather, whereas to-day the whole mountain range was in holiday attire. Nothing was wanting; from thundering avalanches, to its being Sunday, and people dressed in their best going to church, just as it was then.

The hills had only dwelt in my memory as gigantic peaks, for their great altitude had entirely absorbed me. To-day I was struck with amazement at the immense extent of their base, their solid, spacious masses, and the connection of all these huge piles, which seem to lean towards each other, and to reach out their hands to one another. In addition to this you must imagine every glacier, and snowy plateau, and point of rock, dazzlingly lighted up and glittering. Then the far summits of distant mountain ranges stretching hither, as if surveying the others. I do believe that such are the thoughts of the Almighty. Those who do not yet know Him, may here see Him, and the nature He created, visibly displayed. Then the fresh, bracing air, which refreshes you when weary, and cools you when it is warm,—and so many springs! I must at some future time write you a separate treatise on springs, but I have not time for it to-day, as I have something particular to tell you.

Now you will say, I suppose, he came down the mountain again, and is going to inform us once more how beautiful Switzerland is. Not at all. When I arrived at the herdsman's hut, I was told that in a meadow far up the Alps, there was to be a great fête this very day, and I saw people at intervals climbing the mountain. I was not at all fatigued; an Alpine fête is not to be seen every day; the weather said, *yes;* the guide was willing. "Let us go to Intra-men," said I. The old herdsman went first, so we were obliged to climb very vigorously; for Intra-men is more than a thousand feet higher than the Lesser Scheideck. The herdsman was a ruthless fellow, for he ran on before us like a cat; he soon took pity on my guide, and relieved him of my cloak and knapsack, but even with them he continued to push forward so eagerly that we really could not keep up with him. The path was frightfully steep; he extolled it, however, saying that there was a much nearer, but much steeper track: he was about sixty years of age, and when my youthful guide and I with difficulty surmounted a hill, we invariably saw him descending the next one. We walked on for two hours in the most fatiguing path I ever encoun-tered; first a steep ascent, then down again into a hollow, over heaps of crumbling stones, and brooks and ditches, across two meadows covered with snow, in the most profound solitude, without a footpath, or the most remote trace of the hand of man; occa-sionally we could still hear the avalanches from the Jungfrau; otherwise all was still, and not a tree to be seen.

When this silence and solitude had continued for some time, and we had clambered to the top of a grassy acclivity, we suddenly came in sight of a vast number of people standing in a circle, laughing, speaking, and shouting. They were all in gay dresses, and had flowers in their hats; there were a great many girls, some tables with casks of wine, and all around deep solemn silence, and tremendous mountains. It was singular that while I was in the act of climbing, I thought of nothing but rocks and stones, and the snow and the track; but the moment I saw human beings, all the rest was forgotten, and I only thought of men, and their sports, and the merry fête. It was really a fine sight. The scene was in a spacious green meadow far above the clouds; opposite were the snowy mountains in all their prodigious altitude, more especially the dome of the great Eiger, the Schreckhorn, and the Wetter-hörner, and all the others as far as the Blümli's Alp; the Lauterbrunnen valley lay far beneath us in the misty depths, quite small, as well as our road of yesterday, with all the little cataracts like threads, the houses like dots, and the trees like grass. Far in the background the Lake of Thun occasionally glanced out of the mist.

The crowd now began wrestling, and singing, and drinking, and laughing; all healthy, strong men. I was much amused by the wrestling, which I had never before seen. The girls served the men with *Kirschwasser* and *Schnapps;* the flasks passed from hand to hand, and I drank with them, and gave three little children some cakes, which made them quite happy; a very tipsy old peasant sang me some songs; then they all sang; then the guide favoured us with a modern song; and then little boys fought.

Everything pleased me on the Alps, and I remained lying there till towards evening, and made myself quite at home. We descended rapidly into the meadows below, and soon descried the familiar inn, and its windows glittering in the evening sun; a fresh breeze from the glaciers began to blow; this soon cooled us. It is now getting late, and from time to time avalanches are heard,—so thus has my Sunday been spent.—A fête-day indeed!

On the Faulhorn, August 15th.

I am shivering with cold! Outside thick snow is falling, and the wind raging and blustering. We are eight thousand feet above the level of the sea, and a long tract of snow to traverse, but here I am! Nothing can be seen; all day the weather has been dreadful. When I remember how fine it was yesterday, while I earnestly wish that it may be as fine to-morrow, it reminds me of life, for we are always hovering between the past and the future. Our excursion of yesterday seems as far past and remote, as if I knew it only from old memories, and had scarcely been present myself; for to-day when during five mortal hours we were struggling on, against rain and fog, sticking in the mud, and seeing nothing round us but grey vapours, I could scarcely realize that it ever was or ever will be again fine weather, or that I ever lay idly stretched on this wet marshy grass. Besides, everything here wears such a wintry aspect; heated stoves, thick snow, cloaks, freezing, shivering people. I am at this moment in the highest inn in Europe; and just as in St. Peter's, you look down on every church, and on the Simplon, upon every road, so from hence I look down on all other inns ; but not *morally*, for this is little more than a few wooden planks. Never mind. I am now going to bed, and I will no longer watch my own breath. Good night! "Tom's a cold."

Hospital, August 18th.

I have not been able to open my journal for two or three days, as when night came I had no longer time for anything, but to dry myself and my clothes at the fire, to warm myself, to sigh over the weather, like the stove behind which I took refuge, and to sleep a good deal ; besides, I did not wish to try your patience, by my everlasting repetitions of how deep I had sunk in the mud, and how incessantly it rained, and so forth. During the last few days in reality I went through the most beautiful country, and yet saw nothing but thick fogs, and water in the sky, and from the sky, and on the earth. I passed places that I had long wished to visit, without being able to enjoy them ; what also damped my writing mood, was being obliged to battle with the weather, and if it continues the same, I shall only write occasionally, for really I should have nothing to say, but "a grey sky—rain and fog." I have been on the Faulhorn, the Great Scheideck, on Grimsel Spital, and to-day I crossed Grimsel and Furka, and the principal objects I have seen were the points of my shabby umbrella, and I had not even a glimpse of the huge mountains. At one moment, to-day, the Finsteraarhorn came to light, but it looked as savage as if it

wished to devour us; and yet if we were a single
half-hour without rain, it was truly beautiful. A
journey on foot through this country, even in the
most unfavourable weather, is the most enchanting
thing you can possibly imagine; if the sky were
bright, I think the excess of pleasure would be quite
overpowering; I must not therefore complain too
much of the weather, for I have had my full share
of enjoyment.

During the last few days I felt like Tantalus.
When I was on the Scheideck, a glimpse of the
lower part of the Wetterhorn was sometimes visible
through the clouds, and it seemed beyond measure
magnificent and sublime; but I only saw the base.
On the Faulhorn, I could not distinguish objects
fifty paces off, although I stayed there till ten
o'clock in the morning. We went down to the
Scheideck in a heavy snow-storm, by a very wet and
difficult path, which the incessant rain had made
worse than usual. We arrived at Grimsel Spital in
rain and storm. To-day I wished to have ascended
the Sidelhorn, but was obliged to give it up on account of the fog. The Mayenwand was shrouded in
grey clouds, and we had only a single peep of the
Finsteraarhorn, when we were on the Furka. We
also arrived here in a torrent of rain and water
everywhere, but all this does not signify. My guide
is a capital fellow: if it rains, he sings and *jodels;*
if it is fine, so much the better; and though I failed
in seeing some of the finest objects, still I saw a
great deal that was interesting.

On this occasion I have formed a particular friendship for the glaciers; they are indeed, the most marvellous monsters in the world. How strangely they are all tumbled about; here, a row of jagged points, there, toppling crags, and above, towers and bastions, while on every side, crevices and ravines are visible, all of the most wondrous pure ice, that rejects all soil of earth, casting up again on the surface the stones, sand, and gravel, flung down by the mountains. Then the superb colouring, when the sun shines on them, and their mysterious advance—they sometimes move on a foot and a half in a single day, so that the people in the village are in the greatest anxiety and alarm, when the glacier arrives so quietly, and yet with such irresistible force, for it shivers rocks and stones when they lie in the way—then the ominous crashing and thundering, and the rushing of so many springs near and round. They are splendid miracles. I was in the Rosenlaui glacier, which forms a kind of cave, that you can creep through; it looks as if built of emeralds, only more transparent. Above, around, on all sides, you can see rivulets running between the clear ice. In the centre of this narrow passage, the ice has left a large round window, through which you look down on the valley, and issue forth again under an arch of ice, and high above, black peaks rear their heads, from which masses of ice roll down in the boldest undulations. The glacier of the Rhone is the most imposing that I have seen, and the sun burst forth on it as we passed early this morning. This is a suggestive sight, and you get a casual glimpse of the rocky peak of a mountain, a plateau covered with snow, cataracts, and bridges spanning them, and masses of crumbling stones and rocks; in short, even if you see little in Switzerland, it is at all events more than is to be seen in any other country.

I have been drawing very busily, and think I have made some progress. I even tried to sketch the Jungfrau; it will at least serve as a reminiscence, and I can enjoy the thought that these strokes were actually made on the spot itself. I see people rushing through Switzerland, and declaring that they find nothing to admire there, or anywhere else (except themselves); not the least affected nor roused, remaining cold and prosaic, even in presence of the mountains; when I meet such people I should like to give them a good drubbing. Two Englishmen and an English lady are at this moment sitting beside me near the stove; they are as wooden as sticks. We have been travelling the same road for a couple of days, and I declare the people have never uttered a syllable except of abuse; that there were no fireplaces either on the Grimsel, or here; but that there are *mountains* here, is a fact to which they never allude; their whole journey is occupied in scolding their guide, who laughs at them, in quarrelling with the innkeepers, and in yawning in each others' faces. They think everything commonplace, because they are themselves commonplace, therefore they are not happier in

Switzerland than they would be in Bernau. I maintain that happiness is relative; another would thank God that he could see all this, and so I will be that other!

Fluelen, August 19th.

A day made for a journey; fine, and enjoyable, and bracing. When we wished to start this morning at six o'clock, there was such a storm of sleet and snow that we were obliged to wait till nine o'clock, when the sun came forth, the clouds dispersed, and we had delightful bright weather as far as this place; but now sombre clouds, heavy with rain, have collected over the lake, so that no doubt to-morrow the old troubles will break loose again. But how glorious this day has been, so clear and sunny—we had the most charming journey! You know the St. Gothard Road in all its beauty; you lose much by coming down from above, instead of ascending from this point, for the grand surprise of the Urner Loch is entirely lost, and the new road which has been made, with all the grandeur, as well as convenience, of the Simplon, impairs the effect of the Devil's Bridge: inasmuch as close beside it a new arch, much bolder and larger, has been constructed, which makes the old bridge look quite insignificant, but the ancient crumbling walls look much more romantic and picturesque. Though the view of Andermatt is thus lost, and the new Devil's Bridge far from being poetical, still you go merrily downhill all day, on a delightfully smooth road, flying rapidly past the various localities, and instead of being sprinkled by the foam of the waterfall on the old bridge as formerly, and endangered by **the wind, you** now pass along far above the **stream, between two ranges of solid parapets.**

We came past Göschenen and Wasen, and presently appeared the huge firs and beech-trees close to Amsteg; then the charming valley of Altorf, with its cottages, meadows, and woods, its rocks and snowy mountains. We rested at Altorf in a Capuchin Convent, situated on a height; and finally, here I am on the banks of the Vierwaldstadt Lake. To-morrow I purpose crossing the lake to Lucerne, where I hope to find letters from you. I shall then also get rid of a party of young people from Berlin, who have been pursuing almost the same route with me, meeting me at every turn, and boring me terribly; the patriotism of a lieutenant, a dyer, and a young carpenter,—all three bent on destroying France,—was peculiarly distasteful to me.

Sarnen, the 20th.

I crossed the Vierwaldstadt Lake early this morning, in a continued pour of rain, and found your welcome letter of the 5th in Lucerne. As it contained nothing but good tidings, I immediately arranged a tour of three days to Unterwalden and the Brünig. I intend to call again at Lucerne for your next letter, and then I am off to the West, and out of Switzerland. I shall take leave of it with deep regret. The country is beautiful beyond all conception; **and** though the weather is again odious, —rain and storms the whole day, and all through the night,—yet the Tellen Platte, the Grütli, Brunnen and Schwytz, and the dazzling green of the meadows this evening in Unterwalden, are too lovely ever to be forgotten. The hue of this green is most unique, refreshing the eye and the whole being. I shall certainly attend to your kind precautionary injunctions, dear Mother, but you need be under no apprehensions about me. I am by no means careless with regard to my health, and have not, for a long time, felt so well as during my pedestrian excursions in Switzerland. If eating, and drinking, and sleeping, and music in one's head, can make a man healthy, then, God be praised, I may well call myself so; for my guide and I vie with each other in eating and drinking, and not less so unluckily in singing. In sleeping alone I surpass him; and though I sometimes disturb him by my trumpet or oboe tones, he in turn cuts short my morning sleep. Please God, therefore, we shall have a happy meeting. Before that time arrives, however, many a page of my journal must yet travel to you; but even this interval will quickly pass, just as everything quickly passes, except indeed what is best of all !—so let us be true and loving to each other. FELIX.

Engelberg, August 23rd, 1831.

My heart is so full that I must tell you about it. In this enchanting valley I have just taken up

Schiller's "Wilhelm Tell," and read half of the first
scene; there is surely no genius like that of Germany! Heaven knows why it is so, but I do think
that no other nation could fully comprehend such an
opening scene, far less be able to compose it. This
is what I call a poem, and a beginning; first the
pure, clear verse, in which the lake, smooth as a
mirror, and all else, is so vividly described, and then
the slow commonplace Swiss talk, and Baumgarten
coming in,—it is quite glorious! How fresh, how
powerful, how exciting! We have no such work as
this in music, and yet even that sphere ought one
day to produce something equally perfect. It is so
admirable in him too, to have created an entire
Switzerland for himself, inasmuch as he never saw
it, and yet all is so faithful and so strikingly truthful; the people and life, the scenery and nature. I
was delighted when the old innkeeper here, in a
solitary mountain village, brought me from the
monastery the book with the well-known characters
and old familiar names; but the opening again quite
surpassed all my expectations. It is now more
than four years since I read it. I mean presently to
go over to the monastery, to work off my excitement on the organ.

Afternoon.

Do not be astonished at my enthusiasm, but read
the scene through again yourself, and then you will
find my excitement quite natural. Such passages
as those where all the shepherds and hunters shout

"Save him! save him!" in the close at the Grütli, when the sun is about to rise, could indeed only have occurred to a German, and above all to Schiller; and the whole piece is crowded with similar passages. Let me refer to that particular one at the end of the second scene, where Tell comes with the rescued Baumgarten to Stauffacher, and the agitating conference closes in such tranquillity and peace: this, along with the beauty of the thought, is so thoroughly Swiss. Then the beginning of the Grütli—the symphony which the orchestra ought to play at the end I composed in my mind to-day, because I could do nothing satisfactory on the little organ: altogether a variety of plans and ideas occurred to me. There is a vast deal to do in this world, and I mean to be industrious. The expression that Goethe made use of to me, that Schiller could have *supplied* two great tragedies every year, with its business-like tone, always in-spired me with particular respect: but not till this morning did the full force of its signification become clear to me, and it has made me feel that I must set to work in earnest. Even the mistakes are capti-vating, and there is something grand in them; and though certainly Bertha, Rudenz, and old Atting-hausen, seem to me great blemishes, still Schiller's idea is evident, and he was in a manner forced to do as he has done; and it is consolatory to find that even so great a man could for once commit such an egregious mistake.

I have passed a most enjoyable morning, and I

feel in the kind of mood which makes you long to recall such a man to life, in order to thank him, and inspiring an earnest desire, one day, to compose a work which shall impress others with similar feelings.

Probably you do not understand what induced me to take up my quarters here in Engelberg. It happened thus:—I have not had a single day's rest since I left Untersee, and therefore wished to remain for a day at Meiringen, but was tempted by the lovely weather in the morning, to come on here. The usual rain and wind assailed me on the mountains, and so I arrived very tired. This is the nicest inn imaginable,—clean, tidy, very small and rustic,—an old white-haired innkeeper; a wooden house, situated in a meadow, a little apart from the road; and the people so kind and cordial, that I feel quite at home. I think this kind of domestic comfort is only to be found among those who speak the German tongue; at all events, I never met with it anywhere else; and though other nations may not feel the want of it, or scarcely care about it, still *I* am a native of Hamburg, and so it makes me feel happy and at home. It is not therefore strange that I decided on taking my day's rest here with these worthy old people. My room has windows on every side, commanding a view of the valley: the room is prettily panelled with wood; some coloured texts and a crucifix are hanging on the walls; there is a solid green stove, and a bench encircling it, and two lofty bedsteads. When I am lying in bed I have the following view :—

I have failed again in my buildings, and in the
hills too, but I hope to make a better sketch of it
for you in my book, if the weather is tolerable to-
morrow. I shall always consider this valley to be
one of the loveliest in all Switzerland. I have not
yet seen the gigantic mountains by which it is en-
compassed, as they have been all day shrouded in
mist; but the beautiful meadows, the numerous
brooks, the houses, and the foot of the hills, so far
as I could see them, are exquisitely lovely. The
green of the Unterwalden is more brilliant than in
any other canton, and it is celebrated for its meadows

even among the Swiss. The previous journey too from Sarnen was enchanting, and never did I see larger or finer trees, or a more fruitful country. Moreover the road is attended with as few difficulties as if you were traversing a large garden; the declivities are clothed with tall slender beeches; the stones overgrown by moss and herbs; then there are springs, brooks, small lakes, and houses : on one side is a view of the Unterwalden and its green plains; and shortly after a view of the whole vale of Hasli, the snowy mountains, and cataracts leaping down from rocky precipices; the road too is shaded the whole way by enormous trees.

Yesterday, early, as I told you, I was tempted by the bright sun to cross the Genthel valley to ascend the Joch, but on the summit the most dreadful weather set in; we were obliged to make our way through the snow, and this was sometimes anything but pleasant. We speedily, however, emerged out of the sleet and snow, and an enchanting moment ensued, when the clouds broke, while we were still standing in them; and far beneath us, we saw through the mists as through a black veil, the green valley of Engelberg. We soon made our way down, and heard the silvery bell of the monastery ring out the Ave Maria. We next saw the white building on the meadow, and arrived here after an expedition of nine hours. I need not say how acceptable at such a time is a comfortable inn, and how good the rice and milk seems, and how long you sleep next morning.

To-day we have had very disagreeable weather, so they brought me " Wilhelm Tell " from the library of the monastery, and the rest you know. I was much struck by Schiller having so completely failed in portraying Rudenz, for the whole character is feeble, and without sufficient motive, and it seems as if he had resolved purposely to represent him throughout, in the worst possible light. His words, in the scene with the apple, might tend to redeem him, but being preceded by that with Bertha, they make no impression. When he joins the Swiss, after the death of Attinghausen, it might be supposed that he is changed, but he instantly proclaims that his Bertha is carried off, so again he has as little merit as ever. It occurred to me that if he had uttered the very same manly words against Gessler, without the explanation with Bertha having previously taken place, and if such a result had arisen out of this in the following act, the character would have been much better, and the explanatory scene not so merely theatrical as it now is. This is certainly very like the egg and the hen, but I should like to hear your opinion on the subject. I dare not speak to one of our learned men on such matters; these gentlemen are a vast deal too wise! If however I chance some of these days to meet one of those youthful modern poets, who look down on Schiller, and only partly approve of him; so much the worse for him, for I must infallibly crush him to death.

Now, good night; I must rise very early to-mor-

row; it is to be a grand fête to-day in the monastery,
and a solemn religious service, and I am to play the
organ for them. The monks were listening this
morning while I was extemporizing a little, and
were so pleased, that they invited me to play the
people in and out at their festival to-morrow. The
father organist has also given me the subject on
which I am to extemporize; it is better than any
that would have occurred to an organist in Italy.

I shall see to-morrow what I can make of this.   I
played a couple of new pieces of mine on the organ
this afternoon in the church, and they sounded
rather well.   When I came past the monastery the
same evening, the church was closed, and scarcely
were the doors shut, when the monks began to sing
nocturns fervently, in the dark church; they intoned
the deep B, which vibrated splendidly, and could be
heard far down the valley.

August 24th.

This has been another splendid day—the weather
bright and enjoyable, and the bluest sky that I have
seen since I left Chamouni; it was a holiday in the
village, and in all the mountains.   After long-con-
tinued fogs, and every variety of bad weather, once
more to see from the window in the morning the
clear range of mountains and their pinnacles, is in-

deed a grand spectacle. They are acknowledged to be finest after rain, and to-day they looked as fresh as if newly created. This valley is not surpassed by any in Switzerland. If I ever return here this shall be my head-quarters, for it is even more lovely, and more spacious and unconfined than Chamouni, and more free than Interlaken. The Spann-örter are incredibly grand peaks, and the round Titlis heavily laden with snow, the foot of which lies in the meadows, and the effect of the Urner rocks in the distance, are also well worth seeing: it is now full moon, and the valley is clothed in beauty.

This whole day I have done nothing but sketch, and play the organ: in the morning I performed my duties as organist—it was a grand affair. The organ stands close to the high altar, next to the stalls for the "patres;"—so I took my place in the midst of the monks, a very Saul among the prophets. An impatient Benedictine at my side played the double bass, and others the violins; one of their dignitaries was first violin. The *pater præceptor* stood in front of me, sang a solo, and conducted with a long stick, as thick as my arm. The *élèves* in the monastery formed the choir, in their black cowls; an old de-cayed rustic played on an old decayed oboe, and at a little distance two more were puffing away com-posedly at two huge trumpets with green tassels; and yet with all this the affair was gratifying. It was impossible not to like the people, for they had plenty of zeal, and all worked away as well as they could. A mass, by Emmerich, was given, and every note of it betrayed its "powder and pigtail." I played thorough-bass faithfully from my ciphered part, adding wind instruments from time to time, when I was weary; made the responses, extemporized on the appointed theme, and at the end, by desire of the Prelate, played a march, in spite of my repugnance to do this on the organ, and was then honourably dismissed.

This afternoon I played again alone to the monks, who gave me the finest subjects in the world—the " Credo" among others—a *fantasia* on the latter was very successful ; it is the only one that in my life I ever wished I could have written down, but now I can only remember its general purport, and must ask permission to send Fanny, in this letter, a passage that I do not wish to forget. By degrees various counter subjects were introduced in opposition to the *canto fermo ;* first dotted notes, then triplets, at last rapid semiquavers, through which the "Credo" was to work its way; quite at the close, the semiquavers became very wild, and arpeggios followed on the whole organ in G minor. I proceeded to take up the theme on the pedal in long notes (during the continued arpeggios), so that it ended with A. On the A, I made a pedal point in arpeggios, and then it suddenly occurred to me to play the arpeggios with the left hand alone, so that the right hand could introduce the " Credo" again in the treble with A, thus :—

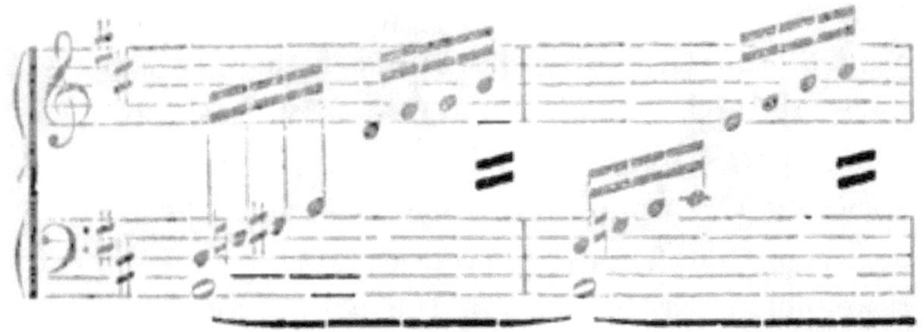

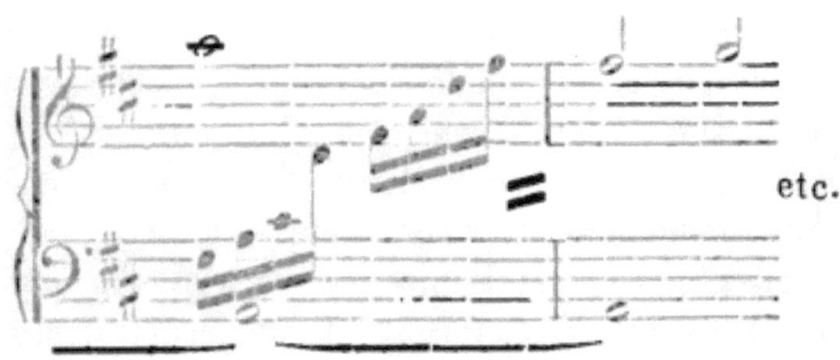

This was followed by a stop on the last note, and a pause, and then it concluded. I wish you had heard it, for I am sure you would have been pleased. It was time for the monks to go to *complines*, and we took leave of each other cordially. They wished to give me letters of introduction for some other places in Unterwalden, but I declined this, as I intend to go to Lucerne early to-morrow, and after that I expect not to be more than five or six days longer in Switzerland.—Your   FELIX.

To Wilhelm Taubert.

Lucerne, August 27th, 1831.

I wish to offer you my thanks, but I really do not know where to begin first; whether for the pleasure your songs caused me in Milan, or for your kind letter which I received yesterday; both however are closely connected, and so I think we have already made acquaintance. It is quite as fitting that we should be presented to each other through the medium of music-paper, as by a third person in society; indeed I think that in the former case you feel even more intimate and confidential. Moreover, persons who introduce any one often pronounce the name so indistinctly, that you seldom know who is standing before you; and they never say one word as to whether the man is gay and good-humoured, or melancholy and gloomy. So we are infinitely better off. Your songs have pronounced your name clearly and plainly; they also disclose what you think and what you are; that you love music, and wish to make progress; so thus perhaps I know you better than if we had frequently met.

What a source of pleasure it is, and how cheering, to know there is another musician in the world who has the same purposes and aspirations, and who follows the same path as yourself; perhaps you cannot feel this so strongly as I do at this moment, who have just come from a country where music no longer exists among the people. I never before could have believed this of any nation, and least of all of Italy, with such rich and luxuriant nature, and such glorious, inspiriting antecedents. But alas! the occurrences I latterly witnessed there, fully proved to me that even more than harmony is dead in that land; it would indeed be marvellous if any music could exist where there is no solid principle. At last I was really bewildered, and thought that I must have become a hypochondriac, for all the buffoonery I saw was most distasteful to me, and yet a vast number of serious people and sedate citizens entered into it. When they played me anything of their own, and afterwards praised and extolled my pieces, I cannot tell you how repugnant it was to me; I felt disposed to become a hermit, with beard and cowl, and the whole world was at a discount with me. In Italy you first learn to value a true musician; that is, one whose thoughts are absorbed in *music*, and not in money, or decorations, or ladies, or fame; it is doubly delightful when you find that, without your being aware of it, your own ideas exist and are developed elsewhere; your songs therefore gave me especial pleasure, because I could gather from them that you must be a genuine musician, and so let us mutually stretch out our hands across the mountains.

I beg that you will also look on me in the light of a friend, and not write so formally as to my "counsel" and "teaching." This portion of your letter makes me feel almost nervous, and I scarcely know what to say; the most agreeable part however is your promise to send me something to Munich, and to write to me again. I will then tell you frankly and freely my honest opinion, and you shall do the same with regard to my new compositions, and thus I think we shall give each other good counsel. I am very eager to see those recent works of yours that you have promised me, for I do not doubt that I shall receive much gratification from them, and many things which are only foreshadowed in the former songs, will probably in these become manifest and distinct. I shall therefore say nothing to-day of the impression your songs have made on me, because possibly any suggestion or question may be already answered in what you are about to send me. I earnestly entreat of you to write to me fully, and in detail, about yourself, in order that we may become better acquainted. I can then write to you what I purpose and what I think, and thus we shall continue in close connection.

Let me know what you have recently composed, and are now composing; your mode of life in Berlin, and your plans for the future; in short all that concerns your musical life, which will be of the greatest interest to me. Probably this will be obvious in the music you have so kindly promised me, but fortunately both may be combined. Have you hitherto composed nothing on a greater scale; some wild symphony, or opera, or something of the kind? I, for my part, feel at this moment the most invincible desire to write an opera, and yet I have scarcely leisure even to commence any work, however small. I do believe that if the libretto were to be given to me to-day, the opera would be written by to-morrow, so strong is my impulse towards it. Formerly the bare idea of a symphony was so exciting, that I could think of nothing else when one was in my head; the sound of instruments has such a solemn and glorious effect; and yet for some time past I have laid aside a symphony that I had commenced, in order to compose on a cantata of Goethe's merely because it included, besides the orchestra, voices and a chorus. I intend now, indeed, to complete the symphony, but there is nothing I so strongly covet as a regular opera.

Where the libretto is to come from I know less than ever since last night, when for the first time for more than a year I saw a German æsthetic paper. The German Parnassus seems in as disorganized a condition as European politics. God help us! I was obliged to digest the supercilious Menzel, who presumed modestly to depreciate Goethe,—and the supercilious Grabbe, who modestly depreciates Shakspeare,—and the philosophers who proclaim Schiller to be rather trivial! Is this new, arrogant, overbearing spirit, this perverse cynicism, as odious to you as it is to me? and are you of the same opinion with myself, that the first and most indispensable quality of any artist is to feel respect for great men, and to bow down in spirit before them; to recognize their merits, and not to endeavour to extinguish their great flame, in order that his own feeble rushlight may burn a little brighter? If a person be incapable of feeling true greatness, I should like to know how he intends to make *me* feel it? And as all these people, with their airs of contempt, only at last succeed in producing imitations of this or that particular form, without any presentiment of free, fresh, creative power, unfettered by individual opinion, or æsthetics or criticism, or the whole world besides; as this is the case, do they not deserve to be abused? and I do abuse them. Pray do not take this amiss; perhaps I have gone too far. But it was long since I had read anything of the kind, and it vexes me to see that such folly still goes on, and that the philosopher who maintains that art is dead, still persists in declaring that it is so; as if art could in reality ever die.

These are truly strange, wild, and troubled times; and let those who feel that art is no more, allow it for Heaven's sake to rest in peace; but however roughly the storm may rage without, it cannot so quickly succeed in sweeping away the dwelling; and he who works on quietly within, fixing his thoughts on his own capabilities and purposes, and not on those of others, will see the hurricane blow over, and afterwards find it difficult to realize that it ever was so violent as it appeared at the time. I have resolved to act thus so long as I can, and to pursue my path steadily, for at all events no one will deny that music still exists, and that is the chief thing.

How cheering it is to meet with a person who has chosen the same object and the same means as yourself! and I would fain tell you how gratifying

each new corroboration of this is to me, but I
scarcely know how to do so. You must imagine it
for yourself, and your own thoughts must supply any
deficiencies; so farewell! Pray let me hear from
you soon, and frequently. I beg to send my kindest
wishes to our dear friend Berger;* I have been
long intending to write to him, but have never yet
accomplished it. I shall certainly however do so
one of these days. Forgive this long, dry letter;
next time it shall be more interesting, and now once
more farewell.—Yours,

FELIX MENDELSSOHN BARTHOLDY.

———————◆———————

Righi Culm, August 30th, 1831.

I am on the Righi! I need say no more, for you
know this mountain. What can be more grand or
superb? I left Lucerne early this morning. All
the mountains were obscured, and the weather-wise
prophesied bad weather. As however I have always
found that the very opposite of what the wise people
say invariably occurs! I tried to make out signs for
myself, though hitherto, in spite of their aid, I have
found my predictions quite as false as those of the
others; but this morning I really thought the weather
very tolerable; still, as I did not wish to begin my
ascent while all was still shrouded in vapour (for
the Faulhorn had taught me caution), I spent the

---

* Ludwig Berger, Mendelssohn's instructor on the piano.

24

whole morning in sauntering round the foot of the Righi, gazing eagerly upwards, to see if the mists were likely to clear off. At last, about twelve o'clock, at Küssnacht, I stood on the cross path leading towards the Righi to the right, and Immensee to the left; and making up my mind not to see the Righi on this occasion, I took a tender farewell of it, and went through the Hohle Gasse to the Lake of Zug, along a charming path, past the water, to Arth; but could not resist frequently glancing at the summit of the Righi Culm, to see if it was becoming clearer; and while I was dining at Arth it did clear up. The wind was very favourable, the clouds lifted on every side; so I made up my mind to begin the ascent.

There was no time to lose, however, if I wished to witness the sunset; so I went along at a steady mountain pace, and in the course of two hours and three-quarters I reached the Culm, and the well-known house. I then became aware that there were about forty men standing on the top, uplifting their hands in admiration, and making signs in a state of the greatest excitement. I ran up, and a new and wondrous sight it was. All the valleys were filled with fogs and clouds, and above them the lofty, snowy crests of the mountains and the glaciers and black rocks stood out bright and clear. The mists swept onwards, veiling a portion of the scenery; then came forth the Bernese Alps, the Jungfrau, the Mönch, and the Finsteraarhorn; then Titlis, and the Unterwalden mountains. At last the whole range was

distinctly visible; the clouds in the val.eys now also
began to roll away, disclosing the lakes of Lucerne
and Zug, and towards the hour of sunset, only thin
streaks of bright vapour still floated on the landscape. Coming from the Alp, and then looking
towards the Righi, it was as if the overture and
other portions were repeated at the end of an opera.
All the spots whence you have seen such sublime
scenery, the Wengern Alp, the Wetter Hörner,
the valley of Engelberg, here meet the eye once
more in close vicinity, and you can take leave of
them all. I had imagined that it was only at first,
when still ignorant of the glaciers, that so great
an impression was made, from the influence of surprise, but I think the effect at the last is even more
striking than ever.

Schwytz, August 31st.

Yesterday and to-day I gratefully recalled the
happy auspices under which I first made acquaintance with this part of the world. The remembrance
of your profound admiration of these wonders, ele-
vating you above every-day life, has contributed not
a little to awaken and to quicken my own perception
of them. I often to-day recurred to your delight, and
the deep impression it made on me at the time. So
the Righi is evidently disposed to be gracious to our
family, and in consequence of this kindly feeling
towards us, conferred on me to-day a sunrise quite
as brilliant and splendid as when you were here.
The waning moon, the lively Alpine horn, the long-
protracted rosy dawn which first stole over the cold,

shadowy, snowy mountains, the white clouds on the Lake of Zug, the clear, sharp peaks bending towards each other in all directions, the light which gradually crept on the heights, the restless, shivering people, wrapped in coverlets, the monks from Maria zum Schnee, nothing was wanting.

I could not tear myself away from this spectacle, and remained on the summit for six consecutive hours, gazing at the mountains. I thought that when next I saw them there might be many changes, so I wished to imprint the sight indelibly on my memory. People came and went, and talked of these anxious, troubled times, of politics, and of the grand mountain range before us.

Thus the morning passed away, and at last, at half-past ten o'clock, I was obliged to go; indeed it was high time, as I wished to get to Einsiedel the same day, by Hacken. On my way, however, in the steep path leading to Lowerz, my trusty old umbrella, which also served me as a mountain staff, broke to pieces; this detained me, so that I preferred remaining here, and to-morrow I hope to be quite fresh for a start.

Wallenstadt, September 2nd.

(Year of rains and storms.) Motto of the coppersmith—" If you can't sing a new song, then begin the old one afresh." Here am I again in the midst of fogs and clouds, unable to go either backwards or forwards, and if fortune specially favours us, we may have a slight inundation into the bargain. When I crossed the lake, the boatmen prophesied very fine weather, consequently the rain began half an hour later, and is not likely soon to cease, for there are piles of heavy, gloomy clouds, such as you can only see on the mountains. If it were twice as bad three days hence, I should not care, but it would be grievous indeed if Switzerland were to take leave of me with so ill-omened an aspect.

I have this moment returned from the church, where I have been playing the organ for three hours, far into the twilight: an old man, a cripple, blew the bellows for me, and except him, there was not a single soul in the church. The only stops I found available, were a very weak croaking flute, and a quavering deep pedal diapason, of sixteen feet. I contrived to extemporize with these materials, and at last subsided into a choral melody in E minor, without being able to remember what it was. I could not get rid of it, when all at once it occurred to me that it was a Litany, the music of which was in my head because the words were in my heart, so then I had a wide field, and plenty of food for extemporizing. At length the consumptive deep bass resounded quite alone in E minor, thus:—

and then came in its turn the flute, high up in the treble, with the choral in the same key, and so the sounds of the organ gradually died away, and I was obliged to stop, from the church being so dark.

In the meantime there was a terrible hurricane of wind and rain outside, and not a trace of the grand lofty rocky precipices; the most dreary weather! and then I read some dreary newspapers, and everything wore a grey hue. Tell me, Fanny, do you know Auber's " Parisienne ?" I consider it the very worst thing he has ever produced, perhaps because the subject was really sublime, and for other reasons also. Auber alone could have been guilty of composing for a great nation, in the most violent state of excitement, a cold, insignificant piece, quite commonplace, and trivial. The *refrain* revolts me every time I think of it,—it is as if children were playing with a drum, and singing to it—only more objectionable. The words also are worthless; little antitheses and points are quite out of place here. Then the emptiness of the music! a march for acrobats, and at the end a mere miserable imitation of the " Marseillaise." Such music is not what this epoch demands. Woe to us *if* it be indeed what suits this epoch,—if a mere copy of the Marseillaise Hymn be all that is required. What in the latter is full of fire, and spirit, and impetus, is in the former ostentatious, cold, calculated, and artificial. The " Marseillaise " is as superior to the " Parisienne " as everything produced by genuine enthusiasm must be, to what is made for a purpose, even if it be with a view to promote enthusiasm : it will never reach the heart, because it does not come from the heart.

By the way, I never saw such a striking identity between a poet and a musician, as between Auber and Clauren. Auber faithfully renders note for note, what the other writes word for word—braggadocio, degrading sensuality, pedantry, epicurism, and parodies of foreign nationality. But why should Clauren be effaced from the literature of the day? Is it prejudicial to any one that he should remain where he is? and do you read what is really good with less interest? Any young poet must indeed be degenerate, if he does not cordially hate and despise such trash ; but it is only too true that the people like him ; so it is all very well, it is only the people's own loss. Write me your opinion of the "Parisienne." I sometimes sing it to myself for fun, as I go along ; it makes a man walk like a chorister in a procession.

Sargans, September 3rd, noon.

Wretched weather ! it has rained all night, and all the morning too, and the cold as severe as in winter ; deep snow is lying on the adjacent hills. There has been again a tremendous inundation in Appenzell, which has done the greatest damage, and destroyed all the roads. At the Lake of Zurich, there are numbers of pilgrimages, and processions, on account of the weather. I was obliged to drive here this morning, as all the footpaths were covered with mud and water. I shall remain till to-morrow, when the diligence passes through at an early hour, and I intend to go with it up the valley of the Rhine, as far as Altstetten.

To-morrow I shall probably have reached, or crossed, the boundaries of Switzerland, for my pleasure excursion is now over. Autumn is arrived, and I have no right to complain if I pass a few tiresome days, after so many enchanting ones, that I can never forget. On the contrary, I think I almost like it; there is always enough to be done, even in Sargans, (a wretched hole,) and in a regular deluge, like that of to-day—for happily an organ is always to be found in this country; they are certainly small, and the lower octave, both in the key-board and the pedal, imperfect, or as I call it, crippled; but still they are organs, and that is enough for me.

I have been playing all this morning, and really begun to practise, for it is a shame that I cannot play Sebastian Bach's principal works. I intend, if I can manage it, to practise for an hour every day in Munich, as after a couple of hours' work to-day, I certainly made considerable progress with my feet (*nota bene*, sitting). Ritz once told me that Schneider, in Dresden, played him the D major fugue, in the "wohl-temperirten Clavier," on the organ, supplying the bass with the pedal.

This had hitherto appeared to me so fabulous, that I could never properly comprehend it. It recurred to me this morning when I was playing the organ, so I instantly attempted it, and I at least see that it is far from being impossible, and that I shall accomplish it. The subject went pretty well, so I practised passages from the D major fugue, for the organ, from the F major toccata, and the G minor fugue, all of which I knew by heart. If I find a tolerable organ in Munich, and not an imperfect one, I will certainly conquer these, and feel childish delight at the idea of playing such pieces on the organ. The F major toccata, with the modulation at the close, sounded as if the church were about to tumble down; what a giant that Cantor was!

Besides organ-playing, I have a good many sketches to finish, in my new drawing book, (one was entirely filled in Engelberg) and then I must eat like six hundred wrestlers. After dinner I practise the organ again, and thus a rainy day passes at Sargans. It seems prettily situated, with a castle on the hill, but I cannot go a step beyond the door.

Evening.—Yesterday at this time, I still projected a pedestrian tour, and wished at all events to go through the whole of the Appenzell. It was a strange feeling when I learned that all mountain excursions were probably at an end for this year: the heights are covered with deep snow, for just as it has rained here, in the valley, for thirty-six hours, it has snowed incessantly on the hills above. The flocks have been obliged to come down into the valley from the Alps, where they ought to have remained for a whole month yet, so that all idea of any footpaths is out of the question. Yesterday I was still on the hills, but now they will be inaccessible for six months to come. My pedestrian excursions are over; wondrously beautiful they were, and I shall never forget them.

I mean to work hard at music, and high time that I should. I played on the organ till twilight, and was trampling energetically on the pedal, when we suddenly became aware that the deep C sharp in the great diapason, went buzzing softly on without ceasing; all our pressing, and shaking, and thumping on the keys, was of no avail, so we were obliged to climb into the organ among the big pipes. The C sharp continued gently humming,—the fault lay in the bellows; the organist was in the greatest perplexity, because to-morrow is a fête day; at last I stuffed my handkerchief into the pipe, and there was no more buzzing, but no more C sharp either. I played this passage incessantly, all the same :—

and it did very well.

I am now going to finish my sketch of the Glacier of the Rhone, and then the day will be at my own disposal; which means that I am going to sleep. I will write to you on the next page to-morrow evening wherever I am, for to-day I have no idea where I shall be. Good night! Eight is striking in F minor, and it is raining and blowing in F sharp minor or G sharp minor; in short, in every possible sharp key.

St. Gall, the 4th.

Motto—"Vous pensez que je suis l'Abbé de St. Gall" (Citoyen).* I do feel so comfortable here, after braving such storms and tempests. During the four hours when I was crossing the mountains from Altstetten to this place, I was engaged in a regular battle with the elements; when I tell you that I never experienced anything like the storm, nor even imagined anything approaching to it, this does not say much; but the oldest people in the Canton declare the same: a large manufactory has been demolished, and several persons killed. To-morrow, in my last letter from Switzerland, I will tell you of my being again obliged to travel on foot, and arriving here, after crossing by Appenzell, which looked like Egypt after the seven plagues. The bell is now ringing for dinner, and I mean to feast like an abbot.

Lindau, September 5th.

Opposite me lies Switzerland, with her dark blue mountains, pedestrian journeys, storms, and glorious heights and valleys. Here ends the greatest part of my journey, and my journal also.

At noon to-day, I crossed the wild grey Rhine in

---

* Mendelssohn jokingly alludes to a poem of *Bürger*,—Der Abt von St. Gallen.

a ferry-boat, above Rheineck, and now here I am,
already in Bavaria. I have of course entirely given
up my projected excursion on foot, through the
Bavarian mountains; for it would be folly to attempt
anything of the kind this year. For the last four
days it has rained more or less with incessant vehe-
mence; it seemed as if Providence were wroth. I
passed to-day through extensive orchards, which
were not under water, but fairly submerged by mud
and clay; everything looks deplorable and depress-
ing; you must therefore forgive the doleful style
of this last sheet. I never in any landscape saw a
more dreary sight than the sward of the green hills,
covered with deep snow; while below, the fruit-trees,
with their ripe fruit, were standing reflected in the
water. The scanty covering of muddy snow, which
lay on the fir-woods and meadows, looked the per-
sonification of all that was dismal. A Sargans
burgher told me that in 1811 this little town had
been entirely burnt down, and recently with difficulty rebuilt; that they depend chiefly on the produce of their vineyards, which have been this year
destroyed by hail-storms, and the Alps also were
now no longer available; this gives rise to serious
reflections, and to anxious thoughts with regard to
this year.

It is singular enough that if I am obliged to go
on foot in such weather, and fairly exposed to it, I
am not in the least annoyed; on the contrary, I
rather rejoice in setting it at defiance. When I
arrived by the diligence yesterday at Altstetten, in

freezing cold, like a day in December, I found that there was no carriage road to Tourgen, to which place I had unluckily sent on my cloak and knapsack on the last fine day. I was obliged to have them the same evening, for the cold was intense, so I did not hesitate long, but set off once more for the last time to cross the mountains, and arrived in the Canton of Appenzell.

The state of the woods, and hills, and meadows, and little bridges, baffles all description; being Sunday, and divine service going on, I failed in procuring a guide; not a living soul met me the whole way, for all the people had crept into their houses so I toiled on quite alone towards Tourgen. To pass through a wood in such weather, and along such paths, inspires a wonderful sense of independence. Moreover I am now quite perfect in the Swiss *jodeln* and crowing, so I shouted lustily, and *jodelled* several airs at the pitch of my voice, and arrived in Tourgen in capital spirits. The people in the inn there were rude and saucy, so I politely said, "You be hanged! I shall go on;" and taking out my map, I found that St. Gall was the nearest convenient place, and in fact the only practicable route. I could not succeed in persuading any one to go with me in such horrible weather, so I resolved to carry my own things, abusing all Swiss cordiality.

Shortly afterwards, however, came the reverse of the medal, which not unfrequently occurs. I went to the peasant who had brought my luggage here, and found him in his pretty newly-built wooden house, and I had thus an opportunity of seeing a veritable and genuine Swiss interior, just as we imagine it to be. He and his whole family were sitting round a table, the house clean and warm, and the stove burning. The old man rose and gave me his hand, and insisted on my taking a seat; he then sent through the whole place to try to get me a carriage, or a man to carry my things, but as no one would either drive or walk, he at last sent his own son with me. He only asked two *Batzen* for carrying my knapsack for two hours. A very pretty fair daughter was sitting at the table sewing, the mother reading a thick book, and the old man himself studying the newspapers; it was a charming picture.

When at last I set off, the weather seemed to say, " If you defy me I can defy you also," for the storm broke loose with redoubled violence, and an invisible hand appeared to seize my umbrella at intervals, shaking it and crumpling it together, and my fingers were so benumbed that I could scarcely hold it fast; the paths were so desperately slippery that my guide fell sprawling full length before me in the mud; but what cared we ? We *jodelled* and reviled the weather to our hearts' content, and at last we passed the Nunnery, which we greeted by a serenade, and soon after reached St. Gall.

Our journey was happily over, and yesterday I drove here, and at night met with a wonderful organ, on which I could play "Schmücke dich, O liebe Seele !" to my heart's content.

To-day I proceed to Memmingen, to-morrow to

Augsburg; the day after, God willing, to Munich; and thus, I may now say, I *have been* in Switzerland. Perhaps I have rather bored you by all the trivial occurrences I have detailed. These are gloomy times, but we need not be so; and when I sent you my journal, it was chiefly to show you that I thought of you whenever I was pleased and happy, and was with you in spirit. The shabby, dripping pedestrian bids you farewell, and a town gentleman, with visiting-cards, fine linen, and a black coat, will write to you next time. Farewell. FELIX.

BURGHER LETTER FROM MUNICH.

Munich, October 6th, 1831.

It is a delightful feeling to wake in the morning and to know that you are to score a grand allegro with all sorts of instruments, and various oboes and trumpets, while bright weather holds out the hope of a cheering long walk in the afternoon.

I have enjoyed these pleasures for a whole week past, so the favourable impression that Munich made on me during my first visit, is now very much enhanced. I scarcely know any place where I feel so comfortable and domesticated as here. It is indeed very delightful to be surrounded by cheerful faces, and your own to be so also, and to know every man you meet in the streets.

I am now preparing for my concert, so my hands are pretty full; my acquaintances every instant interrupting me in my work, the lovely weather tempting me to go out, and the copyists, in turn, forcing me to stay at home; all this constitutes the most agreeable and exciting life. I was obliged to put off my concert, on account of the October festival, which begins next Sunday, and lasts all the week. Every evening there is to be a performance at the theatre, and a ball, so all idea of an orchestra or a concert-room is out of the question. On Monday evening, however, the 17th, at half-past six, think of me,—for then we dash off with thirty violins, and two sets of wind instruments.

The first part begins with the symphony in C minor, the second with the "Midsummer Night's Dream." The first part closes with my new concerto in G minor, and at the end of the second I have unwillingly agreed to extemporize. Believe me, I do so very reluctantly, but the people insist upon it. Bärmann has decided on playing again; Breiting, Mlle. Vial, Loehle, Bayer, and Pellegrini are the singers who are to execute a piece together. The locality is the large Odeon Hall, and the performance for the benefit of the poor in Munich. The magistrates invite the orchestra, and the burgomasters the singers. Every morning I am engaged in writing, correcting, and scoring till one o'clock, when I go to Scheidel's coffee-house in the Kaufinger Gasse, where I know each face by heart, and find the same people every day in the same position; two playing chess, three looking on, five reading the newspapers, six eating their dinner, and I am the seventh. After dinner Bärmann usually comes to fetch me, and we make arrangements about the concert, or after a walk we have cheese and beer, and then I return home and set to work again.

This time I have declined all invitations for the evening; but there are so many agreeable houses, to which I can go uninvited, that a light is seldom to be seen in my room on the parterre till after eight o'clock. You must know that I lodge on a level with the street, in a room which was once a shop, so that if I unbar the shutters of my glass door, one step brings me into the middle of the street, and any one passing along, can put his head in at the window, and say good morning. Next to me a Greek lodges, who is learning the piano, and he is truly odious; but to make up for that, my landlord's daughter, who wears a round silver cap and is very slender, looks all the prettier.

I have music in my rooms at four o'clock in the afternoon, three times every week: Bärmann, Breiting, Staudacher, young Poissl, and others, come regularly, and we have a musical picnic. In this way I become acquainted with operas, which, most unpardonably, I have not yet either heard or seen; such as Lodoiska, Faniska, Medea; also the Preciosa, Abu Hassan, etc. The theatre lends us the scores.

Last Wednesday we had capital fun; several wagers had been lost, and it was agreed that we should enjoy the fruits of them all together; and after various suggestions, we at last decided on having a musical soirée in my room, and to invite all the dignitaries; so a list was made out of about thirty persons; several also came uninvited, who were presented to us by mutual friends. There was a sad want of space; at first we proposed placing several people on my bed, but it was surprising the number of patient sheep who managed to cram into my small room. The whole affair was most lively and successful. E—— was present, as dulcet as ever, languishing in all the glory of poetical enthusiasm, and grey stockings; in short, tiresome beyond all description.

First I played my old quartett in B minor; then Breiting sang "Adelaide;" Herr S—— played variations on the violin (doing himself no credit); Bärmann performed Beethoven's first quartett (in F major), which he had arranged for two clarionets, corno di bassetto, and bassoon; an air from "Euryanthe" followed, which was furiously encored, and as a finale I extemporized—tried hard to get off— but they made such a tremendous uproar that *nolens* I was forced to comply, though I had nothing in my head, but wine-glasses, benches, cold roast meat, and ham.

The Cornelius ladies were next-door with my landlord and his family, to listen to me; the Schauroths were making a visit on the first story for the same purpose, and even in the hall, and in the street, people were standing; in addition to all this, the heat of the crowded room, the deafening noise, the gay audience; and when at last the time for eating and drinking arrived, the uproar was at its height; we fraternized glass in hand, and gave toasts; the more formal guests with their grave faces, sat in the midst of the jovial throng, apparently quite contented, and we did not separate till half-past one in the morning.

The following evening formed a striking contrast. I was summoned to play before the Queen, and the Court; there all was proper and polite, and polished, and every time you moved your elbow, you pushed against an Excellency; the most smooth and complimentary phrases circulated in the room, and I, the *roturier*, stood in the midst of them, with my citizen heart, and my aching head! I managed however to get on pretty well, and at the end, I was commanded to extemporize on Royal themes, which I did, and was mightily commended; what pleased me most was, that when I had finished my extempore playing, the Queen said to me, that it was strange the power I possessed of carrying away my audience, for that during such music, no one could think of anything else; on which I begged to apologize for carrying away Her Majesty, etc.

This, you see, is the mode in which I pass my time in Munich. I forgot, however, to say, that every day at twelve o'clock, I give little Mademoiselle L—— an hour's instruction in double counterpoint, and four-part composition, etc., which makes me realize more than ever the stupidity and confusion of most masters and books on this subject; for nothing can be more clear than the whole thing when properly explained.

She is one of the sweetest creatures I ever saw. Imagine a small, delicate-looking, pale girl, with noble but not pretty features, so singular and interesting, that it is difficult to turn your eyes from her; while all her gestures and every word are full of genius. She has the gift of composing songs, and singing them in a way I never heard before, causing me the most unalloyed musical delight I ever experienced. When she is seated at the piano, and begins one of the songs, the sounds are quite unique; the music floats strangely to and fro, and every note expresses the most profound and refined feeling. When she sings the first note in her tender tones, every one present subsides into a quiet and thoughtful mood, and each, in his own way, is deeply affected.

If you could but hear her voice! so innocent, so unconsciously lovely, emanating from her inmost soul, and yet so tranquil! Last year the genius was all there; she had written no song that did not contain some bright flash of talent, and then M——— and I sounded forth her praises to the musical world; still no one seemed to place much faith in us; but since that time, she has made the most remarkable progress. Those who are not affected by her present singing, can have no feeling at all; but unluckily it is now the fashion to beg the young girl to sing her songs, and then the lights are removed from the piano, in order that the society may enjoy the plaintive strains.

This forms an unpleasant contrast, and repeatedly

when I was to have played something after her, I was quite unable, and declined doing so. It is probable that she may one day be spoiled by all this praise, because she has no one to comprehend or to guide her; and, strangely enough, she is as yet entirely devoid of all musical cultivation; she knows very little, and can scarcely distinguish good music from bad; in fact, except her own pieces, she thinks all else that she hears wonderfully fine. If she were at length to become satisfied as it were with herself, it would be all over with her. I have, for my part, done what I could, and implored her parents and herself in the most urgent manner, to avoid society, and not to allow such divine genius to be wasted. Heaven grant that I may be successful! I may, perhaps, dear sisters, soon send you some of her songs that she has copied out for me, in token of her gratitude for my teaching her what she already knows from nature; and because I have really led her to good and solid music.

I also play on the organ every day for an hour, but unfortunately I cannot practise properly, as the pedal is short of five upper notes, so that I cannot play any of Sebastian Bach's passages on it; but the stops are wonderfully beautiful, by the aid of which you can vary chorals; so I dwell with delight on the celestial, liquid tone of the instrument. Moreover, Fanny, I have here discovered the particular stops which ought to be used in Sebastian Bach's "Schmücke dich, O liebe Seele." They seem actually made for this melody, and sound so touching,

that a tremor invariably seizes me, when I begin to
play it.   For the flowing parts I have a flute stop of
eight feet, and also a very soft one of four feet, which
continually floats above the Choral.   You have
heard this effect in Berlin; but there is a keyboard
for the Choral with nothing but reed stops, so I employ a mellow oboe and a soft clarion (four feet) and
a viola; these give the Choral in subdued and touching tones, like distant human voices, singing from
the depths of the heart.

Sunday, Monday, and Tuesday, by the time you
will have received this letter, I shall be on the "Theresien Wiese," with eighty thousand other people; so
think of me there, and farewell.   FELIX.

Munich, October 18th, 1831.

Dear Father,

Pray forgive me for not having written to you for
so long.   The last few days previous to my concert,
were passed in such bustle and confusion, that I
really had not a moment's leisure; besides I preferred writing to you after my concert was over,
that I might tell you all about it, hence the long interval between this and my former letter.

I write to you in particular to-day, because it is
so long since I have had a single line from you; I
do beg you will soon write to me, if only to say that
you are well, and to send me your kind wishes.
You know this always makes me glad and happy;

therefore excuse my addressing this letter, with all the little details of my concert, to you. My mother, and sisters, were desirous to hear them, but I was anxious to say how eagerly I hope for a few lines from you. Pray let me have them. It is a long time since you wrote to me!

My concert took place yesterday, and was much more brilliant and successful than I expected. The affair went off well, and with much spirit. The orchestra played admirably, and the receipts for the benefit of the poor will be large. A few days after my former letter, I attended a general rehearsal, where the whole band were assembled, and in addition to the official invitation the orchestra had received, I was obliged to invite them verbally in a polite speech, in the theatre. This, to me, was the most trying part of the whole concert; still I did not object to it, for I really wished to know the sensations of a man who gives a concert, and this ceremony forms part of it. I stationed myself therefore at the prompter's box, and addressed the performers very courteously, who took off their hats, and when my speech was finished, there was a general murmur of assent. On the following day there were upwards of seventy signatures to the circular. Immediately afterwards, I had the pleasure of finding that the chorus singers had sent one of their leaders to me, to ask if I had not composed some chorus that I should like to be sung, in which case, they would all be happy to sing it *gratis*. Although I had decided not to give more than three pieces of my composition, still the offer was very gratifying, and the hearty sympathy especially delighted me, for even the regimental musicians whom I had to engage for the English horns and trumpets, positively refused to accept a single kreuzer, and we had above eighty performers in the orchestra.

Then came all the tiresome minor arrangements about advertisements, tickets, preliminary rehearsals, etc., and in addition to all this, it was the week of the October festival. In Munich the days and hours always glide past so very rapidly, that when they are gone, it really seems as if they had never been, and this is more peculiarly the case during this October festival. Every afternoon about three o'clock you repair to the spacious, green "Theresien Wiese," which is swarming with people, and it is impossible to get away till the evening, for every one finds acquaintances without end, and something to talk about, or to look at; a fat ox, target-shooting, a race, or pretty girls in gold and silver caps, etc. Any affair you are engaged in, can be concluded there, for the whole town is congregated on the meadow, and not till the mists begin to rise, does the crowd disperse, and return towards the "Frauen Thürme." The people are in constant motion, running about in all directions, while the snowy mountains in the distance look clear and tranquil, each day giving promise of a bright morrow, and fulfilling that promise; and, what after all is the chief thing, none but careless happy faces to be seen, with the occasional exception perhaps of a few Deputies, drinking coffee in the open air, and discussing the lamentable condition of the people,—while the people themselves are standing round them looking as happy as possible. On the first day the King distributes the prizes himself, taking off his hat to each winner of a prize, and giving his hand to the peasants, or laying hold of their arms and shaking them; now I think this all very proper, as here externally at least society appears more blended, but whether it sinks deep into the heart, we can discuss together at some future time. I adhere to my first opinion; at all events it is so far well, that the absurd restraints of etiquette should not be too strictly observed outwardly, and so it is always something gained.

My first rehearsal took place early on Saturday. We had about thirty-two violins, six double-basses, and double sets of wind instruments, etc.: but, Heaven knows why, the rehearsal went badly; I was forced to rehearse my symphony in C minor alone for two hours. My concerto did not go at all satisfactorily. We had only time to play over the "Midsummer Night's Dream" once, and even then so hurriedly, that I wished to withdraw it from the bills: but Bärmann would not hear of this, and assured me that they would do it better next time. I therefore was forced to wait in considerable anxiety for the next rehearsal: in the meantime there was happily a great ball on Sunday evening, which was very enjoyable, so I recovered my spirits, and arrived next morning at the general rehearsal in high good humour, and with perfect confidence. I started off at once with the overture; we played it over again and again, till at last it went well, and we did the same with my concerto, so that the whole rehearsal was quite satisfactory.

On my way to the concert at night, when I heard the rattling of the carriages, I began to feel real pleasure in the whole affair. The Court arrived at half-past six. I took up my little English *bâton*, and conducted my symphony. The orchestra played magnificently, and with a degree of fire and enthusiasm that I never heard equalled under my direction; they all crashed in at the *forte*, and the *scherzo* was most light and delicate; it seemed to please the audience exceedingly, and the King was always the first to applaud. Then my fat friend, Breiting, sang the air in A flat major from "Euryanthe," and the public shouted "Da capo!" and were in good humour, and showed good taste. Breiting was delighted, so he sang with spirit, and quite beautifully. Then came my concerto; I was received with long and loud applause; the orchestra accompanied me well, and the composition had also its merits, and gave much satisfaction to the audience; they wished to recall me, in order to give me another round of applause, according to the prevailing fashion here, but I was modest, and would not appear. Between the parts the King got hold of me, and praised me highly, asking all sorts of questions, and whether I was related to the Bartholdy in Rome, to whose house he was in the habit of going, because it was the cradle of modern art, etc.*

The second part commenced with the "Midsummer Night's Dream," which went admirably, and excited a great sensation; then Bärmann played, and after that we had the finale in A major from Lodoiska. I however did not hear either of these, as I was resting and cooling in the anteroom. When I appeared to extemporize, I was again enthusiastically received. The King had given me the theme of "Non più andrai," on which I was to *improviser*. My former opinion is now fully confirmed, that it is an absurdity to extemporize in public. I have seldom felt so like a fool as when I took my place at the piano, to present to the public the fruits of my inspiration; but the audience were quite contented, and there was no end of their applause. They called me forward again, and the Queen said all that was courteous; but I was annoyed, for I was far from being satisfied with myself, and I am resolved never again to extemporize in public,—it is both an abuse and an absurdity.

So this is an account of my concert of the 17th, which is now among the things of the past. There were eleven hundred people present, so the poor may well be satisfied: but enough of all this. Farewell! May every happiness attend you all!

FELIX.

---

* *Vide* the letter from Rome of the 1st of February, 1831.

Paris, December 19th, **1831.**

Dear Father,

Receive my hearty thanks for your letter of the 7th. Though I do not quite apprehend your meaning on some points, and also may differ from you, still I have no doubt that this will come all right when we talk things over together, especially if you permit me, as you have always hitherto done, to express my opinion in a straight-forward manner. I allude chiefly to your suggestion, that I should procure a libretto for an opera from some French poet, and then have it translated, and compose the music for the Munich stage.*

Above all, I must tell you how sincerely I regret that you have only now made known to me your views on this subject. I went to Düsseldorf, as you know, expressly to consult with Immermann on the point. I found him ready, and willing; he accepted the proposal, promising to send me the poem by the end of May at the latest, so I do not myself see how it is possible for me now to draw back; indeed I do not wish it, as I place entire confidence in him. I do not in the least understand what you allude to in your last letter, about Immermann, and his incapacity to write an opera. Although I by no means agree with you in this opinion, still it would have been my duty to have settled nothing without

---

* Felix Mendelssohn, during his stay in Munich, received a commission from the director of the theatre, to write an opera for Munich.

your express sanction, and I could have arranged
the affair by letter from here, I believed however
that I was acting quite to your satisfaction when I
made him my offer. In addition to this, some new
poems that he read to me, convinced me more than
ever that he was a true poet, and supposing that I
had an equal choice in merit, I would always decide
rather in favour of a German than a French libretto;
and lastly, he has fixed on a subject which has been
long in my thoughts, and which, if I am not mistaken,
my mother wished to see made into an opera,—I
mean Shakspeare's "Tempest;" I was therefore
particularly pleased with this, so I shall doubly regret if you do not approve of what I have done. In
any event, however, I entreat that you will neither
be displeased with me, nor distrustful with regard to
the work, nor cease to take any interest in it.

From what I know of Immermann, I feel assured
I may expect a first-rate libretto. What I alluded
to about his solitary life, merely referred to his inward feelings and perceptions; for in other respects
he is well acquainted with what is passing in the
world. He knows what people like, and what to
give them; but above all he is a genuine artist,
which is the chief thing; but I am sure I need not
say that I will not compose music for any words I do
not consider really good, or which do not inspire me,
and for this purpose it is essential that I should
have your approval. I intend to reflect deeply on
the poem before I begin the music. The dramatic
interest or (in the best sense) the theatrical portion,

I shall of course immediately communicate to you, and in short look on the affair in the serious light it deserves. The first step however is taken, and I cannot tell you how deeply I should regret your not being pleased.

There is however one thing which consoles me, and it is that if I were to rely on my own judgment, I would again act precisely as I have now done. though I have had an opportunity of becoming acquainted with a great deal of French poetry, and seeing it in the most favourable light. Pray pardon me for saying exactly what I think. To compose for the translation of a French libretto, seems to me for various reasons impracticable, and I have an idea that you are in favour of it more on account of the *success* which it is likely to enjoy than for its own *intrinsic merit.* Moreover I well remember how much you disliked the subject of the "Muette de Portici," a *Muette* too who had gone astray, and of "Wilhelm Tell," which the author seems almost purposely to have rendered tedious.

The success however these enjoy all over Germany does not assuredly depend on the work itself being either good or dramatic, for "Tell" is neither, but on their coming from Paris, and having pleased there. Certainly there is *one* sure road to fame in Germany,—that by Paris and London; still it is not the only one; this is proved not only by all Weber's works, but also by those of Spohr, whose "Faust" is here considered classical music, and which is to be given at the great Opera-house in

London next season. Besides, I could not possibly take that course, as my great opera has been bespoken for Munich, and I have accepted the commission. I am resolved therefore to make the attempt in Germany, and to remain and work there so long as I can continue to do so, and yet maintain myself, for this I consider my first duty. If I find that I cannot do this, then I must leave it for London or Paris, where it is easier to get on. I see indeed where I should be better remunerated and more honoured, and live more gaily, and at my ease, than in Germany, where a man must press forward, and toil, and take no rest,—still, if I can succeed there, I prefer the latter.

None of the new libretti here, would in my opinion be attended with any success whatever, if brought out for the first time on a German stage. One of the distinctive characteristics of them all, is precisely of a nature that I should resolutely oppose, although the taste of the present day may demand it, and I quite admit that it may in general be more prudent to go with the current than to struggle against it. I allude to that of immorality. In "Robert le Diable" the nuns come one after the other to allure the hero of the piece, till at last the abbess succeeds in doing so: the same hero is conveyed by magic into the apartment of her whom he loves, and casts her from him in an attitude which the public here applauds, and probably all Germany will do the same; she then implores his mercy in a grand aria. In another opera a young girl divests herself of her garments, and sings a song to the effect that next day at this time she will be married; all this produces effect, but I have no music for such things. I consider it ignoble, so if the present epoch exacts this style, and considers it indispensable, then I will write oratorios.

Another strong reason why it would prove impracticable is that no French poet would undertake to furnish me with a poem. Indeed, it is no easy matter to procure one from them for this stage, for all the best authors are overwhelmed with commissions. At the same time I think it quite possible that I might succeed in getting one; still it never would occur to any of them to write a libretto for a *German* theatre. In the first place it would be much more feasible to give the opera here, and infinitely more rational too; in the second place, they would decline writing for any other stage than the French; in fact they could not realize any other. Above all it would be impossible to procure for them a sum equivalent to what they receive here from the theatres, and what they draw as their share from the *part d'auteur*.

I know you will forgive me for having told you my opinion without reserve. You always allowed me to do so in conversation, so I hope you will not put a wrong construction on what I have written, and I beg you will amend my views by communicating your own.—Your   FELIX.

Paris, December 20th, 1831.

Dear Rebecca,

I went yesterday to the Chambre des Députés, and I must now tell you about it; but what do you care about the Chambre des Députés? It is a political song, and you would rather hear whether I have composed any love songs, or bridal songs, or wedding songs; but it is a sad pity, that no songs but political ones are composed here. I believe I never in my life passed three such unmusical weeks as these. I feel as if I never could again think of composing; this all arises from the "juste milieu;" but it is still worse to be with musicians, for they do not *wrangle* about politics, but *lament* over them. One has lost his place, another his title, a third his money, and they say this all proceeds from the " Milieu."

Yesterday I saw the "Milieu," in a light grey coat, and with a noble air, in the first place on the Ministerial bench. He was sharply attacked by M. Mauguin, who has a very long nose. Of course you don't care for all this; but what of that? I must have a chat with you. In Italy I was lazy, in Switzerland a wild student, in Munich a consumer of cheese and beer, and so in Paris I must talk politics. I intended to have composed various symphonies, and to have written some songs for certain ladies in Frankfort, Düsseldorf, and Berlin; but as yet not a chance of it. Paris obtrudes herself, and as above all things I must now see Paris, so I am busily engaged in seeing it, and am dumb.

Moreover I am freezing with cold—another drawback. I cannot contrive to make my room warm, and I am not to get another and warmer apartment, till New Year's Day. In a dark little hole on the ground floor, overlooking a small damp garden, where my feet are like ice, how can I possibly write music? It is bitterly cold, and an Italian like myself is peculiarly susceptible. At this moment a man outside my window is singing a political song to a guitar.

I live a reckless life—out morning, noon, and night: to-day at Baillot's; to-morrow I go to some friends of the Bigots; the next day, Valentin; Monday, Fould; Tuesday, Hiller; Wednesday, Gérard; and the previous week it was just the same. In the forenoon I rush off to the Louvre, and gaze at the Raphaels, and my favourite Titian; a person might well wish for a dozen more eyes to look at such a picture.

Yesterday I was in the Chamber of Peers, who were engaged in pronouncing judgment on their own hereditary rights, and I saw M. Pasquier's wig. The day before I paid two musical visits, to the grumbling Cherubini, and the kind Herz. There is a large sign-board before the house: "Manufacture de Pianos, par Henri Herz, Marchand de Modes et de Nouveautés." I thought this formed one, not observing that it was a notice of two different firms, so I went in below, and found myself surrounded by gauze, and lace, and trimmings: so, rather abashed, I asked where the pianos were. A number of Herz's fair scholars with industrious faces, were waiting upstairs. I sat down by the fire and read your interesting account of our dear father's birth-day, and so forth. Herz presently arrived, and gave audience to his pupils. We were very loving, recalled old times, and besprinkled each other mutually with great praise. On his pianos is inscribed: "Médaille d'or. Exposition de 1827." This was very imposing.

From thence I went to Erard's, where I tried over his instruments, and remarked written on them in large letters: " Médaille d'or. Exposition de 1827." My respect seemed to diminish. When I went home I opened my own instrument by Pleyel, and to be sure there also I saw in large letters : "Médaille d'or. Exposition de 1827." The matter is like the title of " Hofrath," but it is characteristic. It is alleged that the chambers are about to discuss the following proposition: "Tous les Français du sexe masculin ont dès leur naissance le droit de porter l'ordre de la Légion d'Honneur," and the permission to appear without the order, can only be obtained by special services. You really scarcely see a man in the street without a bit of coloured ribbon, so it is no longer a distinction.

Apropos, shall I be lithographed full length? Answer what you will, I don't intend to do it. One afternoon in Berlin, when I was standing *unter den Linden* before Schenk's shop looking at H——'s and W——'s lithographs, I made a solemn vow to myself, unheard by man, that I would never allow myself to be hung up till I became a great man. The temptation in Munich was strong; there they wished to drape me with a Carbonaro cloak, a stormy sky in the background, and my fac-simile underneath, but I happily got off by adhering to my principles. Here again I am rather tempted, for the likenesses are very striking, but I keep my vow; and if, after all, I never do become a great man, though posterity will be deprived of a portrait, it will have an absurdity the less.

It is now the 24th, and we had a very pleasant evening at Baillot's yesterday. He plays beautifully, and had collected a very musical society of attentive ladies and enthusiastic gentlemen, and I have seldom been so well amused in any circle, or enjoyed such honours. It was the greatest possible delight to me to hear my quartett in E flat major (dedicated to B. P.) performed in Paris by Baillot's quartett, and they executed it with fire and spirit. They commenced with a quintett by Bocherini, an old-fashioned *perruque,* but a very amiable old gentleman underneath it. The company then asked for a sonata of Bach's; we selected the one in A major; old familiar tones dawned once more on me, of the time when Baillot played it with Madame Bigot.* We urged each other on, the affair became animated, and so thoroughly amused both us and our audience, that we immediately commenced the one in E major, and next time we mean to introduce the four others.

---

* The lady who instructed Mendelssohn in the piano in Paris, when the family resided there for a time in 1816.

Then my turn came to play a solo. I was in the vein to extemporize successfully, and felt that I did so. The guests being now in a graver mood, I took three themes from the previous sonatas, and worked them up to my heart's content; it seemed to give immense pleasure to those present, for they shouted and applauded like mad. Then Baillot gave my quartett; his manner towards me has something very kind, and I was doubly pleased, as he is rather cold at first and seldom makes advances to any one. He appears a good deal depressed by the loss of his situation. I saw a number of old well-known faces, and they asked after you all, and recalled many anecdotes of that former period.

When I was passing through Louvain two years ago with my "Liederspiel" in my head, and my injured knee,* I seized the brass handle of a pump to prevent myself from falling; and when I returned this year in the same miserable diligence, driven by a postilion exactly similar, with a big queue, the "Liederspiel," my knee, and Italy, were all things of the past; and yet the handle of the pump was still hanging there, as clean and brightly rubbed up as ever, having survived 1830, and all the revolutionary storms, and remaining quite unchanged. This is sentimental; my father must not read it, for it is the old story of the past and the present, which we discussed so eagerly one fine evening, and which recurs to me among the crowd here at every step.

---

* Mendelssohn had been thrown out of a cabriolet in London in 1829, and his knee seriously injured.

I thought of it at the Madeleine, and when I went to aunt J——'s, and at the Hôtel des Princes, and at the gallery, which my father showed me fifteen years ago, and when I saw the coloured signs, which at that time impressed me exceedingly, and are now grown brown and shabby.

Moreover this is Christmas Eve; but I feel little interest in it, or in New Year's Night either. Please God, another year may wear a very different aspect, and I will not then go to the theatre on Christmas Eve, as I am about to do to-night, to hear Lablache and Rossini for the first time. How little I care about it! I should much prefer *Polichinelles* and apples to-day, and I think it very doubtful whether the orchestra will play as pretty a symphony as my " Kinder-Sinfonie." * I must be satisfied with it however. I am now modulating into the minor key, a fault with which the " École Allemande" are often reproached, and as I profess not to belong to the latter, the French say I am *cosmopolite*. Heaven defend me from being anything of the kind!

And now good-bye; a thousand compliments from Bertin de Vaux, Girod de l'Ain, Dupont de l'Eure, Tracy, Sacy, Passy and other kind friends. I had intended to have told you in this letter how Salverte attacked the Ministers, and how during this time a little *émeute* took place on the Pont Neuf; how I sat in the Chambers along with Franck, in the midst of St. Simoniens; how witty Dupin was; but no

---

* A " Kinder-Sinfonie," composed by Mendelssohn in the year 1829, for a Christmas family fête.

more at present. May you all be well and happy
this evening, and thinking of me!

FELIX.

Paris, December 28th, 1831.

Dear Madam Fanny,

For three months past I have been thinking of
writing you a musical letter, but my procrastination
has its revenge, for though I have been a fortnight
here, I don't know whether I shall still be able to do
so. I have appeared in every possible mood here;
in that of an inquiring, admiring traveller; a cox-
comb; a Frenchman, and yesterday actually as a
Peer of France; but not yet as a musician. Indeed
there is little likelihood of the latter, for the aspect
of music here is miserable enough.

The concerts in the Conservatoire, which were my
great object, probably will not take place at all, because the Commission of the Ministry wished to give
a Commission to the Commission of the society, to
deprive a Commission of Professors of their share of
the profits; on which the Commission of the Conservatoire replied to the Commission of the Ministry,
that they might go and be hanged (suspended), and
then they would not consent to it. The newspapers
make some very severe comments on this, but you
need not read them, as these papers are prohibited
in Berlin; but you don't lose much by this. The
Opéra Comique is bankrupt, and so it has had

relâche since I came; at the Grand Opéra, they only give little operas, which amuse me, though they neither provoke nor excite me. " Armida " was the last great opera, but they gave it in three acts, and this was two years ago. Choron's "Institut" is closed, the " Chapelle Royale " is gone out like a light; not a single Mass is to be heard on Sundays in all Paris, unless accompanied by serpents. Malibran is to appear here next week for the last time. So much the better, say you : retire within yourself, and write music for " Ach Gott vom Himmel," or a symphony, or the new violin quartett which you mentioned in your letter to me of the 28th, or any other serious composition; but this is even more impossible, for what is going on here is most deeply interesting, and entices you out, suggesting matter for thought and memory and absorbing every moment of time. Accordingly I was yesterday in the Chambre des Pairs, and counted along with them the votes, destined to abolish a very ancient privilege; immediately afterwards I hurried off to the Théâtre Français, where Mars was to appear for the first time for a year past; (she is fascinating beyond conception; a voice that we shall never hear equalled, causing you to weep, and yet to feel pleasure in doing so). To-day I must see Taglioni again, who along with Mars constitutes two Graces (if I find a third in my travels, I mean to marry her), and afterwards I mean to go to Gérard's classical *salon*. I lately went to hear Lablache and Rubini, after hearing Odillon Barrot quarrel with the Ministry. Having seen the pictures in the Louvre in the morning, I went to Baillot's; so what chance is there of living in retirement? The outer world is too tempting.

There are moments, however, when my thoughts turn inwards—such as on that memorable evening, when Lablache sang so beautifully, or on Christmas-day, when there were no bells and no festivities, or when Paul's letter came from London, inviting me to visit him next spring; the said spring to be passed in England. Then I feel that all that now interests me is merely superficial: that I am neither a politician, nor a dancer, nor an actor, nor a *bel esprit*, but a *musician*—so I take courage, and am now writing a professional letter to my dear sister.

My conscience smote me, especially when I read about your new music that you so carefully conducted on my father's birthday, and I reproached myself for not having said a single word to you about your previous composition; but I cannot let you off that, my colleague! What the deuce made you think of setting your G horns so high? Did you ever hear a G horn take the high G without a squeak? I only put this to yourself! and at the end of this introduction, when wind instruments

come in, does not the following note 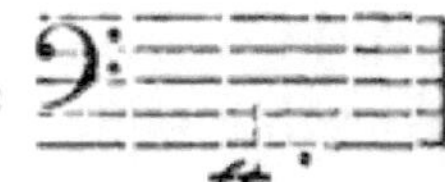

stare you in the face, and do not these deep oboes growl away all pastoral feeling, and all bloom? Do you not know that you ought to take out a license

to sanction your writing the low B for oboes, and
that it is only permitted on particular occasions,
such as witches, or some great grief? Has not the
composer evidently, in the A major air, overloaded
the voice by too many other parts, so that the delicate intention, and the lovely melody of this otherwise charming piece, with all its beauties, is quite
obscured and eclipsed?

To speak seriously, however, this aria is very
beautiful, and particularly fascinating. But I have
a remark to make about your two choruses, which
indeed applies rather to the text than to you. These
two choruses are not sufficiently original. This
sounds absurd; but my opinion is that it is the fault
of the words, that express nothing original; one
single expression might have improved the whole, but
as they now stand, they would be equally suitable for
church music, a cantata, an offertorium, etc. Where,
however, they are not of such universal application,
as for example, the lament at the end, they seem to
be sentimental and not natural. The words of the
last chorus are too material ("mit dem kraftlosen
Mund, und der sich regenden Zunge"). At the
beginning of the aria alone, are the words vigorous
and spirited, and from them emanated the whole of
your lovely piece of music. The choruses are of
course fine, for they are written by you; but in the
first place, it seems to me that they might be by any
other good master, and secondly, as if they were not
necessarily what they are, indeed as if they might
have been *differently* composed. This arises from

the poetry not imposing any particular music. I know that the latter is often the case with my own compositions; but though I am fully aware of the beam in my own eyes, I would fain extract the mote from yours, to relieve you at once from its pressure.

My *résumé* therefore is, that I would advise you to be more cautious in the choice of your words, because, after all, it is not everything in the Bible, even if it suits the theme, that is suggestive of *music;* but you have probably obviated these objections of mine in your new cantata, before being aware of them, in which case, I might as well have said nothing. So much the better if it be so, and then you can prosecute me for defamation! So far as your music and composition are concerned, they quite suit my taste; the young lady's cloven foot nowhere peeps forth, and if I knew any *Kapellmeister* capable of writing such music, I would give him a place at my court. Fortunately I know no such person, and there is no occasion to place you at my right hand at court, as you are there already.*

When do you mean to send me something new to cheer me? Pray do so soon! As far as regards myself, shortly after my arrival here, I had one of those attacks of musical spleen, when all music, and more especially one's own, becomes actually hateful. I felt thoroughly unmusical, and did nothing but eat and sleep, and that revived me. F——, to whom I complained of my state, instantly constructed a

---

* A play upon Fanny Hensel's house, in a court—No. 3, Leipziger Strasse.

musical theory on the subject, proving that it could not be otherwise; I however think exactly the reverse; but though we are so entirely dissimilar, and have as many differences as a Bushman and Caffre, still we like each other exceedingly.

With L——, too, I get on famously. He is very pleasing, and the most *dilettante* of all the *dilettanti* I ever met. He knows everything by heart, and plays wrong basses to them all; he is only deficient in arrogance, for with all his undeniable talent, he is very modest and retiring. I am much with him, because he is a benevolent, kind-hearted man; we should thoroughly agree on all points, if he would not consider me a *doctrinaire*, and persist in talking politics (a subject that I wish to avoid for at least a hundred and twenty reasons; and chiefly because I don't in the least understand it); besides, he delights in hitting at Germany, and in depreciating London in favour of Paris. Both these things are prejudicial to my *constitution*, and whoever assails that, I must defend it and dispute with him.

I was yesterday studying your new music, and enjoying it, when Kalkbrenner came in, and played various new compositions. The man is become quite romantic, purloins themes, ideas, and similar trifles, from Hiller, writes pieces in F sharp minor, practises every day for several hours, and is as he always was, a knowing fellow. Every time I see him, he inquires after "my charming sister, whom he likes so much, and who has such a fine talent for playing and composing." My invariable reply is, that she has not given up music, that she is very industrious. and that I love her very much; which is all true. And now farewell, dear sister. May you be well and happy, and may we meet at the New Year. FELIX.

To CARL IMMERMANN IN DÜSSELDORF.

Paris, January 11th, 1832.

You permitted me to give you occasional tidings of myself, and since I came here, I have daily intended to do so; the excitement here is however so great, that till to-day I have never been able to write. When I contrast this constant whirl and commotion, and the thousand distractions among a foreign people, with your house in the garden, and your warm winter room, your wish to exchange with me and to come here in my place, often recurs to me, and I almost wish I had taken you at your word. You must indeed in that case have remained all the same in your winter room, so that I might come out to you through the snow, take my usual place in the corner, and listen to the "Schwanritter;" for there is more life in it than in all the tumult here.

In a word, I rejoice at the prospect of my return to Germany; everything there is indeed on a small scale, and homely, if you will, but *men* live there;

men who know what art really is, who do not admire, nor praise, in fact who do not *criticize*, but *create*. You do not admit this, but it is only because you are yourself among the number.

I beg you will not however think that I am like one of those German youths with long hair, lounging about listlessly, and pronouncing the French superficial, and Paris frivolous. I only say all this because I now thoroughly enjoy and admire Paris, and am becoming better acquainted with it, and especially as I am writing to you in Düsseldorf. I have, on the contrary, cast myself headlong into the vortex, and do nothing the whole day but see new objects, the Chambers of Peers and Deputies, pictures and theatres, dio- neo- cosmo- and panoramas, constant parties, etc. Moreover, the musicians here are as numerous as the sands on the sea-shore, all hating each other; so each must be individually visited, and wary diplomacy is advisable, for they are all gossips, and what one says to another, the whole corps know next morning.

The days have thus flown past hitherto as if only half as long as they were in reality, and as yet I have not been able to compose a single bar; in a few days, however, this exotic life will cease. My head is now dizzy from all I have seen and wondered at; but I then intend to collect my thoughts, and set to work, when I shall feel once more happy and domesticated.

My chief pleasure is going to the little theatres in the evening, because there French life and the French people are truly mirrored; the " Gymnase

Dramatique" is my particular favourite, where nothing is given but small *vaudevilles*. The extreme bitterness and deep animosity which pervade all these little comedies, are most remarkable, and although partially cloaked by the prettiest phrases, and the most lively acting, become only the more conspicuous. Politics everywhere play the chief part, which might have sufficed to make me dislike these theatres, for we have enough of them *elsewhere;* but the politics of the "Gymnase" are of a light and ironical description,—referring to the occurrences of the day, and to the newspapers, in order to excite laughter and applause, and at last you can't help laughing and applauding with the rest. Politics and sensuality are the two grand points of interest, round which everything circles; and in the many pieces I have seen, an attack on the Ministry, and a scene of seduction, were never absent.

The whole style of the *vaudeville*, introducing certain conventional music at the end of the scene in every piece, when the actors partly sing and partly declaim some couplets with a witty point, is thoroughly French; we could never learn this, nor in fact wish to do so, for this mode of connecting the wit of the day with an established *refrain*, does not exist in our conversation, nor in our ideas. I cannot imagine anything more striking and effective, nor yet more prosaic.

A great sensation has been recently caused here, by a new piece at the Gymnase, "Le Luthier de Lisbonne," which forms the delight of the public.

A stranger is announced in the play-bills; scarcely does he appear when all the audience begin to laugh and to applaud, and you learn that the actor is a close imitation of Don Miguel, in gestures, manner, and costume; he proceeds to announce that he is a king, and the fortune of the piece is made. The more stupid, uncivilized, and uncouth, the Unknown appears, the greater is the enjoyment of the public, who allow none of his gestures or speeches to pass unobserved. He takes refuge from a riot in the house of this instrument maker, who is the most devoted of all royalists, but unluckily the husband of a very pretty woman. One of Don Miguel's favourites has forced her to grant him a rendezvous for the ensuing night, and he begs the king—who arrives at this moment—to give him his aid, by causing the husband to be beheaded. Don Miguel replies, "Très volontiers," and while the Luthier recognizes him, and falls at his feet, beside himself from joy, Don Miguel signs his death-warrant, but also that of his favourite, whom he means to replace with the pretty woman. At each enormity that he commits, we laugh and applaud, and are immensely delighted with this stupid stage Don Miguel. So ends the first act. In the second, it is supposed to be midnight; the pretty wife alone and agitated. Don Miguel jumps in at the window, and does all in his power to gain her favour, making her dance and sing to him, but she cannot endure him, and falls at his feet, imploring him to spare her; on which he seizes her, and drags her repeatedly round the stage, and if she did not make a snatch at a knife, and then a sudden knocking ensue, she might have been in a bad plight; at the close, the worthy Luthier rescues the king from the hands of the French soldiery, who are just arrived, and of whose valour, and love of liberty, ho has a great horror. So the piece ends happily.

A little comedy followed, where the wife betrays her husband, and has a lover; and another, where the man is faithless to his wife, and is maintained by his mistress; this is succeeded by a satire on the new constructions in the Tuileries, and on the Ministry, and so it goes on.

I cannot say how it may be at the French Opera, for it is bankrupt, so there has been no acting there since I came. In the Académie Royale, however, Meyerbeer's "Robert le Diable" is played every night with great success: the house is always crowded, and the music has given general satisfaction. There is an expenditure of all possible means of producing stage effect, that I never saw equalled on any stage. All who can sing, dance, or act in Paris, sing, dance, and act on this occasion.

The *sujet* is romantic; that is, the devil appears in the piece—(this is quite sufficient romance and imagination for the Parisians). It is however very bad; and were it not for two brilliant scenes of seduction it would produce no effect whatever. The devil is a poor devil, and appears in armour, for the purpose of leading astray his son Robert, a Norman knight, who loves a Sicilian princess. He succeeds in inducing him to stake his money and all his personal property (that is, his sword) at dice, and then makes him commit sacrilege, giving him a magic branch, which enables him to penetrate into the Princess's apartment, and renders him irresistible. The son does all this with apparent willingness; but when at the end he is to assign himself to his father, who declares that he loves him, and cannot live without him, the devil, or rather the poet Scribe, introduces a peasant girl, who has in her possession the will of Robert's deceased mother, and reads him the document, which makes him doubt the story he has been told; so the devil is obliged to sink down through a trap-door at midnight, with his purpose unfulfilled, on which Robert marries the Princess, and the peasant girl, it seems, is intended to represent the principle of good. The devil is called Bertram.

I cannot imagine how any music could be composed on such a cold, formal *extravaganza* as this, and so the opera does not satisfy me. It is throughout frigid and heartless; and where this is the case it produces no effect on me. The people extol the music, but where warmth and truth are wanting, I have no test to apply.

Michael Beer set off to-day for Havre. It seems he intends to compose poetry there; and I now remember that when I met you one day at Schadow's, and maintained that he was no poet, your rejoinder was, "That is a matter of taste." I seldom see Heine, because he is entirely absorbed in liberal ideas and in politics. He has recently published sixty "Frühlings Lieder." Very few of them seem to me either genuine or truthful, but these few are indeed inimitable. Have you read them? They appeared in the second volume of the "Reisebilder." Börne intends to publish some new volumes of letters: he and I are full of enthusiasm for Malibran and Taglioni; all these gentlemen are abusing and reviling Germany and all that is German, and yet they cannot speak even tolerable French; I think this rather provoking.

Pray excuse my having sent you so much gossip, and for writing to you on such a disreputable margin of paper; but it is long since we met; and as for a time I could see you every day, it has become quite a necessity to write to you; so you must not take it amiss. You once promised to send me a few lines in reply: I don't know whether I may venture to remind you of this, but I should really be glad to hear how you pass your time, and what novelty a certain cupboard in the corner contains; how you get on with "Merlin," and my "Schwanritter," the sound of which still vibrates in my ears like sweet music; and also whether you sometimes think of me, and of next May, and "The Tempest." It is certainly expecting a good deal to ask you for an early reply to my letter, but I fear that you had enough of the first, and would rather not receive a second; therefore I take courage, and beg for an answer to this one. But I need not have asked this, for you usually guess my wishes before I can utter them; and if you are as kindly disposed towards

me now as you were then, you will fulfil this desire
of mine as you did all the others.—Yours,

FELIX MENDELSSOHN BARTHOLDY.

Paris, January 14th, 1832.

I now first begin to feel at home here, and really
to know Paris; it is indeed the most singular and
amusing place imaginable; but for one who is no
politician, it does not possess so much interest. So
I have become a *doctrinaire*. I read my newspaper
every morning, form my own opinion about peace
and war, and, only among friends, confess that I
know nothing of the matter.

This is however not the case with F——, who is
completely absorbed in the vortex of dilettantism and
dogmatism, and really believes himself quite adapted
to be a Minister. It is a sad pity, for nothing good
will ever come of it. He has sufficient sense to be
always occupied, but not enough to conduct any
affair. He is a *dilettante* on all points, and has a
clever knack of criticizing others, but he produces
nothing. We continue on the same intimate terms,
meeting every day, and liking each other's society,
but inwardly we remain strangers. I suspect that
he writes for the public papers; he is very much
with Heine, and chatters abuse against Germany
like a magpie; all this I much dislike, and as I
really have a sincere regard for him, it worries me.

I suppose I must try to become accustomed to it, but it is really too sad to know where a person is deficient, and yet to be unable to remedy their defects. Moreover he grows visibly older; so this irregular, unoccupied life is the less suitable for him.

A—— has left his parents' house, and gone to the Rue Monsigny,* where body and soul are equally engrossed. I have in my possession an appeal to mankind from P—— in which he makes his confession of faith, and invites every one to surrender a share of his property, however small, to the St. Simoniens; calling on all artists to devote their genius in future to this religion; to compose better music than Rossini or Beethoven; to build temples of peace, and to paint like Raphael or David. I have twenty copies of this pamphlet, which P—— desired me, dear Father, to send to you. I rest satisfied by sending you *one*, which you will find quite enough, and even that one, by some private hand of course.

It is a bad sign of the state of the public mind here, that such a monstrous doctrine, in such detestable prose, should ever have existed, or impressed others; for it appears that the students of the Polytechnic School take considerable interest in it. It is difficult to say how far it may be carried, when there is temptation offered on every side, promising honour to one, fame to another; to me, an admiring public, and to the poor, money; while by their cold

---

* At that time the residence of the St. Simoniens.

estimate of talent, they check all effort and all progress. And then their ideas as to universal brotherhood, their disbelief in hell, and the devil, and eternal perdition, and of the annihilation of all egotism,—ideas, which in our country spring from nature, and prevail in every part of Christendom, and without which I should not wish to live, but which they however regard as a new invention and discovery, constantly repeating that they mean to transform the world, and to render mankind happy. A—— coolly tells me that he does not require to improve himself, but others only; because he is not at all imperfect, but on the contrary, perfect. They not only praise and compliment each other, but all those whom they wish to gain over; extolling any talent or capability you may possess, and lamenting that such great powers should be lost, by adhering to the old-fashioned notions of duty, vocation, and action, as they were formerly interpreted. When I listen to all this, it does seem to me a melancholy mystification. I attended a meeting last Sunday, where all the Fathers sat in a circle: then came the principal Father and demanded their reports, praising and blaming them, addressing the assembly, and issuing his commands; to me it was quite awful! A—— has completely renounced his parents, and lives with the Fathers, his disciples, and is endeavouring to procure a loan for their benefit; but enough of this subject!

A Pole gives a concert next week, where I am to play in a composition for six performers, along with

Kalkbrenner, Hiller, and Co.; do not be surprised
therefore if you see my name mutilated, as in the
"Messager" lately, when the death of Professor
Flegel (Hegel) was announced from Berlin, and all
the papers copied it.

I have set to work again, and live most agreeably.
I have not yet been able to write to you about the
theatres, although they occupy me very much. How
plain are the symptoms of bitterness and excitement
even in the most insignificant farce; how invariably
everything bears a reference to politics; how completely what is called the Romantic School has
infected all the Parisians, for they think of nothing
on the stage now but the plague, the gallows, the
devil, etc., one striving to outstrip the other in
horrors, and in liberalism; in the midst of these
misères and fooleries, how charming is a talent like
that of Léontine Fay, who is the perfection of grace
and fascination, and remains unsullied by the ab-
surdities she is compelled to utter and to act. How
strange all these contrasts are! but this I reserve
for future discussion.   FELIX.

Paris, January 21st, 1832.

In every letter of yours I receive a little hit, because my answers are not very punctual, and so I
reply without delay to your questions, dear Fanny,
with regard to the new works that I am about to
publish.

It occurred to me that the octett and the quintett might make a very good appearance among my works, being in fact better than many compositions that already figure there. As the publication of these pieces costs me nothing, but, on the contrary, I derive profit from them, and not wishing to confuse their chronological order, my idea is to publish the following pieces at Easter:—quintett and octett (the latter also arranged as a duet), "Midsummer Night's Dream," seven songs without words, six songs with words; on my return to Germany, six pieces of sacred music, and finally, if I can get any one to print it, and to pay for it, the symphony in D minor. As soon as I have performed "Meeresstille" at my concert in Berlin, it will also appear. I cannot however bring out "The Hebrides" here, because, as I wrote to you at the time, I do not consider it finished; the middle movement forte in D major is very stupid, and the whole modulations savour more of counterpoint, than of train oil and seagulls and salt fish—and it ought to be exactly the reverse. I like the piece too well to allow it to be performed in an imperfect state, and I hope soon to be able to work at it, and to have it ready for England, and the Michaelmas fair at Leipzig.

You inquire also why I do not compose the Italian symphony in A major. Because I am composing the Saxon overture in A minor, which is to precede the "Walpurgis Night," that the work may be played with all due honour at the said Berlin concert, and elsewhere.

You wish me to remove to the Marais, and to write the whole day. My dear child, that would never do; I have, at the most, only the prospect of three months to see Paris, so I must throw myself into the stream; indeed, this is why I came; everything here is too bright, and too attractive to be neglected; it rounds off my pleasant travelling reminiscences, and forms a fine colossal key-stone, and so I consider that to see Paris is at this moment my chief vocation. The publishers too are standing on each side of me like veritable Satans, demanding music for the piano, and offering to pay for it. By Heavens! I don't know whether I shall be able to withstand this, or write some kind of trio; for I hope you believe me to be superior to the temptation of a *pot-pourri;* but I should like to compose a couple of good trios.

On Thursday the first rehearsal of my overture takes place, which is to be performed in the second concert at the "Conservatoire." In the third my symphony in D minor is to follow. Habeneck talks of seven or eight rehearsals, which will be very welcome to me. Moreover I am also to play something at Erard's concert; so I shall play my Munich concerto, but I must first practise it well. Then, a note is lying beside me, "Le Président du Conseil, Ministre de l'Intérieur, et Madame Casimir Périer prient, " etc., on Monday evening to a ball; this evening there is to be music at Habeneck's; to-morrow at Schlesinger's; Tuesday, the first public *soirée* at Baillot's; on Wednesday, Hiller plays his Con-

certo in the Hôtel de Ville, and this always lasts till
past midnight. Let those who like it, lead a solitary
life! these are all things that cannot be refused. So
when am I to compose? In the forenoon? Yesterday, first Hiller came, then Kalkbrenner, then Habeneck. The day before that, came Baillot, Eichthal,
and Rodrigues. Perhaps very early in the morning?
Well, I do compose then—so you are confuted!

P—— was with me yesterday, talking St. Simo-
nienism, and either from a conviction of my stupidity, or my shrewdness, he made me disclosures which
shocked me so much, that I resolved never again to
go either to him or to his confederates. Early this
morning Hiller rushed in, and told me he had just
witnessed the arrest of the St. Simoniens. He wished
to hear their orations; but the Fathers did not
come. All of a sudden soldiers made their way in,
and requested those present to disperse as quickly
as possible, inasmuch as M. Enfantin and the others
had been arrested in the Rue Monsigny. A party
of National Guards are placed in the street, and
other soldiers marched up there; everything is
sealed up, and now the *procès* will begin. My **B**
minor quartett, which is lying in the Rue Monsigny,
is also sealed up. The adagio alone is in the style
of the "juste Milieu," all the other parts *mouve-
ment*. I suppose I shall eventually be obliged to
play it before a jury.

I was lately standing beside the Abbé Bardin at
a large party, listening to the performance of my
quartett in A minor. At the last movement my

neighbour pulled my coat, and said : " Il a cela dans une de ses sinfonies." " Qui ?" said I, rather embarrassed. " Beethoven, l'auteur de ce quatuor," said he, with a consequential air. This was a very doubtful compliment ! but is it not famous that my quartett should be played in the classes of the Conservatoire, and that the pupils there are practising off their fingers to play " Ist es wahr ?"

I have just come from St. Sulpice, where the organist showed off his organ to me ; it sounded like a full chorus of old women's voices ; but they maintain that it is the finest organ in Europe if it were only put into proper order, which would cost thirty thousand francs. The effect of the *canto fermo,* accompanied by a serpent, those who have not heard it could scarcely conceive, and clumsy bells are ringing all the time.

The post is going, so I must conclude my gossip, or I might go on in this manner till the day after to-morrow. I have not yet told you that Bach's " Passion " is announced for performance in London, at Easter, in the Italian Opera House.—Yours,

FELIX.

Paris, February 4th, 1832.

You will, I am sure, excuse my writing you only a few words to-day : it was but yesterday that I heard of my irreparable loss.* Many hopes, and a

* The death of his friend Edward Ritz, the violin player.

pleasant bright period of my life have departed with him, and I never again can feel so happy. I must now set about forming new plans, and building fresh castles in the air; the former ones are irrevocably gone, for he was interwoven with them all. I shall never be able to think of my boyish days, nor of the ensuing ones, without connecting him with them, and I had hoped, till now, that it might be the same for the future. I must endeavour to inure myself to this, but I can recall no one thing without being reminded of him; I shall never hear music, or write it, without thinking of him; all this makes the rending asunder of such a tie doubly distressing. The former epoch has now wholly passed away, but not only do I lose that, but also the man I so sincerely loved. If I never had any especial reason for loving him, or if I no longer had such reasons, I must have loved him all the same, even without a reason. He loved me too, and the knowledge that there was such a man in the world—one on whom you could repose, and who lived to love you, and whose wishes and aims were identical with your own—this is all over: it is the most severe blow I have ever received, and never can I forget him.

This was the celebration of my birthday. When I was listening to Baillot on Tuesday, and said to Hiller that I only knew one man who could play the music I loved for me, L—— was standing beside me, and knew what had happened, but did not give me the letter. He was not aware indeed that yesterday was my birthday, but he broke it to me by degrees yesterday morning, and then I recalled previous anniversaries, and took a review of the past, as every one should on his birthday; I remembered how invariably on this day he arrived with some special gift which he had long thought of, and which was always as pleasing and agreeable and welcome as himself. The day was a melancholy one to me; I could neither do anything, nor think of anything, but the one subject.

To-day I have compelled myself to work, and succeeded. My overture in A minor is finished. I think of writing some pieces here, which will be well remunerated.

I beg you will tell me every particular about him, and every detail, no matter how trifling; it will be a comfort to me to hear of him once more. The octett parts, so neatly copied by him, are lying before me at this moment, and remind me of· him. I hope shortly to recover my usual equanimity, and to be able to write to you in better spirits and more at length. A new chapter in my life has begun, but as yet it has no title. Your FELIX.

Paris, February 13th, 1832.

I am now leading a quiet, pleasant life here; neither my present frame of mind, nor the pleasures of society, tempt me to enter into gaiety. Here, and indeed everywhere else, society is uninteresting, and not improving, and owing to the late hours, monopolizing a great deal of time. I do not refuse, however, when there is to be good music. I will write all particulars to Zelter of the first concert in the Conservatoire. The performers there play quite admirably, and in so finished a style, that it is indeed a pleasure to hear them; they delight in it themselves, and each takes the greatest possible trouble; the leader is an energetic, experienced musician, so they cannot fail to go well together.

To-morrow my A minor quartett is to be performed in public. Cherubini says of Beethoven's later music, "Ça me fait éternuer," and so I think it probable that the whole public will sneeze to-morrow. The performers are Baillot, Sauzay, Urhan, and Norblin—the best here.

My overture in A minor is completed; it represents bad weather. A few days ago I finished an introduction, where it thaws, and spring arrives; I have counted the sheets of the "Walpurgis Night," revised the seven numbers a little, and then boldly written underneath—Milan, July; Paris, February. I think it will please you. I must now write an adagio for my quintett without delay; the performers are calling loudly for one, and they are right.

I do wish you could hear a rehearsal of my "Midsummer Night's Dream" at the Conservatoire, where they play it most beautifully. It is not yet certain whether it will be ready by next Sunday; there are to be two more rehearsals before then, but as yet it has only been twice played over. I think however that it will do, and I would rather it was given on

Sunday than at the third concert, because I am to play on behalf of the poor on the 26th (something of Weber's), and on the 27th at Erard's concert (my Munich Concerto), and at other places, and I should like my composition to appear first at the "Conservatoire." I am also to play there, and the members are anxious that I should give them a Sonata of Beethoven's; it may seem bold, but I prefer his Concerto in G major, which is quite unknown here.

I look forward with the utmost delight to the symphony in D minor, which is to be rehearsed next week; I certainly never dreamt that I should hear it in Paris for the first time.

I often visit the theatre, where I see a great display of wit and talent, but a degree of immorality that almost exceeds belief. It is supposed that no lady can go to the "Gymnase"—still they do go. Depict me to yourself as reading "Notre Dame," dining with one or other of my acquaintances every day, and taking advantage of the lovely bright spring weather after three o'clock, to take a walk, and to pay a few visits, and to look at the gaily-dressed ladies and gentlemen in the splendid gardens of the Tuileries—then you will have my day in Paris. Adieu. FELIX.

Paris, February 21st, 1832.

Almost every letter that I receive from you now, announces some sad loss. Yesterday I got the one in which you tell me about poor U——, whom I shall no longer find with you; so this is not a time for idle talk; I feel that I must work, and strive to make progress.

I have composed a grand adagio as an intermezzo for the quintett. It is called "Nachruf," and it occurred to me, as I had to compose something for Baillot, who plays so beautifully, and is so kindly disposed towards me, and who wishes to perform it in public; and yet he is only a recent acquaintance. Two days ago my overture to the "Midsummer Night's Dream" was given for the first time at a concert in the Conservatoire. It caused me great pleasure, for it went admirably, and seemed also to please the audience. It is to be repeated at one of the ensuing concerts, and my symphony, which has been rather delayed on this account, is to be rehearsed on Friday or Saturday. In the fourth or fifth concert, I am to play Beethoven's Concerto in G major.

The musicians are all amazement at the honours conferred on me by the Conservatoire. They played my A minor quartett wonderfully last Tuesday; with such fire and precision, that it was delightful to listen to them, and as I can never again hear Ritz, I shall probably never hear it better given. It appeared to make a great impression on the audience, and at the scherzo they were quite uproarious.

It is now high time, dear father, to write you a few words with regard to my travelling plans, and on this occasion in a more serious strain than usual, for many reasons. I must first, in taking a general view of the past, refer to what you designed to be the chief object of my journey; desiring me strictly to adhere to it. I was closely to examine the various countries, and to fix on the one where I wished to live and to work; I was further to make known my name and capabilities, in order that the people, among whom I resolved to settle, should receive me well, and not be wholly ignorant of my career; and, finally, I was to take advantage of my own good fortune, and your kindness, to press forward in my subsequent efforts. It is a happy feeling to be able to say, that I believe this has been the case.

Always excepting those mistakes which are not discovered till too late, I think I have fulfilled the appointed object. People now know that I exist, and that I have a purpose, and any talent that I display, they are ready to approve and to accept. They have *made advances* to me here, and *proposed* to take my music, which they seldom do; as all the others, even Onslow, have been obliged to *offer* their compositions. The London Philharmonic have requested me to perform something new of my own there on the 10th of March. I also got the commission from Munich without taking any step whatever to obtain it, and indeed not till *after* my concert. It is my intention to give a concert here (if possible) and certainly in London in April, if the cholera does not prevent my going there; and this on my own account, in order to make money; I hope,

29*

therefore, I may say that I have also fulfilled this part of your wish—that I should make myself known to the public before returning to you.

Your injunction, too, to make choice of the country that I preferred to live in, I have equally performed, at least in a general point of view. That country is Germany. This is a point on which I have now quite made up my mind. I cannot yet, however, decide on the particular city, for the most important of all, which for various reasons has so many attractions for me, I have not yet thought of in this light— I allude to Berlin. On my return, therefore, I must ascertain whether I can remain and establish myself there, according to my views and wishes, after having seen and enjoyed other places.

This is also why I do not endeavour to get the commission for an opera here. If I compose really good music, which in these days is indispensable, it will both be understood and valued in Germany. (This has been the case with all the good operas there.) If I compose indifferent music, it will be quickly forgotten in Germany, but here it would be often performed and extolled, and sent to Germany, and given there on the authority of Paris, as we daily see. But I do not choose this; and if I am not capable of composing good music, I have no wish to be praised for it. So I shall first try Germany; and if things go so badly that I can no longer live there, I can then have recourse to some foreign country. Besides, few German theatres are so bad or in so dilapidated a condition as the Opéra Comique here. One bankruptcy succeeds another. When Cherubini is asked why he does not allow his operas to be given there, he replies, "Je ne sais pas donner des opéras, sans chœur, sans orchestre, sans chanteurs, et sans décorations." The Grand Opéra has bespoken operas for years to come, so there is no chance of anything being accepted by it for the next three or four years.

In the meantime therefore I intend to return to you to write my "Tempest," and to see how it succeeds. The plan, therefore, dear father, that I wish to lay before you is this—to remain here till the end of March, or the beginning of April, (the invitation to the Philharmonic for the 10th of March, I have of course declined, or rather postponed,) then to go to London for a couple of months. If the Rhenish musical festival takes place, to which I am summoned, I shall go to Düsseldorf; and if not, return direct to you by the shortest road, and be by your side in the garden soon after Whitsunday. Farewell!   FELIX.

Paris, March 15th, 1832.

Dear Mother,

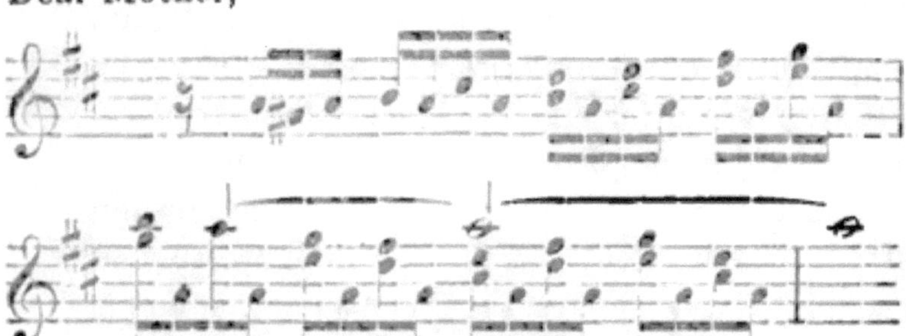

This is the 15th of March, 1832. May every happiness and good attend you on this day. You prefer *receiving* my letter on your birthday, to its being written on the day itself: but forgive me for saying that I cannot reconcile myself to this. My father said that no one could tell what might occur subsequently, therefore the letter ought to arrive on the anniversary of the day; but then I have this feeling in *double* measure, as I neither in that case know what is to occur to *you* on that day, nor to *myself;* but if your birthday be actually arrived, then I almost feel as if I were beside you, though you cannot hear my congratulations; but I can then send them to you, without any other solicitude than that of absence. This too will soon be over, please God. May He preserve you, and all at home, happily to me!

I have now begun to throw myself in right earnest into a musical life, and as I know this must be satisfactory to you, I will write some details; for a letter and a sketch-book that I wished to send you some days ago by Mortier's aide-de-camp, are still waiting, like all Paris, for the departure of the Marshal, which does not however take place. If the letter and the book do eventually reach you through this man, pray give a kind reception to the whole consignment, but especially to the man (Count Perthuis), for he is one of the most friendly and amiable persons I ever met with.

I had told you in that letter, that I am to play Beethoven's Concerto in G major two days hence, in the Conservatoire, and that the whole Court are to be present for the first time at the concert. K—— is ready to poison me from envy; he at first tried by a thousand intrigues to prevent my playing altogether, and when he heard that the Queen was actually coming, he did everything in his power to get me out of the way. Happily all the other members of the Conservatoire, the all-powerful Habeneck in particular, are my faithful allies, and so he signally failed. He is the only musician here who acts unkindly and hypocritically towards me; and though I never placed much confidence in him, still it is always a very painful sensation to know that you are in the society of a person who hates you, but is careful not to show it.

The 17th.

I could not finish this letter, because during the last few days the incessant music I told you of, has been so overwhelming, that I really scarcely knew which way to turn. A mere catalogue therefore of all I have done, and have still to do, must suffice for to-day, and at the same time plead my excuse.

I have just come back from a rehearsal at the Conservatoire. We rehearsed steadily; twice yesterday, and to-day almost everything repeated, but now all goes swimmingly. If the audience to-morrow are only half as enchanted as the orchestra to-day, we shall do well; for they shouted loudly for the adagio *da capo*, and Habeneck made them a little speech, to point out to them that at the close there was a solo bar, which they must be so good as to wait for. **You** would be gratified to see all the little kindnesses and **courtesies the** latter shows me. **At the** end **of each movement of** the symphony, he asks me if there is anything I do not approve of, so I have been able for the first time, to introduce into the French orchestra some favourite *nuances* of my own.

After the rehearsal Baillot played my octett in his class, and if any man in the world can play it, he is the man. His performance was finer than I ever heard it, and so was that of Urhan, Norblin, and the others, who all attacked **the piece with** the most ardent energy **and spirit.**

Besides **all this, I must finish** the arrangement of the overture and the octett, and revise the quintett, as Simrock has bought it. I must write out " **Lieder," and enjoy** the author's delight **of working up my** B minor quartett, for it is to be brought out **here by** two different publishers, who have requested me to make some alterations before it is published. Finally, I have *soirées* every evening. To-night Bohrer's; to-morrow **a** fête, with all **the** violin *gamins* of the Conservatoire; next day, Rothschild; Tuesday, **the** Société des Beaux-Arts; Wednesday my octett at the Abbé Bardin's; Thursday my octett at Madame Kiéné's; Friday, a **concert** at Érard's; Sunday, **a concert at** Léo's; and lastly, **on Monday** —laugh if you choose—my octett is to be performed in a church, **at a** funeral Mass in commemoration of Beethoven. This is the strangest thing the world ever yet saw, but I could not refuse, and I in some degree enjoy the thoughts of being present, when Low Mass is read during the scherzo. I can scarcely imagine anything more absurd than a priest at the altar and my scherzo going on. It is like travelling *incognito*. Last of all Baillot gives a grand concert on the 7th of April, and so I have promised him to remain here till then, and to play a Concerto of Mozart's for him, and some other piece.

On the 8th I take my place in the diligence, and set off to London, but before doing so I shall have heard my symphony in the Conservatoire, and sold various pieces, and shall leave this, rejoicing in the friendly reception I have met with from the musicians here.—Farewell!   FELIX.

Paris, March 31st, 1832.

Pray forgive my long silence, but I had nothing cheering to communicate, and am always very unwilling to write gloomy letters. Indeed, this being the case, I had better still have remained silent, for I am in anything but a gay mood. But now that we have the spectre here,* I mean to write to you regularly, that you may know that I am well, and pursuing my work.

The sad news of Goethe's loss makes me feel poor indeed! What a blow to the country! It is another of those mournful even's connected with my stay

* The cholera.

here, which will always recur to my mind at the very name of Paris; and not all the kindness I have received, nor the tumult and excitement, nor the life and gaiety here, can ever efface this impression. May it please God to preserve me from still worse tidings, and grant us all a happy meeting; this is the chief thing!

Various circumstances have induced me to delay my departure from here for at least a fortnight,— that is, till the middle of April; and the idea of my concert has begun to revive in my mind; I mean to accomplish it too, if the cholera does not deter people from musical, or any other kind of réunions. We shall know this in the course of a week, and in any case I must remain here till then. I believe however that everything will go on in the usual regular course, and "Figaro" prove to be in the right, who wrote an article called "Enfoncé le choléra," in which he says that Paris is the grave of all reputations, for no one there ever admired anything; yawning at Paganini (he does not seem to please much this time), and not even looking round in the street at an Emperor or a Dey; so possibly this malady might also lose its formidable reputation there.

Count Perthuis has no doubt told you of my playing at the Conservatoire. The French say that it was *un beau succès*, and the audience were pleased. The Queen, too, sent me all sorts of fine compliments on the subject. On Saturday I am again to play twice in public. My octett, in church on Monday last, exceeded in absurdity anything the world ever saw or heard of. While the priest was officiating at the altar during the scherzo, it really sounded like "Fliegenschnauz und Mückennas, verfluchte Dilettanten." The people however considered it very fine sacred music.

I am indeed delighted, dear Father, that my quartett in B minor pleases you; it is a favourite of mine, and I like to play it, although the adagio is much too cloying; still, the scherzo that follows has all the more effect. I can see that you seem rather inclined to deride my A minor quartett, when you say that there is a piece of instrumental music which has made you rack your brains to discover the composer's thoughts; when, in fact, he probably had no thoughts at all. I must defend the work, for I love it; but it certainly depends very much on the way in which it is executed, and one single musician who could perform it with zeal and sympathy, as Taubert did, would make a vast difference.—Your

FELIX.

EXTRACT FROM A LETTER FROM LONDON.

London, April 27th, 1832.

I wish I could only describe how happy I feel to be here once more; how much I like everything, and how gratified I am by the kindness of old friends; but as it is all going on at this moment, I must be brief for to-day.

I have also a number of people to seek out whom I have not yet seen, whilst I have been living with Klingemann, Rosen, and Moscheles, in as close intimacy as if we had never been parted. They form the nucleus of my present sojourn; we see each other every day; it is such a pleasure to me to be once more with good, earnest men, and true friends, with whom I do not require to be on my guard, nor to study them either. Moscheles and his wife show me a degree of touching kindness, which I value the more as my regard for them increases; and then the feeling of restored health, as if I lived afresh, and had come anew into this world—all these are combined.*

May 11th.

I cannot describe to you the happiness of these first weeks here. As from time to time every evil seems to accumulate, as it did during my winter in Paris, where I lost some of my most beloved friends, and never felt at home, and at last became very ill; so the reverse sometimes occurs, and thus it is in this charming country, where I am once more amongst friends, and am well, and among well-wishers, and enjoy in the fullest measure the sensation of returning health. Moreover it is warm, the lilacs are in bloom, and music is going on: only imagine how pleasant all this is!

I must really describe one happy morning last

---

* Felix Mendelssohn had an attack of cholera during the last weeks of his stay in Paris.

week : of all the flattering demonstrations I have hitherto received, it is the one which has most touched and affected me, and perhaps the only one which I shall always recall with fresh pleasure. There was a rehearsal last Saturday at the Philharmonic, where however nothing of mine was given, my overture not being yet written out. After "Beethoven's Pastoral Symphony," during which I was in a box, I wished to go into the room to talk to some old friends; scarcely, however, had I gone down below, when one of the orchestra called out, "There is Mendelssohn!" on which they all began shouting, and clapping their hands to such a degree, that for a time I really did not know what to do; and when this was over, another called out "Welcome to him!" on which the same uproar recommenced, and I was obliged to cross the room, and to clamber into the orchestra and return thanks.

Never can I forget it, for it was more precious to me than any distinction, as it showed me that the *musicians* loved me, and rejoiced at my coming, and I cannot tell you what a glad feeling this was.

———◆———

May 18th.

Dear Father,

I have received your letter of the 9th; God grant that Zelter may by this time be safe, and out of danger! You say indeed that he already is so, but

I shall anxiously expect your next letter, to see the news of his recovery confirmed. I have dreaded this ever since Goethe's death, but when it actually occurs, it is a very different thing. May Heaven avert it!

Pray tell me also what you mean by saying "there is no doubt that Zelter both wishes, and requires, to have you with him, because, at all events for the present, it is quite impossible for him to carry on the Academy, whence it is evident that if you do not undertake it, another must." Has Zelter expressed this wish to you, or do you only imagine that he entertains it? If the former were the case, I would instantly, on receiving your reply, write to Zelter, and offer him every service in my power, of every kind, and try to relieve him from all his labours, for as long a period as he desired; and this it certainly would be my duty to do.

I intended to have written to Lichtenstein before my return, about the proposal formerly made to me,* but of course I have given up all thoughts of doing so at present; for on no account would I assume that Zelter could not resume his duties, and even in that event, I could not reconcile myself to discuss the matter with any one but himself; every other mode of proceeding I should consider unfair towards him. If however he requires my services, I am ready, and shall rejoice if I can be of any use to him, but still more so, if he does not want me, and is en-

---

* In reference to a situation in the Singacademie.

tirely recovered. I beg you will write me a few words on this subject.

I must now inform you of my plans and engagements till I leave this. Yesterday I finished the "Rondeau brillant," and I am to play it this day week at Mori's evening concert. The day after I rehearse my Munich Concerto at the Philharmonic, and play it on Monday the 28th at their concert; on the 1st of June Moscheles' concert, where, with him, I play a Concerto of Mozart's for two pianos, and conduct my two overtures, "The Hebrides" and "The Midsummer Night's Dream." Finally, the last Philharmonic is on the 11th, where I am to conduct some piece.

I must finish the arrangement for Cramer, and some "Lieder" for the piano, also some songs with English words, besides some German ones for myself, for after all it is spring, and the lilacs are in bloom. Last Monday "The Hebrides" was given for the first time in the Philharmonic; it went admirably, and sounded very quaint among a variety of Rossini pieces. The audience received both me and my work with extreme kindness. This evening is Mr. Vaughan's concert; but I am sure you must be quite sick of hearing of so many concerts, so I conclude.

Norwood, Surrey, May 25th.

These are hard times, and many are laid low!* May it please God to preserve you all to me, and

---

* He had received the news of Zelter's death.

30*

to grant us a joyful meeting! You will receive this letter from the same villa whence I wrote to you three years ago last November, just before my return.

I have now come out here for a few days to rest, and to collect my thoughts, just as I did at that time, on account of my health. All is unchanged here; my room is precisely the same; even the music in the old cupboard stands exactly in the same spot; the people are quite as considerate, and quiet, and attentive as formerly, and the three years have passed over both them and their house, as peacefully as if half the world had not been uprooted during that period.

It is pleasant to see; the only difference is, that we have now gay spring, and apple-blossoms, and lilacs, and all kinds of flowers, whereas at that time we had autumn, with its fogs and blazing fires; but how much is now gone for ever, that we then still had; this gives much food for thought. Just as at that time I wrote to you saying little, save "farewell till we meet;" so must it be to-day also. It will indeed be a graver meeting, and I bring no "Liederspiel" with me composed in this room, as the former one was, but God grant I may only find you all well.

You write, dear Fanny, that I ought especially to hasten my return, in order if possible to secure the situation in the Academy; but this I do not choose to do. I shall return as soon as I can, because my father writes that he wishes me to do so; I therefore intend to set off in about a fortnight, but solely for *that* reason; the other motive would rather tend to detain me here, indeed, if any motive could do so; for I will in no manner solicit the situation.

When I reminded my father formerly of the proposal of the Director, the reason which he then advanced against it, seemed to me perfectly just; he said that he regarded this place rather as a sinecure for more advanced years, "when the Academy might be resorted to as a harbour of refuge." For the next few years I aspire as little to *this* as to any other situation; my purpose is to live by the fruits of my labours, just as I do here, and my resolve is to be independent. Considering the peculiar position of the Academy, the small salary they give, and the great influence they might exercise, the place of Director seems to me only an honourable post, which I have no desire to *sue* for. If they were to offer it to me, I would accept it, because I promised formerly to do so; but only for a settled time and on certain conditions; and if they do not intend to offer it, then my presence can be of no possible use. I do not certainly require to convince them of my capability for the office, and I neither will, nor can, intrigue. Besides, for the reasons I mentioned in a previous letter, I cannot leave England till after the 11th, and the affair will no doubt be decided before that time.

I beg that no step of any kind may be taken on my behalf, except *that* which my father mentioned concerning my immediate return; but nothing in the smallest degree approaching to solicitation; and when they do make their choice, I only hope that they may find a man who will perform his duties with as much zeal as old Zelter.

I received the intelligence in the morning just as I was going to write to him; then came a rehearsal of my new piece for the piano, with its wild gaiety, and when the musicians were applauding and complimenting me, I could not help feeling strongly, that I was indeed in a foreign land. I then came here, where I found both men and places unchanged; but Hauser unexpectedly arrived, and we fell into each other's arms, and recalled the happy days we had enjoyed together in South Germany the previous autumn, and all that has passed away for ever, during the last six months. Your mournful news was always present to me in its sad reality—so this is the manner in which I have spent the last few days here. Forgive me for not being able to write properly to-day. I go to town this evening to play, and also to-morrow, Sunday, and Monday.

I have now a favour to ask of you, dear Father, in reference to the cantatas of Sebastian Bach, which Zelter possessed. If you can possibly prevent their being disposed of before my return, pray do so, for I am most anxious at any price to see the entire collection before it is dispersed.

I might have told you of many agreeable things that have occurred to me during the last few weeks, for every day brings me fresh proofs that the people like me, and are glad to associate with me; which is gratifying, and makes my life here easy and pleasant;

but to-day I really cannot. Perhaps in my next letter my spirits may be sufficiently restored, to return to my usual narrative style.

Many remembrances from the Moscheles; they are excellent people, and after so long an interval, it is most cheering once more to meet an artist, who is not a victim to envy, jealousy, or miserable egotism. He makes continued and steady progress in his art.

The warm sun is shining out-of-doors, so I shall now go down into the garden, to perform some gymnastics there, and to smell the lilacs; this will show you that I am well.

London, June 1st.

On the day that I received the news of Zelter's death, I thought that I should have had a serious illness, and indeed during the whole of the ensuing week I could not shake off this feeling. My manifold engagements however have now diverted my thoughts, and brought me to myself, or rather out of myself. I am well again, and very busy.

First of all I must thank you, dear Father, for your kind letter. It is in a great measure already answered by my previous one, but I will now repeat why I decline sending any application to the committee.

In the first place, I quite agree with your former opinion, that this situation in the Academy is not desirable at the outset of my career; indeed I could only accept it for a certain time, and under particular conditions, and even then, solely to perform my previous promise. If I solicit it, I am bound to accept the place, as they choose to give it, and to comply with their conditions as to salary, duties, etc., though I do not as yet even know what these are.

In the second place, the reason they gave you why I should write, seems to me neither a true nor a straightforward one. They say they wish to be certain I will accept of it, and that on this account I must enroll myself among the candidates; but they *offered* it to me three years ago, and Lichtenstein said they did so to ascertain if I would take it, and begged me to give a distinct answer on this point; at that time I said *yes*, that I was willing to carry it on, along with Rungenhagen. I am not sure that I should think the same now; but as I said so then, I can no longer draw back, and must keep my word. It is not necessary to repeat my assent, for as I once gave it, so it must remain: still less can I do so when I should have to *offer* myself to them for the post they once *offered to me*. If they were disposed to adhere to their former offer, they would not require me to take a step which they took themselves three years ago; on the contrary, they would remember the assent I then gave, for they must know that I am incapable of breaking such a promise.

A confirmation of my former promise is therefore quite unnecessary, and if they intend to appoint another to the situation, my letter would not prevent their doing so. I must further refer to my letter from Paris, in which I told you that I wished to return to Berlin in the spring, as it was the only city in Germany with which I was still unacquainted.

This is my well-weighed purpose; I do not know how I shall get on in Berlin, or whether I shall be able to remain there,—that is, whether I shall be able to enjoy the same facilities for work, and progress, that are offered to me in other places. The only house that I know in Berlin is our own, and I feel certain I shall be quite happy there; but I must also be in a position to be actively employed, and this I shall discover when I return. I hope that all will come to pass as I wish, for of course the spot where *you* live must be always dearest to me: but till I know this to a certainty I do not wish to fetter myself by any situation.

I conclude, because I have a vast deal to do to enable me to set off after the next Philharmonic. I must publish several pieces before I go; I receive numbers of commissions on all sides, and some so gratifying that I exceedingly regret not being able to set to work at once.

Among others, I this morning got a note from a publisher, who wishes me to give him the score of two grand pieces of sacred music, for morning and evening service: you may imagine how much I am pleased with this proposal, and immediately on my arrival in the Leipziger Strasse I intend to begin them.

"The Hebrides" I mean to reserve for a time for myself, before arranging it as a duet; but my new rondo is in hand, and I must finish those everlasting

"Lieder" for the piano, as well as various other arrangements, and probably the Concerto. I played it last Monday in the Philharmonic, and I think I never in my life had such success. The audience were crazy with delight, and declared it was my best work.

I am now going to Moscheles' concert, to conduct there, and to play Mozart's Concerto, in which I have inserted two long cadences for each of us.

FELIX.

THE END.

JAMES B. RODGERS, PRINTER, PHILADELPHIA.

www.ingramcontent.com/pod-product-compliance
Lightning Source LLC
Chambersburg PA
CBHW021707110726
47902CB00005B/1093